I0563196

THE LEGACY

BOOK 1: THE PREPARATIONS

BOOK 2: THE TRIALS

BOOK 3: THE RETURN

BOOK 4: THE BROKEN

OTHER BOOKS BY
DANIELLE N. MCDONOUGH

The Cursed Half Moon – Book 1

The Cursed Half Moon – Book 2

WWW.THELEGACYBOOKSERIES.COM

THE
TRIALS

DANIELLE N. MCDONOUGH

ILLUSTRATED BY
ANNA CASTRO & ISABELLA INMAN

EDITED BY
REBECCA MARTINEZ & REBECCA BEVERLY
& TERRY MCDONOUGH

Dedicated to all the friends and family who have supported
me on this journey, especially
Anna, Becky, Bradleigh, Bri, Katie, and Kenna.

Special thanks to my mother and sister
for their continuous help.

THE LAND OF THE CLAN

THE VILLAGES

THE PARAMOUNT

THE MAKING

THE BARRACKS

THE GOLDEN FIELDS

RIVERSIDE

THE FARM

THE QUARRY

TREESCAPE

THE NORTH WIND

PROLOGUE
SECURITIES

An old man carefully picked his way along a path coated by snow and rock. The first blizzard of the year had come several days ago, though winter was still nearly a month away. Several inches of white, powdery snow dusted the trail, which wound between high mountains capped by peaks of never-melting ice. In the distance, the sound of hammers striking metal could be heard echoing along the walls of the valley.

From time to time, the old man glanced up, nervously watching for loose stones and chunks of ice that were known to break free of the towering slopes and plummet to the ground with deadly force.

Finally, he reached the source of the noise: a large building with three chimneys, each billowed forth great clouds of black smoke. The door was open, and the air coming from inside shimmered with heat.

The old man paused, gasping for breath. He leaned heavily against the door frame and upon the wooden staff gripped tightly in his hand. Inside, a dozen men were laboring over glowing coals and white-hot metal.

The journey through the valley had been far more taxing than he remembered from past excursions. When last the old man had ventured beneath the shadows of the great mountains, it was spring, and he wasn't alone. A sad smile lit the wrinkled face at the memory of that happier time.

Slowly, he adjusted the object he was carrying. It was a cumbersome burden to him, weighing close to twenty pounds. In his younger years, he could have borne it all day without

1

complaint, but time had laid waste to the once-sturdy frame. He would never have attempted such a treacherous journey now if he had not felt it absolutely necessary.

"Are you all right?" a deep voice asked. It belonged to a broad-shouldered man who stood just inside the doorway. He held a hammer in one hand and appeared to be in the middle of beating something into shape on one of the anvils.

There was another man beside him, holding a pair of tongs. The second man wore a rag tied across his forehead, keeping the sweat from running down into his eyes. He peered out from under it suspiciously at the newcomer.

"I will be fine in a moment," the old man wheezed. "I must speak to the both of you." He nodded back the way he had come, away from the building.

The two men exchanged a glance. The deep-voiced man set his hammer down and approached. He was far taller than both the others, with close-cropped black hair and warm, honey-colored eyes.

The man wearing the rag snatched the metal from the anvil with his tongs and thrust it into a bucket of water, producing a hiss. He had a slim build, and his beady, black eyes shifted constantly as he followed the others.

Each step was slower than the last as the pair escorted the old man along the trail that had brought him there. They didn't stop until the forge and the sound of hammers were far behind them. Only the thick smoke could still be seen, hanging in the air like a low cloud from the sky above.

"What's happened?" the man with the rag asked. He pulled the cloth loose and wiped the back of his neck, revealing a large bald patch in the middle of his head, ringed by short, light brown hair.

"My younger daughter is missing," the old man answered hesitantly. "I fear the worst."

2

The other two men exchanged another glance, but the old man didn't notice. His mind was far from that cold, lonely valley.

"Why have you come to us?" The man replaced the rag on his head as he spoke. "I assure you, we have no knowledge of—"

"I know that," the old man interrupted, coming back to the present. "That is not why I have come. This is." He parted his white cloak to reveal the burden he had carried so far.

"What is that?" the deep-voiced man gasped.

"It is something I intend to leave with you," the old man informed them. "I fear it is no longer safe with me."

The deep-voiced man took the object. It was a polished stone box covered by inlaid gold writing.

"What does it say?" the balding man demanded, peering at what his companion now held.

"You mean you can't read it?" The old man's lips twisted with amusement.

"Learning the 'high language' isn't very *high* on my priority list right now," the balding man snapped. "We've got plenty of work to do here, and not enough help. Hopefully, we'll get a few more Keepers soon and won't have to spend every day working like dogs in this pit." The man spat contemptuously into the snow.

"Yes, you do seem quite busy today," mused the old man.

"It's a ploy to keep us out of the way," the man replied rapidly. He reached up and rubbed his forehead.

The deep-voiced man wasn't listening to the conversation anymore. All his attention was spent studying the box in his hands. He tried to lift the lid but was unsuccessful.

"We can't open it, and we can't read it. What are we supposed to do with it?" he asked in a mystified voice.

"It's not for you to do anything with," the old man told them. "It's not for you or your children or your children's children,

3

but for those that come after. They will find it and, I pray, know what they are meant to do with it."

CHAPTER 1
THE VALLEY OF THE NORTHWIND

"Why are we born to live in this mess of a world? Everything we put our hands to fails, and everyone we love will eventually move on or pass away. Our sole consolation is that we are only here for a brief time. In the end, we are no different; we die like everything else."

The trials were about to begin.

I had waited my entire life for this moment.

Inside my chest, I could feel my heart racing. I longed to run forward, to start the journey which lay ahead, but Core, the First Clan Leader, had not yet given the signal for us to begin.

Glancing to my left, I caught sight of Core's son, Cole, the first leader of my team, and some of the apprehension inside my body lessened. I had lost a lot of people during my sixteen years of life, some to death and some to distance. They all simply faded into the past like flowers that bloom for only a single season.

Cole was the only one left who was important to me. When I looked into his gentle, blue eyes I gained a feeling of peace I couldn't find anywhere else. There was comfort in the fact that he was going to be with me on this journey.

The two of us had grown up together, living our entire lives in the same village, The Paramount. It was the most prestigious village in The Land of the Clan.

The Paramount was where the council—the group of men and women responsible for making decisions for The Clan—lived.

They held long meetings nearly every day to ensure the prosperity and efficiency of our people.

My mother, Myna, was the Second Clan Leader. She'd always been far too busy with her duties to spend much time raising me. For the previous ten years, we had shared nothing but the living space where we both slept at night. That was the extent of our relationship. I learned long ago not to expect anything else. Every time I tried to reach out to her, my heart was cut a little deeper with disappointment, and I found myself building my walls a little higher.

After my father died, I'd felt like the loneliest person in The Paramount, until I had met Cole. Together we had attended school, learned every law of our people, and grown up playing strategy games.

The other four members of our team came from different villages. They had all attended school as well, but no village emphasized law and order as much as The Paramount.

Astra, one of our teammates, shifted impatiently on my right. She was older than I was, and taller, with pale, freckled skin and green eyes. Her long, auburn hair was being blown straight back by the cold air that was streaming out of the valley in front of us.

Personally, I found the cold unbearable, but Astra was from the northernmost of The Clan's villages, The North Wind. It was always cold there; cold and lonely. It was isolated from the other villages by many miles and had few inhabitants. Their only responsibility was to raise, train, and care for the horses used by the rest of The Clan.

Over the previous several days, I had been able to sense Astra's growing anticipation for the trials to begin. With her parents long dead and no family, aside from the community of The North Wind, she wasn't really leaving anyone behind.

I turned my attention forward to where Core was standing. I thought he might have been preparing to give us additional instructions. Instead, he turned slowly to gaze at the other council members who stood in a group off to the side.

About thirty of them had made the trek to the valley's mouth with us. However, Core's eyes were seeking only one person: my mother.

From where I was standing, I saw Myna glance at Core and hold his eyes. They were older than most people whose children were competing in the trials.

Exactly fifty years ago to the day, they had led their own team down this very path and returned as victors. After winning, they became Clan Leaders, as was our tradition. Out of their team of six, only four survived. Never had a winning team returned with all of its members.

I hated to think about the teammates I was likely to lose. Cole, Astra, and I were the oldest and all had a good chance of making it back, but the three younger members seemed so vulnerable.

Kisa was the one I worried about most. At that moment, the little girl was hovering close behind Astra, trying not to let homesickness envelop her before our journey even began. Her face was all but hidden behind the golden hair that cascaded down her shoulders. I couldn't see if there were tears in her blue eyes, but from the way her small frame was quivering, it seemed a safe assumption. She was so young and timid it almost didn't feel right to allow her to compete beside contenders who were so much older and more competent.

Kisa was soft and innocent compared to how I was at the age of thirteen. Even seven years ago, when I was only nine, I'd already been exposed to the harder side of life. With my father dead and a mother who seemed to have forgotten she had a child, survival was up to me and me alone.

My eyes traveled from Kisa back to Core, who was still standing between the thousand plus contenders and the one road leading out of The Land of the Clan. He couldn't have been standing there for more than a couple of minutes, but the time felt like an eternity.

Finally, he let out a long breath, squared his shoulders, and took a dozen steps to his right, carrying him to the group of council members. The moment he ceased moving, teams began surging across the scarlet cord, which had been laid down to mark the starting line of the trials. The first dozen took off running, some carrying or towing the younger, less-willing members of their teams.

Astra thrust her arms out to block us from moving with the first wave. I rolled my eyes at the hand a few inches in front of me. We had already discussed not being among the first rush.

Cole did lay a hand on our lowest ranked team member, Rollan, to restrain him. Apparently, he'd forgotten our plan in the excitement of the moment.

Rollan was ordinary in appearance, with non-descript, light brown eyes and hair. What was remarkable was his endurance and strength. Often during our training, Rollan had been the one to take the least number of breaks, despite his youth.

Whenever there was a task before us, he was the best one at plowing through until the job was completed. I wondered if this gift was something he'd picked up at his village, Treescape. Working all day to fell and haul off trees before chopping them into firewood was certain to make anyone stalwart.

Rollan still bore the remnants of the black eye one of his brothers had given him a few days earlier.

I'd witnessed the five deplorable examples of humanity bullying Rollan during the preparations. He wasn't the youngest, but he seemed to be the most common target of their attacks, both physical and mental.

Some of his brothers were here now, on teams of their own. Rollan hadn't spoken to them or even looked to see where they were. I doubted he'd shed many tears on account of the family he was leaving behind. If anything, he was probably relieved to be free of them for a while.

Rollan's cousin, Joss, was also on our team. He was ranked just below me, and I hoped that he would prove a great asset. Joss had a kind and protective nature, especially when it involved Kisa and Rollan. Even now, he held Kisa's hand tightly in his own.

8

Although they were cousins and both fourteen, the dissimilarities between Joss and Rollan were numerous. Rollan was at least a foot taller—nearly eye-to-eye with me—and probably had about fifty pounds on his cousin. Joss's hair was also brown, but several shades darker, and, while Rollan's was long enough to cover his ears, Joss's was closely shaven. If they hadn't told me they were related when we all first met, I would never have guessed it.

Joss's bright eyes were hazel, and his skin had a nice tan from many afternoons spent swimming in the lake by his village, Riverside. He was gangly and energetic, always bouncing around and planning his next adventure.

The six of us formed one of the one hundred and seventy-five teams chosen by the council to participate in the trials. A handful had been eliminated yesterday when they failed to qualify. The qualifier was merely a written test. I completed it without difficulty. Only one member of our team failed, but that was probably just due to nerves. Since enough of us passed, we were allowed to move on to the trials themselves.

It felt like we watched every other team go before us into The Valley of the North Wind. Part of me was desperate to charge forward. I hated feeling like we were already losing, left behind while others got a head start. Not that we didn't have an advantage already. Astra, who had lived her whole life close to the valley, was secretly permitted to take horses into it for training. She would be able to guide us through the maze of twists and turns with ease.

Cole and I knew the way through as well. When the preparations were announced on Midwinter, we were both so eager to get started that we snuck into the valley to see the lay of the land. It was a forbidden act, and, if caught, we would have been punished with a mark—a symbol of great shame in The Clan—but no one saw us except, annoyingly enough, Astra.

Jase, a friend of Cole's, had come with us too, but he ended up being placed on a different team. I doubted he remembered the way through since he could barely find the way out of his dwelling half the time.

"Come on, Myra," Cole said to me. He and I started forward, and the rest of the team fell into step behind us.

Technically, Astra should have been the one leading with Cole. She ranked above me, second leader to my third. However, Cole and I had been friends for such a long time that we tended to rely on each other more than we did on any of the others.

If Astra minded that I had taken her place, she didn't say anything. When the council assembled the teams, they'd put Astra in a hard position. Joss, Kisa, and Rollan had grown up together. Cole and I had run into Astra a few times when the preparations first began, but we didn't really start getting to know her until we were placed on the same team a month ago. The fact that Astra rarely talked about herself made her still practically a stranger.

She followed just behind me, with Joss, Kisa, and Rollan bringing up the rear. The three who had never been inside the valley before looked around wide-eyed, apparently surprised that the walls were made of ordinary stone.

At first, the path we walked along was fairly broad. There were a couple of other teams close at hand, but the main clump seemed to be somewhere up ahead. It would thin out soon, once teams started reaching the place where the trail divided. The path split many times into long, twisting avenues, most of which were nothing but dead ends. As far as I knew, there was only one way through the maze of paths.

Just before we reached the first split, a team came pushing back past us, heading for The Land of the Clan. Three of their six members were in tears. One of the boys was clutching his hand to his chest. It was red with blood, and he held it at an awkward angle like it was broken.

"Rocks have already started to fall," Astra muttered as they disappeared from our sight.

The valley could be very dangerous; certain paths had frequent landslides, stones could come crashing down with little to no warning, and the stony ground made it easy to lose one's footing.

My friend, Golla, had died in the valley several months back. She snuck in believing the crazy rumor that you could speak to the dead in the valley. I was partially to blame for telling her the rumor, even though I never more than half believed it myself. Despite all of this, Astra promised the main trail was safe enough.

As we reached the first divide and headed to the left, a team came hurtling toward us from the right-hand pathway. Only five members were present. One of them, a lanky boy with dirty blond hair, was supported between two others. His ripped clothes were purple, signifying that he was from The Making. His shirt was stained almost black with crimson blood, and one of his feet was too mangled for him to walk on.

I heard a gasp from Kisa. Her face was completely white as she stared at the ghastly sight. Astra covered the little girl's eyes a moment later and pulled her sharply to the left.

"We should help," she sobbed. "Let me go! I can help!" There was a plea in her voice that was hard to hear without being moved. Before the preparations began, Kisa had been an apprentice healer, a role she was no doubt chosen for because of her empathetic nature.

"There's nothing we can do," I announced, pushing away the twinge of guilt I felt.

"His team will get him back to The Land of the Clan, and the healers there will take care of him," Cole assured her.

Kisa didn't argue, but her forehead puckered with little worry lines. I fervently hoped that she wouldn't realize the team had been missing a member and that we wouldn't see any other injured contenders. Cole was almost as softhearted as Kisa. Nothing would be worse than stopping our journey to help those who had already failed.

At least they couldn't expect us to help carry them back to the healers. The moment we set foot back in The Land of the Clan, we would be disqualified. Cole would never be stupid enough to eliminate our team over something so foolish.

Thankfully, there weren't too many more incidents and none as horrific as the team with only five members. Some of those heading back didn't even have an injured member.

Cowards, I thought reproachfully.

Each time Cole chose a split in the road, he glanced back at Astra to make certain he picked the right path.

"We keep going up," Joss observed a little while later.

"Of course," I told him. "How else did you expect to get over the mountains?"

Joss shrugged as if he had never considered it before.

"We don't have to go all the way to the top, do we?" Rollan asked, glancing at the snow-capped peaks towering high above us.

"Of course not," Cole said. "Just a bit higher; it shouldn't be too bad."

"How do you know?" Joss wondered, oblivious to the fact that Cole and I had been to the valley before.

Cole gave him a blank stare. "What?"

"How do you know what it's going to be like?" Joss repeated his question.

Even though we were all teammates, and technically there weren't any rules during the trials, I still wasn't particularly keen on letting everyone know that we had broken one of the most rigid laws of our people.

"I told him," Astra answered Joss smoothly. "At The North Wind, we train horses in the valley sometimes."

Joss and Rollan turned to look at her in surprise.

"Really?" Rollan gasped.

"How come I didn't know that?" Joss piped up.

"Well," Astra said, "it's not exactly common knowledge, but Myra and Cole witnessed me doing it one day during the preparations."

Astra wasn't being completely honest. We had seen her when she caught us sneaking back out of the valley, but Astra wasn't the snitching type, so she kept that part to herself.

Joss looked like he wanted to know more, but another team came hurrying up behind us at that moment, so he let the subject drop.

Some time after midday, we reached the high point of the valley and could finally see the land beyond. On our last visit to this spot, Cole and I had observed four soldiers from The Barracks guarding the valley exit far below. According to Astra, they were always there, not to ensure that no one left, but to keep the Broken from getting in.

Broken was the word we used for those who were not of The Clan. A handful of them were exiles that had been cast out for breaking our laws. I didn't know where the others—if there were any—came from, but they were people unfit to join our society.

I didn't see the soldiers now. The council must have removed them for the beginning of the trials so no one would be aware of their presence. It was a secret of The Clan.

Only recently had I become aware of just how much The Clan was hiding. Until I started unearthing these secrets, I believed that our society was flawless. Now, I often wondered how much I wasn't being told. Even though I was curious, I held firmly to the belief that everything was done for the good of The Clan. Astra did not share my feelings. She distrusted the council and seemed to think there were hidden agendas in everything they did. Her extreme views made our relationship tenuous, to say the least.

After taking a short break to catch our breath, we began again. The far side of the valley was much steeper and more treacherous than anything we had faced yet. Before long, we found ourselves on a narrow, winding path.

We saw very little of the other teams. At one point, a pair of them came up from behind and passed us before disappearing around the bend ahead. As much as I wanted to sprint after them and be the first team through the valley, I knew it would be folly.

Forty-five minutes later, Astra directed our attention to the trail before our feet.

"Up ahead is a meadow," she said, pointing to where the path vanished around an enormous cliff. "It's full of grass, and there's a brook where we can fill our canteens. It's a safe place, so don't worry about landslides. Once we leave, the path becomes very dangerous. It's steep, and there is one section where the slightest noise will start an avalanche. I've only been past the clearing a few times. Everyone must be as silent as possible. No talking, try to step softly, and, whatever you do, don't drop anything."

We nodded to show we understood, and Astra led us up and around the cliff. The mountain meadow was larger than I had imagined. It was surrounded by short, rock walls and filled with long grass, just as Astra described. The little brook trickled down the stone wall, close to where we entered. I could hear the wind. It was always moving through the valley, but here it was deeper, more ominous-sounding. I found the noise unnerving and wondered what the horses thought of it.

"Is this where you bring the horses?" Cole asked, echoing my thoughts.

"Yes," she said. "Even in the middle of winter, there's hardly ever any snow here. The wind keeps it from piling up more than a few inches."

I knelt and took a long drink from the spring before filling my canteen. The others were doing the same.

"Should we rest a bit?" Joss asked, giving Kisa a worried glance. Joss, who had two little sisters of his own, often acted as the older brother to the little girl.

"I'm fine," Kisa insisted, even though she looked pale from the four-hour hike through the mountain pass.

"We should get out of the valley as quickly as possible," Astra said quietly to Cole. The decision was his to make.

"I agree," Cole nodded. "We'll rest once we're on the other side of the mountains. It doesn't look like too many teams have been here yet, so let's get through before they start showing up. It sounds like the next section is going to be a little tricky, and I don't relish trying to move quietly with another team breathing down our necks."

Joss nodded, and Rollan grunted his agreement. Astra guided us to the correct path out of the meadow; there were six from which to choose. The council had given us a huge advantage when they put Astra on our team. Even Cole and I, who had seen most of the valley before, would never have been able to guide our team this well through the dangerous mountain passages.

No one spoke for the next forty minutes as we continued down the treacherous path. On the left side, the mountain wall rose hundreds of feet above our heads. On the other was a drop at least as far down. I had to work up the nerve to glance over the edge. Below was a bed of broken rocks that must have once rested atop the mountain but had fallen in years past.

We moved haltingly. Astra was in front, setting a slow, steady pace. I figured we were nearly through when, suddenly, she froze a few steps in front of me. I opened my mouth to ask why but remembered quickly not to speak.

Instead, I slipped up beside her and looked ahead. A foot-high layer of rocks and rubble coated the path before us. Another team had beaten us here.

Curiosity got the better of me, and I glanced over the edge to the right again. Even though we were so high up, I thought I could see an arm sticking out from beneath a pile of stones and a foot protruding from under a giant boulder ten yards away.

Contenders had already started dying. Some of them would remain here, in The Valley of the North Wind, forever.

Kisa came to stand beside me. Her jaw fell open in shock. Joss leapt forward and covered her mouth a moment before the scream came. There was still some sound, but most of it was muffled.

Astra gestured for us to keep going. There was nothing we could do for this team. They would be a warning to all those who came after, but they would never return to The Land of the Clan.

Joss slowly removed his hand from Kisa's mouth. She looked stunned but didn't make any more noise. Astra motioned desperately for us to move forward, toward the pile of fallen rocks on the path.

At that moment, the wind picked up sharply for just a second. One of the rocks closest to the cliff was sent hurtling over the edge. I could see the immense danger of such a place if even the wind itself could start an avalanche.

The rest of us hurried forward, but Kisa didn't budge. She stood frozen, face even paler now than in the meadow. Her huge eyes were still taking in the scene of death below.

Cole quietly sidled up next to Kisa and lifted her in his arms. She didn't resist, but a choking sob rose to her lips. Instantly, she buried her face in Cole's shoulder, drowning out the noise.

Astra picked up the pace, and we almost ran down the path. Seeing the bodies must have unnerved even her. After what seemed like an eternity of silence, we finally emerged from The Valley of The North Wind.

Astra stopped. She had led us safely through the valley. Now all six of us stared in awe at the landscape before us. It was less than thirty miles from where we had lived our whole lives, but we had never once seen it.

A plain of short grass covered the land at our feet and stretched away for about half a mile before meeting the tree line. There were several different forests at Treescape and in the lands between the villages of The Clan, but none were like the one that stood before us. The trees were enormous, with huge limbs rising a hundred feet into the air.

The shadows beneath the spreading branches were deep. I looked up to see that the sun was only about two hours from setting. Where had the day gone? Soon, night would close in, and we would be thrown into complete darkness.

CHAPTER 2
THE SCROLL

The thought of the unknown was daunting, but I quickly swallowed my panic. The younger members of my team would be looking to me, and I would not show them weakness.

"What now?" Rollan asked.

Cole had been carrying Kisa for nearly twenty minutes. As we stood together, facing the forest, he gently set her down. There were tear stains on her face, and her cheeks were a little flushed, but her eyes were dry.

"I guess it's time to open this." Cole fished the sealed scroll, which the council had given him, out of his pack. It felt like another lifetime when we stood before the council, and they gave us the parchment. In reality, it was earlier that day when the events took place. While in the council building, we were told not to open the scroll until we were through The Valley of the North Wind.

"Okay," I said, turning to Cole. "What does it say?"

Cole slipped his finger under the edge of the parchment, preparing to break the wax seal.

"Wait," Astra stopped him. "Not here. Let's get to the trees first." She gestured to the forest ahead of us.

"What are you worried about?" Rollan wondered.

Astra shook her head. "I don't know, but I feel that we should not linger in the open. This isn't The Land of the Clan anymore. Anything could be lurking out here."

Her words hit us all. We had spent our entire lives in complete safety. Now, for the first time, we were vulnerable. There wasn't anything to protect us—not a river, not mountains, not The Clan. We were just six children. Alone.

"I agree," I said. Astra and I didn't always see eye-to-eye, but this time she made a good point.

Cole nodded and led us toward the closest patch of trees. A small whine escaped Kisa, but Joss, who was by her side, whispered, "Don't worry Kisa, I'll never let anything hurt you."

I didn't feel any safer once we were beneath the canopy of trees. The forest was ancient and completely still. Not even a breeze could find its way through the enormous trunks to stir the lower branches or leaves.

If anything, I felt less secure. At least in the plain, I could see what was close at hand. Within the thick mass of trees, it would be easy for someone—or something—to sneak up on us.

Cole paused beside a fallen tree. Carefully, he broke the seal on the parchment before laying it across the trunk.

I peered over his shoulder; Joss was trying to join me, but he wasn't quite tall enough. Astra stood on Cole's other side.

The scroll contained several lines of writing. It seemed to be a list of sorts. The entire thing was written in the high language: a second language all those of The Clan were required to learn in school. It wasn't used in day-to-day life but was commonly spoken during ceremonies.

"One," Cole read aloud, translating into the common language as he did. "Follow the rising sun to the east. It will lead you to the edge of the earth, and you will find the ocean: a vast expanse of water with waves that never cease rolling upon the sand.

"Two. Travel north along the coast until you see the great mountain crowned with eleven stone spires.

"Three. Climb the western face of the mountain. There you will find the writing on the rock.

"Four. Read the words carved in stone, solve their riddle, and all will be made known to you."

After Cole finished, we were silent for a long moment. It seemed so simple, yet who knew the obstacles we would have to face? Generations of contenders had read those same words, and almost all of them failed.

"Seems straightforward to me," Joss said. He was peering at the parchment around my elbow. "East is…" He paused as he glanced at the forest around us, and then pointed to the right. "That way. Come on."

I remained where I was, looking at Cole. He was rereading the scroll's words silently to himself.

"Cole?" I asked softly.

Joss had already started toward the east. He spun back around to see why the rest of us weren't following him.

Cole straightened and rolled the scroll back up.

"Let's go," he said, nodding to Joss.

Rollan moved before the rest of us. He sprinted forward toward his cousin.

"I'll lead the way!" he bellowed, passing Joss.

"Not without me!" Joss cried, following him into the underbrush.

Kisa hurried to catch up with the two but was much slower.

"Stay close," Cole called apprehensively.

I wasn't sure the two boys heard him, so I broke into a light jog. If our team got separated in this ominous place, it could take hours to regroup, especially with night closing in. Cole trotted along by my side, and Astra brought up the rear as we followed the trail of broken foliage left by the rest of our team.

Ten minutes later, I caught sight of our three younger teammates and slowed my pace. The trio might have been excited and full of energy but, burdened with their packs and having already gone a great distance that day, it appeared they were content to walk.

As we pressed on, I noticed Cole kept looking down instead of ahead. At one point, he almost walked into a tree. I grabbed the sleeve of his maroon shirt and pulled him out of the way.

"What's on your mind?" I asked, stifling a laugh.

"I don't know," Cole said with a sheepish grin. "I just thought the scroll would say more. I expected to find out something—something—"

"Important?" Astra suggested from behind us.

"Yeah," Cole nodded, glancing back at her.

"That's not likely to happen until we get to wherever the scroll is sending us," I pointed out.

"Where everything will be made clear," Astra quoted, raising one eyebrow skeptically.

We have to get there, I thought. *The answers are there, and I must know them.*

We only continued walking for what I judged to be an hour before the evening was upon us. Although it wasn't dark yet, the sun had vanished into the trees. The days would be shorter than we were used to with the forest encroaching on every side.

Our going would be slow too. Traveling among the trees was a challenge; branches and thickets of undergrowth blocked our path. The ground was rocky and uneven. Already my toes were stubbed, my clothing was filthy, and my boots were caked with mud.

"Should we stop and look for food and shelter?" I suggested. Every second, the shadows were growing longer, and night would not be far behind the setting sun.

"We could go a bit farther," Joss called from a dozen feet ahead of us. "We have food, so why should we worry about that tonight?"

"Look around," I told him. "This is the kind of place that's full of food. The kind of place we should take advantage of so we can save what we have as long as possible."

Cole looked undecided.

"Kisa, do you see any fruit trees around here?" Astra wondered. "I haven't noticed any since we got into this forest. These look more like the trees that grow at Treescape."

"They're mostly oak trees," Rollan observed with a nod. His village, Treescape, was almost entirely enclosed by a massive forest.

"Just in case I wasn't paying attention the whole time we were studying plants and stuff, you can't eat oak, can you?" Joss asked. He wasn't saying it to anyone in particular, and I think he was joking.

"No," Kisa told him, taking his words seriously. She was the one who knew plants the best and had been our teacher at The Golden Fields, where we learned which plants we could eat and which we couldn't.

"There are some edible roots over there, though." Kisa pointed to a row of sprouts sticking out of the ground.

"Excellent. Why don't you start digging them up?" Cole directed. "Rollan, I want you to stay here and help her. Joss and Astra, you guys go that way." He pointed to the north. "See if you can find a water source, or a cave, or anything useful. Come back and meet us here in about twenty minutes. Myra and I will go the other way."

Everyone nodded except Rollan. I heard him grumbling quietly about being left to dig in the dirt while the rest of us got to go exploring.

After spending a bit of time walking through the woods, I was growing more comfortable with the feeling of being surrounded on all sides by trees. I was even getting pretty good at moving quietly. I never realized before how much noise a person could make just by walking in the forest. Back in The Land of the Clan, I hadn't felt the need for stealth, but out here it made me uncomfortable to think that everything could hear my approach.

"Well?" Cole asked after we had walked for a couple of minutes without finding anything remarkable.

"Well, what?" I returned.

"How do you think we're doing?"

I laughed. Cole looked at me in surprise.

"You're asking me this now?" I giggled. "How should I know? We've only just started. Everyone's still alive, so I guess it could be worse."

I was still chuckling when he said, "That was a silly question. I just—I wish I could feel confident."

"About what?"

"Well, the scroll…" he trailed off.

"What about it?" I pressed.

"I don't know. I expected more."

I rolled my eyes. *This again.*

"After we've settled in for the night, we can take another look at it," I suggested.

Cole nodded. We walked on a little farther in silence. Ten minutes later, we headed back. We had found nothing useful.

We returned before Astra and Joss, so we helped Rollan and Kisa finish digging up the roots. They were long, thin, brownish tubers, probably a close relative of the potato. There was quite a pile of them when Astra and Joss got back.

"Anything?" Cole asked.

"Not really," Astra shook her head. "Just more trees."

"Okay," Cole said. He was trying to sound sure of himself, but I could hear his uncertainty.

"I guess we're staying here for the night," I announced, trying to help Cole out. "Kisa," I said, turning to the small girl, "how do we cook these?" I indicated the roots piled nearby.

"Normally, we boil them in water," Kisa answered. "But…" She glanced around as if she thought she might find a pot full of hot water close at hand. "We could probably just wrap them in leaves and cook them like potatoes," she suggested after thinking for a moment.

"Is that what we're going to do?" Astra turned to Cole. She sounded like she didn't agree with my choice of spending the night where we were.

A twinge of resentment pulled at my gut. I suppressed it as Cole said, "Yeah, let's stay here tonight."

Astra nodded but didn't appear pleased.

"I'll get some wood for a fire if you like," she offered.

"I'll help." Rollan popped up from his place on the ground, wiping the dirt from his hands onto his dark green pants. He seemed eager for the chance to get out of the clearing and explore a little.

"Sure," agreed Cole. The two vanished into the woods. It was almost twilight by then, and a little prickle of worry ran down my spine that the pair might get lost.

"What can I do to help you?" Joss asked Kisa.

"We need some big leaves—not dead ones—to wrap the roots. Also, if we can get some of the dirt rubbed off, they'll taste better."

Before Kisa was even finished speaking, Joss was up one of the oak trees like a squirrel. He grabbed handfuls of large leaves and dropped them down to us. A moment later, he was back on the ground. Cole and I started rubbing the tubers in the grass, freeing them of the earth clinging to their skins.

Suddenly, Astra and Rollan appeared, hurrying back through the trees toward us.

"We have a problem," Astra announced. Her hands were empty; she didn't have even one piece of wood. Rollan was puffing behind her. He held several good-sized logs in his arms, proof that there was wood to be found.

"What's wrong?" Cole leapt to his feet, looking around for signs of trouble.

"We can't start a fire," Astra told him.

"Why?" I asked.

"Because we can't," Astra announced.

"Why?" I repeated, slightly irritated.

Astra rolled her green eyes. "Who's going to build it? And how?"

"Rollan's good at—"

"I've always had a flint before," Rollan interrupted me.

What they were poorly trying to explain finally made sense.

"Oh," Cole said.

I turned on Rollan. "You mean you can't make a fire without a flint?" Rollan shook his head. "Didn't you know we wouldn't have one out here?" I tried to keep my tone civil, but I was more than a little annoyed.

"I'm sorry," Rollan replied. "I didn't think of it."

"How could you not think of it?" I snapped. *This was something I actually thought you could do,* I hissed mentally.

Rollan looked away.

"Don't act like this is all his fault," Joss intervened. His voice was gentle but firm as he came to his cousin's defense. "No one else can make a fire without a flint either. We'll have to find another way."

"How are we going to survive without being able to make fire?" Kisa cried, the panic rising in her voice.

"I don't know," Cole admitted. He seemed to be doing better at the "staying calm thing" than I was. "But we'll find a way."

"Or not," I muttered.

Kisa let out a small, worried whimper.

"The river," Joss announced.

Everyone turned to look at him.

"What?" Cole asked. "What river?"

"The river by Riverside, my village," Joss told us. "Sometimes we'd bring in bunches of rocks from the water. The shore is mostly made up of stones, you know."

We were all still staring at him with blank faces, so Joss continued. "We'd sort through them, and some of them would be flints."

"Well, we're a long way from Riverside," I snapped.

"Calm down, Myra," Astra told me and then turned back to Joss. "You were saying?" I narrowed my eyes at Astra, resenting the fact that she was trying to give me orders.

"If there were flints in our river, then maybe we can find some in a river around here." Everyone was silent for a moment. "I'm sure I'd be able to recognize one," Joss concluded.

"Sounds like a good plan," Cole said. "Tomorrow, our first priority will be to find a river or stream or something."

"What about tonight?" Kisa asked.

"We'll just have to go without a fire tonight," Cole told her.

"Should we eat the food in our packs?" Rollan wondered.

Cole was silent for a moment.

"I don't suppose these roots are any good raw?" he asked, picking one up and looking at it skeptically.

Kisa shrugged uncertainly, and Cole took a bite out the tuber in his hand. Tried to take a bite would have been a better way of putting it. The tuber appeared to be as hard as a rock.

Cole sighed. "I guess you can eat some of what you've got in your packs, but only as much as you need." He glanced at the sky; twilight was fading fast. "Best get some rest too. At first light, we're going to start moving again."

I didn't feel hungry at all, just worried. There were so many things for us to do in the morning. We needed food, water, fire, and shelter. Plus, we must be the first team to reach the mountain and return.

The others opened their bags and began looking at the food. I glanced at what Rollan was pulling out. A small, hard loaf of bread, five strips of dried meat, and four apples, not even enough for two days.

Instead of food, I removed the thick cloak from my pack to serve as a blanket. There were several natural niches formed by the roots of one of the great oak trees. Using my backpack as a pillow, I lay down in one and tried to fall asleep. I wished the trees were a little thinner overhead so I could have seen the stars. I loved the stars.

Long before I was asleep, full night closed in, throwing everything into complete darkness. I had slept out in the open once before, in the amphitheater back in The Land of the Clan, but it was different beneath the trees. I didn't feel safe beyond the borders of The Clan, and it was hard to let go of that feeling and surrender my mind to sleep. Every time the wind picked up or a leaf fluttered to the ground, I jumped.

At some point, I must have drifted off, because the next thing I knew, I was opening my eyes in the gray light of dawn. I sat up, unsure for a moment where I was. In a flash, I remembered, mostly because I had a knot in my back from the rocky ground. There was also a light layer of dew on my face. I wiped it away and glanced around.

I was the only one up. Astra was asleep in a pile of leaves with Kisa curled up next to her. Cole was off to my left, and Joss and Rollan were sleeping back-to-back across the clearing.

Silently, I moved to Cole's side and shook him gently. He had said first light, after all. I shook him twice more before he opened his eyes and gave me a groggy stare.

"Myra? What—" Then he realized where he was and sat up. He glanced at everyone else. "Should we wake them?" he asked me.

"You're the leader," I told him.

"They all seemed so worn out yesterday," Cole fretted. "But we need to cover a lot of ground today."

"Let's look at the scroll again; that way they can have a few more minutes," I suggested.

"Great idea," Cole told me. Carefully, he dug the scroll from his pack. As he unrolled it, my eyes skimmed the words once more. I looked for anything unusual that might signify a deeper explanation, but it seemed to be just an ordinary piece of parchment with ordinary writing on it.

"They had to make a lot of these," I observed softly. "One for every team."

Cole nodded. "Guess that's why it's so simple."

His words were true; the scroll was simple. Aside from the lines of instructions, there was nothing, save a pattern bordering the list. Even that was just a series of dots showing all the colors of the villages of The Clan in repetition.

We sat together for several minutes, studying the words. If there was some hidden meaning, I couldn't find it.

After a long moment, Cole sighed. "Well, it was worth a second look. Let's wake the others. Hopefully, today will have a better ending than yesterday."

CHAPTER 3
THE FOREST

Cole and I woke the rest of our team. It didn't take long for us to get everything, except the tubers, into our packs. I looked down at the unappetizing roots and wondered if it was even worth carrying them along with us.

"Take them?" I asked no one in particular.

"Of course," Kisa answered, coming to stand next to me. "They'll be good to eat as soon as we can make a fire."

"Yeah, but I don't like the idea of putting anything this dirty in my bag," I told her, picking one up. Even though we had removed some of the earth the previous evening, it was still fairly grubby.

I heard Astra laugh softly and turned to see her walking across the clearing to join us.

"How long do you think we're going to stay clean out here?" she asked me. "In half a month, we'll all be too filthy to recognize."

"Not if we find water and bathe," I countered, irritated by her tone.

"Won't matter," Astra responded. She knelt, and, gathering up a handful of the roots, started stuffing them into her backpack. Joss came over and began doing the same. He called Rollan to join them.

Fine, I thought. *If you want all your extra clothes covered in mud, do as you like.* I turned away and stood a little distance off, waiting for them to finish. I felt slightly guilty about not helping, but I pushed that thought away. Astra and the boys were used to being dirty. I was not.

We struck out east toward the rising sun, as per our instructions. After about an hour of walking, Joss, who was in the lead again, rushed over to a bush and started picking berries from it.

"Look!" he called in excitement. "Blackberries."

Everyone hurried to join him. We spent ten minutes stripping the bush clean. I had only eaten a few bites of bread for breakfast, so the berries were a delicious treat. We all had bluish-black stains on our hands and faces when we finished. I started to understand what Astra meant about being 'too filthy to recognize'.

Once every berry was plucked from the little bush, we moved on. As the sun rose, the day grew hot. My shoulders were sore from the previous day, and, as we continued to trek relentlessly on, my pack seemed to grow heavier with every step. Sweat was trickling down my neck.

To quench my thirst, I took a sip from my canteen. It was already half empty. We weren't going to last much longer without water.

"This is no good," Astra murmured to Cole and me around midday. "We should stop and rest while the sun is so high. Everyone will dehydrate much more quickly in the heat. Plus, it's hard to tell which direction is east with the sun directly overhead. I'm worried that we will get turned around and end up going the wrong way."

"I don't..." Cole began. He had that unsure look on his face that was starting to drive me insane.

"We need water," I interrupted. "We can't stop until we find it."

"If we rest, we will be able to cover ground more quickly this afternoon. It'll be more efficient," Astra responded.

"We'll dehydrate almost as fast sitting around as we will walking," I shot back.

"She's right," Cole cut in before Astra could raise any more objections. Both of us looked at Cole expectantly.

"Which one?" Rollan bellowed from a dozen feet ahead. Our conversation had started quietly but quickly grown louder. Joss smirked at his cousin's remark like this was all a big joke.

Cole ignored them. "We need to find a river or lake before it gets dark. Even if we can't find a flint and build a fire, we need water. We'll keep moving until night."

"That's a bad idea," Astra told him, coming to a halt. "You're putting all your hopes into finding water today. It's great if we do, but if we don't, we'll be exhausted and out of water tomorrow morning. Then what?"

"We can't stop," I said. "This isn't just about survival; it's about winning. We need speed. We can't take a break every time we're tired or uncomfortable." I was glaring at Astra, not understanding why she was being so difficult.

"Don't fight, guys," Kisa begged in her whiniest voice.

"We're not fighting," Cole assured her. "We're just having a discussion."

Kisa didn't appear convinced. Her face was creased with worried little lines. If she wasn't careful, they were going to become permanent.

Cole glanced around. He seemed painfully aware that everyone was expecting him to make this decision.

"Let's keep going." His words sounded more like a guess than an order. "Drink as little water as possible."

Astra sighed and shook her head, making it clear what she thought of his choice, but she didn't raise any more objections.

We all fell into line again. The afternoon was hot, and it didn't cool off even a little. The humidity was rising too, making it seem as though the forest was trying to smother us.

We had been traveling steadily eastward since entering the woods, but, before much longer, we came to an immense tangle of briars. It was full of thick vines lined with thorns. We had encountered a few similar patches earlier in the day, but none quite so overgrown.

"Should we try to go through?" Joss asked.

"It appears to go on for quite a way," Astra observed, peering into the dense foliage ahead. Her voice was still a little stiff after our earlier argument.

Cole nodded. "Let's go around it."

29

"To the north," I suggested, knowing that we would be heading in that direction after reaching the ocean anyway.

"All right," Cole agreed.

We headed north. The path was not easy, even after we got around the worst of the thistle patch and started traveling east again. The underbrush was thicker than before, and the trees were shorter, allowing the hot sunlight to beat down on our heads. Prickers and thorn bushes grew everywhere, threatening to claw the skin from our arms and legs. In addition, some of the plants sent out runners along the ground, invisible beneath a layer of brown leaves until someone tripped over them.

Kisa was the first to find one. She went tumbling forward with a cry of surprise.

"Kisa!" Joss leapt to her side.

"Ouch!" Kisa said, sitting up and looking down at her leg. She stood tentatively and then winced. Joss carefully freed her foot from the long tendril, which had snared it.

"Are you hurt?" Cole asked.

Kisa took a step and cringed. "It'll be okay, I think."

"Good. We'll all have to be more careful about where we put our feet," Cole observed.

As the afternoon wore on, the forest seemed to become our adversary, as though it were intentionally throwing up barriers for us to navigate around. At one point, we found ourselves on the edge of a deep ravine, the sides of which would have been nearly impossible to scale. While the rest of the team took a break, Joss climbed down a short way to see if there was any water at the bottom. There wasn't.

Between scrambling through briar patches and climbing over mounds of broken rock, I felt battered from head to toe. I could see scratches on my teammates' arms and legs, and bore quite a few of my own. Rollan and Cole had the worst of it. They were clumsy on the rocks and pushed their way carelessly through the brambles. I could only imagine how Jase, Cole's friend from The Paramount, would fare. He was so big and stupid; he would tear himself to shreds on these thorns.

30

There was no indication that other teams had passed this way, but by now most of them were probably clear of the valley and somewhere in the woods close at hand. I could only guess what would happen if we ended up running into any of them. There was nothing in the rules about teams not working together, but only one team could win, so it wouldn't have been a good move in my opinion. My hope was that we wouldn't see any of the other teams—ever.

I tried to keep my mind occupied so that I wouldn't focus on my physical discomforts, but it was impossible to push them away forever. Before long, I caught myself wishing for a nice, cool drink of water. I was used to eating very little, but being without water was a new struggle.

In The Clan, water was never hard to find. There were wells in every village, and the water from the river surrounding the peninsula of our land was pure and sweet.

As the evening was closing in, we drank the last drops in our canteens. Not long after, Kisa started moaning that she wished she hadn't come with us.

"We could go back," she whined when no one, except Joss, took any notice of her complaints. The skinny boy seemed to have an endless amount of patience as he tried to soothe his friend's worries.

The rest of us, who were tired of hearing her complaints, all looked at her with the same expression. She didn't make that suggestion again.

She did, however, keep up a constant whimpering. Half an hour later, Joss looked appealingly to us for assistance, since it seemed that his assurances of everything being okay were wearing thin.

After that, Cole and Astra took turns trying to comfort Kisa with empty words. I attempted to ignore her by keeping my mind focused on more important things, but it was hard. Every one of my muscles ached, and my throat was completely dry. I wasn't particularly hungry, but that was only because thirst was the prevailing need at the moment. I could feel my strength diminishing from lack of sustenance.

Finally, Cole seemed to have had enough of everything, from Kisa's griping to the fatigue we were all feeling.

"Let's stop here for the night," he decided.

"But there's no water!" Kisa practically shrieked. A moment later, she crumbled to the ground, hugging her knees and sobbing.

It was stupid really; she would only dehydrate faster bawling her eyes out like that. Joss crouched next to her, but he didn't have anything left to say, so he just patted her gently on the back.

"We'll do the same thing we did last night," Cole announced. "We'll split into smaller groups and search for water in every direction. Astra, you go straight ahead with Kisa."

It was probably a good idea to pair them together. Astra seemed able to cope well with Kisa's pathetic behavior. I was certainly glad not to be stuck with her myself. I'd known all along she was the weakest link. Some of her skills and abilities might come in handy, but after listening to her fuss all day, I really wished she wasn't a member of our team. Her actions were so selfish, as if the rest of us weren't in as much pain and discomfort as she was.

"Joss and Rollan, you two head south." Cole gestured to me and then to himself. "We'll go north."

Everyone nodded, except Kisa, who was fighting back her tears. Astra replaced Joss by the little girl's side and began talking to her in a soothing voice. I imagined she was using the same tone she would have for an upset horse.

Cole and I didn't stick around long enough to see if Astra managed to get Kisa back on her feet.

Almost as soon as we were out of hearing distance from the others, Cole heaved a great sigh and stopped walking.

"Myra, what have I done?" he asked. "We probably couldn't find our way back now even if we wanted to!" There was

32

panic in his voice, but it was the terrified look in his eyes that scared me.

"Calm down," I almost yelled at him. "I don't need another teammate having an emotional breakdown at the moment."

Cole's shoulders slumped in defeat. He took a deep breath before speaking again.

"You're right; I should be calm. But I understand exactly how Kisa feels." Hopelessness filled his blue eyes. "I'm not doing a very good job, am I?"

"Cole—" I started, but he cut me off with a desperate question.

"What are we going to do?"

"Find water," I said seriously.

"Then what?"

"Find a flint so we can make fire and have some food. That should lift everyone's spirits."

Cole nodded without confidence.

"You make it sound so easy, but if we don't find water tonight, should we keep going east or try a different direction? There has to be water somewhere. I'd hate to think that we are walking parallel to a river without realizing it."

"I don't know," I told him, shaking my head.

Panic crossed his face. He expected me to have all the answers for him, but I didn't. He'd practically given up already. Would I soon do the same? The thought scared me. We had trained for six months and, in less than two days, everything had already gone wrong.

"Myra, I've never been so afraid in my life. Do you think we should—" Cole started.

I couldn't bear to let him finish.

"Stop asking me to know everything!" I yelled, fighting down panic of my own. My breath was coming in great gasps. I wasn't in danger of crying, but I didn't like the feeling of fear Cole's despair brought on me. "It's not my job to make these choices; it's yours! How can I believe in you when you don't believe in yourself?"

Taking a deep breath, I looked up at him. "How am I supposed to trust you?" My voice came out softer as I attempted to get my panic under control.

Cole stared at me in shock. He opened his mouth a few times, but no words came out.

"I—I don't know," he admitted at last. There was something new on his face: pain. I turned away, not wanting to see how much I'd hurt him. Regret filled me, but what was I supposed to do? He had been made team leader; he needed to lead us. I wanted to help him, but he was making it impossible.

"We should—we should keep going," Cole choked out.

I nodded and trailed behind as he continued walking. The only sound was our footsteps as we pushed through the undergrowth.

Silence didn't usually bother me, but this one ripped at my soul. Cole was my closest friend, really the only friend I had left. Even beyond that, I'd hoped that someday we could become more than friends and maybe have a family of our own. Just before the trials began, he had expressed similar thoughts, and I assumed that, after we returned and were of age, we would be together.

Seeing him so ready to give up worried me. I needed him to be strong and brave, someone on whom I could rely when my own perseverance was spent. If he couldn't be that person, were we meant to be together at all? Should I start distancing myself from him for both our sakes? I did not want to push Cole away, but I needed him to be able to stand on his own.

There is no other way, a voice inside my head whispered. Tears almost came then, but I was dehydrated and managed not to shed any.

He needs to learn how to be strong. What you've said will challenge him, help him. He'll thank you for it one day, the voice whispered again. We walked on in silence, both looking straight ahead, pretending to be all right.

You are too close to him anyway, my mind persisted. *You don't want to let him in.* Horror gripped me for a moment, and I faltered. Cole continued as if he didn't notice.

Was I pushing Cole away because I didn't want him to need me or because I didn't want to need him?

I was still frozen, pondering that thought, when suddenly, from ahead of me, Cole called out, "Water!"

Rushing forward, I broke through the tree line and found Cole standing on the banks of a wide river. He looked so relieved that I couldn't help smiling, but in my heart, I felt like weeping.

CHAPTER 4
THE RIVER

After Cole and I both took a long drink from the river, we headed back to meet up with the others.

"This is exactly what we needed," I told Cole.

"Yes," he agreed.

We didn't speak again for the rest of the walk. I had never felt more alone in my life.

Joss and Rollan were waiting for us when we got back to the meeting place. "There's another huge gorge to the south," Joss reported. "We walked along it for a while, but it just went on and on."

"There might be water at the bottom," added Rollan. "We thought we could hear it, but we couldn't see anything. I vote we go back and check it out."

"No need," Cole told him. "We found a river."

"That's nice to hear," Astra said, emerging from the trees with Kisa by her side. Both of them were carrying an armload of little plums. The fruit didn't look quite ripe yet, but even from a distance, the smell coming off their skins was delicious to my empty stomach.

I looked at Cole, expecting him to relax and smile since things were finally on an upward spiral. He did appear pleased, but the beautiful smile I loved so much was nowhere to be seen. I knew it was because of what I had said to him.

The words bothered me too, but they were true. Cole didn't believe in himself, and he lacked conviction. As a rule, I didn't trust people. I'd come closer to trusting Cole than anyone else, but much as I wanted to, I just couldn't.

Trying not to look at him, I went over to Kisa and offered to help carry some of the plums in my pack. The boys did the same, and then we all headed for the river Cole and I had discovered.

Along the way, everyone helped themselves to a few of the little fruits. We reached the water with at least half an hour of daylight left.

The river was deep, slow-moving, and about fifteen feet across. Through the clear water, I could see a rocky bed that I judged to be five or six feet below the surface. The grass, which grew on the banks, was long and wispy. It waved gently in the evening breeze.

I loosened the pack from my aching shoulders and fished out the canteen.

With my back turned, all I heard was a splash as one of my teammates hit the water. I spun around, and, after a second, Joss's head popped up to the surface. He gave an elated whoop and started splashing around.

Joss loved water. He had been an avid swimmer his whole life, so I wasn't particularly surprised by his behavior. Rollan created an enormous wave when he plunged in after his cousin a moment later.

"Come on! The water's great," Joss called. Taking a deep breath, he dove beneath the surface. Water made me nervous, and I couldn't help the tense feeling in my stomach until Joss reappeared with a handful of rocks. After looking them over, he discarded them and dove again.

Kisa was the next one to jump into the water. She had lived in Riverside with Joss for a long time and could swim almost as well as he could.

Cole pulled his shirt off and walked to the water's edge. Instead of jumping, he slowly eased himself into the river.

For a moment, he treaded water, and then he sucked in a mouthful of air and submerged. He wasn't under very long. After dunking himself a few more times, he climbed back onto the bank. Cole ran his hands through his hair, pushing it back out of his eyes, but it inevitably fell forward again as soon as he finished. The tiny strands of gold in his dark locks were impossible to see when it was sopping wet.

Rollan and Joss were competing to see who could hold their breath longer. Kisa was in much better spirits; she giggled as she made sure neither of the two boys cheated.

I turned from the three children in the water to see Cole opening Joss's pack. He removed the tubers we had dug up last night. Next, he moved on to Rollan's bag. Astra brought the ones she was carrying, and the two of them started washing the remaining dirt from the roots in the water. I ached to join them. I wanted to help Cole with whatever he was doing, but I couldn't. Instead, I started filling all the canteens with water.

"Got one!" Joss hollered from the water, holding a clenched fist above his head. Keeping that hand in the air, he paddled unevenly over to the shore and handed a rock to Astra.

"I'm pretty sure it's a flint. I'll look for more," Joss called, disappearing beneath the surface again.

Astra examined the rock without comment before going back to the tubers. Cole didn't even look up. I gathered everyone's packs from where they lay scattered along the riverbank, except for Cole's. It was too close to where he was working beside Astra. The other packs I grouped before replacing the full canteens. I also collected the two shirts and three pairs of discarded shoes left by the swimming trio.

I glanced over my shoulder at Cole; he was speaking quietly with Astra. I wondered what they were talking about, but I couldn't hear because our teammates in the water were making too much ruckus.

Not knowing what else to do, and not wanting to face Cole, I walked over to the river. I removed my boots and dangled my feet in the water. It was deliciously cool.

"Come all the way in!" Kisa called to me. She was beaming, and her blue eyes twinkled with delight.

I shook my head. I hated sleeping with wet hair. Kisa's blonde locks were thin and would dry quickly, but my hair was thicker and would be wet for hours.

Astra joined me on the riverbank a moment later. She and Cole were finished with the roots, and he was laying them out in the grass to dry. His expression wasn't perturbed anymore; whatever Astra said to him must have helped soothe his worries.

I wasn't pleased by that thought. The last thing I'd meant to do was drive the pair closer together.

Astra removed her boots and put her feet in the water, just as I had. Like the rest of her clothing, her boots were black. They were taller than mine, ending mid-calf, while mine only made it an inch or two above my ankles.

"Bet you're glad we kept going this afternoon," I said quickly, hoping to remind her that Cole had listened to me and not her.

"I certainly am," Astra replied calmly. "However, I would hate to see the state we'd be in if we hadn't found the river tonight."

Even though Astra wasn't there to witness the exchange between Cole and me, her words were far too close to the truth. I wondered if Cole had told her what I said. I hoped not; she had no business knowing.

"The river flows to the east," Astra observed mildly. "We can follow it in the morning."

"Naturally," I responded, making it clear that I had already come to the same conclusion.

Astra didn't react to my superior tone.

"Cole and I agree that water—more precisely, the lack thereof—is going to be the biggest challenge we'll face. At least until we reach the ocean."

I scowled at the idea of Astra and Cole making plans without me, even if I was only the third team leader.

"For now," Astra continued, "we believe following the river is our only option."

"Until it starts heading in the wrong direction," I amended.

Astra was silent for a moment. "It's something we'll have to discuss when the time comes," she answered coolly.

There was a period of tense silence between us.

"Let's get some wood," I suggested, ready to change the subject.

The two of us rose and pulled our socks and boots on over our wet feet. Cole was replacing his shirt as Astra and I headed to the forest. There were fallen branches everywhere, and in a matter of minutes, we assembled a good-sized pile.

"Rollan," I called, "come make us a fire." His head was under water so he didn't hear me. As soon as he came up for air, Kisa patted his arm and relayed the message.

He clambered from the river and hurried over to us. Astra and I both jumped back as water droplets scattered from his body in all directions.

"It's just water," he exclaimed, chuckling as he intentionally shook his shaggy head to shower us.

"You'll get the wood wet!" Astra cried, using her body to shield it from the droplets.

Both were laughing at their own antics. I left the pair to light the fire.

Joss and Kisa climbed out of the river as well. Darkness was closing in, and the night air was growing cool.

Joss dug a fresh shirt out of his pack and handed it to Kisa. "Use this for your hair," he instructed her. "You don't want to catch cold."

Kisa nodded and started using the piece of tan clothing to dry the water from her hair.

Joss quickly replaced the shirt he had stripped off before jumping into the water. In one hand, he held several rocks.

"Here," he said, dropping them beside Rollan.

"Thanks. It's always easier to start a fire with wet flints," his cousin grunted. Almost everyone laughed, but not me and not Cole. It would take more than a river and the hope of fire to lift our spirits.

Kisa started wrapping the roots in fresh leaves. I didn't feel hungry at all. The water and plums were enough for me. I opened my pack and pulled out my cloak. The sun was below the tree line, and I felt suddenly cold. I wrapped myself up and sat on the ground with my back against a tree.

Drowsiness clouded my mind as I watched Rollan make several attempts at building a fire. All of them failed. It was nearly pitch black by then, and I could barely make out Kisa's face as the worried expression returned.

"You're doing a great job," Joss said encouragingly to his cousin. He ran to the woods and brought back several handfuls of dry moss. He was trying to help, but it was no good since there hadn't been so much as a spark.

As the last of the daylight died, they gave up. I felt comfortable and warm; the tree trunk was at the perfect angle for resting. I adjusted myself slightly and closed my eyes, wanting to forget the entire day.

Astra was the one who woke me in the morning. It was early, but I was ready to get up. I had not passed a peaceful night.

"We'll follow the river as far as we can," Cole announced as we breakfasted on plums and some of the provisions from our packs. "We need to find a flint."

I glanced doubtfully at the pile of stones Joss had pulled from the river the night before.

Once again, we packed up the roots along with their leaf wrappings. Since they were now clean, I didn't mind carrying some in my bag.

The excitement of finding the river was wearing off, and everyone seemed mellow. Soon, we were going to need something more to sustain us than fruit and water. I was pretty sure most of the boys had already finished the food given to us by the council. There was still a fair bit left of mine, but even after devouring two plums, I could feel a hunger inside me that hadn't been touched at all by the pitiful breakfast.

Before we set out, I took a quick dip in the river. It was cold from the night air, but I felt refreshed when I climbed out afterward. Even though swimming was not my favorite thing, I had learned enough to keep from drowning during the preparations, and it felt nice to be clean.

Half an hour after dawn, we started walking east along the riverbank. Astra kept ordering everyone to drink lots of water. The going was easy while we stayed close to the stream. The grass was long, but it wasn't difficult to push through. Every once in a while, the younger three—usually led by Joss—would jump into the river to cool off.

Around midday, we stopped and took a break. Even with water, the lack of decent food left everyone exhausted. Kisa flopped down and seemed to fall asleep almost immediately. The three boys started trying to make a fire again, which seemed rather pointless to me. It was hot, and surely we didn't plan to stay very long.

"While they try to figure out if they have a flint in that pile of rocks, let's scout around and see if we can find anything useful," Astra suggested to me.

I was so tired that exploring the area was one of the last things I wanted to do, but admitting my exhaustion was even lower on the list. So, after Astra conveyed our plan to Cole, we struck out together into the woods.

Ten minutes had elapsed when suddenly Astra froze and grabbed my arm. Slowly, she raised a hand, pointing to an animal about twenty yards away from us. It looked like a goat, but the horns on its head were twice as thick as any goat I'd ever seen.

Astra smoothly removed the bow from her shoulder and plucked an arrow from her quiver. To my surprise, she handed them to me. Was she too sensitive to shoot the animal? I wasn't sure about that, but what I was sure of was that we needed meat.

I strung the bow and pulled the arrow back. After carefully looking down the shaft, I let it fly, striking the animal in the chest, where, I hoped, the heart was located.

The goat creature leapt into the air and then froze. It took a few hesitant steps before staggering and falling to the ground. I handed the bow back to Astra and pulled out my knife. We approached cautiously, knowing wounded animals could be dangerous, but the creature was quite dead when we reached it.

"Nice shot," Astra praised me, reaching down to pull the arrow from the beast's chest. She didn't flinch as a rush of blood came welling out of the hole left by the shaft.

"Why did you give me the bow?" I asked in confusion.

Astra shrugged, "You're a better shot, and I'm hungry."

I laughed for the first time in days. Astra was so unpredictable.

"Let's hope the boys have gotten a fire started," she announced.

I nodded.

Together, we lugged the animal's carcass back to the riverbank. It must have weighed at least a hundred pounds, and seemed to get heavier and heavier with every step we took.

We were disappointed when we made it back to the others. There was no fire. Instead, Cole and Rollan were crouched over a heap of kindling, trying to produce a spark. Kisa was lying where we'd left her, curled up in a little ball. It took me several moments to locate Joss. He was in the river again, still searching for a flint.

"Let's try these two together," Cole suggested, holding up a pair of rocks. Apparently, they were trying random combinations. None had worked, and neither did this one.

"Why aren't there any sparks?" Rollan demanded in frustration.

Cole didn't say anything, but he looked equally disappointed. For a moment, his eyes met mine. Just as quickly, he looked away, but not before I saw the fear and panic he was drowning in, feelings he didn't want to show me anymore.

Joss came leaping out of the river, splashing water in every direction. Picking up the pair of rocks the other two boys had just set down, he examined them carefully. Suddenly, he seemed to notice the dead animal for the first time.

"Whoa," he exclaimed. "Where did that come from?"

Astra shrugged. "It was just walking around in the woods. Myra shot it."

Everyone, except the sleeping Kisa, looked our way. The fact that we now had meat seemed to cheer them slightly, even though there was no fire with which to cook it.

Cole and Rollan turned back to the kindling as Astra, Joss, and I started to butcher the goat creature. We used my knife for the cutting. Joss tried to help, but he wasn't strong enough to roll the animal's bulk from one side to another without Astra's help. The two of them worked together as I cut away the hide. Once we were finished, the pair began pulling out the guts and tearing the meat from the bones with their bare hands.

There were several grunts of frustration from the fire builders over the following half hour. We were coming along pretty well with the goat creature. The thick fur had been removed from the carcass, and we were now cutting the meat into long strips. It looked delicious, even raw.

"It just won't work," I heard Cole say in a way that reminded me greatly of Kisa. "We'll have to figure out something else."

I glanced back at them. Cole looked completely downcast.

Joss left us to help them out. He held up one of the rocks. "I know this is a flint," he said softly, almost to himself. "So why won't it spark?"

"What?" asked Cole.

Joss glanced at him. "Why does flint spark?"

Cole shrugged. "Because it's flint?"

"No," Joss shook his head. "Otherwise, it would start fires all on its own every time we touched it. We have to hit it against something hard."

"What's harder than another rock?" Cole wondered, clearly not seeing where Joss was going, but I did.

I rose from where I'd been cutting meat from the creature's ribcage.

"Metal," I answered, joining the boys.

Joss nodded. "That's what we always used at home," he said.

"How are we supposed to find metal?" Cole asked desperately.

I bit back a sharp retort, giving him a pass on that one because I knew how tired and hungry he was. But it was a stupid question.

"We brought some," I reminded him quietly.

His eyes widened. "Let me see your knife, Myra," he ordered.

"No," I said, pulling back. "You'll dull the blade if you use it to build a fire. Use your sword."

"It's too long and awkward," Cole argued. "Your knife will be perfect!"

"Then it won't be my knife anymore; it'll only be good for starting fires," I protested.

"Come on," Cole groaned. "We need fire. This is why they gave us the knife. It's so obvious!"

I glared at Cole. Did he really think I was so worthless that the only reason I had been given a knife was so that we could make fire? In his mind, were he and Astra the only ones who had the right to real weapons? If I were to give up my knife, I would have nothing, not even a wooden staff like Joss, Kisa, and Rollan.

"I'm not going to—" I started, but was interrupted.

"Stop arguing!" Astra commanded firmly. Her eyes were not on us but on Kisa. The little girl had woken up and was crying.

"Use this." Astra tossed one of her arrows to Joss.

"Aren't the tips made of stone?" Cole asked in confusion. Astra shook her head.

"The ones we used in practice were, but the seven they gave me are metal."

"I'm going to have to take it apart," Joss warned Astra.

"That's fine," she told him, giving Cole and me each a scathing look. "It's far better than starving to death."

Easy for her to say, I thought furiously. *She has six more arrows. If I had seven knives, I would have gladly given up one to make a fire. I'd like to see her give up her only arrow without a fuss.*

"I'll find you a good, sharp rock to replace this," Joss promised, carefully twisting the metal arrowhead free from the wooden shaft.

Astra nodded as she went to sit by Kisa. I couldn't hear what she said to the little girl, but Kisa's sobs began to subside.

I returned to the animal carcass and continued removing meat from the body. My back was purposely turned on the boys working with the arrowhead and flint.

After what transpired the night before, I had felt distanced from Cole. I was sad and worried that our relationship was growing strained. Now, I was furious with him. He might as well have told the entire team that I was just there so they could use my knife—that I was completely unnecessary, good for nothing except for the tool I carried.

Fuming, I didn't even glance at them when Rollan shouted in excitement. There were several more clinks as rock struck metal, and then I heard the crackle of flames as they devoured the pile of kindling.

Out of the corner of my eye, I saw Cole and Joss head into the woods. They returned a short time later, arms laden with sticks and branches.

Astra helped me finish cutting up the animal. I didn't like how dirty my knife was, but I was able to clean most of the filth away in the river water. It wasn't as shiny as it had been, but being a little dirty was still far better than having the blade dulled from fire making.

Using long sticks, all of us began roasting meat over the flames. It was hard to make the younger team members wait for the meat to be completely cooked before they snarfed it down.

After about an hour, everyone was stuffed and feeling much better, except for me. My anger had dissipated, leaving behind a deep pain. I wanted to believe I was reading too much into Cole's words and actions. However, I couldn't quite accept that when he was sitting beside Astra and wouldn't meet my eyes.

We spent the rest of the afternoon cooking the strips of meat. It was getting late when we finished, and even I didn't see any point in trying to go any farther that day. Settling in for the night, I put some distance between myself and the others. I pulled my hood over my head and tried to push down my hurt feelings.

CHAPTER 5
THE STORM

I woke late the next morning, but I was still the first one up. It appeared everyone was sleeping off the enormous amount of meat we had gorged on the previous evening. Dark storm clouds filled the sky, only letting through a few rays of weak, watery light.

I had little idea what time of day it was, but I knew we'd slept far too long. Surging to my feet, I rushed to my closest team member, Rollan, and began shaking him. Joss was right next to him, and I shook him too. Both boys woke up pretty easily.

They helped me rouse the others. The fire was long dead, leaving only a charred patch of earth. Flies were swarming on the discarded remains of the butchered animal.

The night before, we had stayed up late and roasted all the meat from the goat creature. Astra suggested we try to tan the hide, but I pointed out how impossible that would be while we were on the move.

Working quickly, I pulled the bundle of food I had received from the council out of my pack. It was half gone. Using the cloth, which kept the bread fresh, I wrapped up several strips of meat before stuffing them into my pack. I'd rather have crumbs in my clothes than grease.

"Here," Joss said, handing each of us a stone from his pile. "We should all have one in case someone…" he trailed off with a sharp look at Kisa.

"So that we can all practice making fire," Astra finished for him.

"Exactly," Joss nodded, looking relieved.

It was an extremely practical suggestion. The rock was only two inches long and weighed almost nothing. It wouldn't be much of a burden.

As the others finished their packing, I glanced around and wondered if we should do something with the animal carcass. It seemed weird to leave our campsite waiting here for the other teams to find. Not that it would help them much. Most of the meat from the goat creature was cooked and in our packs. What remained would start to rot before long.

Maybe it would be a good thing if others saw our campsite. Then they would know that there was a team ahead of them who had fire and food. Perhaps it might encourage our competition to give up and go back. One less team would be one less worry.

Half an hour after I'd woken everyone, we were ready to begin. The sun wasn't visible, but we knew the river led east.

The landscape didn't change much as we continued forward; it appeared that the forest went on forever, each tree looking nearly identical to those before it. The river widened and grew shallower. The stone bed beneath its surface was always clearly visible, and I spotted dozens of tiny, silver fish darting in and out of the water reeds.

Sometime in the early afternoon, Cole called a halt. We took a break to eat lunch, but we began moving again after only twenty minutes. The temperature was lovely with the clouds acting as a barrier between us and the sun's intense rays. I was hardly sweating, even though we kept up a good pace.

Before long, the river took a sharp turn to the right. I knew it wasn't flowing east anymore, but didn't argue when Cole continued to lead us beside it.

Soon after the turn, the land began to change. The river suddenly grew narrow and started flowing faster. Its bed deepened into a gorge, too treacherous for us to get near the water. The ground began to rise under our feet. After climbing for nearly half an hour, we came to the base of what looked like a huge cliff. There was no way for us to scale it safely without a lot of rope.

I glanced across the river to the far bank. On the opposite side of the deep ravine, which the river had become, the land also sloped up. The gentle rise was a far cry from the wall of rock blocking our path.

"Should we try to cross?" Joss asked.

"Not here," Cole answered. "It's far too dangerous."

I measured the distance with my eyes. It was at least ten feet across. Our side was higher, but not by enough to make much of a difference.

"I think I can make it," Joss declared.

"Don't you dare," Kisa gasped.

Ignoring her, Joss walked up to the edge of the ravine and looked down.

"Joss, don't," Cole ordered.

The younger boy glanced back at him.

"I can make it," he insisted.

"But not all of us can," Astra pointed out. "And it's not a good idea for you to be over there alone."

"All right," Joss sighed. "So, are we going to backtrack?"

"Looks like it," Cole replied.

Even though the trip back was all downhill, I found it very demoralizing because I knew that we would have to turn around and walk right back up on the opposite bank. It took us nearly forty-five minutes, but eventually, we found a place where we could ford the river.

As usual, Joss was the first one to jump in. He carried his pack above his head to keep it from getting soaked. Much as I didn't want to get wet, we had lost enough time already. The water before us didn't look too deep; it would be easy to wade all the way across, which was good because of the metal we carried.

Everyone knew that metal would pull you down if you couldn't touch the bottom. During my time training at Riverside, the instructors had explained the reasons why to the younger children. That fact, added to my general dislike of water, made me hesitate for just a moment on the bank.

Gritting my teeth, I pulled the pack off my back and held it over my head, just as Joss had. Plunging into the river, I gasped. It was so much colder than I was expecting. The water didn't quite reach my waist, but the current was strong, especially when I reached the middle, where it became a foot deeper.

I glanced back at Kisa to make sure she hadn't been washed away. She was beside Rollan, struggling to keep her pack raised. Their arms were linked so that she could use him for balance.

Joss was already out of the water on the far side. He reached down and took my bag for me, making it easier to climb from the river onto the bank. I stood and started wringing the water from my clothes. My hair and upper body were mostly dry, for which I was very grateful.

I watched with bated breath as the others made their way across. I kept an especially close eye on Cole. He was holding his sword over his head along with his pack. The heavy piece of metal could easily pull him down if he lost his footing.

Cole only stumbled once, and I felt my stomach nearly flip over. A minute later, he was close enough to hand me his sword and pack as he climbed onto the bank.

"Thanks," he said with a nod, taking back his possessions.

"No problem," I told him. Our eyes met, and I could see that he was just as ready to put our disagreements behind us as I was. If it had only been the two of us standing there, I'm sure we would have apologized and made up, but with the others around, it would have been awkward. Maybe if we got a few private moments later I'd be able to say something.

The rest of the team made it across without incident. We were preparing to head back downstream when I heard something that sounded like a branch snapping on the far side of the river. I whipped around, my hand dropping automatically to my hip where I carried my knife.

There was nothing to be seen on the opposite bank. I wondered if the noise could have come from another one of those goat creatures. Not that we needed more meat at the moment; there was plenty left over from last night. Plus, we still had Kisa's tubers. In our excitement over the fire and fresh game the night before, we had completely forgotten to get them out and cook them.

I scanned the opposite side of the river twice before contenting myself that nothing was there. Slowly, I turned to follow the others.

By the time we made it back to the cliff, now on the passable side of the river, darkness was falling over the land. I knew it was too early for nightfall. The clouds swirling above our heads were black and ominous, promising a terrific storm.

We continued a little farther until the ground sloped down and leveled out, allowing us easy access to the river once more.

"It's going to rain soon," Astra said, stating the obvious.

"Should we build a shelter?" Kisa asked.

"That seems like a good idea," Cole agreed. "Rollan, you make a fire. Kisa, why don't you get the tubers out of the packs and start cooking them. Everyone else, let's build a shelter."

Rollan began gathering wood and dry leaves. The rest of us dropped our bags and left them for Kisa. I walked a little way off to see what I could find to use for building materials.

"These trees are so close together, it'll be easy to use them for a shelter." I pointed out a clump of five thin trees with very little space between them.

Astra nodded approvingly. "Look at all the vines around them; it should be pretty easy to weave them together."

"Great, that'll be a good start," Cole said. "Joss and I will go and look for more branches to shore up the walls. You guys can work on what's already here." Cole and Joss vanished into the woods.

Astra and I began removing the sticks and stones from the area where the shelter was going to be constructed. Once the ground was clear of obstructions, we piled up a bunch of dry leaves. They wouldn't be as comfortable as the blankets on my bed in The Paramount, but they would be softer than the ground. Soon, Cole and Joss began dragging large branches back to us. We used the vines hanging from the trees to weave them together into a wall.

Once we finished, I looked at it, unimpressed. I doubted it would keep much rain out at all, but what else could we do?

I thought of the animal skin we had left behind with regret. If only we could tan hides while we were walking, it would have made waterproofing our shelter much easier.

It was starting to sprinkle by the time Kisa announced that the tubers were done. She had found some rosemary to season them with, and the smell was mouth-watering. We each took a few and sat huddled together in the shelter as the rain began to fall.

At first, we remained mostly dry, but I think that was more due to the trees above us than to the shelter. As soon as it started pouring, water began to drip on our heads. Before long, it was falling as fast inside as it was outside. Night came, and it was so dark I couldn't even see my hand in front of my face.

"This is horrible," Kisa whined. No one else said anything.

We didn't bother leaving the shelter as the storm continued pelting rain down on us. The hours stretched on endlessly. All the others managed to drop off to sleep, but I lay awake for a long time. I had put my pack under me as much as possible, even though it made it hard to get comfortable. No matter how wet I got, I felt like I would be okay as long as I had dry clothes for the morning. Not that the morning was likely to be any better.

Someone moved in their sleep beside me. This was the first night we were sleeping close together. It seemed natural enough for the others, even Astra, but for me, who was so unfamiliar with human contact, it was a hard adjustment.

When I was little, I had probably slept with my parents on occasion, but for as long as I could remember, my bed had always been cold and empty. Even during the rare nights I spent with my friend, Rasby, I typically moved to the floor after a few hours of tossing and turning.

I longed to rise and walk away from the others, into the cool night air where I could look up and see the stars. But the sky was covered in clouds, and if I moved, I might wake someone.

Not that I wasn't considering waking Cole.

It had been years since a day had passed when we didn't talk and laugh together. However, we had hardly looked at each other all day, and I couldn't bear it. I didn't want to lose my only friend. Just as I was trying to work out which lump was his head, I finally fell asleep.

It seemed like only a moment later when a crash of thunder jolted me awake. The sound was close by, although the rain had slackened off a bit. I tried to see the others, but everything was pitch black. Judging by the even breathing surrounding me, no one else seemed to have woken up. A flash of lightning lit up the sky and earth for a moment, and I gasped.

People. I could see people outside the shelter, creeping toward us. The lightning flashed again before I even had time to move, and I caught another glimpse of shadowy forms closing in around us. The one in front, a boy, appeared to be holding a sword.

Terror filled my mind, and the scream that rose to my lips was drowned in the following roll of thunder. I started shaking everyone I could reach. They woke groggy and disoriented into blackness. Fervently, I hoped the rain would mask their questioning voices.

"We need to go," I hissed urgently, trying to press them into obedience by my serious tone. I had already shouldered my pack, and I groped for the other packs, shoving them into hands I wasn't sure they belonged to.

My hand fell on my knife. Just as I unsheathed it, they were upon us. I screamed as loud as I could and threw myself at the first one. He was trying to enter the shelter. I needed to keep the entrance clear so no one would be trapped inside.

"Get out!" I screamed to my teammates as I slammed into the large body that appeared in the opening of the shelter.

Whoever I hit stumbled and fell backward, out of the shelter, with me on top of him. In the next flash of lightning, I recognized Toruc of Riverside by his shaggy, blond hair. I only knew his name because he had been the last potential chosen as a second leader. It was rather impressive that I recognized him in the brief moment of light, but adrenaline and fear sharpened my wits.

My knife must have sunk into his flesh because he bellowed with pain and twisted like a fish beneath me. He managed to throw me off a moment later.

I clambered back to my feet, still holding my knife in my hand. Another flash of lightning revealed Kisa disappearing into the woods with a tall girl I didn't know pursuing her.

I heard an angry cry from Astra and the sound of several people rushing around among the trees. I fumbled back toward the shelter and tripped over someone's pack. I snatched it up and kept going.

In the dark, I missed the shelter and found myself floundering in the woods. With my hands stretched out in front of me, I tried blindly to find my way back to our campsite, but all I felt were tree branches clawing my face and scraping my hands. I started to panic.

To my left, I heard a painful scream that sounded like Joss. I turned toward it instantly. There were a few flashes of lightning, but they didn't show me much.

Raindrops were pelting down on me from above, and the wind was whirling so hard I couldn't tell what direction I was going. I heard another cry much closer. Turning, I launched myself toward where I thought the sound had originated. A moment later, I tumbled over several bodies.

"Joss?" I called, shedding the packs I was carrying and dropping my knife so I wouldn't skewer my own teammate. On my hands and knees in the wet leaves, I found someone's upper arm and shoulder.

"I'm here, Myra." Joss sounded winded, and I knew he was not the person I was holding.

The shoulder in my grip started writhing, trying to break free, but I was having none of it. I latched onto the arm with both hands and rolled onto my back, twisting around so my feet were against the torso. I pushed as hard as I could with my feet and pulled the arm toward my head.

There was a strangled yell from whomever it was, and then I heard a sickening pop. The scream that followed was full of agony. I dropped the arm and aimed several kicks at the ribcage beneath my feet.

As soon as I released him, the boy—it sounded like a boy—rose and staggered away. I heard him crashing through the undergrowth.

"Joss," I called again. "Are you hurt?"

"No," came his voice close to me. He sounded like he was in shock.

"What happened?" I gasped.

"He hit me with a stick and- and then tried to choke me." Joss's voice shook, and he lowered it as he continued. "I think- I think he was going to kill me."

I was stunned. They were from The Clan. We might have even known some of them. Why had they attacked us? Before I could think of what to say, I heard someone else crashing toward us. I crouched, ready to leap, but before I did, I heard a voice call out, "Is anyone there?" Whoever it was sounded completely panicked.

"Rollan!" Joss cried.

"We're here," I called. "It's Myra and Joss."

Rollan stumbled over to join us. "Where are the others?" he asked, voice full of relief.

I shrugged before realizing it was too dark for him to see. "I don't know. Everyone scattered."

Painfully, I remembered Kisa being chased into the woods. But she was small, and, hopefully, would find a place to hide.

"We should try to find them," Joss declared.

"Which way would we go?" I countered. Everything was such a blur; I didn't even know the direction from which I had come.

"We have to do something!" Rollan exclaimed.

"All we can do is wait for morning," I told them. Worry was gnawing at me, but what choice did we have? We could end up going the wrong direction entirely. Plus, I didn't want to risk meeting anyone else who wasn't part of our team.

CHAPTER 6
DIVIDED

The storm seemed to go on forever before it blew itself out. There wasn't any more lightning, so the three of us spent the duration of the night sitting in the dark, listening for footsteps in the rain. If there were any, they passed by us unheard.

Finally, I suggested we lie down and try to rest for a few hours. It was to no avail. Every time the wind picked up, I felt my heart begin to race. The sound of water droplets falling from the treetops, along with every twitch of the nearby bushes, triggered my fighting instinct.

I felt wide awake when the somber morning light began to filter through the trees. The others might have slept, but I hadn't. Both Joss and Rollan appeared disconcerted when the gray light of dawn finally allowed me to distinguish their faces. They were muddy, with wet leaves clinging to their clothes and hair. I'm sure I appeared exactly the same.

We were also soaked from the rain. If only the sun would appear in full force and dry our clothing, but the morning did not promise warm temperatures.

My pack and knife were a few feet away, lying where I had dropped them the night before. The extra pack I grabbed was there as well. Upon inspection, we discovered that it was Kisa's.

I was impressed that Joss had managed to carry away both his pack and wooden staff. Rollan only had his staff, but that was better than nothing. Whoever the other boy was that had attacked Joss, he left a staff behind when he fled. I picked it up, thankful for an additional weapon.

"What now?" Joss asked as I handed Rollan Kisa's pack to carry since he didn't have his own.

"We're going back," I declared.

I was slightly worried that we wouldn't be able to find our way to the campsite, but it ended up being pretty easy. We hadn't come that far, and there were several different trails of crushed foliage to follow. We went as swiftly and silently as possible.

I would never have imagined Rollan being able to move smoothly through the woods; however, he was reasonably quiet now that he could see what was in front of him. The saturated foliage helped muffle the sound of our footsteps.

The farther we went, the more anxious I felt. What if someone had been hurt the night before? Or even killed? I still wasn't sure why we were attacked. Did they think we were Broken?

Before long, I could hear the river off to our right. Apparently, in the dark, Joss, Rollan, and I had headed upstream, the opposite direction we were traveling yesterday.

"Let's go up this way," I suggested, gesturing to a rise in the ground. From the top, we would be able to look down on our old campsite, and the long grass would help keep us from being spotted.

Once we were close to the top, we dropped onto our hands and knees and slowly crawled forward.

"No one's there," Rollan whispered, looking down into the empty clearing below.

Even though our old camp appeared deserted, I had the feeling someone was still close by. Several packs were sitting beside what was left of our shelter. Their contents were scattered on the grass close to the fire circle where we had cooked the tubers.

"They've got all my stuff," Rollan muttered glumly. Once he mentioned it, I noticed several articles of Rollan's dark green clothing among the other items. I also saw pieces of Astra's black attire.

Rollan made a move as if to get to his feet, but I pulled him down.

"Be still," I ordered softly.

We lay there and watched. After a quarter-hour, two boys emerged from the woods on the far side of the clearing. They stopped just outside the dilapidated shelter.

"Well?" I heard a harsh voice ask from inside.

One of the boys, who was wearing gold clothing, the color of The Barracks, shook his head. He had light brown hair and freckles on his pale skin. Over his shoulder was a bow; I hoped it wasn't Astra's.

"No sign of Korla," he reported.

The hidden speaker, Toruc, who I had tackled the previous evening, emerged from the ruined shelter. His tan tunic was streaked with dried blood. Some of it tainted his blond hair, darkening the tips.

He doesn't look very good, I noted mentally. *I must have stabbed him a lot harder than I thought.*

"Where is that girl?" Toruc demanded in exasperation.

"She ran off last night after the little one," replied the boy who had not yet spoken. He was wearing the same tan color as Toruc. It signified that they were both from Riverside, Joss's village.

I assumed this Korla-person they were talking about was the one I had seen chasing Kisa. Hopefully, she had fallen and broken her neck.

"What are we going to do?" another boy whined, coming into view for the first time. He was cradling his right arm to his body, and I realized he must have been the one I wrestled with the night before. His face contorted in pain as he stumbled, jostling his arm. He was also from The Barracks, although his clothes were nearly too muddy to make out the color.

"You can keep your mouth shut, Jaren," Toruc growled. "You went running off too and then came limping back to us after being beaten by a girl."

"Maybe the same girl who stuck you," Jaren snapped back.

Toruc didn't hesitate for a second. He struck out with his fist and knocked Jaren to the ground before proceeding to kick him. He would have continued the attack on the smaller boy if the other two team members hadn't intervened.

"Come on, quit," said the one in tan. He grabbed Toruc's arm and pulled him away.

The second boy went to Jaren's side and helped him up. Jaren was crying piteously while clutching his dislocated arm. Toruc started yelling insults and taunts at Jaren and the rest of the team.

I turned to Joss, knowing that the boys in our ruined camp below were making too much noise to hear me.

"Do you recognize either of those two?" I pointed at the pair in tan.

"Yeah," Joss nodded. "Toruc's known for being the biggest bully in Riverside. My friends and I usually steered clear of him and his bunch."

Joss furrowed his brow. "I don't remember him being made a team leader."

"He wasn't," I whispered back. "He was a second leader. Their first leader was a girl from The Making. I don't remember her name."

"Then why does he have a sword?" Rollan wondered.

I shrugged.

"What's the plan?" Joss asked, turning to me. For the first time, I realized that I was temporarily the leader of our group.

"I want my stuff back," Rollan said, looking down at his scattered belongings.

I thought for a minute.

"Let's lay low here for now," I suggested. "Maybe Cole, Astra, and Kisa will find their way back."

I felt a twinge of worry. What if the other team saw them before we did? That twinge of worry turned almost instantly to anger.

Why should I be afraid? I had already gotten the better of half the boys in the clearing below. A new plan began forming itself in my mind, a plan that a true leader would come up with and execute.

I smiled at Joss and Rollan beside me.

"Perhaps tonight, when it's dark, we can make a raid of our own."

Joss grinned. I felt certain he already grasped what my plan entailed.

We remained where we were most of the morning. The fighting amongst the other team only escalated when they divvied up what food was in Rollan's and Astra's packs. Rollan had eaten most of his; a few strips of meat were all they found to quarrel over. There was still half a loaf of bread in Astra's pack, plus several apples. The small amount did little to satisfy the hunger of our attackers.

"How are we going to get more food?" Jaren whined to one of the others when Toruc's back was turned.

The boy shrugged, munching on a core from one of the apples. He was the one from The Barracks.

"And how come we're the only team without fire?" Jaren continued.

"We aren't," Toruc snapped, whipping around.

"This team had fire," pointed out the other boy from Riverside.

"Maybe, Binter. Maybe," Toruc said.

Jaren snorted. "You're not ten feet from a fire ring, and you think they didn't know how to make fire?"

"You better learn to keep your mouth shut, Jaren. Soon even Nolis won't care if I put my sword through your face," snarled Toruc.

Nolis, the boy sitting by Jaren, looked uncomfortable. "Hasn't there been enough of that?" he asked. "We all agreed Reefa was weak, but—"

"He's weak." Toruc jabbed a finger at Jaren.

"You were injured last night too," Jaren pointed out sullenly.

Toruc almost smiled. "Yes, but I'm getting better. You're just going to get worse."

Jaren looked terrified, and neither of the other two boys spoke up in his defense.

Looking down on them, I felt horrified. Our team quarreled from time to time, but not with the hostility brewing below us. In a handful of days, these contenders had gone from peaceful members of The Clan to murderous thieves.

Toruc and Jaren spent much of the afternoon resting. Nolis tried to make a fire by rubbing two sticks together, but he gave up quickly. Binter did some swimming in the river and managed to catch a fish with his bare hands. The group ripped into it raw. It was devoured—bones and all—in a few moments.

"They're so hungry," Joss observed. Rollan had fallen asleep after we ate a little of what remained in our packs. Normally, I would have been unhappy about sharing the food given to me by the council with those who had already eaten all of theirs. However, after having spent the day watching the team below us fight over every crumb, I didn't mind so much.

I began to wonder if we should try to find Cole, Astra, and Kisa ourselves and then come back after dark. The only problem was that I didn't even know where to start. So, we remained on the crest of the hill.

If they are able, why haven't they come back here to look for us? I asked myself.

I was dozing slightly when I saw movement on the edge of the camp. Binter saw it too and let out a sharp cry. A girl dressed in dark blue came staggering out of the woods. She sank to her knees, breathing hard. Binter bounded to her side and was joined by Nolis and the other two a moment later.

"Where have you been?" Binter asked, offering the girl— who must have been Korla—a drink of water. "Did you get the little runt?"

Korla gulped down a quarter of the canteen and then handed it back to him. "No, I went after her in the woods," Korla panted, still breathing hard. She had medium-length, dirty blonde hair and a sharp, little face.

"I almost caught the brat, but then another one of them came at me. I couldn't see anything, and I got my knife into whoever it was. I thought they were dead, but I must have just hit an arm or a leg because, suddenly, my knife was ripped away, and we were fighting with our bare hands."

"Did you kill him?" Nolis asked.

Korla shook her head. "We were wrestling, and I got slammed into a tree or a rock or something. I must have been knocked out. I woke up a few hours ago, and I've been working my way back here ever since." Korla fell silent for a moment. "Any food?" she asked.

Toruc shook his head. "They didn't have any," he lied.

Korla's shoulders drooped. "This is impossible," she moaned. "I'm so hungry."

I almost felt bad for her and the rest of them. But the thought of Korla hunting Kisa, and then stabbing either Cole or Astra, made my sympathy vanish real fast.

"Are we going to move on now?" Nolis asked no one in particular.

"It's too late to go anywhere tonight," Toruc growled. "I need to rest. Binter, you and Nolis get everything packed up so we can leave tomorrow."

"Where are we going to go?" Jaren asked.

"Wherever I tell you," Toruc answered shortly.

"That's a terrific plan," Korla muttered under her breath.

Toruc wheeled on her. "What did you say?"

"We've got no food and no fire. Sure, we picked up a few more sets of clothing last night, but we can't eat those. My head is killing me, and I almost lost my knife. We can't keep going on like this!" Korla was yelling now, even though she hadn't risen from where her knees had given out on her.

I wondered if Toruc would hit her too, but he didn't.

"Quit whining and help the others pack," he ordered, stalking back to the shelter.

Rollan woke up when the shouting started. He looked with sleepy confusion on the scene below as the two boys began filling the packs. It appeared that they were just shoving items into whatever bag was closest without sorting them at all. Instead of helping, Korla sat where she was with a stunned look on her face.

"Keep an eye on them," I mouthed to Rollan. I caught Joss's eye and nodded over my shoulder before moving carefully back down the hill. Joss followed me.

"What are you thinking?" he asked quietly when we made it to the bottom and could speak without fear of being overheard.

"Sounds like someone got hurt," I started. "Whichever of them it was seems to have gotten away, but it could still be serious. We need to help them."

"Then let's go find them," Joss said. "Although, I hate to leave so much of our stuff behind with *that lot*." From his tone, I could tell he was just as disgusted by their actions as I was.

"Agreed," I said. "You still have the fire stuff, right?"

He nodded. "They might have found a flint in one of the bags, but the arrowhead is with me."

"Good. I think we'll wait until nightfall, then see if we can take back some of our supplies."

Joss gave me a crooked smile. "It is so nice of them to pack them up for us."

I grinned back at him.

We rejoined Rollan on the hilltop a few moments later. It was a long, boring afternoon. The group below us did little, except complain about how hungry they were, while we took turns napping.

As evening fell, I heard Binter say to Nolis, "Jaren is getting worse, and Toruc has a fever."

Korla sidled up to them, clearly having overheard their words. Jaren was asleep a short way off, and Toruc was hidden from sight again inside the shelter.

"Maybe we should go," she suggested.

"What do you mean?" Nolis asked her.

"We could go back," she said. "We might be able to make it, just the three of us. The others will only slow us down. It's too late; we can't help them."

Binter shook his head. "Toruc and I have been friends for a long time. I can't just leave him."

"He's lost it," Korla hissed. She'd meant to say it softly, but the force of her words carried them to us. Their voices dropped lower after that, and I couldn't make out what they were saying.

"Let's see how they are in the morning," Nolis suggested, slightly louder. "We wouldn't make it very far before dark anyway. One more night can't hurt us." That seemed to settle the argument. Korla didn't look overjoyed by the idea, but she was appeased.

Night soon followed. I nudged Joss, who was asleep next to me. Rollan, on my other side, was already awake, probably because he had slept most of the afternoon.

Silently, we watched as the three settled down a little way from the shelter. Binter was chosen to keep first watch.

"Let's wait and see if he falls asleep," I whispered.

The moon rose. It was almost full and was shining brightly, in sharp contrast to the previous night's pitch-black sky. An hour or so passed; the moon arced above us, and Binter's eyes twitched.

Just when I was almost sure he was asleep, he rose and started pacing around. Another hour slipped by before he went to rouse Korla. She wasn't fully awake before Binter collapsed into unconsciousness.

After a day of no food and little hope of any the next, Korla didn't even bother trying to stay awake. She just rolled over and went right back to sleep.

Rollan was ready to rush in, but I made him wait. Slowly, we crept down the hill, avoiding as many sticks and leaves as possible. The three packs were still sitting just in front of our old shelter.

We passed the four members of the other team who were sleeping in the open. Two of the boys were snoring, giving us at least a little noise cover. I held my breath as we slipped by them, skirting the fire ring and walking right up to the shelter where Toruc was sleeping.

I was almost within reach of the packs when I heard a snap behind me. I turned and saw that Rollan had stepped on a stick. Toruc stirred inside the shelter. He'd been snoring too, but it stopped suddenly. I could hear his body shift as if he was rolling over.

"Who's there?" Toruc groaned in a groggy voice.

"It's just me, Toruc," I whispered, trying to mimic Korla's nasally voice.

There was silence in response, and I quickly added, "Binter woke me up to keep watch. I tripped over a stupid stick." I tried to add some whine to my voice, hoping it would help add to the illusion.

Apparently, it did. I heard Toruc reposition himself.

"Be more careful next time," he snapped.

"Whatever," I muttered, hoping I sounded surly.

None of us moved for a full two minutes until after the snoring started again.

I inched forward and lifted one of the packs from the ground. The one next to it was poorly balanced and fell over, but it didn't make too much noise. I handed the first one to Joss, who was behind me, and he handed it to Rollan. I picked up the next one and gave that one to Joss as well.

I almost felt conflicted about taking the third pack when this team was already in so much trouble, but we had no way of knowing which of the bags held Rollan's and Astra's stuff. It was a few feet away from the others, and I was forced to take a couple of steps forward to reach it. I held my breath, hoping that nothing would stir from inside the shelter. Carefully, I lifted the last pack from the ground and turned to see Rollan creeping silently away.

Heading after him, I realized that Joss wasn't beside me anymore. I glanced around and spotted him sidling up to the four contenders sleeping out in the open.

What are you doing? I thought wildly, but didn't dare make a sound. He was reaching for something—I couldn't tell what— right next to Nolis. I held my breath, hoping none of them would stir. No one did, and Joss hurried back to my side a moment later with something clutched in his hand.

As soon as he was close, I hurried after Rollan into the trees.

"What next?" Rollan mouthed when we joined him.

"I do not want to be around when they wake up," Joss put in softly.

"What did you go back for?" Rollan whispered.

Joss smiled and held up a fist full of arrows. Rollan laughed a little louder than I was comfortable with.

"I can't believe you did that," I said, shaking my head in mirth.

He shrugged. "Astra will love them. Plus, we can use them to make fire."

"Awesome!" Rollan exclaimed.

Joss certainly was plucky.

"Let's head downstream," I announced, deciding immediately what the best course of action would be. "If the others could have made it back here, they would have done so. Wherever they went, they'll need water. Hopefully, they've continued downstream, and we can meet up with them."

The two boys nodded and fell into step behind me as we marched off into the night. I spent most of the walk pondering what would happen to the team we were leaving behind.

They weren't going to make it. Not all of them, at least. Korla had spoken the truth when she said that they should head back. The two injured members would only slow them down.

If I were in her position, would I be willing to leave Cole or Joss or Rollan? No, I would never leave them.

What about Kisa, the weakling? Or Astra? A nasty little voice hissed in the back of my head. I tried not to think about the answer to those questions as we walked on.

CHAPTER 7
TRIO

We walked all night, until the dawn turned pink before us and the sun was halfway into the sky. At first, our pace was hurried, but after five or six hours of traveling, we were trudging along slower than snails.

I could see that both the boys were dead on their feet, and I felt about the same.

Part of me wanted to push on and get as far as possible from the horrible scene that was most likely already playing out behind us. The three healthy team members might have abandoned the other two at first light, leaving Jaren to face Toruc's wrath. I couldn't imagine what he would do—if he were even still alive. The best-case scenario was that they would give up and head back to The Clan together.

Will they be allowed back in? I wondered.

They tried to kill us, and I was pretty sure they had done something unspeakable to their team leader, Reefa. Murder was the worst offense in our society. It hadn't just been Toruc either; they all went along with it.

No one will ever know, I realized. *They won't tell anyone, and neither can we.* It was forbidden to ever speak of the trials once back inside The Land of the Clan. On top of that, the last thing the Clan Leaders told us when we left was that there were no rules during the trials. Did that mean that what the other team had done wasn't wrong?

Their actions went against everything The Clan stood for. Theft. Murder. Mutiny. Each was considered a serious offense, but out here behavior of that kind seemed almost encouraged.

No. Surely not. This couldn't have been what the council wanted. Something must have been wrong with that group from the start, or at least with Toruc, and he had infected the others. Korla was right when she said that he had lost it. His already weak mind must have been shattered by the lack of food and boundaries. Perhaps it would be better if Toruc never returned to The Clan. How would he ever be able to live a normal life after all the horrible things he'd done?

"Can we stop now?" Rollan asked, cutting into my speculations.

"Sure," I said, coming to a halt. "You guys get some rest. I'll keep watch for a bit."

"Great," Joss replied, dropping both of the packs he carried and lying down right where he was.

"Maybe we should get out of sight a bit," I suggested, trying not to laugh. It was nice to have Joss around; no matter what kind of situation we were in, he was always so lighthearted.

Rollan followed me away from the river, into a clump of trees, where he promptly flopped down and closed his eyes. Joss didn't bother to stand up. Instead, he crawled dramatically on hands and knees to join his cousin.

"I hope Kisa's all right," I heard him mutter.

"I'm sure she's fine," I told him. "It sounds like she got away from Korla, and someone else was with her."

Joss nodded and shut his eyes against the morning light.

While the boys slept, I started going through the packs, because if I stopped moving, I knew I'd fall asleep too. We had six now—I had managed to hang on to Kisa's and mine the first night, Joss had his, and then there were the three we grabbed from Toruc's team. Hopefully, Astra's and Rollan's things were among them.

The first bag I picked up didn't look familiar. It was full of nothing but tan clothing. Judging by the size, they had to be Toruc's, which meant I had taken Toruc's bag by mistake. It must have been the one closest to the shelter. I felt kind of bad for stealing it, but it also seemed like justice.

The next bag I recognized as Astra's. Inside, I found a mixture of black and green clothing, along with two purple shirts.

Purple was the color of The Making, so the shirts must have belonged to Reefa.

The last bag was more of the same, a jumble of clothing. Most of Astra's and Rollan's belongings seemed to be accounted for. Each pack also held a water canteen, and Rollan's still had a flint.

I re-sorted the bags so that all the clothes were separated by color, putting Reefa's and Toruc's things together. I wasn't sure what to do with the purple items, but whatever had happened to Reefa, I doubted she needed her things anymore. Maybe she wouldn't mind us having them.

I stayed awake as long as I could. Once the sun reached its peak in the sky, I couldn't fight my drooping eyelids anymore. I roused Rollan to replace me on watch duty. Joss woke up too.

"I'll scout around a bit," he offered. "I don't feel like sleeping anymore."

I gave him permission, so long as he promised not to go too far. Much as I hated for us to separate, we were going to need food pretty soon. There was also the possibility that he might find some sign of Cole, Astra, and Kisa.

I was asleep in seconds.

It felt like just a moment later that someone was nudging me back to consciousness. I opened my eyes.

"Sorry to wake you," Joss apologized.

The setting sun told me that I had slept long enough, even though my eyelids begged to be closed again.

I sat up and saw that they had made a fire. Even better was the fact that Rollan was roasting three fish on a long stick over the flames.

I nodded approvingly at Joss. "Nice job!"

"It wasn't me, actually," Joss said. "Rollan found it."

"It? You mean the fish?" I asked, coming to sit with them by the fire.

"It was stuck through some of the tan clothes," Rollan chimed in.

"What are you talking about?" I furrowed my brow, confusion growing.

Smiling, Joss held something up. It was small and curved. I blinked and leaned in for a closer look. It was a metal fishhook. A long, thin reed was threaded cleverly through the head. Not as good as a line and reel, perhaps, but functional.

"Where did that come from?" I gasped.

Rollan shrugged.

"Toruc always was a cheat," Joss muttered. "The extra bag we grabbed must have been his."

"Why wasn't he using it then?" I asked. "His team is starving."

We were silent for a moment.

"Maybe it was his last resort," Joss mused. "Perhaps he thought he could use it on the others when they wouldn't listen to him anymore."

"You mean, if they tried to leave him, Toruc would tell them he had a way to feed them all?" I asked.

"Something like that," Joss agreed. "He's just that kind of twisted, too. Waiting until everyone is weak and then suddenly saving them with a fishhook. They'd have to follow him if they wanted to survive."

"How did he get it past the council?" Rollan wondered.

"Wouldn't have been too hard," I realized. "They didn't search us, just our bags. The hook is so small, Toruc could have stuck it through the clothes he was wearing."

"True." Rollan nodded.

"I feel kind of bad that we took it," Joss said.

"Don't," I told him. "They stole our stuff first." I thought for a moment, and then added, "And aren't you the one who took the arrows?"

"Yeah," Joss admitted, "but only four of them. I left some so they could feed themselves."

"Well, they'll have to make do with what they've got," I announced. I wasn't going to admit that I felt kind of guilty too. Stealing was wrong; however, there was no way I was going to march upstream and give them back the fishhook. They had tried to kill us once, and it would be stupid to allow them the opportunity of trying again.

We ate the fish while they were still hot. I didn't realize how hungry I was until my first mouthful. Then I gulped down the rest so fast I almost swallowed several bones in the process.

When we were all finished, it was time to make plans.

"The others are probably close by," I said. Rollan looked worried and started glancing around the riverbank.

"Not *those* others," I amended. "Cole, Astra, and Kisa. I mean, the *other* others are probably close too, but—never mind about that."

"Do you think they went on without us?" Joss asked.

I shook my head.

Astra might, but Cole never would, I thought.

"No," I said aloud. "If anything, we've probably gone farther than they would have. Let's start heading back upstream. We'll travel in the forest and go slowly so we can look for anything that might give us a clue as to where they've gone."

The two boys nodded. Then Rollan piped up, "Can we stay here with the fire tonight?"

"I don't think that's wise," I answered. "If the other team is headed this way, they'll have seen the smoke. Fire is one of the things they want most. We should leave and head back toward our old camp."

"But if they are coming toward the smoke, won't we run into them?" Rollan asked.

"They fight so much, we'll hear them from a mile away," Joss joked.

"Then all we have to do is jump in the bushes and hide until they're gone," I added.

"Let's do this!" Joss exclaimed. Both he and Rollan were grinning.

Rollan smothered the fire while Joss and I packed up our bags and filled all the water canteens. Carrying two packs each was exhausting, but the thought of leaving anything behind to get stolen again was even more distasteful.

There were still a few hours of daylight left when we started walking. The going was much slower inside the tree line, but we made it several miles before sunset.

I called a halt when the twilight was darkening into night. Although I had spent much of the day sleeping, I was still exhausted. I took the first watch again and woke Joss after three or four hours had passed, then I settled down in the leaves with my back pressed against Rollan's for warmth. I didn't want to unpack my bag and get out my cloak in case we needed to make another quick getaway.

Sleep wasn't as instantaneous as it had been earlier that day. Worries came flooding into my mind the moment my eyes closed. Even though it was utterly ridiculous, the thing I was most worried about was my fight with Cole. We had argued plenty of times before, but never so bitterly. I wondered if he was still mad at me—provided he was still alive. If not, then I would never have the chance to apologize.

Rollan shook me awake as the sun was coming up. My days and nights were so messed up that it didn't feel like morning. It didn't feel like any time in particular. We finished what food we had left in our packs before setting out. We moved slowly that day, always on the lookout for our teammates.

I wasn't too worried about finding food. With the fishhook, we could get plenty of fish from the river, so I preferred to stay concealed in the woods as much as possible. What concerned me more was that there was no trace of our missing friends. We couldn't find anything to indicate that they had traveled this way. The only footprints we saw were the ones we had made ourselves the night before last.

Around noon, I was on the verge of suggesting we go to the river and fish when, suddenly, Joss pointed to a tree in front of us. It was an apple tree. We all hurried over to investigate. Most of the apples were small and not yet ripe, but there were ten or twelve in the topmost branches ready to be eaten. Joss was, of course, up the tree in a matter of seconds. He started dropping the ripe ones down to us.

We rested in the shade during the hottest part of the day, munching on several apples each. In the afternoon, we walked on without finding much of anything. We kept watch again that night, but nothing stirred under the moon except wind-blown leaves.

At first light, we took a trip to the river for water and a few fish. The entire time they were cooking, I was torn between anxiety that the other team might attack us at any moment and the hope that Cole would see the fire and find us. No one came.

Later that morning, Rollan spotted more tubers, like the ones Kisa had gathered the first night of our journey. After we dug them up, the boys wanted to go straight back to the river to fish some more and cook the roots, but I wouldn't allow it. We were far too close to our old camp. Instead, we walked at least a mile down the riverbank, away from where the other team might still be lurking.

The afternoon stretched on to evening, creating long shadows in the woods around us. Just before nightfall, we started a fire and prepared the tubers. It was the first time in days we could eat as much as we wanted and still have some left over. Joss just kept pulling fish out of the river, even as he stuffed his face with their kin.

We extinguished the flames and decided to head back upstream a short distance before stopping to make camp. It was tough going because the moon was beginning to wane. Sometimes it was hidden entirely behind thick clouds. The boys didn't complain—at least, not too much. I was starting to get the sense that we didn't have to worry about the other team anymore. I doubted they were still at our old camp, and if they hadn't passed us going downstream, then they must have turned tail and given up.

I was the last one to keep watch that night. As the sky turned from indigo to pink, Joss woke up and came to sit beside me.

"I think we should check the old camp," he said. My stomach clenched, but I knew he was right.

"Yeah, we should," I replied, nodding.

Joss went and woke Rollan.

I stood and stretched; it was so weird sleeping outside. Back in my dwelling in The Paramount, I had slept under a pile of blankets. In the mornings, I always awoke feeling warm and secure. When I woke up outside, I was stiff, cold, and usually covered in dew. It was unpleasant, but I was getting used to it.

Once we had eaten something, several apples and a few fish saved from the day before, we headed for the old camp. We moved more silently that morning than ever before.

No one spoke as we approached our destination. I felt like I was going to be sick.

By mutual consent, we didn't enter the clearing on the nearest side. Instead, we went around and then circled back, so we could approach via the hill, just like we had before.

We all crawled into position to watch. Nothing moved below us for a very long time.

"There's no one down there," Joss finally said.

I had a feeling he was right. Before I could stop him, he stood up and started walking down the hill into the old camp. Rollan and I were right behind him. I would have liked to have grabbed his arm and pulled him back to our hiding place, but I wasn't fast enough. Before I could reach him, we were standing in the empty camp. Still, nothing moved.

"Let's go," I said softly. I pointed to the woods off to our left. "Korla came from there. She said she fought someone. Let's try to pick up the trail."

"Don't you want to see if there's anything useful lying around?" Joss asked.

My eyes slid past him to the ruined shelter, where I could see a cluster of black flies swarming.

I did not want to know what was inside. It was almost as if I could feel the decay of death creeping across the ground toward me.

I shook my head, trying to block the image of dead bodies out of my mind.

"No. Let's just go," I repeated. Joss seemed to understand what I was feeling because all he did was nod as I led them toward the forest once more.

CHAPTER 8
MOVING BACKWARD

Joss, Rollan, and I set out to the northeast, the direction from which we had seen Korla return several days earlier. There were a few prints left in the dirt. The trees grew thicker and thicker the farther we got from the riverbank. Despite slowing our progress, the plants were helpful since there was a clear path of snapped limbs and crushed foliage to follow.

"She must have hit her head pretty hard," Joss observed as the trail twisted back and forth.

"For her to have been unconscious half a day, I would imagine so," I agreed.

We finally came to a place where the trail ended. The moss covering the ground was torn, and a good-sized patch of loam was turned up. I also noticed deep furrows in the dirt. It seemed that a struggle had taken place—anyone could have seen that much—but I couldn't detect any clues as to the outcome.

Joss was the one who pointed out the patch of dried blood. We all stood looking at it wordlessly. It was a lot of blood.

Other than Korla's, there were no visible tracks, so we struck out at random, going northwest, deeper into the forest. We spread out, allowing about eight yards of space between each of us as we walked, keeping an eye out for anything that might give a sign of human life.

I was on the left, and Joss was on the right. Rollan was the least observant, so I stuck him in the middle. Hopefully, if he missed anything, Joss or I would catch it.

The ground started sloping up beneath our feet. Before long, I could see the peak of a mountain in front of us, and I wondered if we were standing on its base. Strange to think that a mountain could begin with something as insignificant as a gentle slope.

As the afternoon slipped away, the mountain's peak vanished into a cloud of fog. Suddenly, something moved on my left.

I hesitated for only a moment and then bolted after it. Out of the corner of my eye, I'd caught a glimpse of maroon.

Behind me, I heard Rollan call out to Joss. I imagined they were racing after me, but I had a good head start.

It was Cole. I knew it was. I could hear him crashing through the brush ahead of me.

"Cole?" I called with what little breath I could spare. "Cole, it's me, Myra!"

I burst into a clearing and saw Cole stopped just ahead of me. He was half crouched, hands braced against his knees. His mouth was open, and he was gasping desperately for air.

I wanted to hug him. Seeing him alive was the best thing in the world at that moment. All my worries of the last four days vanished. I would have gone straight to him and thrown my arms around his neck, but the moment I entered the clearing, our eyes met, and I stopped dead in my tracks.

Something was different. His blue eyes, usually so warm and friendly, were hunted and wary. I stood, not knowing what to do or say.

"Cole?" I breathed, wondering why he didn't recognize me.

He blinked. "Myra?" His voice was hoarse and wonderstruck.

"It's me," I told him, taking a step forward.

Just then, Joss and Rollan came charging into the clearing. Cole's eyes widened in horror until he realized it was them. What had happened to him in the past four days to elicit such a reaction?

I grabbed each of the boys by an arm to keep them from rushing Cole. The last thing I wanted was for him to start running again.

"You're all okay," Cole realized, sounding somewhat like his old self again.

I walked to him slowly, letting go of Joss and Rollan. They followed but remained behind me.

I nodded. "We've been looking for you. Are you alone?"

"Me? No, Kisa and Astra are in a cave nearby."

I felt a smile break across my face. Everyone was all right. We would be together again soon.

"Great!" Joss said a little loudly.

"Shhh," Cole hushed him. "The others might be close." The hunted look came back into Cole's eyes.

I shook my head. "They're gone. We checked the camp before heading this way."

Cole looked surprised. "Are you sure?" He glanced nervously at the forest around us.

"It's empty," I reported. "They were running low on food when they attacked us. I can't imagine things got any better after several of them became injured. I think they must have gone back to The Clan by now."

"How do you know all this?" Cole wondered.

"We hid on the hill by the camp and watched them the morning after the attack," I answered. "They weren't in good shape."

"Then where did you go?" Was that accusation in Cole's voice?

"We headed downstream looking for you," I rushed to explain. I shook my head, not sure why tears were gathering in my eyes. "We thought you'd probably be somewhere close to the river. When we didn't find you, we came back to look and..."

I was forced to trail off. My throat was too tight to speak. Relief filled my entire body as the strain of the last few days faded.

Everything was going to be all right now, wasn't it? I was overjoyed to see Cole, but he didn't seem as happy to see me. I had no clue why. All I knew was that I was about to start crying in front of him and the others, and I really didn't want to.

"Let's go get Kisa and Astra," Joss suggested tactfully.

After a moment, Cole nodded. "We need to get water first, if the others are really gone."

"We have plenty of water," I told Cole, holding up a full canteen.

His eyes widened. I closed the rest of the distance between us and pressed the canteen into his hands.

As he drank, I was finally close enough to see why his face seemed so strange. There were dark, bruise-like circles under his eyes, and he had lost weight. I imagined he must be very dehydrated if the way he was gulping water through chapped lips was any indication.

He stopped after a moment, out of breath again.

"Thanks," he said, sounding much more normal. "I needed that."

Still holding the half-empty canteen in his hand, he began leading us through the woods. We didn't have a long walk, but it was nearly all uphill. Cole was panting and gasping for air before we were even halfway there. I asked him if he wanted to rest for a few minutes, but he insisted on continuing.

The place he took us looked like a giant pile of broken rocks, which must have come from the cliff face above. The trees close by were twisted and bent as if they had felt the impact of falling boulders many times. Moss and lichen grew everywhere, covering large chunks of broken stone.

"Where are they?" I asked, remembering how hard it was to find the cave in The Valley of the North Wind. I had gone there once, looking for Astra when she skipped training because her favorite horse died.

Just as the words left my mouth, Kisa's head popped out of a cleft where two rocks met.

"Joss! Rollan!" I heard her cry softly. She clambered out and scrambled over the rock pile to throw herself into Joss's arms. He laughed with joy as he held her tightly.

Kisa hugged Rollan as soon as Joss released her, and then latched onto me with her quivering body. She looked weak and drained, but not as bad as Cole.

"Do you have any water or food?" she blurted out.

Joss instantly pulled out his canteen for her. Kisa began gulping down water while Rollan fished out our last apple from his pack. Kisa offered some of the fruit to Cole, but he shook his head. Rollan and Joss had a thousand questions for the little girl, who did her best to answer between bites.

"Keep the noise down," Cole advised the youngsters, who were growing louder every second as they all tried to speak at once. Kisa nodded and glanced around with fearful eyes. Joss and Rollan dropped their voices but continued talking over each other as they told Kisa what we had been doing the past four days.

"Come with me," Cole said softly, heading toward the rock pile.

I hurried after him, knowing what I would find and dreading it.

The cave was tiny and coated with dirt and dead leaves. Astra was on the floor, lying flat on her back. Her eyes were closed when I entered, but they snapped open a moment later.

Cole knelt beside her and placed the water canteen in her left hand. He gently helped her raise her head. Astra drank carefully at the awkward angle until the canteen was almost empty. Then she lay back down and turned her gaze on me.

A wry smile flashed across her face.

"You finally found us," she said. "It's about time." I was expecting her to be much worse, but she seemed fine, except for the fact that she didn't get up.

Her body was sprinkled with a thin layer of dust as if she hadn't moved in days. I caught sight of a gash on her right shoulder. There was some green goo on it. Kisa must have found something in the woods to help the wound heal.

"Are you in pain?" I asked.

Astra shook her head slowly.

"No, it's not bad," she replied impatiently, like she'd answered that question a hundred times already. "Where have you guys been?" She didn't sound hostile, just curious.

I quickly related the events of the past few days. Cole had already heard a little of it, but I added all the details I could remember. Both his and Astra's eyes lit up when I told them about the fishhook.

By the end of my narrative, Astra was laughing.

"You stole our stuff back? That's so you, Myra."

I wasn't sure why she thought it was funny.

"Joss grabbed a present for you too," I told her. "He'll have to show you later."

"That was nice of him." Astra finished laughing, but still seemed quite amused. I didn't understand how she could be completely calm while Cole remained so tense.

"What about you guys?" I asked. "Have you been camped here this whole time?"

"Yes," Astra answered. "That night, I saw someone chasing Kisa, so I went after them. It must have been the girl you mentioned." Astra shook her head as best as she could from the ground.

"Why anyone would choose the smallest and try to—" She cut off, and I could hear the anger and disgust in her voice. "Kisa didn't even have anything with her except her staff. I don't know what that coward hoped to gain by killing her, but she seemed intent on it. I didn't dare shoot in the dark, so I grabbed her." Astra glanced down at the wound on her arm with morbid humor. "Apparently, I grabbed the wrong part."

"Korla—the girl—said you fought her like mad," I put in.

"Yeah, that sounds about right. But after I started bleeding, I knew I didn't have very long before I would be too weak to continue. I threw her off, and she crashed into a tree and didn't get up. I think she may have also hit her head on a rock when she landed.

"Kisa was nearby and came back when she heard our yelling. She's such a brave little girl; most would have kept on running.

"And it was a good thing that she did, or I would have been in trouble. She knew what to do and started putting pressure on the wound. I coated it with mud so we wouldn't leave a trail. While we were looking for somewhere safe to wait out the night, we ran into Cole."

"I almost stabbed Kisa," Cole admitted humorlessly. "One second, it was just me in the woods, listening for pursuers, and then she was right in front of me."

"We took shelter in this cave just before dawn," Astra continued. "Every time I got up, my arm started bleeding, so I'm not allowed to move without Kisa's permission. That's why we've been holed up here."

Astra smiled again, but it wasn't quite right. She was leaving something out of her account. I glanced at Cole, wondering if he would tell me what she wasn't. Cole had no comment, nor was he looking at me.

No one said anything for a moment. Astra was the one to break the silence. "Cole, why don't you go see if the boys out there will make a fire? I'm sure that would cheer Kisa up."

Cole looked at her the way he used to look at me when we were communicating without words. He nodded and left without even glancing in my direction. In the narrow space, I was forced to shift my position to let him out through the opening.

I stared after him for a long moment before turning back to Astra. She met my gaze. Her deep, green eyes betrayed none of what she was thinking.

"It has not been a good four days," Astra finally said. "Cole feels very guilty that he wasn't there to help in the fight."

"He told you that?" I asked.

"No, but I can tell it's been eating away at him. Every time he looks at my shoulder, I see it. I'm sure it was hard for him to hear that you and Joss had a scuffle as well. Although, the fact that you are both here and unscathed will, most likely, ease his feelings."

"I don't understand," I replied.

"He's been worried sick about you. The boys, too, but mostly you."

"He didn't seem too worried when we found him," I muttered.

Astra chewed her lip for a few seconds.

"It has not been a good four days," she repeated.

I was tired of trying to figure out what she was hinting at. Her cryptic words gave little away, so I waited silently for her to just spit it out plain and simple.

Finally, she launched into the real story of what had been happening.

"That first night was pretty rough. My shoulder wouldn't stop bleeding. Kisa was crying nonstop because she was afraid I was going to die. Cole didn't know how to help either of us.

"It was so dark, we couldn't see anything, and every noise outside made them jump. A little after dawn, my bleeding finally stopped, and Kisa fell asleep. Cole and I talked then. He felt like the whole thing was his fault because he was a terrible leader."

I nodded. Hadn't Cole confessed those very things to me on multiple occasions?

"I tried to tell him it wasn't true," Astra continued. "But I don't think I convinced him. Kisa slept for a long time, which was good. I dozed on and off, but Cole didn't sleep at all. He paced up and down just outside, torn between staying with us and going back to look for you and the boys.

"He had almost resolved to go; we were discussing it when Kisa woke up and started begging him not to. It soon became clear that he couldn't leave.

"In that moment, when he decided to stay, I think he gave you three up for dead. There was a change in him; I could see it in his eyes.

"We only had one canteen of water and what little food was in Cole's pack to share. We finished nearly all the supplies on the first day. I don't think Cole ate or drank any of it. He wouldn't sleep that night either. I tried to get up and keep watch for him, but my arm began bleeding, which set Kisa off again.

"In the morning, they came. Cole heard them, and we all hid in here. There were three of them and three of us, but neither Kisa nor I would have been much good in a fight. They weren't smart enough to recognize the marks from his pacing and, finally, they left. We hoped they would move out of the area for good.

"The water ran out in the afternoon, so Cole headed back to the river to get more. He wasn't successful, and Kisa cried the whole time he was gone. The other team was still close by and spotted him in the woods. Thankfully, he was able to escape them, but he never managed to make it to the river. He came back after a couple of hours, exhausted and without water. Just having him here made Kisa feel better, although, we were all hungry and thirsty.

"Cole tried again the next day, but the same thing happened. I think they almost caught him. He's got a nasty scratch on his side. According to him, it happened while hiding in a thorn bush, but I think it really came from an arrow or a knife."

Astra stopped for a moment. "He was going to try and get water again today. When you appeared in front of him, it must have seemed too good to be true."

"Why?" I asked. "Surely, he knew we would be looking for you guys. You aren't that far from where we split up."

"Take into account that he hasn't slept, eaten, or drunk anything in over three days."

I nodded. I supposed it was due to the fatigue, but I was still bothered by the fact that Cole was so suspicious of me.

"I'm completely all right," Astra said. I glanced at her, unsure of what she meant. "My shoulder should be fine in the morning. I'll probably stay here until then and get some rest. Why don't you go make sure Cole does the same?"

I nodded, grasping her point, and left the cave.

Joss and Rollan had built a small fire. There was an abundance of wood, and they had collected a sizable pile.

Thinking over Astra's account of the past few days, I suspected the reason Cole's group had been hunted so relentlessly was because we took back our supplies. A feeling of guilt washed over me. It didn't help that I was well-fed and rested while half our team was exhausted and starving.

Cole sat hunched by the fire, staring into the flames expressionlessly. Kisa was sitting on a small rock close by, her head resting on Rollan's shoulder, eyes sealed shut.

"Joss," I called softly, as he went darting by me with an armload of wood. He turned my way, all smiles. In his mind, everything was perfect. We were together again, and he had a fishhook that could feed us forever.

It was that fishhook I was thinking about at the moment.

"Can you and Rollan make it to the river and bring back a few fish before dark?" I asked.

"Sure!" Joss exclaimed. "I was just starting to feel hungry."

I glanced at Cole and Kisa. "It's not really for us," I told him quietly. Joss followed my gaze and nodded. He understood. "Be very careful," I instructed. Thinking about how many times Cole had been attacked in the last few days, I pressed my knife into Joss's hand so he would have a weapon.

"Not a problem," he said to me. "Rollan," he called to his cousin. "Let's go!"

Rollan gently transitioned Kisa's head to the ground without waking her. The two gathered their staffs and the empty canteens before quickly heading out of the clearing.

Cole staggered to his feet, staring after them.

"Where are they going?" he asked nervously.

"To get some food and more water," I answered.

"It's dangerous," Cole cried, taking a few steps as if to follow. I caught his hand and stopped him.

"They'll be all right," I promised. "They aren't helpless, and we need food."

"They shouldn't go. Bring them back!" he almost yelled.

"Cole, you are exhausted," I snapped at him. He froze at my tone. "You need to get some rest." He was already shaking his head in protest as I continued. "I will keep watch, and you will sleep."

Our eyes met and, for a moment, there was a short contest of wills; his crumbled first.

"Okay," he agreed.

I expected him to go to the cave and lay down. Instead, he just sank to the ground where he was and leaned back against a fallen stone. He was unconscious a moment later.

Kisa was staring at me from across the clearing by the fire. She looked like she was about to burst into tears. Cole and I must have woken her.

"It's okay," I assured the young girl, going to stand by her side. "Everything is going to be all right now." She nodded, but she didn't look convinced.

"We're going to be moving closer to the river in the morning," I told her. "If there's anything you can do to help prepare Astra's arm for the trip, you should do it before then."

Kisa nodded, but didn't move. She was completely worn out from lack of sustenance and the stress of the past few days. In less than ten minutes, she fell back asleep. Neither she nor Cole stirred, even when the boys returned.

They'd only caught two fish, but didn't dare stay longer for fear of losing the light. The sky was completely dark by the time the fish were cooked. Our fire lit the entire clearing, throwing strange shadows in all directions among the fallen rocks.

We woke Cole and Kisa so they could eat. I took some of the fish into the cave for Astra as well.

For having gone so long without food, they ate surprisingly little. I didn't allow Rollan or Joss to finish up the leftovers; instead, we saved them for the morning.

CHAPTER 9
TOGETHER

Joss, Rollan, and I agreed to take turns watching throughout the night. After eating, Kisa moved into the cave with Astra. Cole remained where he was, sleeping in the open with the rest of us.

I had the middle watch, which was my least favorite by far. It was worse than the others because as soon as you've been asleep for a couple of hours, someone wakes you. To ensure you don't nod off again, you have to get up and walk around for a bit. Finally, after you've spent your entire watch trying to stay alert, you get to the point where you are really and truly awake just in time for the next person's shift to start. Then, of course, it takes forever to get back to sleep.

After two hours of being awake, I was at the stage where I wasn't sleepy anymore. There was a gentle breeze stirring the air, and I could hear hundreds of crickets and cicadas just beyond the firelight. The sky was patchy with clouds, but a handful of stars managed to peek through.

All of a sudden, Cole began thrashing around wildly in his sleep. I stared for a moment until a low moan escaped his lips. It went up in pitch at the end, sounding like a cry of pain.

I squatted beside him and gently shook his shoulder. I hated to wake him, but I didn't want Rollan and Joss thinking we were under attack. It would have been easy enough to calm them down, but if they disturbed Kisa, she would probably cry for the rest of the night.

Cole didn't respond as I nudged him a second time. Instead, he started trembling, and his breathing accelerated.

"Cole," I whispered, shaking him harder. "Cole, wake up!"

His eyes flew open, wide with panic. He attempted to scramble to his feet but stumbled, ending up on his knees. He looked around in dismay, as if expecting to see enemies everywhere.

"It was just a dream," I said soothingly, reaching out and touching his arm.

He whipped around toward me, eyes still seeing whatever horrible scene he had just left. After a moment, the fear started to dissolve. Slowly, he sank back into a sitting position and closed his eyes in relief. His breathing returned to normal.

"Everything's okay," I promised.

Cole shook his head without looking up.

"We're all together again. In the morning, we'll go back to the stream and keep moving forward," I promised him. I hoped he'd lay back down and get the rest he so desperately needed, but he didn't. Even though my words seemed to quiet his worries somewhat, his face was still strained.

"People are dying, Myra," he whispered.

"People always die during the trials."

"I know, but I didn't think it would be like this. I mean, accidents happen, like in the valley with the rocks, but they were trying to murder us."

I nodded, having no words of comfort to offer him.

"There is evil out here," Cole told me.

I wasn't sure what he meant by that. Evil wasn't really something that existed in The Clan. Sure, sometimes humans did things that were wrong, but it wasn't because they wanted to. Mostly, people just made stupid, little mistakes and were sorry for them. They still had to endure punishment, but most offenses weren't considered *evil*.

"They were desperate," I countered.

"It's more than that. They wanted to kill us—just because they could."

At that moment, I remembered Reefa. She was their teammate; there was no reason for them to hurt her, but they had.

"Maybe there is something wrong with them like there is with the Broken," I suggested.

"Maybe there is something wrong with all of us," Cole muttered darkly.

I didn't know what to say. Much as I wanted to protest, he seemed to have the high ground at the moment.

"You should get some more rest," I responded. Cole still looked exhausted, even though he had slept most of the afternoon, as well as half the night.

Without argument, Cole settled down again. It didn't take him long to fall back asleep, but soon he started moaning once more.

 Instead of waking him, I reached out my hand and ran it gently through his dark hair. It seemed to help calm him, so I repeated the process. His breathing grew more even with my rhythmic strokes.

He didn't have any more dreams after that. At least, if he did, they were silent dreams, which didn't cause him to stir.

I was so caught up in my thoughts, I didn't realize how long I sat there, calmly smoothing Cole's hair and staring into the fire.

The flames burned low, and I was contemplating whether it would be worth getting up to add another log, when I realized the sky wasn't black anymore.

The night was over, and I had let Joss sleep through his watch. I wasn't too worried about it. A few hours of missed sleep wouldn't kill me. Plus, Joss was the one feeding us; it would be good for him to be well-rested.

I waited another half hour, until twilight turned to dawn, before I started rousing the others.

"I thought I was supposed to have the last watch," Joss said when he saw that it was morning.

"I didn't feel like sleeping last night," I told him.

"So nice to be you," Rollan groaned at Joss as he rolled over and sat up. "You're the only one of us three who's gotten a full night's rest in the last five days."

"Because you've been so sleep-deprived," I shot back, sarcasm marring my voice.

Rollan scowled at me playfully; he knew I didn't mean it. Joss laughed at our exchange.

I hated to wake the others, but we needed to make it to the river before night. I left Joss and Rollan to wake Cole and headed into the cave. Astra was still lying in the same position as yesterday, with Kisa curled up close to her side.

Astra was already awake. Her eyes studied the roof of the cave. I was sure she had probably memorized every crack that spanned the low ceiling.

"It's time to go, guys," I said, putting out a hand to shake Kisa.

"What about Astra's shoulder?" the little girl asked after sitting up and rubbing her eyes.

"It's fine," Astra assured her. "I've had plenty of time to heal."

Kisa didn't look convinced. "But it might open up again."

"Then we'll stop the bleeding like we did last time," Astra told her. "I'm going to go crazy if I don't get out of this cave soon."

Kisa nodded as I helped Astra to her feet so she wouldn't have to use her right arm. We joined the boys in the clearing a moment later. They had just finished packing up the seven backpacks. Cole was the only one, other than Joss and me, who had taken his pack with him when we fled in the storm several nights earlier.

I made Cole, Kisa, and Astra split the remains of the previous night's fish. Joss and Rollan watched them eat hungrily. My stomach was growling too, but I ignored it. We would make it to the river soon enough, and then there would be food for everyone.

Kisa took a long-sleeved, purple shirt from the bag we had pillaged. She used it to make a sling for Astra's arm by knotting the sleeves around her neck. Everyone carried their own pack, except Astra. She was willing to sling it over her good shoulder, but Kisa wouldn't hear of it. I had never really thought of Kisa as fierce; however, the young girl was very protective of her patient.

Cole, Joss, Rollan, and I took turns carrying the extra bag and Astra's. I wasn't sure Cole should have been in the rotation, but I didn't want to insult him by suggesting he be excluded.

Just before we set out, Astra handed me her bow.

"This isn't going to do me much good for the next couple of days," she explained.

I didn't know quite what to say, but I took the bow.

"Oh, here," Joss said, putting the extra arrows he'd pinched into the quiver before I looped it over my shoulder and head.

"Nice," Astra exclaimed admiringly, the hint of amusement back in her voice.

We walked slowly, mostly for Astra's sake. Even so, we were all pretty tired by the time we reached the river. Although it wasn't even midday, we elected to take a break.

Joss instantly pulled out the fishing hook and headed for a place where the river formed a little pool of calm water. Rollan and Astra started gathering wood for a fire with their three good hands.

"I want to look around for herbs," Kisa said.

"I'll come with you," I offered. Holding Astra's bow, I felt like it would be easy to defend her.

"Should I come too?" Cole wondered. I could tell he hated the idea of splitting up again.

I waved him off.

"We won't go far," I promised.

He nodded uncertainly and began to help the others with the wood.

Before the two of us were even enclosed by the forest, I heard Joss crow in triumph.

"He must have caught a fish," I guessed.

Kisa grinned.

"Joss is amazing!"

I smiled to myself. It was so cute how Kisa had adopted Joss as her big brother. I wondered if in the future she would come to think of him as something more, or if they would always maintain the same easy relationship. I partially hoped they would never change. What they had was so innocent and carefree yet strong and deep. If they started down another path, they would risk losing everything they had built. And that path would never be easy for anyone.

We didn't find anything to help Astra's shoulder, but Kisa did spy a mint bush. It wasn't the most useful plant out there, but it would be nice to have a taste other than fish in our mouths for a while.

I almost shot a large bird, but I missed by a hair and then had to spend fifteen minutes searching for the arrow.

There was a blazing fire by the time we returned to our newest campsite. Astra was resting against a tree with her eyes shut. Kisa hurried to her side. Cole and Rollan were each roasting a fish over the flames. Joss had just pulled a third from the river. I skewered it on a stick and sat down beside Cole.

"Are we staying here for the rest of the day?" I asked.

Cole looked uncertain, as if he hadn't thought that far ahead. He considered for a moment.

"No. Let's have a rest while it's hot out, and then we can keep moving into the evening."

I nodded. Eager as I was to move on, it was clear that some of the others hadn't regained their strength yet.

After the fish were done cooking, we all ate. Joss caught two more, which we roasted and kept for later. Kisa handed out some mint leaves.

Joss offered to keep watch so everyone else could sleep since he was well-rested. I hated sleeping during the day, but after staying up more than half the night, I was having trouble keeping my eyelids open. I lay down in the shade of one of the large trees by the riverbank. The long, soft grass felt incredibly comfortable— or, more likely, I was just really tired.

By the time I woke up, it was late afternoon. The fire was out, and Joss was packing up his bag. Together, we roused the others and headed downstream.

That night we made camp early. Kisa and Rollan went to look for herbs while Cole and I built a fire.

Now that we were all back together and out of immediate danger, I expected him to be more like his old self, but he wasn't. He hardly spoke, never laughed, and jumped at every noise. I didn't like this new Cole. He was a stranger, not the friend I had known for so long.

I tried to engage him in conversation, to make him smile his beautiful smile and forget whatever horrors he had experienced, but to no avail.

Astra's arm started to bleed, which was the reason we stopped early for the night. It wasn't that bad, but Kisa instructed her to sit still and not move.

I went to work clearing the ground for a fire, while Cole gathered wood. A few of the others went in search of food.

Astra remained seated, but her eyes seemed to follow Cole wherever he went. I tried to ignore her and focus on my work.

Rollan and Kisa came back from the woods beaming. Kisa had found something to help Astra, and, better yet, Rollan carried an armful of pears.

"I spotted the tree myself," he announced proudly.

I went back with Rollan to help him gather more while Joss settled down to fish for something to cook. Kisa took the time to tend to Astra, and Cole finished with the fire.

Sadly, the river here was faster flowing, and Joss didn't manage to catch anything. We ate pears and the two fish from earlier for dinner. Cole announced that he was able to help keep watch that night. Astra said the same thing, but since Kisa wouldn't agree to let her get up and feed the fire, she was excluded. We split the watch into four shifts.

I offered to go first.

"Only if you actually wake people up this time," Cole said. His voice was so serious that it took me a moment to realize he was making a joke. I laughed and saw a smile on his face for the first time in days.

I felt Astra's gaze on me. I turned and glanced toward her. I'd expected to see her giving us a disapproving look, but as she turned away, I saw that she was smirking. I liked that even less.

CHAPTER 10
THE WRONG DIRECTION

Cole woke everyone at first light. We breakfasted while discussing what to do next.

"Let's go back to the pear tree and gather as many as we can carry before heading out," Cole suggested.

"It's a fifteen-minute walk in the wrong direction," I protested. I was eager to move forward. Our progress would already be slowed to a crawl by Astra's injury. I didn't see any reason to hinder ourselves further by trekking the wrong way for a tree that probably grew everywhere around here.

"We need—" Cole started, but I interrupted him.

"We need to keep moving, or the other teams are going to catch us."

It was the wrong thing to say to him. Instantly, he glanced at Astra, which I hated. I'd only meant to suggest that speed was necessary if we were going to win, but he heard a different meaning in my words. I kept forgetting how fragile he was these days.

"If we starve, it won't matter," Astra stated.

I gritted my teeth.

"There's lots of food around here," I argued. "Fish from the stream and probably more fruit trees up ahead somewhere."

Cole was still looking at Astra when he answered me.

"We don't know how long we'll be able to rely on the river for food. Even last night Joss wasn't able to catch anything."

Joss nodded. "If the water stays this rough, there might not be a chance to fish for a while."

I sighed. Clearly I wasn't going to win this argument.

We headed back to the pear tree.

All of us.

Astra suggested she stay behind and wait for our return, but Cole wouldn't hear of it, even if someone stayed with her.

At least Astra moved more quickly that morning. The bleeding from the night before seemed to have been superficial, and her wound didn't reopen. Still, it took us over an hour to make it back to our original starting point. The packs weighed us down even more than before, stuffed to the brim as they were with fruit.

Just before sun high, I noticed Joss struggling to keep up, burdened by the weight of two packs. Since I was carrying the second extra pack, I knew exactly how he felt. I was determined not to complain myself, but was concerned that Joss was going to exhaust himself.

Since I wasn't entirely sure how much Cole had recovered physically, I moved forward, matching my pace with Rollan's. He was far sturdier than his cousin and was now in the lead.

"How long ago did you give Joss Astra's pack?" I whispered under my breath.

"Half an hour," Rollan replied softly. "Why?" He glanced behind us at his cousin.

"Guess I should go get it back from him," he sighed, realizing how much of a toll the load was taking on the smaller boy.

"Be tactful," I advised.

"I'm always tactful," Rollan said so seriously I thought he might have actually believed it.

A few minutes later, I heard Rollan say to Joss, "It's my turn to carry the extra pack again."

"But I haven't even had it for an hour," Joss told him, slightly out of breath.

Rollan shrugged. "The extra weight helps me balance out the one on my back."

I was surprised. Apparently Rollan could be tactful. Would Kisa do something reckless next?

"Don't lie to me," Joss protested. "I know what you're doing."

"I'm not sure what you mean," Rollan said, shrugging.

"You don't think I can carry it," Joss snapped.

"He never said—" Kisa started.

"He doesn't have to," Joss grumbled.

Rollan sighed. "It's a lot heavier now with all the pears in it. Why don't you let me carry it today, and you can have it tomorrow when we've eaten some of them?"

"No!" Joss all but yelled. I'd never seen him upset about anything before.

"Joss," I began firmly, dropping back to join the conversation, "we all have different talents and gifts. That means sometimes we are going to have different responsibilities. Today, yours don't include carrying two packs."

The look on Joss's face when I finished speaking was a mixture of disappointment and misery. Wordlessly, he shoved Astra's pack into Rollan's arms, then jogged past the rest of us to the front of the group. He disappeared into the trees ahead, Kisa hurrying after him.

"Don't go too far," Cole called after the pair.

I glanced at him, wondering if he thought I'd been too harsh, but he didn't say anything.

"It must be difficult for someone like Joss to admit they're not strong enough," Astra commented to me a moment later.

I couldn't help but wonder if her words carried a double meaning.

"He'll get over it," was all I answered.

The rest of that day, Cole, Rollan, and I rotated the two extra bags between us. In the morning, after we'd eaten pears for both dinner and breakfast, the packs were much lighter, and we let Joss join the rotation again.

Before we set out, I stuffed most of the fruit into Reefa's bag, the one Rollan and I were going to switch off carrying. Astra's pack, which Cole and Joss would take turns with, was far lighter. Thankfully, no one noticed.

The day was warm, but we couldn't cool off in the water because the current was far too fast. Even so, we managed to travel many miles to the east while still following the river.

That was how the next several days passed. We lived off fish—when we could get them—and anything else we found that was edible. Astra's arm grew better and better. It wasn't long before she stopped using the sling and wanted to carry her own pack, but Kisa still recommended against it.

One morning, the sun rose far to the left of the streambed. We were no longer heading straight into its light. At some point during the previous day, the river must have begun to angle more to the south than the east.

We'll have to leave it today, I thought.

I saw Cole glance at the sun.

"We should make sure all the canteens are full before we leave the river," I suggested.

Cole shook his head.

"We're not going to leave it."

"What?" I asked. "Our instructions say to head east, and then north. The river is going south."

"I know," Cole replied. "But we should stay with the river. We'll travel faster and farther each day if we don't have to worry about finding water."

"This is a forest," I argued. "There has to be lots of water around. It won't be that hard to find more."

"But it will take time, and what if we don't find any?" Astra interjected. She must have walked up behind me and overheard our conversation.

I whipped around to face her.

"We'll have to cope. The other teams won't be following the river; they'll head straight east. We're going to be left behind. We need to follow the instructions," I told Cole, turning to face him. We had both grown up in The Paramount; following instructions there was as natural as breathing.

Cole looked uncertain, his decision unmade. I could see it in his countenance as he met my gaze. Then his eyes slid to a point behind me, where I knew Astra was standing, and I saw resolve spread across his face.

"We'll follow the river," he announced.

"This is wrong," I snarled. When we had disagreed about going back for the fruit, it was a small thing, and I let it slide, but this would impact the rest of our lives.

"I'm sorry, Myra, but I think this is the right choice." Cole turned away from me and started walking along the river to the south. Astra passed by after him.

My blood boiled at the very sight of her. What game was she playing? Cole was only doing what he thought was best, but with Astra, there was more to it. I hated the fact that I had no choice but to follow in their wake.

The air grew hot much earlier than on the previous day. Before we even made it five miles, I was covered in sweat. Astra seemed much stronger, and Kisa didn't make as much of a fuss over her, so it was almost a pleasant walk, except for the fact that we were going the wrong direction.

We stopped around midday when the heat was nearly unbearable.

"It's going to storm again tonight," Rollan announced.

I dropped the two packs I was carrying before looking up. Dark storm clouds were massing directly ahead of us.

Great, I thought. *Looks like we're in for another pleasant evening.*

The river was slow enough here that the younger boys didn't hesitate to jump in. Kisa seemed nervous about the current, but Joss reported that it wasn't bad.

Astra carefully climbed down the bank and dropped into the water, holding onto a tree root. She submerged a couple of times, then used her good arm to pull herself back out. Rollan went over to help her.

She looked different when she emerged, reddish-brown hair plastered to her face and arms. It took me a moment to realize that the layer of dirt coating her skin was gone. I had grown so accustomed to it that I was shocked to see her clean once more.

It made me think about how grimy I felt. I couldn't remember the last time I'd bathed. My hair was matted, and there was dirt clogging every pore on my body.

Without hesitation, I leapt into the water. It was incredibly refreshing and, even though the current was a bit on the strong side, I felt comfortable paddling around close to the bank.

"Too bad we can't build a boat," I mused aloud. "Then we could just relax and float along."

Joss thought for a moment. "I mean, we could, but I don't know if it would be worth the time and effort."

I laughed. I hadn't been serious. *We shouldn't even be coming this way at all*, I wanted to say.

Once I finished washing away many days' worth of grime, I climbed from the water. I lay on my back in the sun, letting its heat dissolve the moisture from my body. It didn't take long before my skin was completely dry. My clothes and hair continued to be damp for several more hours as we pressed onward.

It was almost time to make camp for the evening when Joss, who was in front again, froze. Glancing downstream, I saw a creature standing close to the river. It was grazing on the long grass with its back to us. The animal looked like a goat that had been stretched out. It had long, skinny legs, brown fur, and the strangest pair of horns I'd ever seen sprouting from its head. They were like barren tree branches.

I wasn't carrying an extra pack at the time, so I grabbed an arrow from the quiver on my back and fit it to the bowstring. Not knowing the anatomy of the creature, I wasn't sure where to aim, but decided middle mass was as good a place as any.

Slowly, I started creeping closer as the animal raised its head. Huge eyes and ears made the animal almost cute. It twitched toward the woods. Immediately, I let the arrow fly before it could vanish into the trees. The shaft buried itself in the beast's chest.

The animal leapt forward and darted away, but we heard a crash in the woods a moment later.

"Excellent," Joss said, practically hopping with glee.

"Let's go and get it," Rollan piped up at almost the same moment.

Cole nodded, and we headed into the woods. The creature's color made it difficult to spot, especially since it had fallen into a bed of dead leaves. It was much heavier than the last animal I shot. We half drug, half carried it back to the riverbank.

With a sigh, I pulled out my knife. I almost regretted killing the beast, because I knew how long it would take to butcher.

After twenty minutes, I took a break and let Joss take over. I went to inspect the head of the animal, still curious about the horns. They were thin, and each of them seemed to be sprouting several horns of their own. The ends came to sharp points.

The dark clouds we had seen earlier were closing in around us, so I started working on a shelter—not that it had done much good the last time. Astra helped me the best she could with only one arm. Kisa assisted as well, but even crippled, Astra was the more useful of the two.

We—mostly I—pulled a fallen log over to a boulder half as tall as I was. It had a cleft on the top. I set one end of the log snugly in the cleft and left the other end on the ground. Next, we leaned sticks against one side of the log, and then covered them in brush to create something of a wall. We did the same on the other side, but left a third of the log uncovered to serve as an entrance. I wasn't sure how effective it was going to be, and I doubted all of us would fit inside.

By the time we finished, more than half the meat was cut up, and some of it was cooking.

We split the first couple of pieces when they were ready. I almost spit out the first mouthful. The meat was a little dry and carried a stronger flavor than I was expecting. It didn't taste bad, but it was unlike anything I had eaten before.

It did rain that night, and we didn't all fit into the shelter.

We were halfway through cooking the meat when the first drops started to fall. I began shoving packs into our little lean-to as the others tried to get as much of the meat cooked as possible. Within five minutes, the rain started pouring down in torrents.

Astra told Kisa to get into the shelter before she caught a cold. The rest of us did what we could, but keeping the fire burning was a losing battle. When it did finally go out, it was too dark to see anything.

We fumbled our way to the shelter, mostly by touch. With Kisa and the packs already taking up half the space, it was easy to tell that only one, maybe two, of us were going to fit inside.

"Let the girls get in," Cole said.

"I don't mind the rain," Astra responded instantly.

"Joss and Rollan are smaller," I pointed out, really meaning shorter. In terms of mass, Rollan was only smaller than Cole. "They'll fit better."

"Fine," Cole sighed. He sounded tired and disheartened, as if he didn't care anymore. No one said anything for a moment. Then Joss and Rollan obediently entered the shelter. If Cole hadn't used that tone, I'm sure they would have objected and insisted that Astra and I join Kisa.

It worried me. Was Cole already worn so thin? We hadn't come that far yet, and the road ahead of us was sure to be far more difficult than the one behind.

I hated the rain and would have been far happier curled up inside the shelter, but I would have rather died than let anyone know that particular fact. Instead, I tried to make the best of it and find shelter under a nearby tree.

Astra really didn't seem to mind the rain and remained where she was in the open to keep the first watch.

Cole joined me under the spreading arms of the oak tree a moment later. He didn't say anything as he settled down. Even though we were barely a yard apart, it felt like I was lying there alone.

CHAPTER II
THE GROVE

When Astra woke me, it felt closer to the morning than midnight, but in the utter darkness, it was hard to tell. After I sat up, I heard her trudge a little way off and lay down. She didn't make another sound until morning.

The rain was falling in large drops, and the wind was whistling through the forest. I was glad it was still summer, otherwise the temperature would have been miserably cold.

Lightning began appearing about an hour after I started my watch. I could see it in the distance long before it reached us. Its slow approach was accompanied by increasingly louder and louder rolls of thunder. The rain picked up too. I was soaked through in a matter of minutes. Not that I had been snug and dry before, but I was now dripping water.

Suddenly, there was a peal of thunder that shook the ground beneath me. I wasn't sure how, but Astra managed to sleep right through it. Not Cole. He leapt up wildly, looking around in panic.

"It's just thunder," I called, speaking over the rain.

In the next flash of lightning, I saw that he had turned toward me, eyes huge with terror.

"You okay?" I asked, half rising myself.

"No," Cole's voice came to me in the dark. "I—I had a dream."

I waited for him to continue, but he didn't. "What was it about?" I pressed.

He made no answer.

"Cole," I said softly, "can't you tell me? You used to tell me everything." Sadness filled my voice as the last sentence left my lips. It hadn't been that long ago—less than a month—but now…

"In my dream, you died," Cole whispered breathlessly. "You all did." I could tell from his voice how much the dream had shaken him.

"I'm not going to die, Cole," I promised gently.

I heard Cole drop to the ground a little to my right. His hands must have been covering his face because his words came out muffled.

"I can't do this," he gasped in the same defeated tone he had used earlier.

I crossed the small space between us to where his voice came from. I extended my hand and found his shoulder.

"Yes, you can," I told him.

I could feel him shaking his head as he protested my words. "I'm not like you. Nothing can stop you, Myra. You've always been so strong and—and able to do the impossible. You never give up. You've never failed. But I have. I'm not—not good enough, not strong enough to do this."

It was easier to be honest in the pitch black that surrounded us, easier to let my walls down a little, easier to believe that this moment wasn't really happening, easier to bare my soul to the only friend I had in the world. A friend I had nearly lost in more ways than one.

"Cole, I'm not what you think. I put on a brave face because I don't want anyone to know the real me. I've learned to hide what I feel because of the things I've had to live through."

I could feel Cole's body trembling slightly under my touch. I reached out my left hand and placed it on his other shoulder so he would know we were facing each other.

"You've been through something horrible. You can choose to be strong and face it, or you can run and let it destroy you." I paused and took a deep breath before continuing. "You aren't alone in this."

Cole stirred under my fingertips. "Yes, I am. You said you didn't trust me." His words were full of pain.

I closed my eyes, although it didn't make any difference.

I'd wanted to challenge him, to help him grow, not snuff out his confidence. Maybe if he managed to struggle through alone, it would make him stronger in the end. However, his pain was not something I could ignore.

"I trust you more than anyone else in the world," I whispered.

How will he ever be strong enough to lead The Clan if he can't even lead his own team? A small voice wondered inside my head. I pushed it away.

"All I want is to help you," I said, trying desperately to assure him of how much I cared about him. "I believe you can make it alone. You have the ability, both mentally and physically. But you don't have to. If you ever need me, I'm here for you. I always will be."

"You're wrong, Myra." Cole's voice was steadier. "I don't have that kind of strength. Not like you. Not like Astra."

I curled my lips at the sound of her name.

"It is you who are wrong," I insisted fiercely. "You do have the strength inside yourself; you just need to find it."

Cole was almost laughing. "It's okay. You don't have to lie to me."

"I'm not!" I practically yelled. Why wouldn't he believe in himself just a little bit?

Cole sighed, serious again. "If what I have endured thus far isn't enough, then I can't imagine what kind of ordeal I would need to suffer for that part of myself to surface."

He thought for a moment. "No, I am sure I would prefer to be as I am now my whole life rather than face what it would take to bring about such a revelation of strength."

I sighed with exasperation. "Cole—" I started, but then stopped. What could I say to that?

"Sorry," Cole replied lightly. He sat back, and my hands dropped from his shoulders.

The worst of the storm was past. The thunder and lightning were growing farther and farther away.

"I don't feel like sleeping anymore. Want me to watch for a while?" Cole offered.

"I don't think I could sleep now either," I told him. "Plus, I'm so soaked that if I lie down, I might drown."

"Let's just talk for a while then," Cole suggested.

We ended up sitting side-by-side with our backs against one of the tree's roots.

"What do you think is going on back home?" he asked.

I shrugged. "The same thing as usual. Our parents are holding meetings with the council; your siblings and mother have their work. Nothing ever changes in The Land of the Clan."

"That place seemed so big before we left. Now, looking back, I realize how small it actually is," Cole said.

"True. It might be small, but it's safe," I reflected.

"Yes, very safe," Cole replied, dropping his voice even lower than before. "I mean, I've been wondering recently if it is possible to survive outside The Clan."

I laughed softly. "You can't be serious! We can barely manage as it is, with all six of us working together. But you'd never be able to do it alone. What about when you got old? There wouldn't be anyone to care for you. When your clothes wore out, how would you get new ones? It's impossible to live long-term without The Clan."

"I suppose. I'm not suggesting we try it; I was just curious." He hesitated for a moment before asking, "Do you miss it?"

I thought about his question for a moment. "No, I guess I don't. I mean, there are times when I miss the rules and order we had there, but I've wanted to participate in the trials my whole life. It would be foolish to spend all that time dreaming of being out here only to start wishing I was back with The Clan now that it's finally happening. This is a new and different experience. I want to enjoy it for what it is, and live fully in the present.

"What about you?"

"I haven't had time to miss much of anything," Cole laughed.

"We've had nothing but time," I pointed out, thinking of how many hours we spent doing nothing but walk.

"And every minute of it I've been worrying about finding food and water."

I smiled. Cole seemed to have relaxed and was beginning to let the horror of the other team's attack go, at least for the moment.

"So, no?" I asked.

"I miss my family. I miss my friends. But I don't miss school or the strict schedule."

"Careful," I warned him. "You're starting to sound like someone from The North Wind."

I was glad Astra wasn't awake to hear our conversation. Her village was known for disregarding rules when the mood took them. The funny thing was, Astra seemed proud of it instead of embarrassed.

"If they kick me out of The Paramount, I guess I'll spend the rest of my days training horses," Cole lamented.

I had to laugh. Cole was great with people, but not good with horses. Something we had in common.

"Do you think we'll miss the trials when they're over?" Cole wondered.

"What?" I asked.

"I mean, they are unpleasant in a lot of ways, but I wonder, will we miss living like this?"

"I think that will depend very much on the outcome," I answered him.

He sighed. "I think my father does. Miss the trials, I mean."

"Really?"

"Yeah, sometimes. He doesn't say anything, but I catch him staring at The Mountains of the North Wind with this distant look in his eyes. As soon as he sees me watching, he looks away. I asked him what he was thinking about once, but he told me he couldn't say, so I always assumed it was related to the trials."

"I guess there is a certain amount of excitement," I conceded.

"It's more than that," Cole said. "I don't know how to describe it, but, in a lot of ways, this is the most amazing thing that is ever going to happen to us."

"When we return, you'll quickly forget and stop missing it so much."

"Why do you say that?" Cole asked.

"Because you'll be too busy worrying about food and water for the entirety of The Clan."

Cole laughed, and it was finally his real laugh.

He cut off suddenly. His voice dropped a bit as he told me seriously, "I meant what I said the other night. There is evil out here."

"I told you, they were just desperate—" I began, but Cole cut me off.

"There was nothing to stop what the other team did. And not just them, but all of us. Without the rules, what is to keep us from doing anything we want, no matter how terrible? Then again, is it actually wrong?"

"Yes," I said. "What they did was wrong."

"Why?"

"Because they hurt other people."

"As you said, they were desperate. And even if they weren't, they'll never have to face the consequences."

"Maybe not external consequences, but that team will have to live with what they've done," I pointed out.

"What makes you think it will bother them?" he asked. "It would bother me, but maybe that's because I come from The Paramount and I've always held the rules to be very important. Perhaps, they won't even care."

"Of course they will," I insisted. "Inside, I'm sure they knew it was wrong."

"But how?" Cole asked. "How can we tell good from evil with nothing to guide us?"

I had no answer for him. All my life, the rules had been my answer. They told me how to act and how to think. In a world without them, was it permissible to do anything I wanted?

110

Neither of us spoke for a while. "Sorry, I keep bringing this conversation down," Cole murmured in a lighter tone. I laughed, more to ease the mood and help dissipate the uncomfortable subject than for any other reason.

We spent another couple of hours talking in that way until dawn came. Not that it was much of a dawn. I hoped the sun would chase the clouds from the sky, but instead, everything was gray and overcast. A drizzle continued to fall, even as we roused the others.

Those in the shelter were damp, and they didn't look like they had gotten much sleep. Our packs fared better; they were mostly dry, but who knew how long that would last.

We debated what to do with the uncooked meat. In the end, we left it behind. There wasn't enough dry wood to build a fire, and no one fancied carrying the bloody, gooey stuff in their pack. We had been able to cook a good portion of it the night before. Hopefully, it was enough to last us at least a couple of days.

Astra deemed herself capable of carrying her pack. The wound on her shoulder was little more than a scar. I was impressed with how well Kisa had treated it. I was not impressed with how far Kisa lagged behind the rest of us when we set out along the riverbank. Most likely, her slow pace was the result of the restless night and the fact that we were finally moving at full speed again.

Nothing seemed to change throughout the entire day. All the woods we walked through were the same. The rain never grew stronger but never stopped. There was a continuous dripping from the leaves above our heads. On our right, the river was swollen from the rainfall. It rushed along, foaming and muddy, carrying tree branches and other pieces of debris.

I don't know what time it was when we found the grove. It felt like morning still, but that might have been because the sky didn't change color all day.

We came to the top of a rise. Below, the expanse of trees spread out for miles. It was obvious the moment we saw the place that something about it was different. Ever since we entered the forest, the trees were a variety of different kinds. Not anymore;

111

now they were all the same. We hadn't found a single peach tree anywhere else in the forest, but here, there were hundreds.

"This is so strange," Kisa gasped when she caught up to the rest of us. "It's just like one of the orchards at The Golden Fields; only the trees aren't in rows."

Cole shrugged. "Maybe they were once, but without someone to tend them, they grew wherever they could."

We made our way down the ridge. Most of the fruit was far from being ripe, but a few trees had peaches that were close enough. Kisa pointed out the ones we should harvest from, and we went to work. There were only a few pears left in our bags, so having something to replace them with was wonderful.

Cole and I strayed into the grove away from the others, gathering all the ripe peaches we could find. I took a bite out of one and let the sweet juice run down my chin. The sun finally emerged from the clouds, revealing that the day was only a few hours from ending. The two of us were lost in a little world of our own when there came a cry from Joss.

The minute we heard the sound, we turned and sprinted toward the source. The others were all there when we arrived. Thankfully, no one seemed to be hurt.

"Don't scare us like that," Cole panted as we came to a halt. "What hap—" He trailed off as his eyes fell on what they were all looking at.

I had never seen anything like it before. It was a box—a huge box—made of something gray and stone-like. There were giant square and rectangular holes in the sides. The entire top was open.

"It looks like part of a dwelling," Astra murmured in a hushed tone.

"Why is it full of holes then?" I asked.

She shrugged.

"Maybe it's falling apart?" suggested Rollan.

"The holes are too perfectly square to be accidental," Cole pointed out.

"You think someone built it?" I asked

"I would say so," replied Astra.

"Nonsense," I told her. "There's no one to have built it."

The others were silent for a long moment. "It could be from—before," Astra suggested quietly. Kisa's eyes grew huge.

"That's impossible," I laughed. "There is nothing left from before. Everything was destroyed, except The Land of the Clan."

No one answered, but Astra suddenly took a step forward.

"Come back!" Kisa called in panic.

"It's okay," Astra said over her shoulder. She walked right up to the box and touched it. "I think it was some part of a building once."

"I told you that's not poss-" I started irritably, but no one was listening. Even Kisa was moving forward to take a closer look.

I sighed and walked up to the box. It was almost twice as tall as I was and at least twenty yards long. If it had been a dwelling once, leaves and dirt buried what would have been the floor. I pushed them away to reveal more of the same type of material that formed the rest.

After a couple of minutes, I gave up poking around. It wasn't all that interesting.

"It's a mystery," Astra said, coming to stand beside me.

"Thank you for stating the obvious," I growled. I didn't know why she had to contradict me every time she opened her mouth. Astra seemed amused by my annoyance, but she didn't say anything.

"We should keep moving," Cole decided a moment later.

Our packs stuffed with peaches, we found our way back to the river. It ran right through the peach grove for a while before splitting in two. The larger branch continued to head due south, but the smaller one headed east.

Finally, I thought. *We can start traveling in sort of the right direction again.*

"Should we follow the larger branch?" Astra wondered.

"Why?" I asked quickly.

"This bit," she pointed to the channel of water heading east, "is so small that it might end at any time."

"The same could be said for the other one," I fired back.

"Still, I think—" Astra started, but I'd heard enough.

"We need to go east," I spat. "You won't go east without water. Now there is water, but you still don't want to go the right way. What is wrong with you? Are you completely stupid?"

"Myra," Cole exclaimed in shock.

"I'm sorry, but this has gotten ridiculous," I told him in a somewhat calmer voice. "We need to go east. We have enough supplies that we could leave the river completely. There has to be more water out there somewhere. But at the very least, we should take the chance that this part of the stream will keep going."

Cole was looking between Astra and me uneasily. He didn't want to pick a side. He never wanted to pick a side. I was sure he would agree with Astra. He never agreed with me anymore. I folded my arms across my chest and glared at the two of them.

Cole was still undecided when Astra spoke up.

"She's right." All of us turned and stared at her in surprise.

"Really?" Cole asked.

Outraged, I turned on him, but he spoke before I could even think of what to say. "That's not what I meant. I meant, you agree with her?"

Astra nodded. "We do need to start moving east. Even if this part of the river dies, it sounds like once we reach the ocean there will always be plenty of water."

Cole nodded. "Good, we all agree then." He smiled at Astra.

Anger stirred deep inside me. She was playing games again. Everything that horse girl did was so calculated. She was trying to be the good guy, giving in to end a fight. Why? What was her agenda?

She wants Cole. The thought hit me like a physical blow.

I'd briefly met a man from The North Wind, a friend of Astra's, who clearly had feelings for her. At the time, I assumed those feelings were returned. Although, the more I thought about it, the more I realized Astra never really gave me any reason to believe that.

Could it be that she was interested in Cole as her life mate? The very idea outraged me to the point that I couldn't even look at her. What made it worse was that she knew how much Cole meant to me. She had often teased me about Cole. Despite that, was she trying to take him away?

I'd see her dead before I let her have him.

CHAPTER 12
AMBUSH

The small branch of the river led almost due east. It curved a few times but seemed to be taking us in the right direction. We followed the water for an hour until we reached the edge of the peach grove.

"We'll camp here tonight," Cole announced. "In the morning, we'll gather all the peaches we can carry before leaving."

There was no point in bothering with a fire that night. The moon was waning, but still half full, providing some light after the sun set. I lay down a stone's throw away from Cole. The grass beneath me was long and soft. It gave off a wonderful scent, even though no flowers grew on the stalks. Nestled there, I was almost as comfortable as if I were in my own bed. Joss, Rollan, and Kisa offered to keep watch.

I was only too happy to agree. I couldn't remember the last time I had slept through an entire night. Astra volunteered to help if they ended up needing another person.

Shortly before dawn, a strange sound startled me awake. My eyes flew open, and I saw a large bird perched overhead in one of the trees. As I looked at it, I wondered where the sound had come from until it opened its beak and let out a loud call.

Slowly, I sat up to get a better look. The feathery creature let out another cry before spreading massive wings and flying silently away into the morning mist that filled the grove.

"That's an owl," Rollan whispered from across the clearing. I could easily make out his figure in the twilight, sitting with his back against a peach tree, a half-eaten fruit in his hand.

I rose and walked over to him. "I've never seen a bird like that before," I admitted.

Rollan nodded. "They live in forests," he told me. "We have some in Treescape."

"Why didn't I ever see one there?" I wondered.

"They're nighttime hunters. They only come out after dark and usually vanish before the dawn."

"What do they hunt?" I asked.

"Mice, rats, squirrels, small children."

I gasped. "They eat people?!"

Rollan laughed. "No, I'm kidding. They aren't dangerous."

I scowled at him, but that only made him smirk. The creature was larger than any hawk or eagle I had ever seen, but there was no way it was large enough to carry off even the smallest of babies.

"On the contrary, we like having them in the woods," Rollan told me. "They are good for keeping the rodent population down."

"Like the cats at The North Wind," I recalled.

He nodded.

I started getting my things together and began piling up large numbers of peaches. Due to the hazy mist filling the grove, I didn't wander very far. Rollan filled the extra pack to the brim with fruit.

As soon as the first golden rays of sunlight came over the treetops, he roused the others. We sat in a loose circle and ate the last of the pears along with some peaches and a few strips of meat.

After breakfast, Kisa examined Astra's wound.

"It's completely healed," she exclaimed. "There's always going to be a scar, but otherwise, it's as good as new."

"Excellent," Astra replied, flexing her arm.

Much as I was reluctant to give up the bow, I knew it was time to return the weapon to Astra. She took it with a smile.

"Hopefully, you won't have the chance to use it again," she told me with a wink.

I didn't much care if she got hurt again or died. After my realization from the previous night, I didn't care what happened to her at all.

With full bellies and bags, we left the grove. Joss had an extra peach in his hand, which he munched on as we went. Rollan held a fruit in each hand. Once the boys finished and threw the pits away, they washed the sticky juice from their fingers in the water.

In contrast to our fears, the river did not dwindle but grew broader. Several smaller streams, which we were forced to jump over or wade through, joined it, swelling the water level until the river was larger than ever before.

Even though it was still early in the day, I could tell it was going to be a blazer. The mist, which had covered the landscape in the morning, was quickly burned up, and it wasn't long before Kisa started lagging farther and farther behind.

Around midday, we reached a place where the long, soft grass gave way to short, ugly stuff. The trees surrounding us didn't have many leaves and were twisted and knobby. Needless to say, we didn't linger very long. Instead, we each ate a peach or two and a little of the meat before continuing our journey. There wasn't much meat left. Soon, Astra or I would have to go hunting.

The hours seemed to drag on far longer than they should have. Since the undergrowth was too thick to allow us passage beneath the trees, we were forced to walk right on the edge of the river. The sun beat down mercilessly. I saw the sweat soaking the clothes of my companions and felt it running down my face and the backs of my legs.

Kisa fell so far behind she was often lost to sight by the winding river and stray trees, which grew close to the water.

Joss was hanging back too, but not quite as far, as though trying to keep an eye both on her and us. He wore a fretful expression.

I wasn't worried. I was annoyed. Kisa wasn't that much younger than the rest of us and should be able to keep up. It wasn't like we were running, just walking, and everyone was dealing with the same heat and fatigue.

I glanced at Cole and wondered if he would call a halt soon. My heart nearly stopped when I caught sight of him in the lead with Astra. The two were conversing together quietly. Rollan, who was just in front of me, didn't seem to be listening to what they were saying, and I could hear none of it.

Anger twisted my stomach. Since when did Cole confide in her instead of me? Hadn't we talked and worked out our differences the night before last? Yet there he was, speaking with Astra, and only Astra.

Part of me wanted to pass Rollan and join their conversation, but I wouldn't give Astra the satisfaction. I shouldn't have to be the bumbling idiot, arriving too late to an already finished conversation. If they wanted to talk and have their secrets, then that was fine.

For the next hour, I walked in angry silence, glaring at them. They might have noticed if the river hadn't suddenly taken a turn through a willow grove. At least we weren't in the sun anymore. Instead, we were walking through long streamers of willow leaves, and the conspiratorial pair were often lost from view.

Rollan was the only one I could see at all times. Joss and Kisa were somewhere behind us. Every once in a while, I could hear the sound of their progress.

Soon, a clearing appeared ahead of us. Cole stopped in the middle and looked over his shoulder in concern. He must have been too busy with his new friend to realize what the rest of us were doing.

Astra didn't stop until she was across the open stretch of ground. She glanced back, but all she was looking for was Cole. I made my move quickly. I dodged around Rollan and went to stand beside Cole in the center of the clearing. Now Astra would have to join us.

"Where are the others?" Cole asked.

I shrugged. "Behind us."

"I'll see if there's any game around this place," Astra said. Without waiting for a response, she dropped her pack and headed off, away from the river with just her quiver and bow.

Several minutes after she left, Rollan headed to the water's edge. He knelt and started filling his canteen. The water was flowing very quickly, almost as fast as the river that surrounded The Land of the Clan.

I heard a twig snap behind us. Turning my head, I expected to see Kisa or Joss enter the clearing. A figure did come rushing out from under the trees, but it was not one of our teammates.

It was a boy, not quite as tall or broad as Cole, but larger than me. He wore no shirt or shoes, and his pants were stained and ripped. They might have been brown once, but now they looked closer to black. A mass of dark brown hair grew from his head. But what really caught my attention was the knife he held in his hand. It was shorter than mine and curved. I had never seen a knife like it.

All this I perceived in an instant, because the second after he sprinted into the clearing, he intentionally slammed into Rollan, shoving him headfirst into the river.

Rollan disappeared under the water with a cry and bobbed to the surface a moment later. He tried to swim back to shore, but the strong current carried him downstream and out of sight.

It took a moment for Cole and me to react, so unexpected was this wild boy's arrival. We both lunged forward. Cole was closer. Instinctively, he moved to grab the boy's knife hand.

The boy was quicker. He dodged Cole's outstretched fingers and spun away, slashing with his blade as he did so. I heard Cole cry out in pain and saw blood splatter on the grass. In the next moment, Cole crumpled to the ground, hands pressed to his stomach.

I literally saw red along the edge of my vision. Pulling my knife, I charged the attacker with a scream. He saw me coming and braced himself to meet me. I was ready for the slash he made at my stomach. I countered it neatly with my blade. What I wasn't prepared for was his other fist, which collided with my head as our knives met. The blow knocked me off my feet, and everything went from red to black in a moment.

I struggled to my knees, vision blurry, and saw the boy kneeling over Cole with his back to me. He was holding Cole by the front of his shirt. The horrible, curved blade was positioned directly over Cole's head.

"No!" I screamed. I tried to get to my feet but couldn't. The entire world felt like it was shaking, or maybe it was just my own limbs. The boy didn't move but remained frozen with the knife posed above Cole.

All of a sudden, Astra exploded out of the woods. Before the boy could even turn around, she brought her elbow down on the back of his head. While he was still stunned from the blow, Cole reached up a blood-covered hand and latched onto the hilt of the boy's knife. Astra seized him from behind and succeeded in dragging him back a couple of feet, leaving the boy's weapon in Cole's hand.

The boy thrashed around wildly and managed to wrench away from Astra. As he did, she gave him a shove. Unbalanced, he fell to the ground, landing flat on his back. Without hesitation, Astra lunged forward across his stomach and hit him in the face as hard as she could. Blood flowed freely from the boy's mouth as Astra hit him again with her other hand.

I finally managed to get to my feet and stagger a couple of steps toward them. Astra's fist connected with the enemy's head twice more.

"Kill him! Kill him!" I screeched. The blood roared in my ears. I was angry—no, furious. I wished I was the one on top of the boy, beating the life out of him. My heart was racing, adrenaline making my whole body feel powerful and weak all at once.

As Astra pulled her fist back to hit the boy again, her other hand came up automatically for the counter swing.

"Kill him!" I cried, but Astra paused mid-swing.

She didn't move from her position, crouching over the boy, her fist raised and her breathing heavy. Slowly, she lowered her arm, eyes not leaving the boy's face. It was then that I caught my first real look at him.

He was younger than I would have supposed from his violent actions. His age was hard to determine, but I guessed he wasn't that much older than I was. Every rib and bone was visible beneath the tan skin of his lean body. The face was hard to see beneath the smears of blood and dirt. Sweat soaked his hair, causing it to cling to his forehead. In the dark brown depths of his eyes, I saw terror.

He had to be a Broken.

I couldn't understand why Astra had stopped hitting him. She slowly rose, leaving the bleeding, trembling boy on the ground.

Hatred filled me. I felt my face twist in rage, and I leapt forward to finish what she'd started. Her hand caught my wrist, and she held me back from the boy. I struggled with her for a moment, but she twisted my arm and shoved me to the ground.

"Enough," she declared firmly. "It's done."

I didn't understand. I rose, ready to rush at him again, but Astra stepped between the boy and me.

"What are you doing?" I yelled. "He's the enemy! He tried to kill us! Why are you defending him?"

I expected her to scream back, but her voice was rigid and forceful when she replied. "Get a hold of yourself."

For just a moment, I saw Myna standing in front of me instead of Astra. They had the same ice-cold tone of disapproval.

She turned her back on me. My fury was so great I wanted to attack her. If she had been anyone else, I might have punched her. I knew she was waiting for it, and I knew I would lose our fight. When we had sparred together in practice, I came out on top nine times out of ten, but at that moment, I somehow knew I would not win this fight.

Astra slowly walked away from me and went to Cole's side. To my surprise, Joss and Kisa were kneeling beside him. I hadn't even noticed their arrival. The boy on the ground twitched slightly, like he might try to get up. Astra turned her hard, green gaze on him, and he froze instantly.

I joined the others, keeping one eye on the Broken. Cole had a shallow cut across his stomach. Kisa was applying pressure to it with a shirt. To my great satisfaction, the shirt was black. I expected Astra to complain, but she didn't even mention it. Cole winced as Kisa pressed harder, trying to stem the flow of blood.

Something came crashing through the woods ahead of us. Astra stood and turned, drawing her bow in one swift movement. It was a pity she hadn't used it the first time, although she might have shot Cole by accident; her aim wasn't as good as mine.

This time, she notched an arrow and waited. Rollan came barreling into the clearing. He was soaking wet and looked as angry as I felt. Astra lowered her bow instantly.

It took a long moment for Rollan to take in the scene before him. Then he took a step toward the boy on the ground. The boy's eyes widened, and he started scrambling up.

"Stop," Astra said in a commanding tone. Both boys froze, Rollan poised to attack and the Broken halfway to his feet, ready to bolt.

Rollan stared at Astra in confusion, but she wasn't looking at him. Her eyes were on the boy. I was shocked to see that he was crying.

"Why?" Rollan growled at Astra. His voice was a lot calmer than mine had been, but the word carried a mutinous edge to it.

"What are you going to gain by killing him?" she asked, turning her eyes to Rollan.

He met her gaze steadily. "He won't ever try to kill me again."

His line of reasoning sounded pretty good to me.

Astra glanced at the boy once more before replying. "I don't think he's going to try to kill anyone again."

Rollan was silent for a moment.

"Cole?" he asked, turning to our leader, clearly not satisfied with Astra's ruling on the subject.

Cole was silent at first. I supposed he didn't want to go against his new confidant, Astra, but there was only one right choice. Couldn't he see that? Astra was wrong; her decision to let the Broken live was crazy. Now was Cole's chance to step up and be a leader.

Cole looked at me suddenly, as if guessing my thoughts. I felt the anger inside me lessen slightly. I shook my head, showing that I did not agree with Astra. It took him a long time to consider his words. No one moved. Cole slowly turned his eyes from me to the bloody-faced boy on the ground.

If Cole ordered Astra to kill the pathetic excuse of a human, I wondered if she would obey him. Considering her track record of disrespecting authority and breaking the rules, I imagined she wouldn't.

"I don't think there is any need for more violence today," he said softly.

"Well, I do," I hissed stubbornly, looking to Rollan for support since I wasn't getting any from Cole. "You believe there's evil out here? You're looking at it!"

Shock crossed Cole's face at my words, but they did not change his mind. Rollan didn't say anything, but he met my eyes, and I could tell he was unhappy with the decision.

Astra ignored us and walked to the boy's side, where she knelt. Rollan and I followed her across the clearing, pausing a few feet away. The boy didn't get up but leaned back as far away from her as he could. He was sobbing, the tears making paths through the dirt on his face.

"Please don't kill me," I heard him beg.

Astra ignored his words. "Are there more of your people close by?" she questioned him.

The Broken shook his head vigorously.

"Why did you attack us?" she asked.

The boy provided no answer; he was crying too hard. Astra continued to look at him. Her green eyes seemed to pierce his flesh.

After a moment, he managed to calm down a little, and she asked again, "Why?"

"For my rite," he answered, his voice a strangled whisper.

"I don't know what that is," Astra replied, clearly demanding the boy go on.

The Broken hesitated and looked everywhere but Astra's eyes.

Astra's gaze didn't waver.

"Explain," she commanded.

Finally, he spoke.

"The rite of manhood." His voice had a strange accent that took concentration to understand.

"The rite of manhood? What does that have to do with attacking us?"

He had to swallow before answering. "I was trying to—"

"Kill us," Rollan interjected angrily.

The boy snapped his mouth shut.

"Is that true?" Astra pressed. "Were you trying to kill us for your rite?"

Shutting his eyes tightly, the boy nodded once.

A hiss escaped my lips.

"Why?" demanded Astra.

"I must prove my worth as a man," the boy explained in his strange voice. "Killing another in battle and bringing back proof is one such way of winning honor."

Astra furrowed her brow. "What kind of proof?"

The Broken still would not look up. He licked his lips before answering.

"Four canines," he choked out.

I was confused. What was he talking about? Canines? Being a man? It made no sense. He was probably insane; most Broken were. This was part of his fractured mind leaking out of his mouth.

"Canines?" Rollan wondered. "Like the teeth?"

The boy nodded.

"You need to kill one of our people?" Astra asked. "For their teeth?"

"It doesn't matter who. I just need to kill someone," the boy whimpered from the ground.

"So, you could have killed any one of us?" Astra wondered.

The boy nodded.

There was sudden movement on the other side of the clearing. I whipped around, but it was just Kisa. She had run to the river to get water for Cole.

Instantly, my attention was on the Broken again. Astra had glanced back as well. Her eyes remained on the little girl for a long moment, and then she turned to the boy. Silently, she studied him and didn't speak for a long moment.

"Are you going to attack us again?" she asked.

The boy shook his head.

"How can we believe him?" I snapped at Astra. I had cooled down considerably. Killing the boy didn't sound nearly as appealing as it once had, but I didn't know what else we could do with him.

The Broken shook his head again.

"Please," he gasped. "I swear by the snows of winter, the flowers that grow in the spring, the waves of the sea that wash the sands in summer, and the leaves that fall in autumn, I will never hurt any of you if you will let me go."

Astra wasn't going to trust a Broken, was she? He would return and try to finish us off as soon as night fell!

I was about to voice my objections when I noticed Astra was staring at the boy in amazement.

"The waves of the sea that wash the sands? Do you mean the ocean?" she asked.

The boy nodded. "Ocean, sea, same thing."

"You know where the ocean is?" she demanded. Suddenly, I had a bad feeling I knew where this was going, and I did not like it.

Nodding, the boy raised his hand and pointed to the east.

"Good," said Astra. "You are going to take us there by the quickest route possible."

"Wait, no," I protested. "We are not taking *him* with us."

I stepped forward to where Astra was crouching. She looked up at me with a cold light in her eyes.

"Why ever not, Myra? I thought you wanted to win?" she pointed out.

I was shaking with rage as I turned to Cole. "This can't be allowed. He'll murder us all in our sleep!"

Cole looked uncertain. "If he can help us win, it might be worth the risk."

"Or—" I started, but Cole's blue eyes met mine, and I could tell that killing the Broken wasn't an option he would consider.

You're too soft-hearted, I thought. *You will regret this.*

"What's your name?" Astra asked the boy.

"Todicmadaya," he replied, sounding more like he'd sneezed than told us his name.

Astra thought for a moment.

"We'll call you Todd," she said in a voice that was a million miles away. "You're going to show us the way." The boy nodded, accepting the responsibility Astra was giving him, along with the new name.

Todd. I knew I'd heard that name before, but I couldn't think of where.

CHAPTER 13
ADDITION

I won't let this happen, I thought desperately, stalking across the clearing to Cole's side.

"This is a horrible idea," I told him.

"I agree," Rollan added, arms folded across his chest.

Cole was sitting up now. With Joss's assistance, Kisa had gotten most of the bleeding to stop. I could see that the wound on Cole's stomach wasn't nearly as bad as I had feared during the fight.

Astra was ignoring us and still conversing with the Broken.

Cole dropped his voice to a whisper, and I was forced to lean in to hear what he said.

"If we let him go, he might ambush us again. Surely, it's safer to have him where we can keep an eye on him."

I snorted in disbelief.

"I can think of a better way to keep everyone safe," Rollan muttered, eyeing the sword laying on the ground at Cole's feet.

"If we just chased him off, there's no way he'd attack us again," Joss pointed out. "There are six of us, and we'd be ready for him."

His argument sounded quite reasonable. It wasn't such a bad idea since it provided a perfect compromise. The boy could live, but far away from our team.

One look at Cole and I knew he wasn't going to change his mind. Perhaps there was a way I could get rid of the boy on my own. In fact, I was sure I'd be able to figure something out.

I didn't bother arguing anymore. They had made up their minds, and so had I. Soon, it would be time to take the situation into my own hands.

We stayed in the clearing the rest of the day; no one wanted Cole's wound to start bleeding again, and we were all pretty shaken up.

Cole kept an eye on the recently designated Todd, while the rest of us made camp. I gathered wood for the fire, but I didn't stray far from the clearing. If the Broken made one wrong move, I wanted to be there so I could do what Astra had failed to do earlier.

However, the boy did nothing except lie on the ground, huddled in a miserable ball. I heard him sniffling from time to time and wondered how long he was going to cry.

Soon, I had piled up a huge stack of firewood. I went to stand by Joss, who was sitting on the riverbank holding a long reed with the fishing hook attached to it. He hadn't caught anything, and the current was so fast I wasn't sure he would. He gave me the arrowhead we used to make fires. I had a flint, and I soon got a spark to catch in the dry moss. Hopefully, it wouldn't be for nothing, and we would end up with something to cook over the flames.

Rollan and Kisa returned a little later. They had been looking for herbs and edible plants. They brought back some more of the potato-like tubers. I helped wash the mud off and wrap the roots in leaves before setting them in the fire to bake.

Astra returned with something even better: a rabbit. It wasn't as fat as the ones back home, but there was still plenty of meat on it. She had gone out with Kisa and Rollan and remained in the woods to hunt. The animals outside The Land of the Clan were nervous around humans, so hunting was harder than I had imagined it would be.

At The Farm, where animals were raised for The Clan, most of the creatures were friendly with people, especially when the people brought food with them. You could pretty much choose the one you wanted, and it would follow you to the slaughter.

Astra dropped the rabbit.

"I'll see if I can get another," she said, heading back to the forest.

"But—" Cole began.

She didn't even turn around. "I won't go far."

Cole didn't look too pleased.

Good, I thought. The last thing I wanted was for him to be happy with Astra. I certainly wasn't. She always made a mess out of everything.

I set about butchering the rabbit with Rollan's help. While I stripped off the pelt, I directed him to find some large sticks and build a spit to go over the flames.

Once both of us finished our tasks, we skewered the rabbit and set it over the fire. Rollan rotated it from time to time to make sure the meat cooked evenly and didn't burn, while Kisa added some herb I didn't recognize for seasoning.

Soon, Joss gave up fishing and came to stand by the fire, waiting for the delicious-smelling food to be ready. With a long stick, Kisa pulled one of the leaf-wrapped tubers from the embers.

"They're done," she announced. She and Joss carefully removed the others. There was maybe another half hour of sunlight left. I hoped Astra was lost in the woods and would never return. Once the tubers cooled off, we began eating.

I took a bite out of a rabbit leg, but the taste didn't even register. I could feel the Broken watching me. Out of the corner of my eye, I saw him hungrily staring at us.

Maybe if we don't feed him, he'll run off during the night.

Just as I thought it, I realized I was too late. Cole had called Joss over and was directing him to take some food over to the boy. It was so easy for him to forget that not even five hours earlier the Broken had sliced his stomach open.

Joss approached with caution. The Broken was bigger than him. I'd already felt the strength of his fist and knew that, despite his tears, he was no weakling. My hand tightened on my knife as Joss approached.

The wild boy made no move to rise when offered a chunk of rabbit, a tuber, and two peaches. As Joss walked away, I saw the boy quickly gulp down the food. He was so skinny I could count his ribs. I had assumed it was a result of a recent growth spurt, but, from his rate of consumption, I decided it was more likely he hadn't eaten in days. Not that I cared, but he was sure to stick around if we continued feeding him.

Astra returned just before dark. She carried two more rabbits. One of them looked like it hadn't been killed when her arrow pierced its hide. The head was a bloody mess. She must have wounded the animal and then finished it off with a rock or something.

We started cooking the two additional rabbits while Astra ate. There was no conversation around the fire that night. It was strange having a newcomer within hearing range. It didn't feel safe to talk like we usually did.

I took the first watch. The evening was pleasant and fine, and I would have enjoyed the time to myself, but the presence of the intruder nagged at me. I kept the fire burning brightly, wanting to ensure the Broken was always visible. He was lying with his back to me, on the edge of the firelight.

My team was sleeping closer to the fire than usual, except Joss and Astra. They always complained that they had trouble falling asleep with so much light. I could barely make out what I guessed to be their sleeping forms farther off in the clearing.

About an hour and a half into my watch, I heard someone sniffling. At first, I thought it was Kisa, but it was coming from the wrong direction. A moment later, I realized it was the boy, Todd.

It seemed so laughable to me. He'd attacked a group of six people, going directly for the only one larger than himself, then he managed to get caught, and now he was huddled in the darkness, sobbing.

I remembered the night I had found Larna crying, back before any of this began. That was different; even as much as I disliked Larna, she was part of The Clan.

This boy was a Broken. There was something wrong with him. I suddenly wondered if he could have been part of The Clan once. It was very unusual for someone so young to be exiled. None of us recognized him, but there were other villages than ours he could have lived in. If he hadn't been a part of The Clan, then where did he come from? Surely it wasn't possible that two

Broken could have found each other and started their own family. The thought repulsed me.

I remembered the murderer I'd seen exiled not too long ago, Geal. He begged his family to join him. They refused, but what if they had said yes? Maybe that happened sometimes. There could be small family groups living outside of The Clan like savages.

Hadn't Cole suggested it might be possible to live beyond the borders of The Clan not that long ago? Would I be willing to join him if he asked? I tried to shake those kinds of thoughts from my head. They were useless. What mattered was making sure the Broken didn't hurt anyone during the night. If he wanted to run away, I was more than happy to turn a blind eye. However, running didn't appear to be his plan; he just lay there and sniffled.

He was still at it an hour later when I woke Kisa for her watch. She glanced in his direction, and I leaned close to whisper in her ear, "He's been crying for hours."

Instead of disgust, concern lit on Kisa's face.

"Really?" she whispered back. "Maybe Astra hurt him worse than she thought."

I shook my head. "He's either a coward or he's trying to trick us," I informed her.

Kisa nodded, eyes huge and mouth puckered with worry. I settled down a short distance off and closed my eyes.

Clearing my mind wasn't easy after such an eventful day. I rolled over a couple of times, trying to get comfortable, and was almost asleep when I heard something move.

My eyes snapped open. I saw Kisa making her way over to the boy. I sighed mentally but got up to follow her to where the Broken lay on the outskirts of the clearing. I wasn't going to risk anything happening to Kisa, even if she was asking for trouble.

I half expected the boy to attack when Kisa drew close to him, but he just curled into a tighter ball and rubbed his face with his hands. Kisa stopped beside him and then knelt down.

"What's wrong?" she asked gently. He didn't answer. Instead, he pulled away from her, hugging his knees tightly to his

132

chest. Slowly, she reached out and put a small hand on his shoulder.

"Are you hurt?" she pressed.

The boy still made no reply.

"Leave him," I ordered. "He's not worth your time."

Kisa ignored me. "Are you afraid?" she persisted, speaking to the Broken.

I saw him turn his head slightly and look up at her for the first time.

"Yes," he whispered in a cracked, husky voice.

"Then you're a coward," I told him harshly, curling my lip in revulsion. "Fear limits you. I have never been afraid of anything."

The clearing was still for a moment.

"I have been." All three of us nearly jumped out of our skins at the unexpected voice that came from the darkness to my left. Astra seemed to quite literally appear just in front of me as she stepped out of the night.

"I have been afraid of many things and have had to struggle to face my fear. But the struggle is what makes us strong." Her words didn't seem to be directed at any one of us, but I felt a sting as she said them. She had been far more honest than I.

The truth was that I had also been afraid many times in my life. Each time, I hated that feeling of fear, so I pressed it away and pretended to be brave. In truth, I still struggled, not that I would ever admit it to anyone.

"Why don't you all get some sleep?" Astra cut into the silence once more. "I'll watch for a while."

Kisa nodded and went back to her sleeping spot. I didn't move for a moment. Astra turned her green gaze on me.

"Not tired?" She asked in her superior tone.

"I was just making sure Kisa wasn't harmed by this mongrel." I nodded toward the boy.

"I think he could have killed her already if he wanted to," Astra announced.

I glared at her. Was she insinuating to my face that I couldn't protect Kisa from the Broken in a fight? He might be larger and stronger than I was, but I had a knife and months of training.

Too angry to speak, I turned and went back to where my cloak and pack were. I lay down and listened to hear if Astra would say anything to Todd. Either she spoke too softly, or I fell asleep too quickly, because if any words passed between them, I never knew.

The next morning, Joss woke me. I glanced over and saw that the Broken was still among us. He was in the same position he had been in all night and appeared to be asleep. I considered kicking him to make sure, but I figured that would set Astra off. Not that I cared what Astra thought, but I imagined Cole wouldn't like it either.

Astra woke the boy a short time later and gave him a peach for breakfast. Once again, he snarfed the food down in a matter of moments.

The rest of us ate at a more leisurely pace. Once we finished, Kisa checked the cut on Cole's stomach.

"It seems to be fully scabbed over," she reported cheerfully as the rest of us packed up the camp. "Just don't exert yourself too much, or it might open up again."

Cole handed Joss the Broken's curved knife. Since he was the fourth team leader it seemed appropriate.

"Here," Astra said, giving the extra pack to the boy. I hoped there wasn't anything important in it. I could just see him running off with our supplies. The boy shouldered the pack without comment.

I hadn't noticed before, but there was a thin, leather cord around the Broken's neck. A chunk of oddly shaped rock was tied to it. I wondered if it was a flint for starting fires, but the stone didn't look like flint.

"Which way?" Cole asked, coming to stand beside Astra and the boy.

The Broken raised his hand and pointed toward the rising sun. "To the east." The path he indicated angled away from the stream.

"Is there water?" Astra wondered.

The boy nodded. "There is a lake three days from here."

"Fill your canteens," Astra ordered. "We're going to be without water for a while."

Everyone did as instructed.

Wordlessly, Astra began to walk in the direction the boy indicated, away from the river we had followed for so long. The Broken and Cole trailed behind her.

I ground my teeth in frustration. Hadn't I been saying all along that we needed to go east, and that we would be sure to find plenty of water along the way? They hadn't listened to me at all. Now, this Broken was telling them to head east, and suddenly it seemed like a good idea?

I stayed in the back of the group most of that day. I couldn't bring myself to look at Astra, the Broken, or even Cole. Why did he trust someone who had tried to kill him more than me?

CHAPTER 14
FEVER

We traveled all day in the same silence that had prevailed the previous evening. At one point, we climbed over a pile of boulders and halted on the other side because Cole's wound began bleeding. Kisa made him lie on the ground while she applied pressure.

After that, we moved slowly, frequently stopping so Kisa could check for bleeding. Cole didn't complain, but his face was drawn, and I wondered if the wound pained him. I couldn't help glaring at the Broken, knowing that all this was his fault.

The terrain was level and grassy until the late afternoon when it started to slope upwards, and the ground beneath our feet turned gravelly. The trees grew thinner and thinner. I could see several rises ahead, but nothing beyond.

As night fell, we made camp in one of the few patches of trees still to be found. There was no water to refill our canteens, of course. Everyone had been conserving what they could all day, leaving us tired and weak.

Sleeping in the open, without the forest surrounding us, felt strange. I advised against building a fire, and the others agreed. Unless we cut down one of the trees, there wouldn't have been enough wood to keep the flames lit for more than a few hours.

The next morning, the land grew harsher. It was rocky with only a few scraggly shrubs. Traveling was hard, even when we were going downhill instead of up. We continuously came to cliffs and ridges that were all but impossible to descend. I cringed to think how arduous the return journey would be when we were forced to climb back up.

Cole was pale and panting hard, but he continued doggedly on, despite Kisa's protests that he should be taking things easy.

Only the fact that there was no more bleeding kept the little girl from insisting on a halt.

Everyone was hot, tired, and dirty by the time we stopped for a rest in the early afternoon. There was no stream to cool off in, so we sought shelter under a couple of gnarled trees that were hardly large enough to provide shade. My mouth tasted like dirt and felt gritty.

Astra sat next to the Broken, and Cole settled down on her other side. He smiled at me, inviting me to join them. I wasn't fuming anymore, but after two days of difficult travel, I certainly wasn't in a good enough mood to deal with any of them. If Cole had been alone, I might have considered it. As it was, I pretended not to notice and joined Kisa, Rollan, and Joss under the second tree a little way off.

"This is too hard," Kisa whined, rubbing a crumpled-up leaf on her scraped knees.

I had a few scratches of my own, but I was gifted with long arms and legs, so all the climbing wasn't as difficult for me.

"I don't like it," Rollan murmured. Kisa handed him a leaf from her pack, and he started on his own knees and elbows. "He could be leading us into a trap."

"I don't think he'd try anything like that," Joss put in, taking a swig from his canteen. "He seems pretty terrified of us, especially Astra."

I glanced over at the others. The boy was sitting as far away from Astra as he could get. Astra and Cole looked to be in deep conversation. Part of me yearned to hear what they were saying. In retrospect, I should have sat with Cole as he had wanted. Now I was grouping myself with the lower end of the team.

"Guess I'll see what the plan is," I announced, standing and walking to the other tree.

Cole and Astra halted their conversation when I approached. I ignored Astra's eyes following my every move as I lowered myself onto the stony ground next to Cole.

"Kisa and the boys are having trouble with the terrain," I informed them.

"We need to find water," Cole added.

Astra nodded and turned her head to the boy. "Todd, how far away is the lake you mentioned?"

Todd glanced at us, and I could see what Joss meant. He was timid and hesitant to even look in our direction. I couldn't say we were all that comfortable with him either; although, Astra seemed perfectly at ease sitting beside him.

"It's a little more than a day's journey ahead," he answered quietly.

"Our supplies should hold out until then," Astra told Cole. "As long as we're very careful."

He nodded.

A shadow crossed my mind, and I wondered if Rollan was right. What if this boy was leading us into some sort of trap? What if there was no water?

We did not remove very many miles from between us and the supposed lake that afternoon. We stopped early and made camp on the edge of a massive cliff. It was going to be a treacherous task to climb down, and everyone was too exhausted that night.

No one bothered to build a fire; there was nothing to cook. We had spent the entire day sweating, so the fresh night air was a relief.

With no trees, I felt exposed and vulnerable. Everything about the place was uncomfortable. We had nothing to sleep on but the bare rock. It was warm under my back as I laid down and looked up. For the first time since leaving The Clan, I had an unobstructed view of the night sky.

The stars had always been special to me. I had only a few memories of my father, but one of them was on a similar evening. He'd awakened me in the middle of a warm summer night, carried me outside in his arms, and pointed upward. I remembered laughing with delight.

Hand in hand, we walked away from The Paramount to the amphitheater, where it was completely dark. My father stretched out on his back, lying across one of the stone seats. He pulled me on top of him, and we spent several hours looking up at the night sky. Maybe that was why the amphitheater became my special sanctuary after he died less than a year later.

The memory of us being there together helped soothe my bruised feelings from the past few days. I fell asleep watching the stars and thinking of my father.

Astra shook me awake in the middle of the night. I sat up groggily.

"Something's wrong with Kisa," she whispered to me.

"What?" I asked, rubbing the sleep from my eyes. The moon had risen, but it wasn't full enough to give much light. With no more explanation, Astra seized my wrist and pulled me from the ground over to where she and Kisa had been resting. Kisa seemed to still be asleep.

Cole was there, crouching beside Kisa's body. I could see three other forms lying a short way off. One was snoring; I assumed it was Rollan.

"When Cole woke me for my watch, I noticed that she was burning up," Astra told me softly, dropping to the ground beside Kisa. I knelt and reached out to touch her hand. There was a sickly heat coming from her skin.

"What can we do?" Cole asked. "Neither of us could recall an herb that would be good for fevers."

"I remember the names of a couple," I answered. "The only one I know by sight is thyme, and I haven't seen any recently. She'll need lots of water too, and we don't have that much left."

Astra nodded in agreement.

"Can we ask Kisa if she knows of any?" I suggested. Kisa had a vast knowledge of the healing properties of plants.

"I woke her up when I felt how hot she was," Astra replied. "But she didn't make any sense, and she thought she was talking to her mother."

"Today must have been too much for her," Cole put in, sounding dejected.

"Today was hard on everyone," Astra told him. "Kisa's body is the weakest. It's not surprising that she got sick."

"We need a plan," I said, rising. "Let's wake the others."

"Is that a good idea?" Astra wondered. "I don't want anyone to panic."

I turned back to her scornfully. "It's Joss and Rollan. No one's going to panic, but they'll want to know. Especially Joss."

"I agree," Cole said, siding with me for once.

I roused the other two, and Astra filled them in on the situation.

Even though I hadn't shaken him, Todd woke up too. He moved closer so he could hear what was going on, but he didn't join us as we huddled around our friend.

"She might be better in the morning," Rollan suggested.

Joss shook his head. "I doubt it; a fever like this could last days." He took Kisa's head onto his lap and gently combed out her pale, blonde hair with his fingers.

"She needs rest, and we are all going to need water soon," I told them. "Neither of which we'll find here."

"We should try to get her to the lake. I could carry her," Cole suggested.

"It'll be impossible with all the cliffs and ridges," Astra pointed out.

"Especially this one," I couldn't help agreeing, as I pointed to the huge cliff in front of us. It was going to be impossible enough to get down without falling on our own. There was no way we would manage to get an unconscious girl safely to the ground below.

"If we wait for her to get better, we might not reach the lake before we run out of water," said Cole.

"What are we going to do if she gets worse?" Joss asked. His voice was steady, but I could hear the depths of his concern.

Rollan's eyes widened. "She won't die, will she?"

"I don't know," Astra answered no one in particular.

"If only we could get her down this cliff, then we'd have a chance. So long as we move as quickly as possible and drink as little as we can, we might be able to make it to the lake before…" Cole cut off with a look at Joss.

"Before what?" he asked. "Before Kisa's dead?"

140

There was a moment of silence.

"Why don't you leave her?" I had forgotten the Broken was listening to our conversation. "She's weak and nothing but a burden. You could go on without her," he pointed out.

"You—" I had never heard such a furious tone in Rollan's voice before.

He spun around and struck Todd full in the face. The Broken fell backward with a gasp of pain, but regained his feet a moment later as Rollan swung at him again.

This time, Todd dodged nimbly before kicking out with his foot. He caught Rollan in the leg with his bare heel. I saw the Broken glance at the cliff to his left. He repositioned himself so that Rollan was closer to it than he was, and then braced himself for another strike. Rollan bellowed and made to rush at the other boy, but Astra leapt between them.

Cole moved to join her.

"That's enough," she spat at the pair, glaring at each in turn.

"But he said—" Rollan began in protest.

"It doesn't matter what he said," Cole cut him off.

"It was actually a good idea," Astra announced. Five pairs of eyes stared at her in astonishment.

"You can't be serious," Cole gasped.

"Not all of us," Astra amended, seeing our horrified faces. "If a couple of us went as quickly as possible, they could reach the lake in less than a day. Right, Todd?"

"Easily," the Broken said softly. He turned his head and spat out a mouthful of blood. There was already a fresh lump rising on his cheek where Rollan had punched him. It wasn't that noticeable since he still had considerable swelling from the beating Astra had given him.

"We should send the fastest," Astra suggested. "They can go, get water, and look for any useful plants. That way, we can let Kisa rest. The fever may even have broken by the time they get back."

"Excellent," Cole nodded. "Who should go?"

"I will," I volunteered. There was nothing I wanted to do less than sit around feeling helpless.

Astra looked at me with approval and nodded. "Todd will have to go too, since he knows the way."

I wasn't pleased with the idea, but maybe this was my chance to get rid of him, especially if Astra didn't join us.

Joss appeared torn, as if he couldn't decide whether to go or stay.

"I'll go," Cole offered, noticing Joss's anxiety. "You should stay with her."

"Bad idea," Astra told him. "If something happens and we need to move her down the cliff, you're the only one who might be able to manage it."

We were silent for a moment. She had a point. Astra and I were strong enough to lift Kisa, but I doubted we would have the arm strength to climb down the cliff face holding that much weight. Joss looked particularly disturbed by Astra's words.

"I'll go instead," Astra told him.

Great, I thought. *My two favorite people.* I was beginning to regret volunteering before the rest of the group had been chosen. My only consolation was that at least Astra wouldn't be left behind with Cole.

"Do you want me to come too?" Rollan asked.

Cole shook his head. "Three should be enough," he decided. "You stay here. If we have to move her, I'll need all the help I can get."

Rollan nodded, looking relieved. I was beginning to understand that heights weren't really his thing.

"When do we leave?" I asked. The sky was starting to turn from black to blue with a few traces of pink in the east.

"Immediately, I should think," Astra replied.

I nodded.

It didn't take us long to sort out the packs. We had seven canteens. We filled two of them with water for those staying behind, leaving barely a mouthful of water in each of the five we took. It would have to last us all the way to the lake. Astra and I left our packs behind. The Broken didn't carry one either.

Before we started the climb, we each ate a couple of peaches and took a few strips of meat for the journey.

Climbing down the cliff was every bit as bad as I had imagined. Worse, because it was still dark and had to be done mostly by feel. The three boys staying behind lay on the ledge above us, watching our progress.

Todd was the best climber. He moved as if he had been scaling mountains his whole life, which, for all I knew, might have been the truth. It took more than half an hour for us to make it to the bottom. Astra slipped once and almost fell. I grabbed her but wouldn't have been able to keep her from falling if her other hand didn't already have a firm grip on another outcrop. She thanked me anyway.

Once we reached the bottom, I waved up at the rest of our team. They were so far away that I couldn't even tell them apart in the dim light of dawn.

Turning from the cliff, the three of us started toward the lake. Our progress was swift. There were a few rises and dips but nothing even close to the cliff we had just descended.

A little before midday, trees began appearing ahead of us. Shortly after that, we entered another forest. *Why couldn't Kisa have gotten sick here?* I wondered. *Nothing ever seems to go right.*

We didn't rest. None of us were particularly tired. It was much easier to travel all day without the burden of a pack. The sun was hidden behind a thick cloud bank, and it seemed like rain would start falling at any moment.

I could tell we were getting close to the lake when the ground started growing soft and marshy underfoot. Clumps of reeds popped up in the wettest spots.

"There." Astra pointed to a space between a couple of trees where water was visible. The lake was huge, easily as large as the one close to Riverside, surrounded by a dense forest of pines.

Just before I stepped out of the trees, I heard something and froze. Todd bumped into me from behind, knocking me to my knees with his larger bulk.

"I'm sor—" he started, sounding terrified.

"Shhh," I told him.

There it was again. Voices.

"What is it?" Astra asked.

"There are others here."

CHAPTER 15
THE LAKE

Todd froze in surprise. Astra threw herself to the ground and pulled the Broken down beside her. Just as quickly, I ducked behind a large bush.

I was in front and moved forward slowly on my hands and knees for about twenty yards until I saw the other team off to the right. Glancing back, I realized that the Broken wasn't with us anymore. After a moment, I spotted him ten yards behind Astra, kneeling on the ground. With eyes closed and head raised, he mouthed silent words to no one.

Astra looked to see what had caught my attention. We both stared in surprise at the boy, clueless as to why he'd suddenly lost his mind and started speaking to the sky.

"Todd," Astra hissed. "What are you doing?"

The Broken opened his eyes and crept up to us carefully. He seemed almost as terrified as he had been the first night he spent in our camp.

"I was praying," the boy whispered to Astra.

"What?" she asked in confusion.

"I was praying for safety and—"

"Enough," I interrupted him, not caring what explanation he was trying to offer for his insane behavior. "Tell us about it later. We need to get water and get out of here."

I focused my attention back on the other team. They were standing in the open, close to the lake, fifty feet from where we were concealed by the trees. A large number of rocks stood between them and us. They went all the way down to the lake.

"We can use these for cover," I suggested, pointing.

Astra nodded. Moving with great caution, we crept toward the cluster of boulders while staying hidden by the trees as much as possible. Once we reached the rocks, the other group was even closer, and I was able to get a better look. A wave of relief passed through me. Half of them were wearing the maroon color of The Paramount. It was Bala, Jase, and Tiera's team.

The three were friends of mine that I had known nearly all my life. Well, not friends exactly. Jase was Cole's best friend and, as such, we spent a lot of time together. I was on good terms with Bala, although she was slippery as a fish. I trusted her about as far as I could have thrown her. Tiera was someone I always avoided. Young, whiny, and annoying, she made Kisa look like a stalwart and hardy contender. Even though we weren't intimately acquainted, they were something familiar; I felt safe around them.

I would have stepped out and greeted them, but Astra, sensing my intentions, grabbed my arm.

"What?" I hissed, shaking her off. "I know them."

Astra still shook her head. "I don't care. We should get the water and leave." I was about to open my mouth to argue with her, but she didn't give me a chance.

"What do you think they will do to him?" she asked, nodding toward Todd. The Broken's dark brown eyes were wide with fear.

What we should have done with him, I thought rebelliously.

I remembered that once Jase had vowed to kill any Broken he found. Somehow, that didn't seem quite as right now as it did then. If Todd hadn't tried to murder us, wouldn't it be just as wrong to kill him as to kill a member of The Clan?

But he did try to kill us, I reminded myself. *Because he's a Broken; they are all the same.*

I was still considering revealing myself to the other team as I crawled to the water beside Astra and began filling the canteens I carried. From our hiding place, we could hear what they were discussing.

"I think we should just go back," Tiera whined. "We haven't had any food in days." She obviously hadn't changed much.

146

"We're not going back," Bala growled, sounding even more out of sorts and short-tempered than she usually did.

"That's right," a deep voice agreed. It must have belonged to the boy from The Quarry, who was their team leader.

"I'm sick of your sniveling," he continued. "We have water; that's all we need. More food will turn up soon. Now, let's get a move on."

Astra and I each took long drinks from the canteens before topping them off again. Todd, who had already drunk his fill, was moving back to the tree line, keeping a wary eye on the others.

"I'm not going," Tiera cried.

"Yes, you are," said the deep voice of the leader. I tried to recall what he looked like, but the only thing that came to mind was his dark hair and grim face.

"No!" Tiera screamed.

"Then you can stay here," he bellowed in return.

"I will, and I'll head back alone. You've been nothing but cruel to me since we started," Tiera shrieked.

There was silence for a moment.

"That won't work." I barely heard the words Bala spoke. "If she manages to make it back, we'll all be eliminated."

I was suddenly glad that I hadn't revealed our presence to the other team. It didn't seem like a good time for them, and I was sure our appearance would have only inflamed the situation.

When Astra and I finished filling the canteens, we began silently moving toward the trees. Todd was waiting for us, still watching the other team intently.

"She's correct." I was getting to my feet when I heard the boy from The Quarry reply to Bala's words.

"Then we all lose. Serves you right," Tiera snapped rudely. "None of you would make good Clan Leaders anyway. I'm not going to try to help you win. I'm going home!"

"You little brat," I heard the team leader hiss furiously. "You're not going anywhere."

"Yes, I am!" Tiera shouted. "Try and stop me."

Suddenly, I had a sinking feeling in the pit of my stomach. I couldn't help looking back at the other team to see what was going to happen.

Bala and the first team leader moved in on Tiera.

"Don't touch me," she cried.

"Jase," Bala said with an eerie calm in her voice, "kill her."

Horror made me halt. I knew Bala was almost as intent on winning as I was, but to order the death of one of her own teammates? Would I ever have gone that far? I hoped not. Surely, even without the rules to guide me, I would always know the difference between right and wrong. Jase too. He was a good person; he had followed the rules all his life. Jase would never kill the girl who was not only from The Clan and his village but also on his team, would he?

My internal question was answered a moment later as Jase grabbed Tiera in his massive arms. She screamed and cried, pleading for mercy. In a matter of seconds, her shrieks were cut off by the sound of a sickening snap as Jase broke her neck like it was a twig.

Her lifeless body tumbled to the ground as he released her. A scream was building in my throat, but I clenched my jaw, determined to hold it in. I managed to do so, but it lingered just behind my lips. I knew we needed to get away as quickly as possible. The Broken was staring at the clearing, mouth hanging open. Astra had turned away from the horrible sight.

"Let's go," she whispered.

I followed wordlessly and only glanced back once to see the other team dragging Tiera's body off into the woods. I wondered what they would do with it there. Hide it, probably. They would want to hide what they had done from everyone who came that way and from themselves.

I was still in shock as I stumbled through the woods, away from the lake.

Jase.

Cole's best friend.

If I knew any of them, it was him. I couldn't believe what he had just done.

What am I going to tell Cole? The thought scared me almost as much as what I had witnessed.

If no one told him, he and Jase could go on being friends once we made it back. But could I let that happen? Wouldn't I want to know if it was my friend? I was still battling with my indecision when Astra stopped. The Broken and I grouped around her.

"We aren't going to tell anyone what we've just seen," she ordered.

The boy nodded.

"Myra?" Astra asked.

I met her green eyes with my gray ones for a long moment. She seemed to know that I was still making my decision on that, but didn't press me any further.

"Right," she said. "Let's hurry."

We weren't worried about the other team; they would be heading in the opposite direction. However, after seeing something so horrific, I was eager to get back to my friends. I hoped all of them were safe.

Instead of walking as we had before, we ran. The rain that had been threatening to fall for the past couple of hours started. It wasn't a storm, just a light drizzle. I hoped the cool water would help bring down Kisa's fever.

We were forced to stop for the night because the moon was sheathed in clouds. The huge cliff that marked the end of our journey was just barely visible in the distance when the last of the light faded from the sky.

We found a small cave among the boulders and crags nearby. I hated the idea of sleeping so close to a Broken, but the alternative was to sleep in the rain.

There didn't seem to be much point in keeping watch, so I lay down as far from the others as I could.

Just before I fell asleep, I heard Astra talking to the Broken. Their conversation was too faint for me to hear all of it, but I could make out a small portion.

"Did you really think we would leave one of our own behind?" Astra wondered.

"No," Todd answered. "I didn't think you would, but I was curious as to why not. That was the reason I asked."

"Rollan thought you were making a suggestion," Astra told him.

The Broken didn't respond.

"Would you have left her behind?" asked Astra.

"I don't know," Todd's reply came slowly. "She's going to be a beautiful young woman, but only if she lives."

"We're going to make sure that she does, and for a very long time," Astra told him.

Todd made no answer that I could hear. Not long after, I fell asleep.

In the morning, the rain was gone. We made it to the cliff before the sun had cleared the tree line. I dreaded the thought of climbing up.

"I'll go and take the water," Todd offered. I glanced at him suspiciously. Was he trying to catch us with our forces divided?

Astra nodded. "We'll be right behind you."

Todd shimmied up the wall, making it look easy. Astra and I scrambled up after him, taking twice as long. The others were waiting for us at the top.

Cole beamed when he saw me. I smiled back, but I couldn't help instantly thinking of Jase, so the smile was forced.

Kisa was awake but very weak. Joss had just finished giving her a drink of water from one of the bottles we'd brought back.

"Thanks for getting water," she told us with a weak smile. "I'm feeling much better now."

"Good," Astra said. She nodded to Cole and then glanced back at me. The three of us stepped a short distance away from the others. Rollan was trying to coax Kisa into eating a peach, which

Joss was cutting up with the knife we had taken from Todd. The Broken was perched on a boulder a little way off. He was looking in their direction, but his expression was glazed as if his thoughts were somewhere else.

"We need to try and make it down this cliff," Astra reminded us both as if our focus for the last twenty-four hours hadn't been that very descent.

"I don't know if she's strong enough," said Cole. "She's better now, but—"

"I agree," I piped up. It wasn't safe to wait where we were. Another team could come upon us at any moment. The thought of that was more worrisome to me than falling from the cliff.

"I wish we had a rope or something. We tried to make one yesterday, but we couldn't find anything strong enough," Cole told us.

"If we go now, while it's still cool out, she can make it," I said, trying to sound more confident than I was.

Cole glanced at me. He seemed to sense that something had happened. I mean, how often did I immediately agree with Astra on anything?

He was right, of course; something had happened. The experience by the lakeside made Astra and me of the same mind. That team wasn't desperate. They killed Tiera—murdered her, really—simply because they considered her an annoyance and a threat.

I could only imagine what they would have done to us. I wasn't sure if even my friendship with Jase would have been enough to protect me.

"If you both think we should try it, we will," Cole decided.

We rejoined the others. Kisa was in the middle of consuming the peach, while Joss was chattering happily with her. Both he and Rollan looked quite pleased with themselves for getting her to eat.

Cole waited until Kisa finished, and then he announced, "It's time to go. Pack up."

"Wait, what?" Joss asked. "Kisa's not ready yet. We should wait a few more hours."

Cole shook his head. "The hotter it gets, the worse she'll feel. We need to go now, while it's cool."

"But—" Joss started. Kisa put a hand on his arm.

"It's okay. I feel strong enough," Kisa said. Her voice was steady, but her eyes betrayed her fear.

In that moment, I had to admire her. She was so different from Tiera. She would never give up on her team. Although, it seemed as though Tiera's team hadn't been very supportive of her from the start.

We lined up on the clifftop, looking down at the dizzying drop below. I kept telling myself that I had already climbed up and down it once, so I shouldn't have any problem doing it again. However, it was unnerving to actually be able to see exactly how far it was to the ground.

"I'll start climbing down, and you come right after me," Joss told Kisa. "If you start to slip or anything, I'll catch you."

Kisa nodded trustfully.

"You're not big enough to stop her if she's falling," Cole told Joss. "I will do it."

Joss looked uncertain. "But- you're not that great of a climber, no offense."

"I still have more of a chance than you do of catching her," Cole pointed out. The uncertainty in his voice told me exactly how worried he was about Kisa and his ability to help her.

"I'd still feel better if I was the one—" Joss started, but he was interrupted.

"I can do it." All six of us turned to look at the Broken. "I've already climbed down once, and I know where the footholds are." He wasn't looking at any of us, just standing on the edge of the cliff, staring at the dead drop below. The Broken was a good bit larger than Joss and had proved to be an agile climber. He was the logical choice.

"Wait—" Joss started, but he was interrupted again, this time by Cole.

He went down on one knee in front of Kisa so that he could look her in her eyes.

"What do you think?" he asked her.

"I don't like this at all," Rollan spat, glaring at the Broken.

Kisa glanced at each of the boys in turn. "I—"

"I'll keep you safe," Todd said, looking directly into Kisa's eyes, probably for the first time.

After a moment, she nodded. "Okay."

As he began climbing down, followed closely by Kisa, I couldn't help remembering what he had told us about needing to kill someone for his rite. This was a perfect chance for him to get the weakest of us alone. I bit my tongue to keep from voicing my accusations. The rest of my team was ready to trust Todd, so I was forced to accept him. However, if anything happened to Kisa, no one would be able to stop me from taking revenge on the Broken.

Joss insisted on being the next one to go. Cole went after him, carrying Kisa's pack as well as his own. Next was Rollan, then me and, finally, Astra. The climb was much easier the second time, even though my arms were sore and tired from climbing up that morning. All the way down, I kept my ears pricked, dreading that I might hear a scream or the sound of a body hitting the ground.

I glanced down a couple of times, but I couldn't see much past Rollan and Cole. Finally, I spied Todd and Kisa safely on the ground. Kisa was sitting on a log, breathing hard. Joss and Cole were with her a few moments later. The rest of us reached the bottom in safety.

Kisa tried to stand, but her legs were wobbly from the exertion of the descent.

"It's okay; I've got you," Cole said, catching her before she could fall.

"Thanks," Kisa gasped, looking at both Cole and the Broken.

We redistributed backpacks so that Cole wouldn't have to carry any. In exchange, he hoisted Kisa up onto his back. She fell asleep a short time later with her arms clasped loosely around his neck and her head resting on one of his shoulders.

The day grew hot, but we didn't stop. Every so often, Astra would place a hand on Kisa's forehead. Based on her expression, it was unlikely that Kisa was improving.

We made it to the forest in the late afternoon. I wondered whether Astra would say anything about having seen another team. She didn't, but I observed her having a few quiet words with Todd. He started steering us a little more to the north after that, away from the shore where we had seen the other team. It was just as well; I had no desire to come upon Tiera's body.

We caught sight of the lake a few hours before the sun set. The surface was calm and smooth with only the faintest ripples appearing now and then as unseen fish darted to and fro. Lily pads sprouted in the shallows. Among them were a few purple water flowers. I hadn't noticed the absence of bugs until we arrived at the water's edge. The air was teeming with gnats and flies. I shook my long ponytail to keep them away from my face.

After walking for another fifteen minutes, we found a cozy, little hollow close to the water where the ground was dry.

Astra talked the boys out of making a fire. I was pleased she managed to do it without revealing the presence of the other team. It would have been a waste of time anyway since we didn't have anything to cook. Despite the lack of food, I didn't feel hungry, just exhausted. I flopped down under the nearest tree, thankful that there was a soft layer of moss between myself and the ground.

I heard the others settle down too. Astra volunteered for the first watch. Cole chose a spot about three feet away from me, beneath a different tree. After his breathing had grown steady, I rolled over to face him. He looked so peaceful while wrapped in sleep. Would he still have been able to find that peace if he knew what I knew? If he had seen what I had seen?

I rolled onto my back and looked up. The stars were masked by the tree's branches, which stretched high above my head. I didn't have the energy to rise and find a place where they would be visible. Instead, I closed my eyes and didn't open them until morning.

We spent the following day making slow progress around the lake. Kisa was still very weak, so we stopped often and rested for several hours during the afternoon. It was nice to take it easy for a bit, but the constant worry that other teams were around and ahead of us ate away at me.

The plus side was that, while we were stopped, Joss managed to fish up an enormous haul from the lake. There were also several apple trees along the shore. I was surprised Jase and Bala's team hadn't realized the food potential of the place.

In the early evening, we called a halt. The small glade we chose smelled amazing. Pine needles blanketed the ground. We were within a stone's throw of the lake, but the land around us, which was twisted by many ancient tree roots, was a foot above the surface of the water.

While Kisa napped, Astra took her bow and headed out to see if she could find any red meat. Todd accompanied her, whether by her choice or his, I wasn't sure.

Rollan and Joss caught half a dozen fish in the first hour. Afterward, they abandoned the task and splashed around in the shallows, trying to dunk each other. It made me nervous. The lake was pretty large, but it would be hard for anyone passing by to miss their noisy, half-clothed forms wading around in the water.

Even though the fish were already cooked, I sat by the fire, keeping the coals alive in case Astra returned successfully from the hunt. Nearby, Cole was resting with his back against a tree. Kisa lay on the ground close beside him. The illness she was fighting made her sleep fretful and agitated. Cole had soothed her to sleep when we first stopped, and then seemed to have nodded off himself.

The previous evening, his sleep had been peaceful, but from where I sat, I could see his body was starting to stiffen. His lips twisted into a grimace, and I heard a painful gasp escape his lungs. His dreams didn't seem to be getting any better. I wondered if anyone else had noticed them.

Swiftly, I rose and touched his arm. He woke instantly. At least he had reached a point where the panic from his dreams didn't remain with him in the waking world.

He let out a long sigh and glanced at Kisa. I returned to my spot by the fire and wasn't surprised to see Cole follow me. He sat on the pine needles close by. The fear may not have carried over, but there was still a shadow across his face.

"Cole?" I murmured softly.

He turned his eyes toward me. "Yes?"

"What happened?" I asked.

He shrugged. "It was just a bad dream."

"No," I said. "What happened those few days we were apart? There's something you haven't told anyone. What was it?"

"It was—intense—" Cole told me haltingly.

I shook my head. "I don't believe that's all it was. Astra and Kisa don't have nightmares every night." Cole couldn't meet my gaze. "You don't have to talk about it if you don't want to, but if it'll make you feel better, I'll be happy to listen."

"I—" Cole began, but he trailed off. I waited for him to continue. "I just don't want to burden you."

My eyes moistened at his words. "Cole, I'm your friend," I told him. "Or at least, I thought I was. Don't you know that I would do anything to help you?"

Cole nodded and met my eyes. "I know," he whispered. "And I can't explain how much that means to me. I'll tell you, but I don't want the others to know. It would be too terrible if any of them found out." His eyes slid to the lake where Rollan and Joss were still playing in the water.

"I promise," I whispered.

It took Cole a while to continue, but I remained patiently silent. I held a long, thin stick in my hand, and I began poking at the fire absentmindedly.

"It was really—intense," he began, using the same words from earlier. "I—I thought you were dead." Cole's voice broke.

I left the rock and moved to sit close beside him on the ground. Gently, I reached out and took his hand. His grip was warm and strong.

"Kisa and Astra needed me," he continued. "But I couldn't seem to find a way to get them water or food. The other team continued to hunt us, and we lived in terror."

Cole paused and licked his lips as if remembering the thirst of those days. "The first two times they spotted me, I was far enough away to outrun them, but not the third time."

I leaned closer to Cole, the fire completely forgotten. The haunted look in his eyes returned as he re-lived the chase.

"They surprised me while I was trying to get to the river. One of the boys had a bow and grazed my side with an arrow. A few inches over, and it would have killed me. As it was, the adrenaline kicked in, and I was able to sprint away, but they were too close for me to outdistance them for long.

"I hadn't eaten in days, and I was completely dehydrated. Plus, my side was bleeding, and I couldn't tell how bad the wound was. There was no way to outrun them, so I hid in a hollow log.

"I hoped they would pass my hiding place, but they didn't. There were three of them: two boys and a girl. They stopped to catch their breath and—and I heard what they were planning."

Cole broke off and stared into the fire for a long time; his hand still held in mine. I didn't move a muscle. Slowly, Cole turned his gaze to Kisa. He lowered his voice even more before continuing.

"I thought it was strange that the girl followed Kisa that first night when she didn't have a pack or weapon to steal." Cole's voice was calm when he spoke, but then he raised his blue eyes to my face. I saw all the horror he had felt hiding in the log as if it were my own.

"But I found out why. They'd seen us earlier that day before they attacked us. They watched us cross the river and planned their attack very carefully. They knew they wouldn't be able to catch us all in the dark. Instead, they wanted to get a hold of Kisa and—" He cut off and took a deep breath before continuing. "They were going to break her legs and leave her in the clearing as a trap for the rest of us."

I felt the blood drain from my face at the ghastly words.

It was disturbing and genius all at once. If Kisa were lying in the woods screaming, we would have come for her. Even if we knew it was a trap, we would have come.

"What did they hope to accomplish?" I gasped.

Cole shook his head. "I don't know. They may have wanted to thin out the competition, or they could have been planning to make us help them."

As we're using Todd and his knowledge of the forest, I thought.

"I didn't think such a horrible thing could ever be conceived, much less planned and acted on by those of The Clan," Cole admitted.

"That's why you think there's evil in the world," I observed.

"Not just in the world," Cole amended. "In us."

Wait a minute, I wanted to say. *That was them, not us.* But how could I? Hadn't I just thought how genius their plan was? Hadn't I watched Jase, someone I'd known all my life, act similarly?

"It's true," I whispered, more to myself than to Cole. It wasn't just the Broken who had evil in them; it was in all of us.

CHAPTER 16
CROSSING

It took most of the following day for us to finish rounding the lake. Todd said that there were lots of streams and rivers in the land ahead. He predicted that we would reach the ocean in about fifteen days.

Just before we left the water's edge, the Broken raised his hand and pointed at two distant mountain peaks on the horizon.

"That is the way I came," he reported.

"Yeah, I vote for the road where we don't have to scale a mountain range," I snorted.

"There is a path between them," Todd explained. "Going around will take far longer."

I considered for a moment. He was probably telling the truth, provided his only goal was to get us to the ocean so he could go free. Although, if Todd wanted his freedom so badly, he could have tried running away. Did he really think we would bother hunting him down? He wasn't worth our time.

Everything went smoothly after we left the lake. It seemed we couldn't walk more than a couple of hours without coming across little brooks and streams. The land was green and teeming with food. We lacked neither meat nor edible vegetation.

Kisa's fever was all but gone two days later, so our progress increased again. I had feared the illness would leave the little girl weak, but instead, it seemed to have made her stronger. She didn't lag behind so much and was always spotting edible plants.

There was no sign of other teams; still, I kept a sharp eye out for them. Hopefully, they would all go around the mountains while we passed through them. I didn't want to meet another team any time soon—or ever.

My worries faded as the land shifted to fields of green grass and small clumps of trees. All the while, I had the impression that we were climbing; however, the slope was gradual enough to be mostly unnoticed.

The weather was lovely. Huge, puffy clouds of swirling white mist filled the sky above. Gentle breezes from the east crossed the land, stirring the fields of flowers but barely moving the stout branches of the mighty oaks.

One evening, Astra and Todd brought back another of the thin-legged, goat creatures. A few more walked right by our camp that night as darkness veiled the sky. It was pointless to shoot them; we would never be able to carry all the meat, so we let them pass in peace.

The Broken told us that the creatures were called "deer". Rollan wasted no time telling the Broken that he called them "dinner". Everyone laughed, including Todd. It was the first time I'd seen him look even slightly pleased.

With the swelling from the beatings Astra and Rollan had given him going down, I could see that he had a beautiful face, in a wild, savage sort of way. Cole offered to let him borrow a shirt, since he didn't have one, but the boy declined. It appeared he was comfortable going around half naked.

It also didn't appear to bother him to be barefoot. Over grass, thorns, and rocks, he trekked on as if he didn't feel a thing on the soles of his feet. It was just another part of his strange ways, like the rock he wore around his neck. I'd seen his hand clutching it a few times, but I was yet to see him do anything useful with it.

Several nights after leaving the lake, we came to a fast-flowing river, which was too deep to wade through. It was evening, so we resolved to wait until morning before figuring out how we were going to get across.

Everyone set about making camp. I was down on the riverbank filling all the canteens when I heard it—a strange, eerie cry—coming from across the water. I straightened quickly and peered at the opposite shore.

160

Dusk had already fallen, and the far bank was well over a hundred feet away, but I was certain that I saw a dog-like creature moving among the shadows. Its fur was dark, and I caught a flash of green eyes before it vanished into the trees.

Instantly, I remembered the monstrous beast I had seen once before, giving the same cry. There was a river between the creature and myself then too, but that hadn't kept me from being frozen with shock.

This time, I didn't feel any of that. I felt happy. The sound was beautiful—if a bit lonely. This world was amazing. It was full of creatures that I had never seen before, creatures whose existence I would never have even known about if not for the trials.

"What was that?" I heard Kisa say from where she was helping gather kindling for the fire.

Before I could answer, the Broken did. "It's a wolf."

"What's a wolf?" Kisa sounded nervous.

"A predator, like a dog, but bigger and wilder," the boy told her.

"It's on the other side of the river," I informed them as I climbed back up the bank, arms laden with full canteens.

Kisa nodded, but I heard the Broken mutter, "Great, it'll eat us tomorrow instead of tonight."

"Eat us?" Kisa squeaked. "Dogs don't eat people."

"Well, wolves do sometimes," the boy replied.

"Really?" Joss asked. He and Cole had returned from a nearby pear tree with enough fruit for everyone.

Todd nodded. "I've never known anyone it has happened to, but there are stories."

"What are you talking about?" I asked suspiciously.

Just then, Rollan got the fire to catch, and there was a sudden blaze of light. As it died down, it left the clearing with an eerie feeling. I saw Kisa shudder slightly, but she leaned forward, her eyes intently watching the Broken's face.

The boy cleared his throat before continuing. "There was a wise man's son who was in charge of his father's flock of sheep. He loved each and every lamb and knew them all by name. Every day, he'd lead them out to the beautiful pasture where they grazed. It was a long way off, and he took the sheep up a steep hill to get there, but the pasture was surrounded by rock walls, and it was safe.

"After many years of doing this, the son grew up and had other, more important things to do for his father. They entrusted another boy to watch the flock for them.

"The new boy didn't feel like climbing the steep hill every day when there were plenty of green pastures that didn't require such an effort to get to. Without telling the man or the son, he stopped taking the sheep up the hill. Instead, he let them graze in different pastures that weren't protected.

"At first, he just did it from time to time, but eventually, he gave up climbing the hill completely and never took the sheep back to their original pasture. What's more, he grew pleased with himself, thinking how clever it was for him to save so much effort.

"Then, one day, the wolves came."

Kisa's eyes grew huge at Todd's ominous words and tone.

"One of the youngest lambs was the first to catch the wolves' scent. It let out a cry and ran toward the boy, hoping for protection. The other sheep also smelled the wolves and crowded around the boy. The father and son had taught the boy how to fend off wolves, but not so many at one time.

"The boy wished for the protective stone walls of the meadow where he used to graze the flock. But he knew they were far away and he could not reach them in time. The wolves started to attack, dragging off the sheep one by one."

Kisa gave a cry of horror, and I wondered if maybe this wasn't a good thing for her to be hearing. However, if we were going to face wolves, we needed to know about them.

"The boy did all he could," Todd continued. "But the attacks came from every side at once, and he was too weak to defend the flock. Before, when he used to climb the hill every day, it built his strength, but it had been a long time since he made the journey, and the boy had grown weak.

162

"Soon, his entire flock was devoured, down to the last lamb. But the wolves were still hungry. The boy despaired and sat down, waiting for death.

"'Giving up so soon?' asked one of the wolves. 'Aren't you going to fight?'"

"Wolves can talk?" Kisa interrupted in surprise.

Todd seemed confused by her question. "No, not in real life, but in a story—"

"Liar!" I spat. "None of this is true!"

The boy looked surprised. "Of course it's not true. It's just a story."

"But if it's not true, then why would you say it?" Cole asked.

The Broken opened his mouth but didn't seem to know how to answer.

Just then, Astra walked into the clearing carrying a rabbit. I had forgotten that she was off hunting. She stopped when she saw the scene in front of her. Cole and I were glaring at a speechless Todd.

"What's going on?" she asked.

"Todd has just finished telling us a number of lies," Cole explained to her.

"I didn't mean to," Todd said desperately. "I didn't realize you'd think it was true. It's just a tale my father told me when I was little to scare me into doing what I was told. Didn't your parents tell you made-up stories?"

Kisa, Rollan, and Joss all shook their heads together.

"What do you mean a tail?" Joss asked. "Isn't that part of an animal?"

"No," Todd explained. "It's like a fable or myth—"

"There are no such words," I interrupted. I'd memorized the entire language book in our school, so I was certain those words did not exist.

The boy looked utterly confused and astonished. "I—I—" he stammered.

Joss jumped in, almost like he felt sorry for the Broken and wanted to help him out. "Maybe they forgot to put them in our books."

"That's probably because they have a bad meaning," Cole guessed. "Lying is wrong, so why would they need multiple words for it?"

Astra laughed. "Not like we haven't all lied before," she said, turning back to Todd. "Do you not think it's wrong to lie?"

"Well, sometimes," the boy answered. "But I've never considered a story to be untruthful. I didn't mean to make anyone think it was true. I just—it's something we do for fun."

"You sit around and lie to each other?" I asked.

Todd shook his head and seemed to think hard before answering. "It's not like that. A story—a tale—it can take you to another place. Let you experience things that aren't real."

I snorted. "That's so stupid."

"I did feel a little scared when he talked about the wolves surrounding the sheep," Kisa admitted kindly. "Is that what you mean?"

The boy nodded. "Yeah, exactly."

"I felt the same way," Joss said. "It was kind of fun."

"I didn't," scoffed Rollan.

"It is a fascinating concept," Cole conceded.

"That doesn't mean it's not against the rules," I insisted stubbornly.

"There are no rules," Astra reminded me. "At least, not right now."

"Maybe there should be!" I practically yelled. "Without rules, everything is misguided, like the other teams."

"Teams?" Cole looked surprised.

"If one team is murdering and stealing, why wouldn't the others?" Astra put in smoothly. Instead of being grateful, I grew even angrier. I didn't need her to cover for me. I could manage on my own.

"We must remember the way we were raised," I insisted. "That is probably the true test of the trials, to see who can follow

164

the rules and lead a team in the way of The Clan. If the Clan Leaders could see us now, they would be ashamed. We're supposed to be struggling for the future of The Clan. Instead, we sit here listening to the lies of a Broken."

Everyone was silent for a moment after my outburst. I felt the heat drain from my face. Perhaps I had been too harsh.

"What are the trials?" Todd asked.

"That's what we're doing right now," Astra explained to him. "It's how The Clan decides its new leaders every fifty years. That's why we need to find the ocean."

"Oh." The boy thought for a moment. "What happens when you find the ocean?"

Cole shrugged. "Nothing special. That's just the first part. Next, we have to head north and find a mountain with—"

"Don't tell him!" I cried, horrified that Cole would share secrets of The Clan with a Broken.

Astra let out a sigh. "I'm sure he means to beat us to the mountain and become a Clan Leader on his own."

"You—" I started, but was too choked on disgust to get out another word.

"Don't fight," Kisa begged.

I glared at Astra. I had never met anyone who could infuriate me with just a couple of words.

"Let's finish getting camp set up," Cole suggested tactfully.

"Yes," Joss agreed. He took out the knife that had belonged to the Broken and started to butcher the rabbit.

The next morning, we were faced with the challenge of crossing the river. Of course, Joss plunged in without hesitation. He swam around a bit and then called up to those of us on the bank, "It's fine. The current isn't very strong."

"Is it deep?" Astra asked.

"Let me check." Joss plunged beneath the surface, only to reappear a moment later. "About eight or nine feet," he shouted to us.

"And he's not even that far out," I muttered.

"If we go farther down, will it get shallow enough for us to walk across?" Astra questioned Todd.

"I'm not sure," Todd shrugged. "This is where I crossed last time."

"How are we going to get the metal across?" Cole wondered aloud.

That was the biggest concern. More food could be found, and clothing would dry, but Cole's sword, Astra's arrows, mine and Joss's knives, plus the fishhook, were irreplaceable.

Rollan shrugged. "I guess we aren't."

"Maybe we should walk along the bank and look for a place we can ford," I suggested, not wanting to relinquish my weapon.

A soaking wet Joss scrambled up the bank. "The river is so big, I doubt we'll find a better place to cross," he told us.

"We have to," I argued. "I don't want to leave my knife behind. We might need it again."

"Why would you leave it behind?" the Broken asked.

"It's metal," Rollan told him. "There's no way to get it across the river. If you try to carry it while swimming, it'll pull you down."

"No, it won't," the boy argued.

"Trust me," Joss said. "I've spent my whole life by a lake. We never take anything metal out on the water. You can use it from the shore and in the shallows, but when the water gets too deep, the weight of the metal will drown you."

"That's the stupidest thing I've ever heard," Todd muttered under his breath.

I scowled at him, wanting to propose we let him carry some metal across the river if he was so sure he knew what he was talking about. As it turned out, I didn't have to, because, with his next breath, the Broken made the suggestion himself.

"I'll prove it to you," he said. "Give me my knife. I swam across with it last time, and I'll do it again."

"Nice try," I told him. "Do you think we're stupid?"

"I was just going to show you," Todd exclaimed innocently.

"Here," Joss said.

I almost started to protest, but saw that what Joss put into Todd's hand was the fishhook. Much as I didn't want to lose the hook, at least the Broken couldn't attack us with it.

"Wait," Astra said, catching the Broken by his arm. "Are you sure?" she asked him.

"Of course," Todd answered.

She released him, and all six of us huddled together to watch as the boy made his way down to the water. He jumped in without hesitation.

After a tense moment, he reappeared, swimming toward the middle of the river.

"Why isn't it pulling him down?" Rollan demanded.

I shrugged.

"Do you still have the fishhook?" Joss called.

In answer, Todd held up a hand, which was still gripping the small piece of metal.

"This doesn't make any sense," Cole said.

Todd made his way back to us.

"Well, maybe this river is different," Astra suggested.

Joss shook his head. "I don't understand, but it's certainly better for us if we can take the metal across. Now, how are we going to keep the food dry?"

I glanced around, and my eyes lit upon the unused firewood from the night before. "We could build a raft," I suggested.

Rollan shook his head. "It would take too long."

"Not if it was a small one," I replied.

"Yes," Cole agreed. "Something we could put the packs on and pull across the river." He smiled his beautiful smile at me, and I couldn't help but blush. I saw Astra watching, but I didn't mind. I was happy she saw.

It didn't take us long to build the raft out of the wood we had assembled and to secure our packs on top. In truth, the raft was really just a large number of branches and sticks all woven together.

Carefully, we laid the metal weapons beside our packs. If something did happen, at least we would only lose the raft and not our lives.

It took all of us to maneuver the craft to the river. Joss guided it out into the current. Rollan and Astra joined him immediately; they were the strongest swimmers in the group. Kisa was right behind them.

I hadn't even thought to be nervous about the water until that moment, watching my team swim away from me with our supplies. Could I make it?

Of course, you can, I told myself. *You can do anything you put your mind to.*

I jumped into the river with Cole beside me. Todd dove in after us.

The Broken quickly overtook and passed me, heading for the raft. He swam up alongside Joss and began helping him steer. Todd had smooth, powerful strokes and moved skillfully through the water. After watching for a few moments, I wondered if he were better than all of us.

Once the raft was in the middle of the stream, the current started to pull at it. Cole and I caught up with the others and held on with all our might. It was a battle that took nearly twenty minutes, but we finally reached the other shore.

I emerged on the far bank, thoroughly exhausted, and crawled up onto the grass. My limbs felt heavy as stone, and I was gasping for breath.

Joss, who had done much of the work, joined me. Cole, Astra, Rollan, and Todd were equally worn out. Kisa started unloading the bags. Cole and Astra got up to help, but I didn't have an ounce of energy left.

After the bags were unloaded, they released the raft. I watched it lazily drift down the stream. It didn't get too far before becoming entrapped by a group of rocks jutting from the water.

"I never thought the whole 'metal is too heavy' line made sense," Astra announced, handing Cole his sword and collecting her arrows. No one made any comment on her statement.

The day wasn't particularly warm, and I was starting to feel cold. I rose shakily to retrieve my knife and pack. From the latter, I drew forth my maroon cloak. Much as I hated putting it on when I was soaking wet, catching a cold would be worse still. Everyone rested a bit longer before we continued to the east.

CHAPTER 17
STORY

The woods were far denser on the new side of the river, and I felt like the ground was sloping down. By the end of the day, we were still surrounded by closely packed trees, so I had no way to see what lay ahead of us. The two mountains Todd had said we would pass through were hidden from view.

We chose to spend the night underneath a giant oak tree. It was large enough that all of us, not including the Broken, could barely have reached around the trunk if we were holding hands.

Joss and Rollan built a fire and then began gathering acorns from the ground. After the fire was going strong, we roasted the nuts. Every once in a while, one would get too hot and explode. When this happened, Kisa would inevitably give a little cry of surprise. Joss and Rollan found it hilarious. At first, Kisa was indignant about their laughter, but after a few more episodes, she couldn't help but join in.

We gorged on the nuts along with the fruit and meat in our bags. We were growing used to eating well. It would be hard to readjust when food became scarce again. I tried to put that worry aside for the time being. The others were in a good mood and chattered away as twilight fell.

Mostly, I just listened, content that things were finally going well. I settled onto my back and looked up. It saddened me that the stars overhead were once again blotted out by the tree branches, which spread thickly above us. Memories washed over me, and I dozed slightly.

"Well, I didn't get to hear the first one," Astra was saying when I opened my eyes several minutes later.

"But isn't it wrong?" Kisa asked.

"I can't think of why," Astra announced. "Cole?"

I rolled onto my side, wondering what they were discussing.

"I don't know. I suppose there's no harm." Cole spoke quietly. He glanced at me with a guilty look.

"What's going on?" I wondered in confusion.

"Todd's going to tell us another story," Astra explained.

I felt too tired and too at peace to argue for once. Sighing, I rolled onto my back again. I moved my hands behind my head and stared straight up. Much as I didn't want to, I couldn't help overhearing what the Broken said in his strange, accented way.

"Once, there was a boy named Beheen, born into The House of The Warrior. He was in love with a beautiful girl named Majida. In all the land, she was the loveliest, and every man for many miles wanted her to be his for always. Her hair was the golden color of the sunrise and fell to the floor in long curls. She had skin so white it put the snow to shame. Her eyes were twin pits of violet flames."

I wasn't sure about the others, but that was the strangest description of beauty I had ever heard. Who would want hair that fell to the ground? Mine only came halfway down my back, and I had to wear it in a ponytail, or it got everywhere. Plus, someone with such white skin couldn't have done any work outdoors. Her body would be soft and without muscle.

"Beheen had passed Majida many times in the street," Todd continued. "But never once said a word to her. For a while, it was enough for him to just watch the lovely girl go about her family's business on market day. Soon, it became too hard for him to watch any longer. He spoke to her father and asked how he could make Majida his wife."

"What's a wife?" Kisa asked.

"I think it's like a life mate," Joss observed. "Someone that you can start a family with and live with forever."

Out of the corner of my eye, I saw the Broken nod before going on with the lies he was telling.

"Majida's father told Beheen that only the bravest and most worthy man would be allowed to marry his daughter.

171

"In the next moon, Beheen set out to pass his rite of manhood. What Beheen did not know was that all the days he had been watching Majida and her beauty, someone else was watching him. The morning he set out to prove himself, that same person set out as well.

"It was a girl named Aleen. She did not have a head full of long golden curls, nor fair skin and violet eyes, but she had a heart full of love for Beheen. They were childhood friends, and she had grown to love him over the years, even as he fell in love with another.

"She followed him from the village because she couldn't bear the idea of being separated from him and because she was worried that he might need help. Beheen didn't realize he was being followed. He traveled every day farther to the west, the place where the wild things of the world dwelt. He planned to slay a mighty beast and prove how good he was in battle."

"A beast like a wolf?" asked Rollan.

"No," Todd said. "It's bad luck to kill a wolf. They have friends and family who will come after you if you do.

"Beheen wanted to kill a bear. A great, brown bear."

"What is luck?" Kisa asked.

At the same moment, Joss said, "What's a bear?"

I glanced over and saw that the Broken seemed a little perplexed when answering their questions. "Luck is when things are going well for no reason. If things are going badly, and you don't know why, it's called having bad luck," he answered Kisa.

"I'm not sure I understand," Kisa admitted.

"Let him get back to the story," said Astra.

Todd cleared his throat and began again. "Beheen was going to hunt the great brown bear."

I saw Joss open his mouth to repeat his earlier question, but Todd held up a hand to silence him.

"What is a bear, you ask? It is a creature so massive it can blot out the sky when it stands on its hind legs. Its paws are large enough to crush a man's skull, and its claws are sharp enough to cut through rock. Only the bravest warriors have enough courage

172

to defeat the great brown bear. Few who face them live to tell about it afterward.

"With this in mind, Beheen traveled many days to the west. Aleen followed him by night, tracking his footsteps. In his eagerness to win Majida's hand, Beheen hadn't thought about what time of year it was. He left only a few weeks before winter. It was a bad time to travel, and the snow started falling before he even reached The Western Woods, where the silver stag was slain.

"The first snows of winter soon covered the land. Beheen would have frozen to death that first night, for he did not even bring a blanket. As he lay on the icy ground, in a fitful sleep, a shadow crept up to him and placed a blanket over his body before stealing away back into the night.

"When he woke and found a blanket covering him, he thanked the gods and—"

"What are the gods?" Kisa asked.

I heard Todd gasp. "You don't know who the gods are?"

Something in his altered tone struck me. I sat up and looked over to where the others were gathered in a group around the Broken as if he were a true member of our team.

The boy was staring at all of us in wonder and fear. "I've— I've never known anyone who did not know of the gods," he stammered.

"Well, who are they?" Astra pressed curiously. "Are they the leaders of your people?"

The Broken shook his head. "I'll explain about them some other time," he promised. "Forget I mentioned them."

There was a pause while the boy composed himself and picked up where he had left off.

"When Beheen woke and found a blanket covering him, he was very pleased with his good luck. He didn't know how it had come to him, but he took it as a sign that he was going to be successful.

"Many times over that terrible and bitter winter Beheen would have died without Aleen watching out for him. She left him food when he couldn't find any and added logs to his dying fire at night when he slept. Beheen noticed some of these things but thought they were all his good luck. He never realized that Aleen was there in the woods with him. As brave and determined as Beheen was, he was not very clever.

"All winter, Beheen traveled west without finding even the trace of a bear. If he had known anything about bears, he would have known that they sleep all winter in their dens because they don't like the cold. No matter how much he searched, there were no bears to be found.

"Even still, he diligently worked each night to fashion a weapon with which to confront his foe. He selected a large chunk of stone, sharpened it, and attached it to a shaft to make a spear.

"Aleen knew that Beheen was seeking a bear. She also knew that bears sleep during the winter. Much as she did not wish to aid Beheen on his quest to wed another, she could see that he was growing more troubled each day. So, even though she feared for his life, one night, she scouted out a bear's den, then left a trail of bright, red rocks in the snow from Beheen's campsite to the lair. In the morning, Beheen saw the trail and followed it to the cave.

"He bravely started throwing the red rocks into the dark opening. The bear awoke from his sleep and emerged from the den in a terrible fury. The monster stood on its hind paws and blotted out the sky. Beheen was ready with his spear and stabbed at the beast. He cut deep into its body, but this only made the bear angrier. It raised one massive paw to swipe at Beheen.

"If the blow had fallen, Beheen would have been torn in two and never would have made it back to his sweet Majida. Suddenly, a rock flew through the air and struck the bear on the head. The creature was distracted and turned to look in the direction from which it had come. At that moment, both Beheen and the bear saw Aleen.

"The bear charged for her, claws outstretched. Aleen dodged, but the massive claws did not miss entirely. They opened four long wounds on her side. While the bear was distracted with Aleen, Beheen ran up beside the creature and stabbed his spear into the only vulnerable spot on the bear's body, its throat.

"The animal fell to the ground, dead. Beheen rejoiced that he had proven victorious and could now return a man and marry Majida. But then he remembered Aleen. She was sitting on the ground, holding her side.

"'What are you doing here?' he asked her.

"'I have followed you for many moons. I have brought you food when you had none and kept you warm when you were cold. All this I have done because ever since we were young together, I have loved you.' Even while speaking, Aleen's blood was spilling out.

"Beheen did not know what to think. He had fond memories of Aleen from when they were young together, but she was plain to look at, and her hair was brown instead of gold. Her skin wasn't white, and her gray eyes were a far cry from violet. Also, Beheen didn't know what people would think of a warrior who needed a girl's help to kill a bear.

"It was with these thoughts in mind that Beheen said to Aleen, 'You should not have come. I did not ask for you to follow me, nor do I love you. I will go home now and marry Majida.'

"So saying, he cut off the bear's head and carried it back with him toward his home. Spring was returning to the land, and Beheen was able to feed himself from the fruit on the trees and the animals in the forest.

"When Beheen made it back, he appeared before his people on the great stone dais and told them the account of his success, leaving out the part Aleen had played. When he showed them the head of the bear, they declared him a man.

"Majida's father was very impressed with the courage and strength of Beheen. In three moons, Beheen and Majida were married. They had a fine farm, and Beheen grew the plants of the field to feed them. After nine years, Beheen was blessed with six golden-haired children, four of which were good, strong boys, each a better warrior than the next.

"Aleen never returned, and Beheen never thought of her again. She died in the forest beside the bear's body. It wasn't the wounds which killed her, those would have healed quickly and left hardly a scar. It was her broken heart. She simply lost the will to go on. She never rose from the spot where Beheen had left her, and, two days later, she closed her eyes for the last time."

Todd stopped speaking, and there was a moment of utter stillness. I contemplated the story silently. It disturbed me, and I certainly thought the ending was strange.

"That's so terrible." Kisa sounded like she was on the verge of tears.

"Are all—stories that sad?" Rollan asked, stumbling over the unfamiliar word.

"No," Todd told him. "Some are happy, and some are funny. But I was never very good at telling those. I like tragedies better."

"What was the point?" Cole asked. "You said the one about the boy and the wolves was to teach children the importance of hard work. I fail to see any similar themes in this one. If anything, it seems to reward disloyalty and foolishness."

"This story is meant to teach young women that their place is in the home, and even if they do love someone, it is better to let that person go than to pursue them," Todd answered.

I almost joined the conversation, but Astra said exactly the thing I was thinking. "It teaches exactly the opposite about young men," she countered.

Todd nodded. "Of course. Men should seek what they want."

"But not women?" Astra sounded curious. Had I been the asker, I would have sounded hostile.

"Well…" Todd considered for a moment. "Women are weaker. They should be prepared for whatever the stronger gender bids."

I would have snorted, but I held it in. I was interested to see what Astra would have to say about such a statement.

"While it's true that women are physically weaker, I have always found that they can make up for it in determination and aspiration," she pointed out. "The story you told illustrates that pretty well."

176

"The females here—I mean, the women of your people—are different from other women." Todd was choosing his words very carefully, as if he hadn't realized he was being insulting until it was too late.

There wasn't much conversation after that. I fell asleep a little later. Joss woke me several hours before dawn for my watch.

I hated to admit to myself how deeply the story had affected me, but I couldn't get it out of my mind. I spent the hours of my watch thinking about what a fool Aleen was to throw away her life and love on someone as worthless as Beheen.

When it came time to wake the others, I went to Todd first. Resisting the urge to nudge him with my foot, I put my hand on his shoulder to rouse him. He sat bolt upright, looking at me with wide eyes.

"What's wrong?" he asked timidly.

"Nothing," I whispered. "I want to know something. Why did Aleen die? It's not possible to die from a broken heart. She might have grieved for a long time—forever, even—but if she was clever enough to follow him all that way and care for both of them, why didn't she just move on with her life?"

In some ways, I knew my question was ridiculous. It involved people who had never lived. This was why stories were forbidden in The Clan. They were pointless and distracted one from what was real.

Todd took the question very seriously. "It was for the sake of the story. Otherwise, it wouldn't have been over."

"But that's not fair," I protested, completely irrationally.

Todd's deep, brown eyes met mine. "I suppose she had to die, however unfairly, because it wasn't her story. In the end, it was about other people, and she was just a character that helped them along the way.

"There are lots of characters like that. They are guides to the others, and, even though they are not the focal point, we truly feel something when they are lost."

I turned away from the Broken. He had spoken more to me in the last three minutes than ever before, but I found that I was not content with his answer.

Aleen had died because it wasn't her story?

CHAPTER 18
DESCENT

For several days, traveling remained pleasant. The land was mostly flat, and there were numerous rivers and small streams, which Todd called "creeks". The days were warm, but there was often a breeze coming from the east. Astra successfully hunted almost every night, Joss fished when he could, and all of us spotted fruit trees from time to time.

Best of all, everyone was getting along really well. There wasn't a single quarrel. We were traveling east, which made me happy, I wasn't persecuting the Broken too much, which made Astra happy, and Astra and I weren't fighting, which made everyone happy.

Everything would have been perfect if the fear that we might meet another team wasn't constantly nagging at the back of my mind. I succeeded in blocking it out most of the time, but every once in a while, it would gnaw its way into my thoughts. The image of Jase snapping Tiera's neck was never far enough away.

A morning came when we started out going east as usual, but suddenly, Todd paused. "We need to head a little more to the north," he announced.

"Why?" I asked. I'd never been able to completely shake the feeling that we were being led into a trap.

Todd pointed ahead. "It took me quite a while to find the way between those mountains," he said. "As far as I know, there is only one path that leads through. There are still cliffs, but they are manageable. I think I remember the trail being a bit farther north."

My eyes narrowed. Now that we were closer, the mountains' sides looked all but impassable. If there was a path between them, it would have to be tiny and well hidden. However, we were likely to save a lot of time by going through the mountains instead of over or around them.

"How well do you know this land? Do you travel here often?" Cole asked.

Todd shook his head. "Not often. This is my first solo journey into The Western Woods, where the silver stag was slain. But I've always been good with direction and finding my way in the forest. I came through here about two moons ago. I did not travel as quickly as you. I explored a great deal of the land between here and the great river we crossed, where the wolves prowl."

Much of what the Broken said made little sense to me. I often had a hard time following his words. Usually, Kisa was the one who asked for an explanation, but she was too out of breath to voice any questions at that particular moment.

"Do you live by the ocean?" Astra wondered as our footsteps turned to the north.

"Sort of," Todd replied.

"So, close by but not right next to it?"

"Sure." Todd didn't seem very keen on talking about himself, and Astra let the subject drop.

We traveled north for a day and a half, and then turned again to the east. It took us two more days to reach the path between the mountains.

On the morning of the third day, we found the cliffs Todd had spoken of. I was sad to leave behind the gentle fields and shaded woodlands. Even though the Broken talked about an easy way through, we still did quite a bit of scrambling to get up, down, over, and across the boulders and crags blocking our path. There were some skinned knees and elbows along the way.

It started getting dark, and we still hadn't found a suitable place to make camp. The path we were on was perilously close to a sheer drop. I stepped over to the edge and glanced down. I could see lots of broken stones at the bottom. Looking ahead, I observed that all of the terrain in the area was just as inhospitable as the rocky patch on which we stood.

"What should we do?" I asked.

"Camping here on the cliff will be pretty uncomfortable," Cole remarked.

"What about that cave?" Rollan suggested, pointing to a small hole in the rocks about twenty feet ahead of us.

"Good eyes," Cole praised him. "Let's check it out."

"What if there's a bear inside?" Kisa asked nervously.

I laughed. The Broken's story must have frightened her.

Cole glanced at Todd. "Is it possible?" he asked.

"I doubt it," the boy told him. "They usually live in the woods."

Cole still drew his sword before entering the cave. Astra was right behind him with her bow loaded and ready. I followed too, but didn't bother unsheathing my knife. It was dark inside, especially since the light in the sky was dying as quickly as the day. The three of us stooped low to get through the entrance, but the interior was much larger than I imagined it would be from the nondescript hole Rollan had spotted.

Once we looked around—there wasn't much to see—we called the others. It wasn't half as nice as a bed of soft moss, but it was cozy, sort of, and it was loads better than falling off the cliff in our sleep.

I volunteered for the first watch.

"We don't need a watch tonight," Cole said. "No one is going to try to come this way by night. Plus, I doubt they'd be able to find the cave in the dark."

I agreed, but it still took me a long time to fall asleep. Cole was almost certainly correct as far as other teams were concerned. I was more worried about what Todd might do. I never liked to leave him unobserved.

I still didn't care if he decided to run off; we probably wouldn't have that much trouble finding our way to the ocean from where we were without him. My main concern was that he would try to attack one of us. It was true that he hadn't attempted anything of the sort since the day we met him, but I still didn't trust him. A lot was going on behind those dark eyes of his.

The following day, we faced more cliffs and more skinned knees. It soon became hot work, since the sun-baked stones were uncomfortable to the touch. I thought ruefully of the shady glens we had left in our wake. The woods, no matter how dense, were far more pleasant than this.

"I thought he said we would be skipping the cliffs," I heard Rollan grumble to Joss.

"I'm sure he's doing the best he can," Joss replied generously. "He'll get us there in no time, probably before any of the other teams."

We spent another night among the rocks, but at least we were able to find level ground on which to camp. The area was closer than I liked to a sizable drop, but we were all too exhausted to look for a better place.

There was one advantage to that particular campsite: it had water. A thin trickle was running down the rock face and creating a small puddle. We spent a very long time filling our canteens with what water we could catch. It took even longer because we were all so thirsty from the day's travel that we kept emptying them.

We didn't make a fire that night since there wasn't much wood. Not that we had any need of one. There was plenty of food in our packs, and the rocks were still warm from the day's heat. I wondered how much longer we would have to endure this uncomfortable leg of the journey.

The next day, I had my answer. It was even more miserably hot than the day before. We climbed down one ridge and then scrambled back up another, higher ledge. It was as if the land didn't know whether it wanted to rise toward the sky or sink away from it.

I was ready to stop for a midday rest and was just turning to Cole to see if he would agree with me, when Astra pointed ahead.

"Look," she said, gesturing to the Broken above us.

Todd, who had been climbing the steep, rocky wall ahead, was motioning for us to come up quickly and join him. I muttered under my breath as I took hold of the rocks above me before pulling myself up with a great heave.

182

Astra was on my right, and Cole was just below us. Rollan and Joss were a little behind him, helping Kisa. She was doing her best, but her short legs and weak arms made the climbing harder for her than any of the rest of us.

Astra made it to the top of the ridge first. She pulled herself up and stood beside Todd. I heard her gasp as she looked out to the east.

With my curiosity piqued, I dragged myself over the top of the ledge and rose to my feet. "Unbelievable," Astra murmured softly.

Nodding, I was forced to agree with her. The landscape before us took my breath away, leaving me unable to form any words of my own.

I hadn't known so much water existed in the entire world, and yet there was a never-ending expanse of it spread out in front of me. Waves—huge waves, not the little ones we saw on the lake sometimes, but waves taller than I was—crashed onto the land below us.

"It's just like the scroll said," Cole whispered as he joined us on the ledge.

I could have stood there all day watching the water lap at the shore, but Todd was already on the move again. On the far side of the ridge, the land sloped easily down beneath our feet. As we followed after Todd, I could still hear the sound of the waves even though we momentarily lost sight of the water behind another rise.

From behind us came several elated cries. I turned to see our other three teammates on the crest of the cliff. Joss was grinning, and Rollan was cheering. Kisa, standing between the two, looked happy as well, but her face was pale, and I knew that she was battling with the strain of the past several days.

We waited for the others to join us at the top of the next rise; they weren't long in coming. In their excitement, Joss and Rollan seemed to have forgotten all weariness. Kisa wasn't quite as energetic as they were, but she ran up the slope with them all the same.

"We did it!" Joss panted. "We found the ocean!"

"What's the next step?" Rollan asked.

"First, we have to get down," I pointed out, glancing toward the ground. There was one last cliff separating us from the water. It looked more treacherous than any we had descended yet. Kisa was staring at it in despair.

"Let's rest first," suggested Astra.

"I'm fine," Kisa insisted. "We should get down to the water."

"Are you sure?" Cole asked her.

Kisa glanced at Joss. His eyes were glowing with anticipation. She nodded. "Yes, I'm ready."

I wasn't convinced, but the others were eager to reach the water. Todd went first, as usual, with Astra close beside him. They were followed by Kisa, Rollan, and Joss. I was glad to see that even in the midst of their excitement, the boys were still helping Kisa.

Cole paused on the brink of the cliff. He turned back to look at me with warmth in his blue eyes.

"We made it," he whispered.

I couldn't help but smile back.

"Yes, we did," I agreed, stepping up alongside him. Carefully, we began the long descent to the sandy shore.

"I bet we got here before any of the other teams," Cole added, feeling for handholds in the rocks. "Having someone knowledgeable about the land was very helpful. Everyone else probably went around the mountains. I can't imagine how long that would have taken."

"Yes, but we did lose a few days going south and when Kisa was sick," I pointed out. "We can't assume no other teams have made it this far. We still need to—" I was cut short by a scream from below.

It was Kisa.

I looked down to see her legs flailing in the air, hands desperately gripping the cliff face. My heart stopped for just a moment until I saw Joss and Rollan secure her hold on the stone wall.

It appeared that the rock beneath her feet had broken loose, almost taking her down with it. The boulder plummeted toward the ground. It skittered off a rocky outcrop, missing Astra by a hair and colliding with Todd.

Astra reached down and tried to grab him, but she wasn't close enough. With a screech of terror, Todd fell from the cliff and dropped to the sands below, where he lay without moving.

CHAPTER 19
THE OCEAN

Everyone was frozen for three agonizing seconds, and then we all sprang into action. Astra was still at least thirty feet up, but it took her less than a minute to get close enough to jump to the ground.

She rushed to Todd's side. "He's alive," she called to us.

Kisa, Rollan, and Joss reached the ground moments after Astra.

"I'm sorry!" Kisa kept repeating. "I went too quickly and didn't notice the rock was loose! I'm so sorry!"

Astra took the young girl by both shoulders and looked her directly in the eyes. "It wasn't your fault; stop blaming yourself. You're the only one who can help him now, so you need to keep it together."

Kisa nodded and started checking Todd for injuries. Cole and I didn't dare jump as Astra had; there were too many people on the ground below us.

Once we reached the bottom, Cole rushed to Kisa's side.

"What can we do?" he asked.

"Nothing just yet," Kisa told him. Her voice was calm, but it carried a tiny tremble in it. She was terrified but keeping it under control.

There was a gash on Todd's head. Either the boulder had struck him there, or he had hit it when he landed. Kisa pressed one of her shirts to Todd's wound to stanch the flow of blood.

I didn't see blood coming from anywhere else. I hoped that was a good sign. Much as I disliked and distrusted Todd, I didn't want him to die. I didn't want anyone to die.

"How bad are his injuries?" Astra inquired. She was cradling Todd's head in her lap and took over applying pressure to his cut, freeing Kisa to check the rest of his body.

"Head injuries are tricky. We won't know much until he wakes up," Kisa said gently. "I think his arm is broken too. I saw him land on it."

I glanced at Todd's left arm, which was curled beneath his body. "As soon as his head stops bleeding, I'll set the bones. It'll be better to do it before he wakes up."

"Why?" Joss asked. He regarded Todd with a grave expression, the ocean completely forgotten.

"Because it's exceedingly painful," Astra told him.

I knew from experience she was right. Even though it had been many years ago, I still remembered the awful pain I endured when the healer set my broken arm. I was given some plants to eat, which I was assured would dull the pain. Even with the herbs, it was the single most painful experience of my life, physically, at least.

Kisa nodded, and Astra removed the wadded-up shirt so she could check the wound. It was still bleeding, but not nearly as heavily.

"Astra, can you keep the pressure on his head while I take a closer look at his arm?"

Astra nodded and reapplied the bloodstained fabric. Cole helped Kisa lift Todd's body enough to free his left arm. A faint groan escaped his lips as Kisa straightened it and began to feel the muscles and bones. I was just glad none of them had come through the skin.

"Do you know what to do?" Astra asked.

Kisa nodded. "I think so. Cole, help me hold him."

Joss came over to help as well. Together, the pair held Todd in position as Kisa instructed. I turned away when she began to set his arm. It brought up unpleasant memories, making my stomach churn. However, there was no way to miss the sickening sound that followed as she set the bone. Todd groaned again, louder this time.

I looked back and saw his eyelids flutter, but not open. Kisa asked Astra for her headless arrow to use as a splint. With some of the extra clothing we had, she wrapped Todd's left arm before fashioning him a sling identical to the one Astra had worn when her shoulder was injured. Kisa then proceeded to check the rest of Todd's body for additional injuries but didn't find any.

"We'll have to camp here tonight," Cole announced. "Let's see about getting a fire and filling the canteens with water."

Rollan, Joss, and I headed down to the shore. Our exuberant spirits were gone. All we had left was the will to complete the tasks assigned to us. The sand was blisteringly hot in the afternoon sun. Close to the cliff, where the rest of our team remained, a great shadow was cast by the towering rock, sheltering them from the heat.

The boys started gathering pieces of wood, which lay inexplicably on the sand just out of reach of the waves. From a distance, the water looked blue, but close up, it was more of a brown color. I wondered if this was because there were tiny particles of sand floating in it. Not wanting to put sandy water in the canteens, I cupped my hands full of liquid and lifted them to my face for closer examination. The water looked fairly clear, so I raised it to my mouth and took a drink. The moment the first drop passed my lips, I was gagging and spitting it back out.

"What's wrong?" Joss called from the shore. He started wading into the shallows toward me.

I was still spluttering as I tried to rid my mouth of the foul-tasting substance. "There's something wrong with the water," I told him, wiping the back of my hand across my mouth.

"What's wrong with it?" Joss asked.

I shook my head. "I don't know, but it tastes awful."

Of course, the first thing Joss did was lean down and take a giant gulp of ocean water. I'd thought him to be one of the more intelligent of the group; I must have been mistaken.

His reaction was similar to my own and, actually, quite humorous.

"Yeah, that's no good," he said ruefully.

188

I sighed. It wasn't like I hadn't warned him.

"So much for having plenty of water all the way to the mountain," I lamented.

"It'll be all right. Every team who has ever won the trials came this way, and they must have found water somewhere," Joss pointed out.

"True," I agreed. Perhaps he wasn't unintelligent, just a bit too curious. "Let's break the news to the others."

We trudged back up the beach to where the rest of the team still huddled around Todd. Joss gathered up a quick armload of wood. I took some too, but couldn't carry as much since I was already weighed down with everyone's canteens.

Todd was awake. His eyes were wide and looked like those of a cornered animal. Kisa had tied the shirt around his head but was still kneeling beside him.

"Does anything hurt?" she asked gently.

I couldn't hear what Todd muttered back to her.

"I'm so sorry," she responded to whatever he said.

"Bad news," I announced as we approached.

"More?" Astra asked. Both she and Cole turned toward us.

"What now?" Cole groaned, looking both of us over to make sure we were uninjured.

"The water's sour," I told them.

"Of course, it is," Astra growled blackly.

Cole didn't say anything, but I could see that the words hit him pretty hard. We had all expected the most difficult part of our journey to be over, but it looked as though it was just beginning.

"Every team from the past trials who made it this far found water along the way," Joss reminded them.

"It's also possible that the water wasn't sour when they were here," Astra pointed out. "Something might have died in it."

I felt about ready to retch. The idea of drinking water that contained a rotting carcass was repulsive.

"If that's the case, once we start moving, we should be able to get around the bad part," Cole said. "Farther on, I bet the water will be good."

"No," Todd murmured in a distant voice. "You can never drink water from the ocean. It's full of salt."

We all turned to look at him.

"Why didn't you tell us?" Astra wondered.

Todd grimaced in pain and cradled his arm tightly to his chest. "I assumed you knew. You said your people had been here before. Why didn't they tell you the water was salty instead of fresh?"

"It's forbidden," I told him.

"I don't—understand." Todd looked utterly defeated. He was in a half-crouched position as if prepared to spring to his feet. Suddenly, he sank backward. Kisa reached out and stopped him from falling over completely. Astra, who was closest, came to her aid and helped ease Todd down. There was a layer of sweat over his body, and he was shivering at the same time.

"Wake up!" Kisa yelled suddenly. She reached forward and tried to pull Todd into a sitting position. Joss dropped to his knees beside them and helped get Todd up. His eyes opened languidly.

"Don't fall asleep," Kisa ordered him. I'd rarely heard Kisa sound so forceful; it was rather shocking.

"Build a fire. We're camping here tonight," Cole instructed Rollan. "Astra, Myra, I need to talk with you. Joss, you help Kisa, and call us if anything happens." The pair on the ground nodded, and Rollan set about building a fire.

Astra and I followed Cole a short distance away. When we were far enough to escape being overheard by the others, he spun to face us. I could see that between the trauma of Todd's fall and the discovery that we couldn't drink the water, Cole was quickly reaching the end of his rope.

"We need to make a new plan. It's going to be impossible to travel with such a burden," he announced.

"How can you say that?" Astra demanded hotly. "We can't abandon Todd!"

"Of course not! I wasn't talking about him," Cole snapped at her, and then winced, seeming to realize how sharply he had spoken. "I was referring to the situation of the water. What are we going to do?"

"We go north," I told them calmly. "Those were our instructions. That is what we must do."

"How can we go without water?" Cole argued. "If we head back to the woods, we could still head north."

Astra shook her head. "Todd would never be able to climb up the cliffs."

"And that's not what our instructions say," I put in. "We were told to—"

"Follow the coastline, I know," Cole interrupted. "But we could follow it from up there." He pointed to the cliffs the way we had come.

I shook my head, looking at the maze of ledges and peaks we would have to cross. "Not very easily."

"But we could survive there," Cole urged. "We weren't trained to survive with sour water and barren sands. All of our training was on how to survive in the forest."

I considered his words for a moment. I didn't see a way to find food or water where we were.

"You're not entirely correct," Astra told him, meeting his blue eyes with her green ones. "We weren't taught to survive in the forest. Many teams who trained beside us didn't manage. Our training was to teach us to learn how to survive. We adapted to the forests and the cliffs; we can readjust here as well."

Both of us were silent for a moment. "I don't—" Cole began.

I interrupted him as a new idea dawned on me. "That's what the trials are really about," I realized. "They don't want to see how much we've learned; they want to see how much we can figure out and adapt to."

Astra nodded in complete agreement. Cole still didn't seem quite so convinced.

"You both feel this way," he mused to himself, considering. After a moment, he stepped forward, passing between us. I thought he was heading back to the others and turned to follow him, but he paused and cupped his hands around his mouth.

"Joss!" he called.

I saw Joss's head lift from where he was still sitting with Todd and Kisa. Cole beckoned to him. Joss rose and started running toward us.

"I want one more opinion," Cole explained, with a guilty look at us.

Astra nodded, and I tried to hide a smile. I already knew what Joss would say: that we would be able to find a way to survive on the coastline. Hadn't he already told us that much?

"What's up?" Joss asked, coming to a stop, panting slightly from his run.

"Joss," Cole started, "we're at a bit of an impasse and could use another point of view. You're the fourth leader, so I want to hear what you have to say."

Joss seemed surprised; this was the first time he had been part of the decision-making process.

"Sure," he agreed amicably.

"It seems to me that surviving here, on the beach, would be pretty hard. I'm not sure if it would be better to head north from here, or to head back to the forest first," Cole explained.

Joss took a moment to consider. "There are advantages and disadvantages to both. I think we will be able to find water, even if the ocean water is undrinkable. There was that trickle down the cliffs last night. Why couldn't there be something like that along here?" Joss gestured to the extensive rock wall that cut us off from the trees and grasses.

"I'm sure there's food as well. We always found food on the shores of the lake. This isn't quite the same, but there has to be something to eat. Plus, we won't have to climb any more mountains," Joss added.

Cole nodded. "Looks like I'm outvoted. We'll stay on the coastline and head north."

If I had been Cole, and my whole team went against me on a vote like this, I think I would have been sullen and hostile about

192

it, but Cole was the opposite. It seemed that a huge burden had been lifted from his shoulders. I supposed he didn't care whether he was right or wrong, so long as the decision was made.

A moment later, he was giving everyone their instructions.

"Joss and Astra, see what you can find to eat. Myra, let's help Rollan gather more wood."

Everyone nodded and headed to their various tasks. It didn't take long for Cole and me to amass a sizable pile of fuel for the fire. Rollan had already given us a good start, so our task was completed fairly quickly.

Joss and Astra waded out into the waters of the ocean. After finishing with the fire, Rollan splashed through the shallows to join them. I wasn't sure what they were hoping to find out there, but it would certainly be nice if they were successful.

Cole and I went to stand by the fire. The late afternoon sun made the temperature extremely hot but, tucked in the shadow of the cliffs, I was comfortably cool.

"How is he?" Cole asked Kisa, nodding toward the Broken.

"I don't think he's in danger from his arm," Kisa said gently. "I'm more worried about his head."

Todd was staring into the fire; he seemed oblivious to the conversation. However, I noticed a tension in his shoulders that offset his calm appearance, betraying the fact that he was paying careful attention.

"Todd," Cole said, turning to him. The boy was huddled by the fire, his broken arm strapped across his bare chest. He looked up at Cole through the dark, shaggy hair that fell into his eyes.

"We asked you to bring us to the ocean, and you did that. There is no reason you have to continue traveling with us."

A shadow of fear crossed Todd's face.

He thinks Cole's going to send him away, I realized.

If Todd understood Cole even slightly, he would have known how ridiculous that notion was. Although, earlier Astra had jumped to the same, irrational conclusion. I thought they were closer than that.

"We need to go north," Cole told him.

Panic showed in Todd's eyes for just a moment.

"I won't be able to help you," he admitted somberly. "I've never been any farther north than this. I don't know what lies in that direction."

"I understand that," Cole acknowledged. "But you aren't going to survive very long on your own with a broken arm."

Todd looked away from Cole and stared sullenly at the fire once more.

"Then, if you have no use for me, what do you want from me?" he asked so softly I had to strain to catch the words.

"Nothing," Cole told him. "But you can still come with us if you would like."

Todd's eyes flashed back to Cole's.

"Are you playing with me?" he snarled.

Cole blinked in confusion. "I don't understand."

"There is no sense in you taking me with you. I'm no good to you anymore; I can't help you. I'll be nothing but a hindrance, and you expect me to believe that you'll just let me come along?" Todd's voice was filled with fury driven by fear.

"Well, I'm not going to leave you here to die!" Cole almost shouted. He collected himself a second later and walked to Todd's side, where he crouched beside the Broken so they were on the same level. The boy shrank as far away as he could, not taking his dark eyes off Cole.

"Todd, you aren't part of this team, but you're still one of us now. We take care of our own; so, we aren't going to leave you behind, unless that's what you want."

Kisa and I were silently observing. Neither of us moved or even breathed. Finally, Todd looked away from Cole. He seemed shaken, unsure if he was hearing the truth.

Cole reached out slowly and placed a hand on Todd's good shoulder. "You can trust me," he promised.

CHAPTER 20
SUNRISE

No one found any food that night. We were still fairly well supplied from the forest, but Cole encouraged us to eat as little as possible.

Todd was silent the remainder of the afternoon and evening. He hardly responded when Astra offered him a pear and some strips of meat. I doubt he would have eaten them if Kisa hadn't started fussing over him. I wasn't too surprised to see the boy toss a portion of the food into the fire when he thought no one was looking. I was the only one who seemed to have noticed his action.

The firelight cast eerie shadows on the sands as the sun set. Curiously, some of the wood pieces we added to the fire burned colors other than orange. There were tongues of green and blue flames, with an occasional tint of purple. All of us sat transfixed by the flickering colors.

"Can I sleep now?" I heard Todd ask Kisa quietly. It was the first time he had spoken since his conversation with Cole.

"How do you feel?" Kisa asked. "Nauseous at all?"

Todd shook his head. "Just tired."

"It's probably okay then," Kisa said. "If you feel sick or anything tonight, you can wake me up."

Nodding, Todd moved a short distance from the fire, closer to the cliff, and lay down with his back to the rest of us.

It wasn't long until the others followed his example. I took the first watch and remained sitting with my eyes fixed on the colors swirling amidst the flames. Because I was so close to the fire, it took me a while to realize how much the temperature dropped. There was a cold breeze coming continuously off the ocean.

195

Was it that close to winter already? I panicked for a moment and tried to count back the days. I couldn't recall the exact number, but winter should still have been far away. Perhaps it was just an unusually cold night.

I woke Rollan after a few hours passed. When I lay down, I found the sand to be surprisingly comfortable, but the sound of the waves on the shore kept me awake for quite a while. I supposed that, in most of the other villages, it wasn't unusual to hear the noise of water from the river. Joss was probably the most accustomed to it, since Riverside was built directly on the shores of the lake. In The Paramount, we were miles away from the river and never heard the water. The nights there were still and silent.

Astra woke all of us before dawn. "Get up," she ordered, shaking me before moving on to the next person.

"What's happening?" I asked, sitting up wearily. It was just starting to turn light, and I couldn't understand why she had awakened us so early.

"That water's risen during the night, and it's still coming," Astra reported.

I squinted at the dark expanse of the ocean. She was right; it was much closer. I leapt to my feet and started groping around for my things. The others were doing the same. I hoped we would have time to make it to high ground before the water reached us.

Astra roused Todd last, and he looked around in confusion.

"The water?" he asked groggily.

"It's rising," Astra explained, pointing to where the waves lapped ten feet higher on the shore than they had the previous night.

"Oh, that's all," Todd said, lying back down.

"He must have hit his head harder than you thought," I heard Joss whisper to Kisa.

"It's just the tide coming in; it won't reach us here. It's probably about as high as it's going to get." Todd rolled over, careful of his arm, so his back was to us and the water once again.

We all stared at him.

"Are you sure?" Kisa asked.

"Yes," Todd muttered. "You can go back to sleep."

Joss, Rollan, Kisa, and even Cole managed to settle back down. I was too awake even to bother trying. Plus, the waves were closer, and therefore much louder, as they crashed onto the shore.

As ever, Astra was wearing her long, black cloak. Once the others settled down again, she seated herself on the sand, intently watching the water.

Instead of pretending to go back to sleep, I picked up my own cloak, which I was using as a blanket, shook the sand from it, and went to sit beside her, my knees drawn up to my chest.

She glanced at me in surprise. "Not tired?"

I shrugged. "If I managed to fall asleep again with all this noise, I'm sure it would be just in time for the sun to come up."

"I know what you mean," Astra sympathized. "The Paramount has got to be much quieter than this."

I nodded slowly. "The North Wind too; it's just about as far from the river."

"True," agreed Astra. "And it might be quiet among the dwellings, but the stable is never silent."

"The horses kept you up?" I asked.

I remembered that she and several others slept in the hayloft above the horse stalls instead of in proper dwellings.

Astra laughed. "You could say that. Although, there's something incredibly comforting about sleeping that close to so many living creatures."

"Really?" I asked, thinking of my solitary bedroom.

"Sure, and even when they aren't snorting and stamping, there was always the wind. I miss the wind; the way it used to make the old stables talk." Astra smiled sadly.

I shuddered, pulling my cloak closer. How could I have forgotten the wind? Every time I had gone to The North Wind, it was blowing across the land, sucking the warmth from all creatures. I couldn't imagine anyone missing it. Cold and never-ending, it was kind of like the breeze coming off the ocean, but even worse.

"There's plenty of wind here," I pointed out.

"I love it," Astra told me, grinning. Her long, coppery hair was hanging around her shoulders, moving gently when the wind chanced to catch it. My hair was tied up in its usual ponytail. I could occasionally feel it lifted from my back by the stronger gusts.

We were quiet for a moment. Twilight had broken upon the land while we were talking.

"What do you think we're going to find at the mountain?" I wasn't sure why I asked her that question, but I felt that if anyone might be able to conceive the road ahead, it was Astra.

"Truth," was Astra's immediate answer.

"What do you mean?" I pressed.

"There's some secret, about us, about our people, that we must find; something that will explain who we really are." She wasn't looking at me but out at the ocean instead.

I pondered her theory for a moment. "If that is so, it must be well hidden," I mused. "Because only one team will ever be able to learn what it is. Otherwise, how will the Clan Leaders know who has won?"

My thoughts ran so deep that Astra's next question took me completely by surprise.

"Why don't you and your mother get along?"

"What?" I gasped in shock. My hands were resting on my knees. Unconsciously, I clenched them into fists, nails biting into my palms.

She looked at me and seemed to read the tension in my face and body.

"Sorry I asked," she said. "It's none of my business."

She faced the ocean; however, she seemed to be battling with herself about whether to say anything else. I would have preferred her to let the subject drop, but apparently, that wasn't the choice that won out in her head.

She sighed deeply before speaking. "It's just that, I know what it's like to be without parents. If one of them was still alive, I can't imagine isolating myself from them."

Astra's green gaze was on me again, asking a question I didn't think I would ever be able to answer. I didn't look at her. My eyes were fixed on the stretch of sand between my feet and the water. Of course, what she said sounded sensible. I was certain that if anyone else was my mother, the divide would never have opened between us. But Myna was my mother, and it had.

"I guess my family was never meant to be," I explained softly, not caring if Astra could hear me over the waves. "Myna— she never loved my father. I don't even know if she loves me."

"I'm sorry," Astra whispered. The sun began to rise, turning the water to fire. We sat for a while, watching the crimson waves lap the sandy shore.

"What were your parents like?" I finally asked, suddenly curious. I had answered her question; wasn't it fair that she answer mine?

Astra smiled. "They were wonderful."

I'd never heard Astra talk about her parents before, but as she did, her whole face lit up.

"How old were you when…" I trailed off awkwardly.

"My mother died when I was born and my father when I was two," she replied smoothly.

"But you remember them?" I asked.

Astra didn't answer for a long time, and I started to wonder if she ever would.

"No," she admitted at last, so quietly I strained to catch the words. "I don't have any memories of them. I only know what people have told me, and what I've seen in my dreams."

"Your dreams?" I asked.

She nodded. "When I was very young, I used to dream about them quite often. I still do from time to time."

"I've never dreamed of my father," I admitted. I never really dreamed at all.

"I know it's not actually them," Astra told me, "but I used to pretend, and it still brings me comfort to think they left a piece of themselves in my dreams."

"Why did they stay at The North Wind after your mother got pregnant?" I wondered.

Astra laughed. "Because they loved it. I know you can't imagine that, but my mother grew up there. Her name was Aislin, and she learned to ride before she could walk.

"My father was born Travis of The Barracks. Everyone says his eyes were the same green color as mine."

"Did he transfer to The North Wind to be with your mother?" I asked.

"No," Astra answered. "He fell in love with The North Wind itself before he fell in love with my mother. It brought them together, made them happy. They wanted to live there forever and grow old among the fields and stables."

I wished my parents had such a story. The little I had gleaned from Myna over the years was nothing like this beautiful account of love that Astra described. For the first time, I felt sorry for Astra. At least I could remember my father, but she had nothing more to hold onto than a shadow of her imagination.

"I always loved The North Wind too," Astra told me. "All the more so because they did. It's the only way I feel close to them. That's why I always swore I'd never leave." She paused. "Only, now I have."

Astra's voice broke, and she looked down.

"We'll make it back," I assured her.

"I believe we will." Astra's smile was distant. "But it will never be the way it was before. Especially after what happened to Rickie."

I nodded, recalling that Astra's favorite horse, a golden gelding named Rickie, had died. Astra believed he was poisoned, but she couldn't fathom who would have done it or why. I was certain the incident made her feelings about The North Wind pretty complicated.

Astra ticked me off sometimes, but everyone else seemed to love her. I couldn't imagine who would want to hurt her so badly.

Although, judging by what we had seen in the trials so far, some contenders would do anything if it put them closer to victory.

Things are different in The Clan, I thought.

But are they? A little voice asked me.

More questions I couldn't answer.

"Do you want to win?" Astra asked me.

"Of course," I blurted out. "Don't you?"

Astra sighed. "In some ways. I have a competitive nature, which is one of the biggest reasons I told the council I wanted to have the chance to be a contender. So, yes, part of me does want to win, but the other part isn't so sure."

"Yes," I mused, remembering the day Astra was referring to. "What happened when you met with them? The council?"

She shrugged. "It started the evening before. Your mother—or Myna—came to The North Wind at the request of our representatives. When training began, I wasn't able to keep up with my normal duties, and people began to grow concerned that I would be made a contender."

"Why just you?" I asked.

Astra shifted uncomfortably. "The North Wind has never done very well in the trials. Normally, not even half the children there are made contenders. The other villages think it's because we are slow and witless, but I believe there is another reason.

"Most of the other potentials from The North Wind did very little training, from what I observed. Instead, they continued to focus on their duties around the stable. Ironically, the council probably marked them off as lazy."

"But you focused more on training," I guessed.

"Yes. I was older than most of the others, almost too old. Much as I love The North Wind, I was curious to see what was out there. I started slipping on my duties back home. My friend, Gann, helped cover for me as best he could, but there was no way for us to keep up. Before long, it came to the attention of the village elders. They went before the council to ask that I be removed from the trials entirely."

"They did it against your will," I guessed.

"I didn't know anything about it until Myna showed up. Then they told me that I was an essential member of the village and that they wanted me to consider stepping down from the trials. Myna wouldn't hear of it and denied their request.

"After she left, they conspired all night. The following afternoon, Litis dragged me to The Paramount."

"I remember," I said. It was right after my friend, Rasby, and I stopped speaking to each other, another side effect of the trials.

That evening, I had witnessed Astra and Litis leaving the council building.

"Litis was certain that the council would side with her. She was sure I would side with her too, but no one even stopped to ask what I wanted. When we went before the council, Litis stepped forward to make her speech. Myna let her get out about a sentence and a half before stopping her.

"Poor Litis. I've never seen her so furious, but Myna didn't even seem to notice. She and the other Clan Leaders spoke together, just the four of them. They talked for nearly forty-five minutes. All the while, Litis was stewing and planning out exactly what she wanted to say next.

"I don't know what the Clan Leaders were discussing, but I think Core was unhappy about the decision because, as soon as they were done, he left. The others sat back down and heard Litis out. She talked for another forty-five minutes. After she finally finished, it was my turn.

"I didn't have to say much. The first question Myna asked me was whether I still wanted to be a potential. I told her yes and figured that was all she would need to know, but she kept asking things."

"What did she ask?" I wondered.

"Lots of stuff. She wanted to know exactly how tall I was, if I could swim, if I was allergic to any plants or bugs, whether I was afraid of heights. None of it seemed relevant to me, but I didn't want to be rude.

"In the end, they voted unanimously to keep me as a potential. Litis was unhappy, but you observed that for yourself."

"It wasn't your fault," I pointed out. "Once the preparations were announced, you should have been free of your other responsibilities."

"Myra," Astra began, "don't take this the wrong way. You grew up in The Paramount, so I don't expect you to understand—"

"Of course not." I rolled my eyes and glanced at the sun; it was halfway above the horizon. The entire ocean was reflecting its light. I couldn't remember ever having seen a more beautiful sunrise.

"Hear me out," she insisted. "In The Paramount, there weren't many tasks you could have done, since I'm sure they don't let children help with the record keeping. So, when you weren't at school or studying, you could do whatever you wanted. Other places aren't like that. Joss, Kisa, Rollan, and I all pitched in with the work of our villages."

I opened my mouth to object, but couldn't find anything to say. I had never thought of it that way. Could it be that I had had it easy growing up in The Paramount?

"It probably wasn't as intense for the others; they are still young. But at The North Wind, you can be considered an adult as early as the age of fourteen. That was how it was with me. I rarely went to school and spent most of my time working. There is always so much to do in the stables."

"So, the other villagers couldn't stand that you weren't working all the time," I concluded.

"Something like that," affirmed Astra. "You're thinking about it differently than they do. You see the trials as an adventure, an opportunity to secure your position in The Clan. To them, the trials are just an interruption. Our positions are already set, every one of our days planned out far in advance."

She glanced at me with sympathy. "It must be hard living in a village where there is no sure path to the position you want, even if you're the person best suited for it."

"It can be," I told her.

"Did you always want to be a Clan Leader?" she asked.

I nodded. "For the most part."

"Why?"

"I don't know. I've just always felt like it was something I was meant to do."

"I know what you mean," Astra replied. "When they announced the trials, I felt the same way. Maybe that's why I devoted myself to the preparations the way I did."

For the first time, I wondered if Astra and I were really as different as I had always thought. Another question popped into my head.

"Why do you wear black clothing?" I asked. It was a mystery I had been unable to solve in all the time that I'd known her.

Each village had its own color. The color of The North Wind was gray, but Astra always wore black instead. There were others, just one or two people, at The North Wind who did the same.

Astra opened her mouth to speak, but then changed whatever she was going to say.

"It would take too long to explain," she finally answered. "Ask me again when we have more time."

I glanced at the sky. The sun was fully up now. "Should we wake the others?" I suggested.

"I suppose so," Astra agreed.

We rose at the same moment, and I thought how nice it had been to talk about the places we came from. It was something we rarely did. The Land of the Clan was behind us. It belonged in the past and the future, but it was only a distraction in the present.

CHAPTER 21
PROVISION

Astra and I woke the others. We ate a scant breakfast and began heading north. Walking along the beach was harder than walking on stone or dirt because the sand wasn't solid. It tugged on your legs every time you lifted a foot. At least it was mostly level, and there were no hills to climb.

After about half an hour, I heard Astra ask Todd if there was anything else we should know about the ocean.

"Like what?" he wondered. He didn't sound grumpy or sullen anymore. Kisa had checked his injuries earlier and said that everything looked like it would heal in about a month.

"I don't know," Astra answered. "Something along the lines of 'you can't drink the water' or 'it rises and looks like it's going to cause a flood sometimes'. That sort of thing." She sounded slightly stern, but I could see an amused gleam in her eye.

Todd glanced at her uncertainly. "It goes on forever," he finally said.

"In which direction?" she asked him.

"North, south, east. I've even heard that if you walk west long enough, you'll find it there too."

"How far west?" Astra wanted to know.

Todd shrugged. "A long way. Even farther than where we met for the first time."

I loved the way he made it sound all innocent. We had "met" there, not like he tried to kill us or anything.

"You live even farther west, right?" Todd inquired.

Astra nodded.

"If you have never seen the ocean before, then it must be even farther than where you come from," Todd concluded.

"Can fish survive in the ocean?" Joss asked, coming up next to me, behind Todd and Astra.

"Yes," Todd replied, glancing over his injured shoulder at Joss. "There are lots of fish. Some of them are bigger than I am."

Joss laughed. "Very funny," he said.

Todd seemed confused again. "They really are. I've seen them."

Joss stopped laughing, but he couldn't seem to figure out whether Todd was telling him the truth or not.

"How do we catch them?" Astra wondered.

"The easiest way is with a net," Todd told her.

"We use those back home," Joss said wistfully. "I don't see how we can make one out here; we don't have any rope."

"You could use dried seaweed," Todd suggested.

"What's seaweed?" asked Astra.

"It's a plant that grows in the water. There are lots of different types. Some are good for making rope and nets. Others you can eat, but they don't taste very good." Todd's face twisted with disgust.

"That's helpful to know," Astra said. "When you're hungry enough, anything tastes good."

"You've never eaten seaweed," I heard Todd mutter under his breath.

The coolness of the night quickly faded, leaving the air hot and dry. Joss, Kisa, and Rollan took off their shoes and walked on the damp sand, which was wetted constantly by the waves.

Before long, my throat was parched and almost felt like it was full of sand; although, I had no idea how it would have gotten there. We didn't even have the option of walking in the shade since the sun was yet to move behind the cliffs and offer shelter from its searing rays.

About midday, when a patch of shade finally began growing against the cliff, Astra suddenly pointed ahead.

"Look," she called. There was a thin torrent of water coming down one of the cliffs, running across the sand in front of us. Without a moment's hesitation, she and I raced over to investigate.

"Where are you going?" Cole called from the back of the group.

"Water!" I answered, my mouth too dry to say more than the single word.

"Perfect," Astra announced as we reached the cliff. There was a small pool of clear water—more of a puddle really—that was being fed by a trickle running down the rock face.

I cupped some water in my hands and raised it to my mouth. The liquid was refreshing and delicious.

"It's drinkable," I reported to Astra.

She smiled and took a handful for herself. By the time the others joined us, and we all filled our canteens and stomachs, the puddle was almost completely diminished.

Sitting in the thin strip of shade was delightful. I glanced at Kisa and Rollan. Kisa was lying on her back with her eyes closed; her skin was red, and she looked overheated.

"I think we should rest for a while," I suggested to Cole, who was standing next to me.

"I agree," he replied, sinking onto the sand. Our backs were to the cliff, and we faced the water.

No one did much talking. The day just kept getting hotter and more miserable. We were fine in the shade, with water close at hand, but I knew the moment we started walking, everyone would begin feeling fatigued again. I wondered if there was anything we could do to stay hydrated. A plan started to form in my mind. In the forest, we had rested during the heat of the day, but it was different on the beach. There was little shade, and the heat seemed to rise up from the ground itself.

After about half an hour passed, Cole rose to his feet.

"We should go," he announced. Joss, Todd, and Astra stood, following his lead. Kisa and Rollan seemed to have fallen asleep because neither of them moved.

"Wait," I said, rising and moving to stop Joss from rousing the sleeping pair. "This is foolish. We don't know how much longer we'll have to walk until we can find more water, and we'll run out too quickly in the heat."

Cole glanced at me. "What choice do we have?" he asked. "You wanted to stay on the beach."

"And I still do," I told him. "But I think we should travel at night and rest during the day."

Everyone was silent for a moment.

"How are we going to travel without being able to see anything?" Joss asked.

"We'll have the moon," I pointed out.

"Not always," Cole commented, but I could see he was considering my plan.

"We won't need to see that much," I explained, supporting my stance. "This isn't like the forest. There aren't any tree roots or rocks to trip over here. We can use our ears to know exactly where the water is and which way to go."

Cole nodded. "I guess we could give it a try. If that's the plan, then we should all attempt to get some sleep now. As soon as it starts cooling off, we'll move out."

I stretched out gratefully in the sand. Sleep was more appealing to me now than it had been the previous night. The sound of the waves was softer, and I was comfortably warm. Joss offered to keep watch, so I allowed myself to doze off.

It felt like only a moment later when I heard Kisa cry out, "Why didn't you wake me up earlier?"

I sat up and saw that the shadows were growing long. Even though I still felt exhausted, several hours must have passed. Joss was asleep, and Rollan was keeping watch. His cousin must have explained our plan to him, but apparently, Kisa had been asleep during the conversation.

"It's okay, Kisa," I called gently, hoping to keep her from waking the others. I motioned for the little girl to come with me as I withdrew a short distance from the sleeping forms of our teammates.

"What's going on?" Kisa asked in alarm. I quickly explained the plan to her. She seemed crestfallen. "Are you doing this because of me?" she wondered in a small voice.

"What?" I asked.

"I'm sorry I can't keep up and get so tired; I'll try to do better."

"Kisa, it's not like that at all," I promised her.

"Yes, it is. I'm always lagging behind. I always need to be helped. I wish I was stronger, more like you and Astra, but I just can't be." With those words, Kisa dissolved into tears.

Rollan glanced over at us. I gave him a helpless look, unsure of why Kisa was so upset. He came over to join us.

"What's wrong, Kisa?" he asked.

"I'm so useless," she sobbed. "I can never do anything right!"

"That's not true at all," Rollan insisted. "You do lots of things to help us that no one else could."

"Like when you saved Todd's life," I suggested. "He probably would have died without you."

I was hoping to comfort her, but my words just made Kisa cry all the harder.

"It was my fault he got hurt in the first place!" she moaned.

I wished Joss weren't asleep; he always knew the right thing to tell Kisa to calm her down.

"You also helped Astra when she got hurt," Rollan reminded her.

"But she was protecting me, so that was my fault too," Kisa sobbed.

Time to wake Joss, I thought. I didn't know what else to do. Comforting people was not something I had ever been very good at.

"Accidents happen," Rollan said. "People get hurt. That's why I'm glad you're on my team. So that when they do, I'll have you here to help me."

"Really?" Kisa asked, her tears slowing momentarily.

"Yes," Rollan continued. "There isn't anyone kinder or more soothing. You've got a healer's touch."

"Plus, you've helped feed us," I chimed in.

"That's right," Rollan agreed. "On the very first night, you found those roots. Even though we couldn't cook them, it gave us hope just knowing that we would be able to survive and find food on our own."

I was surprised at how encouraging Rollan could be. He and Kisa had butted heads a couple of times in the past, and I hadn't noticed how strong their relationship was growing. Joss might have some competition in the future.

"Plus, you make everyone so happy," Rollan continued. "If you weren't on the team, we'd all miss your smile and your laugh."

Kisa stopped crying and wiped her nose on her sleeve.

"Thanks, Rollan, Myra. I'm sorry I got so upset, but I hate it when everyone has to make special allowances for me. I won't just try to keep up anymore. I'll do it. I promise."

"You shouldn't worry about it, Kisa," I told her. "Everyone is different and has different needs."

"Plus, we're your friends," Rollan added. "You don't have to change; we love you the way you are."

"More like a family," I said softly. Kisa and Rollan nodded. We went back to join the others, who were beginning to stir.

I thought about the meaning of what I said to Kisa. Were we a family? I'd never had a family before, much as I longed for one. It was the only thing I had ever wanted almost as much as winning the trials.

However, even if we lost, wouldn't it have been enough to be part of this group? Would our bonds last once we returned to The Clan? Or were we simply drawn together by mutual hardship? Only time would tell.

There were still a few hours of daylight left when we set out. It was much more pleasant walking in the evening. The heat was dissipating, and there was a breeze coming from the ocean. Todd pointed out to us that the tide was going to start coming in again soon.

"Does it always come in at night?" Cole asked.

"No," Todd answered. "It changes from time to time, but you can see a mark on the sand where it will stop."

It was amazing to me how little the landscape changed on the shore. In the forest, we had passed from clumps of pine trees to oaks and birches. There were rocks to climb over and hills to ascend. Along the beach, it was nothing but mile upon mile of sand. During the day, my eyes had ached from the glare of so much white; yet another reason traveling by night was such an attractive idea.

When the sun began to set, I could see that we would have some moonlight that evening. It reflected off the waves, which almost doubled the amount of light. The ocean was quite beautiful under the silver moon.

As Todd predicted, the tide continued to wash higher and higher on the sand. I could well understand why Astra had woken us the previous night in fear of the rising waves. However, the water never made it past the mark in the sand Todd pointed out as the "high-tide line".

Once the moon set, the going was harder. We still had a touch of starlight, but it wasn't very helpful. Even still, since the sand was white, we were able to make it out in the faint light.

We walked close together to keep from getting separated. Several people—including myself—were stepped on before we worked out proper spacing. Now and then, a dark patch would appear ahead of us when driftwood, as Todd called it, was lying across our path. Cole was in front, and he would give an alert if we were going to come close to any pieces. A few times, he didn't spot them, and someone would trip over one.

The hours of darkness went on longer than seemed possible to me. It was still summer, and the nights were supposed to be short. Every minute, I expected to see twilight spreading from across the water to our right. Maybe the night just felt long because I had walked half the day and only slept for a couple of hours in the afternoon.

Finally, the stars faded away, and dawn began to grow in the east.

"We should keep going," Cole said. "Until it starts to get hot."

Time passed much more quickly once I was able to mark its passage by the rising sun. The tide was going out again; each wave receded farther than the last.

Suddenly, Todd gave an exclamation of joy and took off running down the beach toward a hunk of driftwood. I didn't know what made him rush forward like that. It appeared he was trying to drag the driftwood away from the water with his good arm.

"Help me! Quick!" he called to us.

Cole and Joss, who were in the front, surged forward. Astra and Rollan rushed past me from either side. I sighed and, tired as I was, ran toward him as well. With the assistance of the others, Todd managed to drag the driftwood away from the foaming water.

I looked down to see what was so special about this particular piece of wood and realized it was something completely different. It appeared to be a large, circular rock. At least, part of it did. There were extensions coming out of several holes in the side of the stone, and the top only came up to the middle of my calf.

"What is it?" Kisa wondered as she jogged up behind me.

Just then, the entire thing moved. I'm not sure if it was Kisa or myself who squeaked. We both jumped, but everyone looked at Kisa, so I was pretty sure I wasn't the one who had made the high-pitched noise.

"It's a sea turtle," Todd said. "We can eat it."

"That's great!" Joss exclaimed in delight. "Good find, Todd!"

The boy glanced down, seeming slightly uncomfortable with Joss's praise.

I re-examined what I now realized to be an animal. It was somehow wedged very tightly in the stone, and that was why I hadn't realized it was alive at first.

"How do we get it out of the rock?" I ask.

Todd looked at me in confusion. "What rock?" he asked.

"This one." I reached forward and put my hand on the rounded top. It felt strange, like nothing I'd ever touched before.

"That's its shell," Todd told me. He sounded like he was holding back a laugh. I didn't think it was very funny.

"Shell- like a snail?" Kisa asked, after thinking for a moment.

"A little, I guess," Todd answered. "But these are delicious. Snails, not so much."

Absently, I wondered how he knew what a snail tasted like.

"All right," Cole directed, "let's make camp by the cliffs again so that we can sleep in the shade."

After depositing their packs by the cliff, Astra, Kisa, and Joss gathered wood and started a fire. Under Todd's direction, Cole began to butcher the sea turtle after dispatching it. Since the creature was so massive, Rollan and I helped. It took all three of us to pull off the massive top shell, which turned out to be something like a large bowl.

"You can cook the meat in the shell with water," Todd told us. "Or you can cut it into strips, like you did with the deer and rabbits."

Since we didn't have an abundance of fresh water, we went with the latter proposal. The sand was a bloody mess by the time we finished. In the forest, the blood had blended into the earth, but on the beach, there remained deep, red stains along the ground. We didn't have any good sticks with which to build a spit, so we placed some large, flat rocks beside the fire and laid the meat on those to cook.

We sat in a loose circle around the flames, waiting for the turtle meat to be ready. I was curious to find out what something that came out of the ocean would taste like, but the meat cooked far slower on the rocks than if we had been able to use skewers.

"I'm so tired," Joss said. "I might nod off before the food is ready." He yawned to show how serious his threat was.

Kisa, who sat next to him, sighed. "I don't think I've ever been up all night before."

"I could fall asleep in ten seconds if I wasn't so hungry," Rollan put in. He was lounging on the other side of Kisa.

"This is taking forever." Joss poked impatiently at one of the still-raw bits of meat.

"Todd," Kisa began, turning toward the boy on the opposite side of Joss, "will you tell us another story while we wait?"

"Good idea," Rollan said.

"Last time you said something about 'the gods'," Joss recalled. "Who are they?"

Todd glanced my way, but I knew it was pointless to try to stop him.

"The gods are the most powerful of all beings," Todd explained.

"Are they like soldiers?" Rollan asked.

"I don't know that word," Todd responded, shaking his head.

"A soldier is someone from The Barracks," Rollan clarified.

"That won't mean anything to him," Astra chided Rollan. "It's someone who trains in combat skills and knows how to fight," she explained.

Todd shook his head. "No, they are much stronger than that. They have powers that no human has. Some of them can control animals; others can set things on fire just by thinking about it."

"But how can they do those sorts of things?" Kisa asked.

"Ummm…" Todd seemed at a loss from all the questions. "It might be easier to understand if I just tell you a story about them."

"Okay," Kisa agreed enthusiastically.

CHAPTER 22
THE GODS

"The greatest of all the gods is Arsh, the king, he that is the crown upon the head," Todd began. "Long before the gods came to earth, Arsh spent thousands of millennia ruling over the heavens."

"What does he look like?" interjected Kisa.

"He is tall and proud, with flowing golden-brown hair," Todd told her. "His skin is bronze and his eyes golden. With his keen sight, Arsh can pierce the flesh of other beings and see into their hearts. It is said that when he pronounces death for any mortal, that person will die instantly."

Kisa caught her breath at Todd's description.

"There is only one strong enough to stand against him: Husam, the edge of the sword, the warrior god."

"And what does he look like?" Kisa interrupted again.

"Husam is huge and has bulging muscles. Dark hair grows on his head, and his eyes are the color of freshly spilled blood. Wherever a battle is fought between men, he can be found there, helping to slaughter both sides.

"The pair were once great friends, closer even than brothers, but then the warrior betrayed the king. Ever since that day, malice has grown between them, and they have never ceased striving to destroy each other."

"Why did the warrior betray his friend?" Joss asked.

"That's a very long story," Todd replied. "Maybe I'll tell it next time."

Joss nodded, and I hoped there wouldn't be any more interruptions. The day was starting to grow hot, and I was about ready for some sleep, whether the turtle meat had finished cooking or not.

"The two met in battle many times, but neither was ever able to best the other," Todd continued. "Over hundreds of years, the bond they once shared turned to nothing more than bitterness, and the memory of their friendship was all but lost.

"Arsh, the king, has a younger brother named Todkala. He is the god for whom I am named."

Todd held up the little chunk of stone he wore around his neck.

"Todkala is the fox creeping through the night, the trickster, the maker of mischief and confusion."

Leaning closer to look, I realized for the first time that the stone was in the shape of an animal, a fox. I had only seen a fox once or twice. Some of them lived in the forest at Treescape. They were harmless enough there, but if one found its way to The Farm, where The Clan's animals were kept, chickens and rabbits would start to go missing.

"The trickster," Todd continued, letting the stone drop back to his chest, "has a countenance far younger than his brother, the king. He has dark brown hair and bright, purple eyes.

"Todkala supported Arsh in the war between the gods. Often, he would attempt to gain his brother's favor by aiding him in the fight against Husam.

"One day, an idea came to Todkala of how to defeat the warrior. He chose the largest mountain in the world and shaped it into a body.

"Growing in The Western Wood, he found the two oldest pine trees, each three hundred feet tall. He pulled them up and stuck them in the sides of the enormous mountain-body to serve as arms.

"For a head, he selected a piece of granite, enormous in both weight and size. So vast was the stone that Todkala could barely lift it. With great difficulty, he positioned it upon the shoulders of the mountain.

"Next, he took a mighty river and wrapped it with care around the middle of his creation to bind it together. All that was left for him to do was find a heart, and his new weapon would be complete.

"As Todkala set out in search of a heart, Tohopke, another of the gods, came to the place where the two pine trees were ripped from the ground.

"Tohopke, the beast hidden in the woods, the wild one, cares little for humans but instead prefers the forests and untamed places of the world. To see the gaping holes where the two ancient pines were uprooted angered him greatly.

"He began to follow Todkala's trail, vowing vengeance upon whoever had caused such desecration. The wild one came upon Todkala just as he ended the life of a great, brown bear. Without realizing he was being watched, the trickster cut the still-beating heart from the bear's body and hurried back to his creation.

"Tohopke again followed, growing more furious all the while. He had never forgiven Todkala for the death of the silver stag, and to see him cutting down trees and killing beasts in The Western Woods made the wild one's blood boil.

"When Todkala reached the mountain, he carefully cut open its chest and placed the heart inside. The trickster can give life to inanimate objects and control them. Carefully, he began embedding life into his mountain creature.

"Tohopke saw what Todkala was doing and guessed all that he planned to do. The wild one detested the king, Arsh, nearly as much as he loathed Todkala. Without thought, he charged into the clearing and attacked.

"Now, Tohopke is like a great man with a tangle of wild, brown hair. When he goes into a rage, his strength is tripled. As he charged Todkala, he lashed out savagely. The blow would have been a mighty one, but Todkala turned at the last moment and raised his arms in defense. The force of Tohopke's attack struck against the power Todkala was amassing to put into his creation.

"The sudden surge of sheer fury caused Todkala to lose control of the power, and it shot into the mountain, bringing the mass to life with ten times the amount of strength Todkala alone could have given it.

"Both gods froze as the mountain stood and turned toward them. Todkala did his best to control the monster, but his will was no match for so much power. It charged for the two gods. Each braced for a fight, but they could not withstand the might with which the living mountain struck them.

"The blow flung Tohopke halfway across the world. It took him nearly half a moon to find his way back to The Western Woods.

"The same blow hit Todkala, and he was thrown against another mountain. The impact was so hard that he did not rise for many days.

"The monster was created to slay gods, so it began to search for fresh prey, leaving a trail of destruction in its wake.

"Arsh heard of this creature a few days later. He came to where the abomination was born and saw the shattered earth and flattened forests. The king began to follow the monster's trail. The brute had no sense of direction and wandered here and there, often re-crossing its own path.

"Finally, the king caught up with it and attacked. The monster flailed out a long pine tree arm at him, and Arsh was knocked to the ground. Never had the king felt such a great power before. Even still, he rose to his feet, determined to find victory.

"He struck at the rock atop the mountain and, with his great sword, cleaved a chunk of stone from the creature's head. The king hoped this wound would slow the monster, but the mountain appeared to feel no pain and persisted in its attack.

"Though Todkala's creation was not quite as fast as the king, it was relentless. It swung its great arms again and again, never taking a moment's break. Repeatedly, Arsh struck the head and body; however, no matter what kind of damage he caused, the monster would not stop.

"The day turned to night, and the hours stretched on until dawn came upon the land. Still, the two battled, each trying to slay the other.

"Arsh grew fatigued as dusk fell on the second day. His movements were more sluggish, and the monster managed to land a blow that knocked him back a hundred feet and into a fast-flowing river. The current carried the exhausted god away.

"Many miles downstream, he was at last able to drag himself free of the water. On the banks, Arsh found a pomegranate tree and, after devouring several of the fruits, his strength was replenished."

Todd paused briefly to snarf down a few pieces of the turtle as Cole removed it from the fire. I laid more raw meat on the stones before taking a few bites for myself. The meat tasted unusual but good. It was a little chewier than I was accustomed to, but edible.

Todd swallowed, cleared his throat, and then continued the story.

"Most of the other gods would have chosen to flee, but the king was too proud. He resolved to kill the creature or perish trying.

"It was not hard for him to find the trail left behind by the mountain. As he closed in on his quarry, something unexpected caught his eye: fresh blood.

"Arsh paused to examine it, then heard a familiar battle cry. It was the cry of the warrior, Husam, his mortal enemy.

"The king charged forward, ready to confront whatever he found in the clearing. To his surprise, Arsh saw his old friend struggling against the monster.

"Husam's spear was broken and his clothes torn. As Arsh watched, the abomination flung the warrior to the ground and raised one stone foot to crush him. The king saw his chance and leapt forward, sword drawn. He smote off a hundred feet of the creature's right arm, upsetting its balance and causing it to miss the warrior by inches.

"The mountain stumbled, and Arsh found himself kneeling beside Husam. The gods' eyes met.

"'Let us defeat it together,' Arsh declared.

"Husam, too winded to speak, nodded his agreement.

"As one, the pair rose and then divided, so as to come at the creature from both sides. Husam drew his sword and hacked away at the monster's feet, while Arsh brought his blade crashing down on the granite head. A great crack was made, and a tremor passed through the mountain.

"The monster turned and struck toward the king. As it did, the warrior lashed out at the left arm, shearing most of it away and leaving only a knobby stump.

"Arsh dodged the great blow thrown at him, then looked over to see a thin trail of blood dripping from the spot where Todkala had placed the bear's heart. With a mighty effort, the king thrust his sword into the heart, hoping to end the conflict once and for all.

"His attempt was useless. The heart was sealed inside the creature by powers unknown to Arsh.

"Husam saw the king's intention and attempted to strike the heart himself, but it was invulnerable to both their attacks.

"Just then, the right arm came sweeping toward the two gods. It flung them together against a nearby rock. As they crashed into it, the solid stone splintered and cracked.

"An idea came to Arsh. He glanced at Husam, and understanding passed between them. Wordlessly, they divided again. The warrior drew the monster's attention as Arsh found a great tree. It was not nearly as large as the pines Todkala had given the monster for arms, but it was tall with a slender trunk.

"Taking a great leap, Arsh flung himself into the tree and climbed to the top in a matter of moments. As he climbed higher, the pine began bowing under his weight.

"Holding tightly to the top of the tree with one hand, he used the other to take hold of a thicker tree trunk nearby. Very carefully, using both hands and feet, the king pulled the top of the tree all the way to the ground. He made certain to maintain an iron grip on the second tree.

"Husam looked toward his old friend and saw that he was in position. Quickly, he sheathed his sword and darted between the stout legs of the mountain to reach Arsh's side. Just as the warrior took hold of him, the king released the second tree trunk.

"The pair were flung hundreds of feet into the air. Arsh turned his body so that his sword was facing down. As they fell to earth, Husam placed his hands alongside Arsh's on the sword.

"Together, they brought the blade down directly on the monster's head into the crack Arsh had made earlier. With a sound louder than a thousand peals of thunder, the granite head shattered.

"Neither god let go of the blade as it continued to cut into the mountain, dividing the heart perfectly in two. The power of the creature was released in a mighty rush, and the gods were hurled to the ground.

"When Arsh rose, he saw that the enormous mountain had crumbled into eleven pieces, each large enough to be a mountain in its own right. (*Once, on a hunting trip, I saw these very mountains.*)

"Now that the creature's life was vanquished, the king turned to Husam, and the two looked upon each other.

"'It was a good day to fight beside a friend,' Husam said at last.

"'Indeed, it was,' Arsh agreed.

"'There can never be peace between us,' the warrior began. 'But need there always be war? Surely, a day like today, where we stand side by side once more, could be allowed in remembrance of what we did here and all that we have done together in the past.'

"Arsh nodded. 'Every year, on this day, we will put aside our feud, and things will be between us as they used to be. We are enemies now, but once we were friends, and that should be remembered.'

"So saying, the two made a vow. This is a serious thing because gods cannot break the vows they make. That is why each year a festival is held on the day that the king and the warrior are at peace.

"It's one of the best days of the year! Held at the close of summer, just before the harvest begins."

A wistful smile appeared on Todd's face. His eyes grew distant as if he was recalling the event he described.

CHAPTER 23
STRIFE

There was a long moment of silence after Todd finished speaking. I glanced over at Kisa, surprised she wasn't overflowing with questions. Her head was resting on her folded arms, eyes closed, already fast asleep. Rollan and Joss looked close to joining her.

"I'll keep the first watch," Astra volunteered quietly.

Cole, who was removing the last of the turtle meat from the cooking rocks, nodded and said, "Wake me in a couple of hours."

"I can watch after you," I offered.

He nodded and smiled at me, but his eyes were clouded with weariness. As I settled down, I could feel the late morning sun touch my skin. Before long, it would disappear behind the cliffs, but until then, I would enjoy the warmth.

As I drifted off to sleep, I watched Todd and Astra cover the cooked meat with a few pieces of purple clothing to keep the sand off. To my surprise, Todd threw a piece of the meat into the fire. I sleepily wondered if part of the animal that wasn't good to eat had accidentally gotten mixed in and cooked with the rest.

Cole woke me sometime later. Every inch of my body felt terrible as I rose and took a drink of water. My stomach was churning uneasily, and my head felt as if it was filled with fog. I supposed it would take some time for my body to understand that days and nights were reversed.

The sun wasn't on our little group anymore. I missed its heat, but the afternoon air was warm enough that I was comfortable. The fire had long since died, and there wasn't enough wood lying around to keep it going for long, even if I did build it back up.

Despite my disquieted stomach, I nibbled on a little bit of the turtle meat. It was surprisingly mild in taste. I expected something coming from the ocean to be salty or have a fishy flavor. However, the turtle tasted much like the animals that lived on land their entire lives.

In school, I had always been at the top of the class. It was important for me to prove I was the best and brightest student, so I worked hard. Never had I felt as ignorant or unprepared as I did now. Why weren't we taught about the ocean in school? For that matter, why didn't they teach us about anything outside our borders? Was Astra right? Did they keep everything a secret just so that we would have to figure out how to survive? Or was there another reason?

I pondered these questions and others for several hours, but never came to any conclusions.

By the late afternoon, I couldn't keep my eyes open anymore. I glanced over to where Rollan was lying and decided to wake him for the next watch.

I rose and began to make my way toward him, but saw movement out of the corner of my eye. Turning, I observed Todd sit up.

"I can take the last watch," he offered, perceiving my intentions.

"Not a chance," I retorted.

"Why?" Todd wondered, as if he was really mystified. "I'm not as worn out as they are." He nodded toward where the younger half of the team slept.

I didn't disagree with him; it would have been nice to let Rollan, Joss, and Kisa sleep. If my body was struggling, I couldn't imagine how theirs were handling everything.

My gray eyes met Todd's brown ones as I considered my options. It wasn't likely he would decide to run away; Cole had already given him that option. On his own—with a broken arm and no weapons—he wouldn't last very long. In his present state, he was hardly a match for Kisa, not to mention the rest of us. If he did attack anyone, I would kill him myself.

I didn't trust Todd, but I did trust that he wanted to live, and if he did something stupid, it would only make it harder for him to achieve his goal.

"Fine," I growled at him. "Wake us when it starts getting dark."

I settled down and closed my eyes almost all the way. Through one slit, I watched Todd for a while. He sat with his back to me, looking out toward the water.

I could have imagined it, but something about the slope of his shoulders appeared more relaxed than usual. If he were telling the truth, and his people did live close to the ocean, then this place must remind him of where he came from.

Even though it was the middle of the afternoon and the waves were not even twenty yards away, I fell asleep quickly once I finally closed my eyes.

It was Astra who shook me awake several hours later as twilight was settling on the land. I wasn't particularly surprised that Todd was too scared to lay a hand on me. Cole was shaking Joss and Kisa. Rollan was already awake, packing as much turtle meat as he could into his bag and mouth simultaneously. Cole and Joss joined him. I put some in my pack, but didn't feel like my stomach was going to let me eat anything ever again.

We left our campsite before it was completely dark. The refreshing night air began to help me feel a bit better. We walked for a long time in silence. There were a few bits of conversation here and there, but it was cloudy, and in the near pitch dark, it seemed strange to break the stillness.

"I kind of fell asleep last night—I mean this morning—and didn't hear the end of the story," Kisa admitted when dawn was only a few hours away. "What happened?"

I listened with amusement as Joss and Rollan tried to repeat the ending of Todd's story about the gods. They didn't get the details quite right, but they finally managed to convey the gist of it.

"So, they still wouldn't be friends even after risking their lives for the other?" Kisa wanted to know.

I think Todd shook his head, but the moon had already set, so it was hard to tell for sure.

"That's so sad," Kisa lamented. "It would be like Joss and Rollan becoming enemies."

"That'll never happen," Joss promised quickly.

"Yeah," Rollan agreed.

"It might," Todd told them. "Something you can't even imagine could divide you in the future."

"I doubt it," Joss chuckled at the same time Rollan demanded, "Like what?"

"Women, position, power, mon—"

"None of those things are important to me," bellowed Rollan without letting Todd finish.

"Maybe not right now," Todd countered, "but someday they could mean more to you than anything, even your friends."

"Not likely," Rollan argued.

"If you say so," Todd replied. "But people change. Everyone has their price. Everyone has something they'd gladly kill their brother for."

"How dare you!" Rollan snarled.

From the tone of his voice, I thought it might be time to change the subject.

"You're no more perfect than anyone else," Todd went on. "Given the necessary incentive, you might even be willing to kill Joss or Kis—"

Before Todd had even finished speaking the girl's name, I heard the impact of a fist to a body and a sudden gasp of pain.

Great, I groaned mentally. *Everyone's fighting again.*

It was hard to see who had hit who, but I guessed it was Rollan going after Todd.

"I would never lay a finger on her!" Rollan screamed, confirming my suspicions.

"Hey, cut it out!" Cole called. I think he was trying to find the pair in the dark.

I couldn't see them, but I moved toward Rollan's voice to help break up the scuffle.

There was the sound of another blow and then a blood-curdling scream. Adrenaline shot through my body as I heard it, making my feet rush forward. I nearly tripped over something on the ground. It moved. I crouched down to find Todd writhing in pain.

"What's wrong?" I demanded as a loud gasp passed his lips.

"Rollan, what did you do?" Astra demanded. She was close at hand but completely invisible, garbed in her black clothing.

There was no answer from the darkness.

"Kisa, come here," I called.

A moment later, both she and Astra were beside me. I backed away to give them room.

"What hurts?" Kisa asked in a small voice.

"My arm," the boy answered through gritted teeth.

"Let me see." I had the vague impression of Kisa putting out a hand to find Todd's arm.

I heard Cole and Rollan talking in raised voices not too far away, but I couldn't make out their words.

"I'll have to reset the bone," Kisa whispered a moment later. "Can you both help hold him?"

"Sure," Astra replied, moving to place her hands on Todd.

I reached forward more hesitantly, unsure of exactly what to do. After finding Todd again in the dark, I helped pin down his shoulders while Kisa got into position.

"This is going to hurt," Kisa warned Todd.

Both Astra and I tightened our grips and braced ourselves. The last time was bad enough, with Todd unconscious and several feet away from me.

This time, I felt Todd's body spasm as Kisa forced his arm back into place. Another scream of pain escaped the boy's lips, and bile rose thickly in the back of my throat.

"It's done," Kisa murmured.

I slowly released Todd. He was lying flat on his back, gasping for air. Astra remained by his side while Kisa re-wrapped his arm.

Unable to bear it any longer, I staggered a few feet away and retched into the sand. After I finished, my body felt lighter, not that my stomach had been holding much. I cleaned my mouth with some water, but didn't use as much of the precious liquid as I wanted.

Slowly, I made my way back to Astra and Kisa.

Cole and the other boys joined us.

"We'll have to stop and rest here," Cole announced grimly. "Let's head over to the cliff and try to get some sleep."

Even without much light, it was easy to find the cliffs.

"Rollan, come here." I'd very rarely seen Cole angry, but the tone he used to call Rollan made it clear that he wasn't pleased.

Wordlessly, I heard Rollan trudge across the sand.

"You'll sleep here," Cole ordered.

After walking a dozen paces and having Todd join him, Cole gave him the same instructions.

"Neither of you is to move until it's time to leave," Cole commanded both boys. "Joss, you have the first watch. I'll go second, Kisa third, and Myra last," he told the rest of us.

Cole settled down between the two boys he had separated. Joss and Kisa moved closer to Rollan, while Astra took a place between Cole and Todd.

I chose a spot close to Cole but still nearer to Rollan. There wasn't any doubt who had thrown the first punch, but I was more loyal to my teammate than some stranger who shouldn't have been mouthing off.

Despite my exhaustion, the fact that my sleep schedule was completely altered resulted in me lying awake for a very long time.

I was just dozing off when something moved. The dim light of dawn showed me it was Joss. He rose and stretched before settling down farther from the sleeping bodies of his friends, closer to the ocean, where he would have a better view.

Sleep had almost claimed me when, again, there was movement. This time it was Rollan. Despite Cole's orders, the boy left his assigned sleeping spot to go and sit beside his cousin.

I didn't care enough to intervene. My eyelids were too heavy and sleep was too near.

"What if Todd's arm doesn't heal right?" Rollan asked, breaking the silence.

I sighed internally and gave up on the idea of sleep altogether for the time being.

"Kisa told me that he would probably be fine," Joss said, trying to comfort his cousin.

"I wish I wasn't so much like my brothers!" Rollan dropped his head into his hands.

"You're not like your brothers," Joss promised.

"Yes, I am. When I don't like something, my only answer is to hurt other people," Rollan sighed.

"That's not true," Joss protested. "Do you remember when our fathers used to make all of us play together?"

"Your mother didn't like it," Rollan recalled, his head still hanging low.

"No, she didn't," Joss agreed. "She was afraid you and your brother's manners would rub off on Jess and me."

Rollan nodded miserably.

"I'll tell you a secret," Joss continued. "My mom wasn't the only one who didn't like it. Jess hated it too; he never really got on with any of your brothers, even the ones who were close to his age. For a while, I was the same. I dreaded visits from your family.

"But one day, we all went swimming together. Jess and I were the best swimmers, so we didn't hang around with you guys. Your brother, Rossin, always tried to dunk everyone, so Jess and I swam to another part of the beach. Do you remember that day?"

"Not really, we went swimming a lot," Rollan muttered.

"Yes, but that was the day you and your brothers found the duck nest."

Rollan flinched at Joss's words.

"I remember," he whispered so softly I almost didn't hear.

"Your oldest brother, Relan, caught one of the ducklings and drowned it while Rossin and the others fended off the mother.

"I watched from down the shore and wanted to stop them, but they were so much bigger than me, and I wasn't brave enough." Joss turned his head toward his cousin. "But you were."

Rollan raised his head to meet Joss's gaze.

"You swam over and started yelling for them to stop. They wouldn't, of course, and I saw you tackle Rellis, who was holding two more ducklings. Then the other four came at you, and I couldn't just watch anymore."

"You blindsided Relan when he was about to grab me," Rollan recalled. "I've never seen him look more surprised." A smile spread across Rollan's face as he relived the memory.

"We didn't fend them off for very long," Joss admitted. "But it was long enough for the mother duck to get her babies out onto the lake, where your brothers couldn't reach them."

"I got one of the worst beatings of my life that day," Rollan murmured.

"Me too," Joss told him. "But it was totally worth it."

"Because we saved the ducklings?"

"No," Joss shook his head. "Because that was the day we became friends. I saw you make a choice that day; you chose not to be like your brothers. Every day since then, I have watched you make the same choice over and over again.

"When my mother saw what your brothers did to me, she had a fit. She didn't want us playing together anymore, but I couldn't wait to see you again. Ever since, you've been my best friend, and you always will be, no matter what."

"Why?" Rollan asked, looking down at his hands. "I'm not worth it."

Joss reached out and put a hand on his cousin's shoulder.

"Yes, you are. I've seen enough of your brothers to know exactly who you could have become. I know everything you've overcome, and let me tell you, not many people could have done that.

"Yeah, you make mistakes sometimes. You shouldn't have hit Todd, especially with his broken arm, but—"

229

"I was just so angry that I didn't think," Rollan interrupted. "I didn't mean to hurt him so badly, but the very idea that I might ever murder someone…" Rollan trailed off.

Joss thought for a moment. "I think it's important to understand that Todd was raised very differently from us. To him, murder doesn't seem like such a big deal. I doubt he even realized he was insulting you."

"That might be true," Rollan admitted.

"The only way to help him understand that it's wrong is to explain it to him, not attack him."

Rollan had no answer for that.

"Besides, Todd's not so bad," Joss insisted. "If he had been born in The Clan, I bet we would have all been friends."

"I don't know about that," muttered Rollan.

"Oh, come on, he has the most fascinating mind. I want to know more about him and his people."

"I guess," Rollan agreed half heartedly.

Dawn was breaking, and both boys seemed in much better moods. They sat in silence for a few minutes.

"What do I do now?" Rollan asked as the sun cleared the horizon.

"I'd start by apologizing," Joss suggested. "And the next time Todd—or anyone—makes you angry, try to see things from their perspective."

"Okay, I will." Rollan rose and then turned back. "Thanks. For everything. Thanks for being my best friend." With those words, he half tackled, half hugged his cousin.

"Get off me, you great lump," Joss complained from underneath his cousin's bulk.

Rollan laughed softly and rolled away. Joss gasped dramatically as he sat up, both boys chuckling.

"Better get some rest now," Joss suggested a moment later.

Rollan nodded and returned to the place Cole had told him to sleep. He lay down carefully so he wouldn't wake Kisa.

I closed my own eyes, hoping to at last find peaceful rest.

CHAPTER 24
DAYS AND NIGHTS

Kisa woke me in the early afternoon. As soon as I sat up, she walked over to where Joss and Rollan were sleeping back-to-back. With weary movements, I saw her flop down on the sand by their heads.

The air was warm and the wind gentle. Everything about the afternoon invited sleep. I stood and walked down to the ocean. The cold waves lapping on my bare feet helped my body remain alert.

I closed my eyes and listened. Above the sound of the waves, I could hear the cry of birds. Not the usual chirping calls I associated with the winged creatures, but high-pitched shrieks that were both captivating and slightly annoying.

A few silver birds perched on the cliffs above my sleeping companions. There were no other signs of life to be seen. This place was so forlorn. Was survival here really possible?

I needed to believe it was if we were going to be able to complete our quest.

After a quarter-hour of wading in the shallows, I wandered back to my team. The sand clung to my wet feet, but there was no point in trying to wipe it away. After my skin dried, it would fall off on its own.

The shadow of the cliff grew longer on the sand as the day passed. Cole was the first to wake. He came to sit by me. Without saying a word, I leaned against his shoulder, resting in his gentle presence.

Finally, when the shadow reached the water line, he spoke. "What do you think I should do about what happened last night?"

I didn't raise my head from his shoulder, my eyes watching the rolling waves.

"I wouldn't worry about it," I answered. "Joss and Rollan had a long talk, and I think everything will be all right now. If anything, maybe try to have a few words with Rollan, but I wouldn't be too harsh."

Cole sighed. "I don't want to punish him, but he needs to know that his actions were unacceptable."

"He does," I replied. "But just like when he was too rough with Kisa during training, if you come down hard on him, he'll close himself off to you."

"Because of his brothers?"

I lifted my head and nodded. "Yeah. In his heart, he knows you aren't like them, but sometimes his head forgets. Gentle words are what he'll respond to best."

"You're probably right," Cole agreed.

I put my head back on his shoulder, and we sat like that for another half hour.

"We should wake the others," I finally said, although I wished for nothing more than to remain by Cole's side.

"Yes, we should," he agreed. Still, neither of us rose.

It wasn't until I heard someone moving beneath the cliff that I lifted my head to glance back. Astra was awake, being careful not to look at us as she packed up her bag.

Slowly, I stood and stretched. Cole headed toward Joss, Kisa, and Rollan. He roused them and asked Kisa to check Todd's arm. She nodded, and Joss went with her.

"Will you come with me for a moment?" Cole asked Rollan.

The younger boy nodded, and the two walked down the beach a little way.

Kisa was finished examining Todd, and all the bags were packed by the time Cole and Rollan returned. Soon, we set out along the beach.

Slowly, the stars began to appear in the indigo sky, little points of white light, rivaled only by the rising moon. Under the silver glow, our progress was rapid.

Again, we spoke very little, allowing the long hours to be filled only with the continuous sound of the waves. Joss walked in the front of the group, keeping an eye out for driftwood or rocks in our path. Kisa and Rollan flanked him.

Todd was the one who lagged behind the group. I caught myself feeling sorry for him—just a little. Remembering his attack on Cole abated my sympathy considerably, but not entirely. Much as I didn't care for the Broken, I hated the idea of anyone being in pain.

Dawn came sooner than I expected. Since we'd slept so long the evening before, Astra suggested we go as far as possible. Our efforts were rewarded when we found a tiny waterfall running down the cliff. A stone pool, about a yard across, caught the water before it flowed out to the ocean.

As we made camp, I saw something that set my hair on end. A small pile of ash and a few half-burned pieces of driftwood.

Cole's face grew grim when I showed him my find.

"Another team must be close by," he muttered.

"And they're ahead of us," I hissed.

"That's good, though," Joss remarked. "They won't be heading toward us. At least we won't be surprised by them."

I nodded and managed not to point out that we were losing.

"Let's see if we can find something to eat," Cole suggested.

Everyone spread out and started searching the area.

I noticed Rollan square his shoulders and walk over to Todd. Although Cole followed Rollan with his eyes, he made no move to interfere.

Todd stiffened but didn't retreat.

"I'm sorry about the other night," Rollan said. "I let my temper get the better of me, and I was wrong."

Todd nodded, seeming at a loss for words.

"I hope we can put it behind us," Rollan continued. "Maybe we can even be friends?" His statement came out more like a question.

For a moment, Todd remained silent. "All right," he agreed.

Rollan smiled and held out his hand. With only a brief hesitation, Todd accepted it.

A twinge of discomfort pulled at my stomach. Something about the exchange didn't seem right, but I wasn't able to put my finger on it. I knew Rollan was sincere, but I had no idea what Todd was thinking. Was it wise to allow ourselves to become so familiar with a Broken?

The tension inside me continued to grow. More than anything, I was worried about meeting another team. We didn't see any more signs, but I couldn't imagine we were as alone as we felt.

Several days later, in the dead of night, we came to a large body of water covering the beach ahead. Todd said he thought it was a lagoon. We decided to wait for dawn before trying to cross. Joss and Rollan waded out into it but didn't make it very far before turning back. Even they didn't dare swim for an unknown destination in the pitch black.

"Hopefully, it won't be more than a few hours until first light," Cole commented.

No one made any answer. Instead, we all settled onto the sandy ground.

"Todd," piped up Joss a moment later, "will you tell us about the one god, the warrior…" he hesitated as if trying to recall the name.

"Husam," Todd told him.

"Yeah, that one," Joss continued. "Why did Husam betray his friend…"

"Arsh."

"Yes, why did Husam betray Arsh?"

"I want to know that too!" Kisa added enthusiastically. "Will you tell us?"

"All right," Todd agreed.

It took him a moment to compose his thoughts.

"Long before men came to live beside The Brimming Lake, all of the gods lived together in the sky," he began, his voice altered—more elegant—as if he were repeating words he seemed to know by heart.

"Lived in the sky?" Kisa cut in.

"Yes," Todd answered. "Their home was far above the clouds in a wonderful, perfect haven. After they created the earth, they dwelt above it for many millennia, watching all that took place below. There were nine of them. Eight descended from the sky and found themselves trapped on the earth."

"Why only eight?" Kisa interrupted again.

"Let him tell the story and ask questions afterward," Astra ordered impatiently.

"Sorry," Kisa murmured.

"It's okay," Todd told her before continuing. "The gods scourged the earth in anger—"

"Were they angry because they were trapped on the earth?" Joss asked.

I sighed.

"Really? You too?" Astra muttered.

"Well, I want to know!" Joss protested.

"That's another long story," Todd replied. He seemed to think for a moment before answering Joss's question. "Without going too much into the history of it, their anger was mostly caused by human arrogance.

"The gods had already given mankind a second chance, but still, a large number of them refused to worship the gods.

"As a result, the gods—Arsh and Husam, especially— hounded mankind nearly to the brink of extinction. If the pair had gone on that way, completely unchecked, my people, The People of the Brimming Lake, would have been wiped from the face of the earth.

"There was a wise man named Peter. He was the one who had begged the gods for a second chance and saved humanity the first time. It was his two sons—"

All six of us gasped at Todd's words.

"Peter? It can't be!" Cole exclaimed.

CHAPTER 25
THE SLAYING OF THE SILVER STAG

"It must be a coincidence," Astra remarked hesitantly, as if even she didn't believe the words.

"What?" Todd asked, sounding thoroughly mystified.

"In the history of The Clan, there is also a man named Peter," Kisa explained.

"He saved humanity too," Joss added.

"I thought your people didn't tell stories," Todd recalled in surprise.

"This one's a history," Rollan told him. "It's true."

"So is the story I'm telling," Todd said.

"What?" I asked, furrowing my brow. "You mean, you expect me to believe that there used to be some great and mighty beings with strange powers rampaging around the earth?"

"No," Todd answered nervously. "There didn't *use* to be; they're still alive. If you don't give them the proper respect, they'll smite you."

I laughed.

"Let him tell the story," Astra intervened. "If everyone keeps interrupting, we'll never get anywhere."

There was a pause before Todd continued.

"After Peter died, his two sons were the ones who turned the gods against each other. They knew that no human would ever be able to wound or kill a god; only another god could do that. So, they convinced their people to no longer worship Arsh, the king, and to instead turn their praise to Husam, the warrior. In this way, they hoped to drive a wedge between the king and the warrior.

"Husam had never before received such worship. He was arrogant and greatly enjoyed the praise that the people lavished on him. He became prouder with each passing day as Arsh grew more and more jealous. The friendship they had always borne for each other became strained.

"Finally, the king appeared to the two sons of Peter. In a fit of passion, Arsh prepared to strike them down in front of all the people for their blasphemy.

"One of the pair instantly dropped to his knees and recanted. Before the other could do anything, Husam arrived. Fury burned in his red eyes, for he knew what Arsh was trying to do and for what reason. The two gods began to exchange angry words and then blows. The humans ran and hid, for the fight was terrible to behold. Arsh was the stronger of the two, but Husam was the fiercer.

"The pair used to spar against each other, but never had they fought like this. No one knows who would have won if the other gods had not intervened.

"Jiya, the heart in the chest, the fair one, most beautiful of both woman and goddess alike, stepped between the two and begged that they would not fight. It disturbed her greatly to see Arsh and Husam at odds, for Jiya is the wife of the king.

"The fair one called to Tohopke, the wild one, who I have already told you about. He was close by and came to help her bring the battle to an end.

"At their intervention, Arsh and Husam ceased their fighting and went their separate ways. Jiya went with her husband, Arsh, and Tohopke went with the warrior.

"On the shores of the sea, Jiya assured Arsh that he was the king and no one should ever say otherwise. All night, she filled her husband's ears with praises and promises of his preeminence. Arsh was soothed by her presence and appearance, for Jiya was ever so lovely to look upon, with midnight hair and sapphire eyes. No mortal man can see the beauty of the fair one without falling completely in love with her.

"That same night, the warrior and the wild one spoke together of the king. Husam's pride now drove him to desire the kingship for himself, and so usurp his old friend's throne. With Tohopke's help, he knew his goal would be possible. However, as with the animals of the world, Tohopke was undisciplined. He cared little for Husam's disagreement with Arsh and would make no promises. Instead, he returned to the wilderness he loved so much, where his wife awaited him.

"Her name is Zeruiah. She is the pain in the wound, the torturer of man, beast, and god alike. If Jiya is the image of beauty, then Zeruiah is the image of suffering and fear. Her black hair is straight and does little to hide her gaunt figure. Her white, bony fingers are often clutched around the hilt of a weapon, for she revels in the pain of others.

"When Tohopke came to her, the torturer could see that her husband's mind was burdened. Before long, he told her what had transpired. They did not know it, but another heard all that was said as well.

"It was Todkala, younger brother of the king, whom you will remember from the last story. As he listened, a plan began to form in the head of Todkala.

"The trickster knew that there was a good chance this fight would blow over if Tohopke did not choose a side. Then the king and the warrior would be friends again.

"Todkala did not want this. In his heart, he hated Husam because Arsh loved the warrior more than he did his younger brother. The king hardly ever took notice of Todkala and rarely sought his company. Many times, the trickster had watched Arsh and Husam go on ventures together and leave him behind.

"It took several days for Todkala to build up the courage to take action, but finally, in the dead of night, he rose and wrapped himself in darkness. That is one of his gifts; he can disappear and pass through the land without leaving a trace.

"The trickster came to the shores of the sea, where Arsh and Jiya were staying. They did not realize he was there until he removed the shroud of darkness, and they saw the moonlight reflected in his purple eyes.

"Todkala told his brother that the entire world was speaking of how Husam had challenged Arsh and was trying to claim kingship for himself. He insinuated that Husam was planning to attack and dethrone Arsh. The king grew angrier and angrier with each report the trickster gave him.

"His face darkened in fury, and his fists clenched in rage. Todkala paused, afraid of what his brother might do. The king demanded Todkala proceed. At his brother's invitation, the trickster spoke of his plan to ensure that Arsh would remain king and defeat the warrior.

"Both Arsh and Jiya listened. The fair one's lip curled in disgust at the conclusion of Todkala's words, for she despised the actions he suggested. Jiya would have dismissed him immediately, but the king believed there to be merit in his brother's scheme.

"Jiya departed in a fit of passion from the seashore while the king remained and spoke with his brother. In the end, he vowed to do all that Todkala suggested. Only then did the trickster return to his lair, The Undying Garden.

"Now, before I tell you their plot, it is important to know that Tohopke has a sister named Sur. She was in the flower of youth, very much like a girl on the cusp of womanhood. As with her brother, she was wild at heart and dwelt in The Western Woods.

"Sur was in love with another of the gods, Dezi. Tohopke was not aware of this, for he paid little attention to his sister and never noticed how much time the two spent together.

"Sur and Dezi wanted to be married but hadn't yet confessed this to Tohopke. The two were plotting a way to obtain the wild one's blessing. Sur knew her brother would be hard to persuade, for Tohopke hates change above all things.

"Four days after the trickster visited the king, Arsh went to Tohopke. He dared not ask directly for what he wanted, in fear that the wild one would reject his request. So, instead, the king, the crown upon the head, issued a challenge to Tohopke.

"Since the time that the world began, there was one animal in the forest that was swifter than the wind and harder to find than a pearl. It was the silver stag, called the spirit of the forest.

"The silver stag was the only creature Tohopke had no control over whatsoever. For he that is the beast hidden in the forest could call any other animal to him and have it do his bidding.

"Arsh proposed that whoever captured the stag first would be the winner and get to demand a favor of the other. Tohopke loved the excitement of the hunt, so he agreed readily to the contest. Todkala's plan was for his brother to win and use his request to gain the allegiance of Tohopke, his wife, Zeruiah, and his sister, Sur. With the support of so many gods and goddesses, he knew Husam would stand no chance of ever claiming the kingship.

"When dawn broke the next day, the two gods began to search the woods. Tohopke knew the forest well and went alone, seeking signs that the spirit of the forest was near.

"He was not aware that Todkala already knew the place where the stag grazed each day and slept every night. As soon as the wild one was out of sight, he brought his brother, the king, to the secret meadow in which the silver stag was waiting.

"When it saw the gods, the stag rolled its black eyes in terror and fled. Its heels were quick as lightning, but the two gods pursued it, never giving the creature a moment's rest.

"The beast ran for a day and a half, until its mouth dripped foam and its flanks were dark with sweat. Carefully, the two gods chased the stag into the trap Todkala had laid. The canyon where they drove the beast had high, stone walls. The day before Arsh made his challenge, the trickster blocked the passage, creating a dead end.

"In that place, in a dark hour, Arsh struck down the silver stag. Todkala was overcome with delight and composed a poem for its death, which he sang over and over as the king carried the carcass to Tohopke. The song goes like this:

Quietly in the green field stands the silver stag
The fox alone observes, following along at a lag
The stag's secret ways he studies without shame
Not long 'til the start of the hunter's deadly game

Fervently we chase him into the dead of night
To the place we have designed with no escape in sight
Survival will require that he defeat us there within
But he knows it is a battle that he can never win

Streaks of red blood stain the stag's silver hair
His panicked black eyes look wide in a stare
The deep wounds in his flesh will never be healed
His life is cut short by the sword the king doth wield

Once so majestic and such a fine sight
This creature that walked unheard in the night
Yet the proudest of beasts has too become prey
The silver stag will not again see the light of another day

I stared at Todd in amazement. I had never heard anything like the sound he was making. It was a sort of recitation, only his voice changed. It went higher, then lower, but in a completely smooth and seamless manner.

"What was that?" Kisa gasped. The rest of us just stared.

"It was the song that Todkala made up," Todd answered.

"What is a 'song'?" Astra asked.

"You mean your people don't sing?" Todd appeared thunderstruck.

I shook my head. There were a lot of words from his story that I hadn't recognized; "husband", "pearl", "sing", and "song" were among them. I knew every word recorded in the language books from school. These were not included, so where had they come from?

"Is 'song' what you just did?" asked Joss.

Todd nodded. Twilight was beginning to fill the sky, and I could see that he was gaping at us.

"I sang a song; it's called singing."

"It was nice," Kisa told him.

"I'm not that good," Todd confessed. "There are some people who can sing so beautifully it will bring tears to your eyes."

"How do you do it?" Rollan wondered, trying to make his voice change in the way that Todd's had.

Kisa giggled as Joss tried as well. A moment later, she joined in herself.

Cole began chuckling, and I couldn't help but laugh as well. The trio sounded like a herd of unhappy goats. Astra was shaking her head and smiling. Soon even Todd was laughing.

Finally, they stopped.

"How was that?" Rollan asked, completely out of breath.

"It was something else," Cole told him.

"Can you teach us?" Kisa pleaded.

"Sure," Todd agreed.

I glanced at the horizon; it would be light in less than an hour. "How about finishing the story now and teaching us later?" I suggested.

"Yeah, we'll need to be moving on soon," Cole agreed. "Let's hear the end of the story."

Todd was silent for a moment, as if trying to recall where in the story he had left off. After a brief pause, he began speaking once more.

"When Arsh and Todkala found Tohopke, the king threw the stag's carcass at his feet in triumph. He was unprepared for what happened next. The wild one fell to his knees in grief. When the challenge had been set forth to capture the silver stag, he never dreamed that anyone would think of slaying the beast. Its death was a terrible blow to him. For, as I have already told you, the silver stag was the very spirit of the forest itself.

"Tohopke was too grieved to rise from the ground and remained that way for two whole days, lamenting the loss of such a

242

creature. The king and the trickster could get nothing out of him in all that time.

"Finally, as the sun rose on the third day, he that is the beast hidden in the woods stood and looked on Arsh and Todkala with fury.

"He would have attacked them right then and there, but gods must keep the vows they make; even the trickster must do this, though it is against his nature. So, Tohopke asked what request the king would make of him.

"Instantly, the king demanded Sur as a wife. With great despair in his heart, Tohopke agreed to give her over—"

"But Sur was in love with a different god," Kisa blurted out. "Didn't she get a choice?"

Todd shook his head. "It is decided by a woman's closest male relative who they will wed."

"Wait," Rollan jumped in. "The king guy- Arsh- wasn't he already bonded to the beautiful goddess?"

"So?" Todd asked.

"Well, you can't have more than one life mate—or whatever you call it," Rollan explained.

"Why not?" Todd inquired.

"Because it's wrong," Astra told him. "Two people should be completely committed to each other when they are in that sort of a relationship. Adding a third can only cause trouble and pain."

"That's not true," Todd protested.

"Does it work out well for the gods in this story?" Astra wondered.

"Well, no," Todd said hesitantly. "But that doesn't mean it's always bad," he insisted.

"Astra, let him finish the story," Cole interjected. "You two can argue as much as you want after we've crossed the water and the rest of us are asleep."

"Fine," Astra sighed and glared at Joss, Kisa, and Rollan. "No more interruptions," she announced as if they had been the ones mincing words with Todd.

"Go on," Cole instructed with laughter in his voice.

Todd nodded and spoke again. "When Sur learned of the arrangement, she was beyond furious, and Dezi was heartbroken. The following day, Sur wed Arsh. It was then that she swore love would never enter her heart again. She became the dagger in the soul, the one filled with hatred.

"Sur blamed Tohopke more than the king. She had once loved her brother dearly, but after his betrayal, she could never again think of him with tenderness. A bitter seed was planted in her against her kin, which grew stronger every day.

"Instead of binding Tohopke to the king as Todkala planned, the wild one was filled with guilt and went to Husam, pledging to help him instead.

"Along with his wife, Zeruiah, Tohopke conspired with the warrior on how they might slay him who is the crown upon the head, thus freeing Sur.

"Dezi also joined them, though he was broken in spirit and mind. He became the sorrow of the world, the weeper. Every morning when he rose from slumber, there were tears in his eyes as he thought of the beautiful girl he loved with a longing that was never to be fulfilled.

"Indeed, he spent much of his time sleeping, preferring to walk in dreams rather than in the real world.

"With the three gods and one goddess aligned against them, the king and his two wives, along with Todkala, began to prepare for an attack.

"They didn't have long to wait. The warrior and those that supported him made their move in less than a moon. They attacked at night, hoping to catch the others unprepared, but they were disappointed.

"Arsh himself was standing guard. When he saw them coming, he gave a great battle cry and charged straight for his old friend, Husam. Their swords clashed, sending up sparks in the darkness.

"Zeruiah, the torturer, moved to help the warrior strike the king, but Jiya leapt to her husband's defense, and the two goddesses began a battle almost as fierce as the gods'.

"Todkala was not strong in battle. He stood on the sidelines, uncertain of what to do. Tohopke spied him. He had brooded upon all that occurred, and he was confident that the trickster was at the bottom of the stag's death and his sister's ill-suited marriage. The wild one rushed forward and attacked Todkala so furiously that it was all the trickster could do to ward off each blow, retreating with every advance.

"Dezi then emerged onto the field and prepared to attack the first figure he encountered. He swung as someone approached him, but checked the blow when he realized it was Sur. Her hair, which was once long and chestnut, was now shorn away, the ragged ends bouncing around her burning brown eyes.

"With a cry of anguish, the weeper threw himself to the ground, sobs wracking his body. She that is the dagger in the soul did not even notice her old love, lying face down in the dirt. Her eyes only sought her brother. When she beheld him fighting against Todkala, she rushed forward and nearly ran him through with her blade. Her brother turned to face this new opponent. This distraction allowed him that is the fox creeping through the night to flee from the battle in fear.

"Tohopke could not bring himself to fight his own sister, especially since he knew the grief he had caused her, so he also ran. Sur pursued him, screaming for the wild one to turn and face her.

"Jiya and Zeruiah were well-matched for battle. The two didn't fight with swords as the other gods did, but with long knives instead. Finally, Jiya drew blood from Zeruiah. The torturer was not used to being injured. She had never before felt pain, and the sensation was too much. She deserted Husam and ran from the field.

"It was then two against one, and Husam was losing ground. His defeat was hastened by the return of Sur. The hater was filled with wrath from not having been able to find her brother. She threw herself toward Husam. The warrior knew when he was outmatched and followed his companions into the woods.

"Arsh raised a cry to the heavens. All his enemies were run away, save Dezi, who did nothing but lay on his face and sob. He cried not for his own grief, but for how much Sur had changed. Heartbroken as he was to lose her, it was ten times worse to see the girl he loved so filled with anger and rage that she did not even know him.

"Sur approached Dezi then. You might imagine they would share a few tender words, but she who is the dagger in the soul had removed all feelings, save that of hatred, from her heart. She looked upon him with cold eyes and even raised her sword to strike. He who is the sorrow in the tears would not have stopped her, but Arsh did. He spared Dezi's life and sent him to the warrior with a message, a message proclaiming that there would never be peace in the world until the warrior and his followers were dead.

"Over the centuries, the gods have clashed many times as the warrior and the king strive for power. This was the first battle of their great war, which will continue until the end of the world."

CHAPTER 26
SIGHT

At the conclusion of Todd's words, everyone remained still for a long moment. The sun was clearing the horizon, illuminating the azure pool of water before us. It was like a small lake, fed by a waterfall cascading down the cliff.

"That's not much of an ending," Kisa pointed out, turning to Todd. "How does it end? Who wins?"

Todd shrugged. "We won't know until the end of time."

"The end of time?" Joss echoed.

Todd nodded. "There will be a final battle here on earth. The victorious gods and their followers will ascend into the heavens for all eternity."

"Followers?" Cole asked.

"Yes, my family belongs to The House of the King. We oppose those who follow the warrior. My father and older brother are named for the king, just as I am named for the king's brother."

"Wait," Joss broke in. "I thought you said all the people decided to follow the warrior."

Todd nodded. "For a time, they did, but only to turn the gods against each other. In the end, the older of Peter's sons, the one who recanted, along with his family and many others, turned back to the true king, Arsh. Peter's younger son and those foolish enough to follow him choose to continue worshiping the usurper, Husam."

Todd spat onto the ground.

"I don't understand," Kisa said. "Have you met the gods? Have you talked to them?"

"Not exactly." Todd shook his head. "They're invisible most of the time, and I've never seen one, but they are always watching over those who worship them."

"Then you follow someone you've never met without any proof that they ever existed?" I asked incredulously. "Why?"

Todd hesitated for a moment. "My family always has."

"Why?" I repeated. "If the gods were so bad that the people had to turn them against each other in order to survive, why follow them?"

"We must," Todd insisted. "We can't live without them!"

"Why?" I wondered again.

Todd sighed. "It was only because of disbelief that the gods turned away from humanity. But to their believers, the gods grant power and good fortune. Once my ancestors regained Arsh's favor, he blessed their new land, The Brimming Lake, and caused them to prosper."

I narrowed my eyes.

Cole shook his head. "Enough of this. We should get moving now that there's some light. It looks like it will be easier to get to the waterfall on the other side of this—what did you call it, Todd?"

"A lagoon," Todd informed him.

"Right," Cole recalled.

As it turned out, all of us were able to wade across the pool of water except Kisa. She had to start swimming in the very center, where the sandy bottom curved downward. Rollan took her pack and held it over his head along with his own so it wouldn't get soaked. The rest of us did the same with our bags and weapons. Cole took care of the extra pack Todd was carrying since he only had one good arm.

On the far side, we headed for the place where freshwater fed into the lagoon. Much as I hated to think about the amount of time we'd lost during the night, I couldn't deny that sleeping now would be a good idea. The air around me was already getting hot, and the sun had barely crested the horizon.

We divided up the watches. I didn't have one for a change, and everyone went off to sleep except Kisa, who was the first watcher.

248

I woke in the late afternoon to find someone had built a fire. At first, I couldn't understand the need. As I'd suspected, the day was quite warm. We wouldn't have gotten very far if we'd tried to journey beneath the blazing sun.

A moment later, I noticed that two fish were cooking on a large stone close beside the flames. I examined them and saw that they were nothing like the fish we found in our lake. Their bodies were longer and flatter with far more fins.

Joss was sitting on the edge of the lagoon with Todd, discussing fishing techniques. Rollan was down on the beach, gathering firewood. I went to join him since I doubted I'd be much help with fishing.

"Look at this," Rollan said, holding up a hand as I drew near.

The object he presented was the strangest shape. I came closer to get a better look. At first, I thought it was a colorful stone, like the ones I'd seen in Astra's hidden cave back in The Valley of the North Wind, but it wasn't.

"It's a seashell," he announced. "Todd showed them to Joss and me earlier. He said that small animals live inside them, just like the turtles in their shells."

"Oh," I replied. "Where did you find them?"

"Look down," Rollan laughed.

I did and instantly realized that what I'd taken for pebbles were actually hundreds of seashells. Some were smaller than flower petals, while a few were the size of my hand. Each was unique and fascinating.

"I bet Kisa will like them," Rollan murmured, gathering a few more.

I suppressed a smile as I started picking up pieces of driftwood.

Joss managed to catch two more fish, so everyone was well-fed and full of energy. In high spirits, we left the lagoon before nightfall.

"Todd, what did you mean when you said the gods created the world?" Kisa asked.

"Exactly what I said," Todd replied. "At the dawn of time, the nine gods worked together to create the earth."

"How?" Rollan demanded.

"With their powers," Todd explained.

"This is all ridiculous," I told him. "You can't seriously mean to tell me that any of you believe a word of it. The gods aren't real."

"Of course they are," Todd insisted. "If I blasphemed them, the gods might strike me down."

"That seems a little far-fetched," Cole muttered. "Plus, I don't understand how a being such as a god could exist. There's no evidence."

"There is evidence," Astra put in before Todd could come up with an answer.

"What?" I asked in surprise.

"Well," Astra said, with a gesture at the moonlight-bathed world around us, "where did all this come from?"

I waited for her to expound, unsure of what she was trying to say.

"There has to be more to this world than meets the eye," Astra continued. "And it must have come from somewhere."

"Of course," Cole said. "Everything has a beginning."

"But, by that logic, the gods would need to have a beginning too," I stated, my mind churning as I wondered if it was possible for the world to have been around forever.

For a moment, the only sound other than the waves was our feet crunching in the sand.

"Maybe," I heard Astra reply softly. "Humans have a beginning, just like trees and animals. But we follow the same physical rules they do, like gravity and needing to eat food. If there are beings out there who defy physics, their existence wouldn't necessarily be defined by the same rules as ours."

Astra's statement was met with silence.

"What are you trying to say?" Cole asked at last.

"How could all this come from nothing?" Astra seemed to be reasoning everything out as she spoke. Her words were rather nonlinear, and I wasn't sure anyone else was able to follow them.

"That's not what we've been taught," I pointed out.

Astra sighed. "Yes, but no one in The Clan knows anything about *before*. Even what history we are told is vague. How are we ever supposed to understand when we know so little?"

"We know enough," I argued, not liking the direction the conversation was taking.

Even in the dark of the night, I could feel Astra's gaze turn on me. "We know almost nothing," she responded. "And our people have made no effort to learn."

"I've learned enough to know that there are no gods," I declared.

"An ant or a beetle is as ignorant of our doings as we would be of an individual who was that superior to us," Astra mused.

"However, ants and beetles can actually see us," I shot back, growing annoyed. This was a stupid thing to argue over. It was obviously untrue, but I had no more evidence to disprove Astra's words than she could provide to support her view.

"Only if they had eyes to see and wisdom to perceive," Astra answered me.

"But—" I started to protest.

"Quiet," Astra ordered.

Growing angry, I opened my mouth to object to her interruption, but I didn't get a chance. Cole, who was just in front of me, came to a sudden stop, and I narrowly avoided tripping over him.

"What—" Kisa began to say from the back of the group.

Even though she spoke softly, Astra shushed her immediately.

There was just enough moonlight for me to see Astra raise a hand and point down the beach.

Someone was out there. Far in the distance, a fire was burning.

"What do we do?" Joss whispered as quietly as possible.

251

"Are they going to attack us?" Kisa asked fretfully.

"Whisper, Kisa," I told her. "They can't attack us if they don't know we're here."

The little girl nodded but didn't say anything. I could well imagine how her face looked, even though it was too dark to see. She would be pale, her eyes huge and round with fear.

"Let's take a closer look," Cole whispered.

"We should walk in the wet sand," I added, "so the water will erase our footprints." I removed my shoes, and the others did the same, those who had been wearing them at least. Astra, Joss, Rollan, and Todd were already barefoot.

Cole took the lead; I stayed close by his side. Just behind us were Astra and Todd. The other three brought up the rear.

"Who are they?" I heard Todd whisper to Astra.

"They might be another team from The Clan," she answered.

"If so, then why would they attack you?" Todd wondered.

"It's complicated," Astra replied.

The boy considered for a moment. "Should we attack them first?" he asked.

"No," Astra told him instantly, putting an end to the conversation.

The fire was farther off than I originally thought. It was almost twenty minutes before we were close enough to make out the figures lit by the orange glow. I shuddered to think how visible we had been when it was us sleeping around the flames. We would be building no more fires by night; I would make sure of that.

Cole and I stopped when we were about a hundred yards from the campsite. The figures weren't moving. All of them seemed to be asleep, except for one, who was looking out toward the ocean. If we ventured much closer, we might be spotted.

I glanced at Cole, not sure of what to do. Cole studied the situation wordlessly without meeting my eyes.

The moon wasn't very bright, but the idea of being seen made my pulse race.

There were only four sleeping figures. This team had already lost a member. For one horrible moment, I wondered if it could be Bala and Jase's team. I tried to make out the colors of the contenders' clothing, but we were too far off.

Astra came up beside us and put her mouth close to Cole's ear. I leaned in to hear what she was going to say.

"If we go one at a time and stay out of the firelight, it is unlikely that we will be noticed."

Cole nodded as Astra pulled her hood over her head and wrapped herself in her black cloak. She was all but invisible only three feet from where I stood.

Astra moved stealthily forward. Kisa and Rollan tried to follow, but I stopped them. I held my breath as Astra passed the part of the beach right in front of the watcher. He never stirred.

Cole placed a hand on my arm, pushing me forward slightly. I understood and began making my way across the wet sand. Astra was still moving ahead of me. Once she was well out of reach of the firelight, I saw her draw her bow and notch an arrow.

As I came closer, I couldn't help staring at the group. I was fairly certain at least two of the figures were wearing brown. The one on watch was wearing dark green. One of the last two was either in the same dark green or royal blue. I couldn't tell anything about the fifth. It wasn't much, but at least I was reasonably certain that I didn't know any of them.

I could see that they had caught and cooked something that evening because there was a pile of bones beside the fire. For a brief moment, I wondered if I should suggest a raid. We could use more food and were always in need of water.

I pushed the thought down just as quickly as it sprung up. Cole would never allow such an attack. Deep down, I knew it would be wrong.

Astra was standing less than twenty feet ahead of me. I glanced back and saw Todd creeping along about the same distance behind me. His tan skin blended into the night far better than mine. I wondered how Kisa would do. She was blonde, pale, and wearing the lightest color.

To my relief, when she started walking, Rollan was beside her. His dark green clothing was far less conspicuous. Even together, Kisa had a better chance of going unnoticed with him shielding her.

Joss followed behind them, then Cole. We all made it. We were all safe, at least for now. When the sun rose, and we made camp, the tables would turn. We had the advantage of numbers, but neither Kisa nor the injured Todd would be much good in a fight.

Speed was our best defense. We would have to outdistance them. Cole must have been thinking the same thing. After passing the other team, he picked up the pace considerably. I glanced at Kisa and wondered how long she would be able to keep up such a gait. We stayed in the shallows with the waves washing around our feet. In the morning, the other team would walk the same path without ever knowing we had been there.

The going was harder in the wet sand. With each step, I sank up to my ankles in the gooey substance, which clung relentlessly to my feet. I was so completely absorbed in my struggles that I almost tripped over Cole for the second time that night when he pulled up short in front of me. Without a word, he turned around and started walking in the wrong direction.

I stared at him, wondering if he had seen something I missed. Then I realized he was going back for Kisa. She had fallen at least ten yards behind. Joss and Rollan were beside her, trying to help her keep up.

Cole didn't say anything as he approached the three. The campfire was long out of sight, but everyone was feeling apprehensive. After handing his pack to Rollan, Cole lifted Kisa onto his back, and we continued forward again.

I felt guilty for not noticing how fatigued Kisa was, especially since I had known that she wouldn't be able to keep up.

Cole didn't lead quite as quickly as before since he was now weighed down with Kisa, but we still made good time. The moon disappeared in the early morning hours. The tide reached its high point and started going out. Finally, there was the faintest glimmer of light across the water, yet we continued marching through the sodden sand.

"How much farther are we going?" Astra asked when the entire sky was the color of a pale rose. She didn't whisper, and her voice sounded impossibly loud in the stillness of the morning.

"As far as possible," Cole replied.

I knew how much he feared an attack. Astra and I exchanged a glance; we couldn't let him drive us to exhaustion.

After another hour, the sun was beginning to arc its way across the sky.

"Look," I said, pointing at the cliffs to our left. A trickle of water was running down the rocks.

There were a number of large stones close to the water source where we would be safe from the eyes of the casual observer.

"Perfect," Astra said, and the two of us turned toward the water.

"Let's make camp," I suggested.

"No," Cole ordered. "We should go a little farther."

"We need water," Astra told him.

"Then let's fill up and keep moving."

I shook my head. I hated to defy Cole, but I had no choice.

"Cole, we must stop," I told him. "We can hydrate here and sleep. If the other team is going to catch us, we should be rested and have someone on watch that can keep their eyes open."

Cole still looked uncertain.

"It'll be all right," I promised. "Not all teams are like the one that attacked us."

My words persuaded him; Cole yielded and followed the rest of us to the cliff. I sighed inwardly, doubly thankful I hadn't told him what Astra, Todd, and I witnessed at the lake.

CHAPTER 27
ENGAGEMENT

I didn't know how Cole could sleep in such a situation. He'd been ten times more unsettled by the presence of the other team than I was, yet he was the one who was sound asleep while I tossed and turned on the sand. After about half an hour, I gave up.

Joss was keeping watch.

"Go ahead and get some rest," I told him, standing up with a sigh. The sun wasn't even halfway into the sky yet, but it already felt warm.

"Are you sure?" Joss wondered. "Your watch doesn't begin for a couple more hours."

"I can't sleep, so you might as well."

"Okay," he said, settling down in the sand. "Wake me if you get tired."

I nodded and sat with my back to the cliff and my slumbering companions. Even though I knew the other team wasn't likely to reach us until the afternoon, I kept a sharp eye out. We were all safely hidden behind the cluster of rocks, but I wasn't going to take the chance of being surprised.

Ideally, the other team wouldn't come far enough to find us. We had covered a lot of ground the night before. Plus, traveling during the cooler hours allowed us to go without breaks. Hopefully, they wouldn't be able to keep up. I already knew they weren't moving as quickly as we were, since we had been able to pass them. Now we just needed to extend our lead. We *must* reach the mountain first.

It had been a long time since I'd thought of victory instead of just survival, but I wanted to win, more so now than ever before. We were getting closer every day, not that any of us could gauge the distance. Our destination could be hundreds of miles farther up the coast. However, our path was secure; there was only one direction to go.

I mulled these thoughts over for hours. Finally, when the sun was almost directly overhead, I felt that most of the tension had left my body. After taking a long drink, I set my canteen under the dripping water to refill.

I shook Joss gently. He sat up and nodded at me. I lay down and fell asleep almost at once.

When Cole roused me, it felt like only fifteen minutes had passed. I could tell from his face that something was happening. Instantly, I was wide awake and sprang to my feet. Long shadows spread out in all directions, signifying that it was only a few hours before sunset.

Todd, Joss, and Kisa were still asleep, but everyone else was awake. Astra crouched behind one of the rocks closest to the ocean. She was gazing back the way we had come.

"What's going on?" I asked quietly.

"They're coming," Rollan answered.

"Should we leave?" I whispered to Cole.

Astra, who darted over to us, answered for him. "Too late for that."

"Maybe they won't attack us," Rollan said.

"I don't know," Cole answered. He was frozen with fear.

"Wake up Joss and the others," I ordered Rollan. "We need our weapons."

Astra already had her bow on her shoulder. Rollan snatched up his wooden staff and woke the others as Cole quickly retrieved his sword. My knife was never far from my side.

"What are you thinking?" Astra asked me.

"We should stay out of sight," I told her. "If they start to come over here looking for water, we'll use a show of force. Hopefully, they'll leave us alone."

Astra nodded. Everyone was awake and grouped around Astra and me, weapons at the ready.

"All right," I said, trying to remain calm for their sakes. "We're going to hide behind the rocks and not move a muscle when they pass by. If they start to head our direction, Cole, Astra, Joss, Rollan, and I will jump onto the rocks with our weapons."

The others were nodding as they listened to me. I licked my dry lips before continuing. "We'll try everything to make them leave peacefully, but if we have to fight, then we will. And—" My voice hesitated as the next words came to my lips. "And if we fight, we must kill them."

Cole looked shocked, but Astra nodded again, giving my words her full support.

"Todd and Kisa," she said, turning to the pair, "stay hidden. It's better if they don't know that you are here."

"If they see Todd," I began, picking up where Astra left off, "they'll probably attack us immediately." Kisa's eyes were huge with fear. Todd looked nearly as terrified as she was.

"They're getting closer," Joss whispered beside me.

"Hide everything," Cole ordered. Now that we had a plan, he seemed better able to cope with the situation.

I decided it would be best to remain close to him. We crouched together behind one of the largest rocks. Astra was a few feet to my right, concealed by another of the boulders. Rollan was a little way beyond her. Joss was on my other side, to Cole's left.

All the packs were stashed close to the rock where Kisa and Todd hid.

The seconds ticked passed, marked only by the beating of my heart and the crashing of the waves. I strained to hear the other team's footsteps. Seconds turned to hours; every minute felt like an entire day.

I glanced at Astra. She was peeking out around her rock. I couldn't help but do the same. It was evening, and my hair was dark, so it probably wouldn't be easily spotted.

After an eternity, the other team came into view. Two average-looking guys from The Farm were in front. Behind them walked two girls from The Quarry. One was a short, dirty blonde, while the other was of average height with black hair. The second girl carried a sword identical to Cole's. Bringing up the rear was a larger guy from Treescape. I hoped Rollan didn't know him, or, at least, that they weren't good friends. Not that Rollan had many friends in his village. Most of his free time before the preparations seemed to have been spent with Joss in Riverside.

The other team trekked forward without glancing in any direction. They had nearly passed us entirely when one of the girls—the short one—said something and pointed in our direction. The black-haired girl turned toward us. I quickly pulled my head back a little, but not far enough that I couldn't see them. The boys in front stopped and seemed to be considering something. After a couple more minutes, the girl with the sword nodded, and the group headed toward the rocks.

Maybe Cole had been right all along; we should have filled our canteens and left. The water was attracting them to our position. However, we were safer hidden behind the rocks than if we had encountered them on the open beach.

I met Astra's eyes. Her gaze was steady as we listened to the other team approaching our hiding spot. She gave me a sudden nod and turned to do the same to Rollan on the other side.

I nodded to Cole and Joss, and then the five of us leapt as one upon the rocks. The other team froze. Astra's bow was drawn and pointed at the boy from Treescape, who was the second leader of his team. He fumbled to load his own bow.

"Stop," Astra commanded, and he froze, seeming to notice for the first time that he was in her sights. He slowly lowered the weapon.

"Are you going to shoot us?" the black-haired girl asked after a moment of silence. The long sword at her side, which marked her as the team leader, was undrawn, but her fingers ran listlessly over the hilt.

"Not if I don't have to," Astra replied.

"Will you allow us to fill our canteens with water?" she asked.

Astra shook her head.

"No," Cole called. "We can't let you do that." If the other team reached the water, they would see Todd, and then we would be in big trouble.

"We are camped here for the evening," I said, hoping to conceal the fact that we traveled at night. "Go back the way you came. In the morning, we will leave this place, and you can have the water to yourselves."

The leader of the other team considered for a moment.

"We need water tonight," she countered. "Our canteens are all empty, and we have come a long way today."

Even though it was growing dark, I could see several of the team members' canteens. From the way they dangled on their cords, I found it highly unlikely that the leader was speaking the truth.

"Throw us one of your empty canteens, and we'll fill it for you," Cole suggested. "That should be enough water to hold you over until the morning."

I didn't like the offer. One of us would have to get down and fill the canteen with our back to the other team, but it did seem reasonable.

I watched as the black-haired girl mentally searched for a reason to object.

"How do we know you won't put something bad in the canteen?" one of the boys from The Farm asked.

"You'll just have to trust us," Astra growled.

"But you clearly don't trust us," countered the team leader.

Cole didn't answer the accusation.

"The choice is yours," was all he said.

The leader glanced between Cole and Astra for a long moment, as if trying to decide on a course of action. We had the high ground, so an attack would have been stupid. Finally, she dipped her head to Astra.

"We will have to move on since you will not allow us access to the water." She began to edge away slowly, and the others did the same.

Instead of heading back the way they had come, they headed forward, the way we needed to go. My heart sank. We would have to pass by them again that night, and their watch would be much more studious now that they knew we were close at hand. Plus, these encounters would be repeated over and over again, until one of us attacked the other out of desperation and fear. I could already tell that this was not going to end well.

I glanced at Astra; her face was grim. She'd come to the same conclusion as me. As soon as the other team was almost out of sight, Astra jumped off her rock.

"Rollan, keep watch," she ordered. Everyone except Rollan climbed down.

"We've got to go," Cole announced.

"Why?" Kisa asked, emerging from her hiding place with Todd by her side.

"I can't imagine they won't be coming back for the water," I told them. "Even if they were lying about not having any, it's impossible to know how long it will be before more can be found."

Cole nodded.

"Unless they find some almost immediately, they probably won't risk going on without it," he said. "Our only chance is to follow and try to slip past them while they're waiting for us to fall asleep."

"I hope that works," Todd muttered.

"We have to try. Everyone, pack up," Cole ordered.

"And keep your weapons close at hand," I warned. "They might attack at any moment."

It didn't take long for all the bags to get packed. A few strips of turtle meat were handed around to give everyone strength, and we all drank from and refilled our canteens.

"Let's build a fire," Todd suggested.

"What?" I asked, at the same time Astra said, "Good idea."

She and Todd started gathering wood, Todd with only one hand. Joss and Cole jumped in to help them. Once they had amassed a good-sized pile, they got a fire burning. It was almost fully dark by then.

"That'll provide a good distraction," Cole announced as we walked away from the orange flames.

"We should stay in the wet sand again," I instructed.

261

Everyone nodded, and we started off, traveling even faster than on the previous night. The moon was smaller, for which I was very grateful, but I still felt impossibly exposed. I knew that with every step I took, I was getting closer and closer to death. In all likelihood, if there were an altercation, someone was going to die, a lot of someones probably.

It seemed that in my life, all I had ever done was lose things. Much as I hoped my team would make it through unscathed, I needed to prepare myself mentally just in case.

What if it's Cole? The horrible thought popped into my head unbidden. I could just see him getting himself killed trying to protect somebody like Kisa or Todd. It would be so like him.

I wasn't stupid. Going into the preparations, I had understood that there was a very real possibility that I would have to watch teammates die. To that end, a small part of my mind was already prepared to lose someone I cared about, but not Cole.

Maybe because I didn't remember a time before I had known him, maybe because he was my only tie to The Paramount and my childhood, or maybe just because he was the most precious thing in the world to me.

I could not accept the thought that he might die. I knew it was weakness to have something I could not stand to lose, but I could not force myself to feel otherwise.

"If we meet them here, on the beach," I said softly to my team, "drop your packs and stand ready with your weapons. Kisa and Todd, hide if you can."

Everyone nodded wordlessly.

We had only traveled for about twenty minutes when I finally saw what I was dreading. Movement ahead.

At least the waiting was over.

Astra saw it too and froze. There was nowhere for us to hide, so we put our backs to the cliff, removed our bags, and drew our weapons. My heart was hammering in my chest as the figures grew nearer and nearer. I wondered if they might possibly miss us all together. We were hidden in shadows and pressed close to the stone wall, but the cliff was less than twenty yards from the water. The other team would pass by not ten yards from where we stood.

Todd was mostly shielded from view behind Astra. Rollan and Joss were standing protectively in front of Kisa. All we could do was wait.

It didn't take long for them to reach us. They stopped about fifteen yards away.

"Planning an ambush?" their leader called. I couldn't make out much in the dim light, but I could see the moon reflecting off the blade of the sword she held in her hand.

"Just the opposite," Cole called back. "We were trying to avoid one." There was silence for a moment. "We don't want to fight," he added, truth ringing in every word.

"That's not what it looks like from where I'm standing," growled one of the boys. The voice was deep, and I assumed it belonged to the big guy from Treescape.

"Let's not do this," Astra called from my right. Even as she spoke of peace, I could see her pinpointing a target with her bow. "You go back to the water, and we'll be on our way."

"No good," came the leader's voice.

"Why not?" Cole asked.

"Two reasons," she replied. "First, we left all our packs at our new campsite, and we can't let you go along and take them."

"I promise we won't touch them," Cole declared.

Someone moved among their group. It was one of the boys, not the second leader from Treescape, but the taller of the pair from The Farm. I wasn't sure, but it looked like he had raised his arm over his head.

"I don't have any reason to trust you," the first leader told Cole.

"Come on," Cole responded, taking an unconscious step forward. "We're from The Clan. All of us. It shouldn't be this way. We're brothers and sisters."

"Pretty words, but not true. Out here, we're all enemies. The second reason we can't let you go is because then you'd be in the lead."

I didn't like the way she said the last sentence. I could hear her mouth twist into a smirk. The other team came a step nearer. Something flashed in the hand of the boy with the raised arm. I realized too late that it was a knife.

No! I thought, springing forward, trying to reach Cole and push him out of the way. I was too slow; the boy's hand came forward. At the same moment, I heard the sharp twang of a bowstring, and Astra dropped to the ground on my other side.

CHAPTER 28
BLOOD AND SAND

I expected Cole to lurch when the blade of the knife pierced him, but he only whipped around to look at where Astra had fallen.

I didn't dare take my eyes off the enemies before us. The boy who had thrown the knife vanished suddenly, and I couldn't tell where he was. The other contender from The Farm was crouched low on the ground.

I didn't have time to figure out why, because a second arrow came whizzing through the darkness, missing me by only a few inches. It struck the rocks and clattered to the ground.

All the training I had done during the preparations came back to me in a rush, and I charged forward. I had the sense that I was being followed, but I didn't know by whom. Another arrow went streaking through the night, this one from our side. Either Astra wasn't as severely injured as I feared, or someone else was using her bow.

The black-haired girl came to meet me. She had a sword, and I only had a knife, but I didn't feel afraid. Every beat of my heart filled my limbs with adrenaline. The tension was gone; there would be no more sneaking around, just the wild frenzy of battle. This was something I had spent a lot of time training for. This was something I knew how to do.

I dodged the first swing of the team leader's sword and tried to slash at her hand. I wasn't quite fast enough, though, and only connected with a bit of the blue cloth from her sleeve. I twisted around quickly to counter her next blow. It was a struggle to keep my footing in the sand, but I managed.

We backed away from each other, circling slowly, each looking for a chance to strike. Out of the corner of my eye, I saw Cole grappling with the smaller of the boys from The Farm. The other girl, the blonde one, was trying to fend off both Joss and Rollan with her staff. I didn't see any of the others, and my attention was called back to my own fight.

The black-haired girl leapt forward. I raised my knife to ward her off, but she dodged at the last minute, leaving me slightly off balance. She turned and struck. This time, I nearly didn't block her thrust, only managing to knock the blade away at the last second. My attempt was weak, and I felt the sword nick me on the leg. It stung, and I was sure to have a terrific bruise, but I didn't think I was actually cut.

Sticking out a foot, I managed to catch the girl's leg, and she stumbled several steps away. After a moment, she regained her footing, and we began circling again. I heard a cry from my left and resisted the urge to turn and look. It sounded like Joss, but there wasn't anything I could do to help him. My opponent risked a quick glance. Either she couldn't tell exactly what was going on, or she wasn't pleased with what she saw, because a scowl crossed her face. I used her moment of distraction to dart forward, but not quite quickly enough. She raised her sword and blocked my strike, almost knocking the knife from my hand.

I staggered away, trying not to fall. It took me only a few seconds to regain my balance and whip around. Sure enough, the girl was upon me, sword raised. This time, I hit the ground on purpose and twisted away, kicking out at her nearest leg. I didn't hit it hard enough to do any serious damage, but it forced her to halt, and I sprang to my feet.

She struck again, but I easily dodged her blow. Her mistake was that she kept looking exactly where she was going to strike. Before her muscles even contracted, I could tell precisely where her sword would fall. The next time, as the blade went by, I struck out, catching the edge of her hand with my knife.

The cry she let out was more of a gasp than a scream as the metal of my knife sliced into her hand. She instantly swung again, her eyes fixed on my head. I sidestepped, but the direction of her blade changed midair. Her eyes had deceived me this time.

She struck so quickly that the blade wasn't fully rotated. I didn't have time to dodge away, but all I received was the flat of the weapon. The blow fell on my right arm, my fighting arm, just above the elbow. I leapt backward, almost bumping into someone else. I didn't have time to turn and see who it was. I could sense that there was chaos and battle all around, but for me, it was just the two of us, and I would not let her win.

It felt like something wet was running down my arm. It could have been my imagination, or I could have been bleeding to death; there was no way for me to know. The girl advanced on me, sword held high, eyes glittering in the darkness.

I did the last thing she expected; I lowered my center of balance and charged her. She was too surprised to even lift her sword as my shoulder planted itself in her chest. I whipped around and slashed with my knife, aiming for where I assumed her counterstrike would come.

I severely misjudged.

Her build wasn't as solid as mine. The blow to her chest impacted her more than I anticipated. She had dropped to her knees, and my follow-up slash slit her throat as neatly as if I had planned the entire thing from beginning to end. In the dim moonlight, I could see the blood darkening her neck and even coming out of her mouth. Her expression was ghastly. Shock and fear mingled with pain and horror.

I stood frozen, the bloody knife still clenched in my grip. I couldn't believe what I had just done. I had killed someone; I had broken the greatest law I knew. This girl was just like me. She was of The Clan. We belonged to the same people.

The few seconds it took for her to finish dying were the worst of my life. The following moments, when her body collapsed limply to the ground, were equally horrible, as was every second after that.

More than a minute passed before I realized I was screaming. I tried to stop myself, but I was still in shock. I couldn't take my eyes from the crumpled form in front of me that used to be a living human being.

Another scream reminded me that I was in the middle of a battlefield, and my teammates were still in danger. I whirled toward the sound. Rollan was fighting the blonde girl alone, but they'd stopped when she let out the second scream.

She rushed forward, straight at me, fury filling her eyes. I was too stunned even to raise my knife, but she didn't attack me. Instead, she dropped to her knees in the sand beside her fallen leader.

There were quite a number of dark shapes lying on the beach. I desperately searched for Cole, hoping that he was all right. I finally made him out a little distance away; he was pinning a dark figure to the ground. I took a faltering step toward him and stopped. The figure struggled free from Cole and rose.

"You're beaten," Cole yelled furiously. "Get out of here!"

The figure hesitated and then began to back away. Once he was out of striking distance, he turned and ran.

A black shape loomed on the edge of my vision. I jumped and spun, knife raised, but it was only Astra. To my surprise, she wasn't limping at all. I hadn't even been sure she was alive during the battle.

Astra ignored me. Instead, she walked to the blonde girl, who was crouched over the body of her friend, sobbing.

"Get out of here," Astra hissed. "Go back to the water. We'll still leave your packs if you want to come back and get them."

The girl didn't move. Astra seized her by one arm and dragged her from the corpse.

"Leave!" she snarled.

The girl got uncertainly to her feet and ran after the boy, who had already vanished into the night.

"They'll have a better chance if they go together," Astra said in a quiet, dull voice.

"Is anyone injured?" Cole called.

"Joss got hit really hard," Rollan answered.

"Where is he?" Cole asked.

Rollan shook his head. "I don't know."

268

Everyone started investigating the figures lying closest to them. Everyone except Astra and me; we knew what was there, between us in the sand.

"Here he is," Rollan said in relief, which turned to panic. "He's not moving!"

Kisa hurried toward his voice. I heard her sniffling and knew she had been crying. Not that she had a real reason to cry. She'd spent the entire fight huddled against the cliff. She hadn't hurt anyone; she hadn't—killed anyone.

"Is everyone else accounted for?" Cole asked.

My throat was too dry for words, but Astra spoke for both of us. "Myra and I are here. Where's Todd?"

"I'm here." Todd's voice came from the cliff. He hadn't joined the fight either.

"That's everyone then," Cole said in relief.

I glanced around. There were three figures on the ground besides the girl with the sword. One was Joss; the others were a boy from The Farm and the one from Treescape.

Cole, Kisa, and Rollan crowded around Joss.

"Is he going to be okay?" I heard Rollan ask.

"Where did he get hit?" Kisa wanted to know.

I took a step forward to join them; however, my legs had grown weak and wouldn't support me. My knees gave out, and I ended up sitting in the sand. I didn't care. There was nothing I could do for Joss. If anything, it was better for me to stay away and give Kisa room to work.

I tried to calm my heartbeat and focus on what my teammates were saying, but no matter what I did, I couldn't stop seeing the girl's face. I didn't even know her name. Maybe that was for the best. I didn't want to know who it was that would never return to The Land of the Clan, whose family would always wonder what had happened to her. They would never know that I was the one who killed her, but I would never be able to forget it.

When Golla, a childhood friend of mine, died in The Valley of the North Wind, I blamed myself for not going with her or stopping her altogether. This was completely different. This time it was personal. I had struck her down with my own hand and watched her die with my own eyes.

I don't know how long I sat there. The others were silent. It felt like hours later that a gasp from one of them brought me back to myself.

"Can you hear me?" Kisa asked.

"Yeah," Joss answered.

Even in my shocked state, I felt some level of relief to hear Joss's voice. I also realized I was cold. Goosebumps covered my arms and legs, but I didn't bother doing anything about it. I just didn't care.

"That's good," Kisa continued. "Tell me what hurts."

"My side, mostly, and my head." Joss's voice was hoarse. Todd hurriedly brought him some water.

I suddenly realized Astra wasn't with them. I glanced over my shoulder to the last place I'd seen her. She was there but farther away. Her back was to me, and she was looking out at the horizon.

I closed my eyes. The girl's face was there. I opened my eyes and stared blankly at the group in front of me.

Finally, Cole and Rollan helped Joss get up. Dawn was approaching. Even with my back to the east, I could see the stars beginning to vanish. Soon it would be morning, and I would have to look at what I had done in the light of day.

The thought terrified me. They would all know. I couldn't hide it from them. Maybe if I hadn't spent the night sitting next to the corpse, I could have pretended that she somehow was killed in the melee.

I could still say that—pretend that it wasn't my fault, but I didn't want to deceive them. The truth, hideous and horrible, was still better than a lie that would fester inside of me for the rest of my life.

Joss's voice was growing stronger, and Kisa seemed more relaxed, so he couldn't have been in too much danger. They all seemed so happy, glad even, that all of us were okay. Didn't they understand? We had killed members of The Clan. Nothing would ever be okay again.

I could have gotten up and joined them. I was sure my legs would have held me, but I wanted no part of their happiness. Only once the entire sky was full of light did Cole turn my way. The relieved expression on his face vanished when he saw me sitting on the ground, my knees pulled up to my chest.

He began to walk over.

"Myra?" he said uncertainly.

I glanced at him without really looking.

"Are you okay?" he asked.

What a stupid thing to say.

He glanced over at the corpse of the black-haired girl as he lowered himself to the ground at my side.

"It wasn't your fault," he told me gently, reaching out to put a hand on my shoulder.

"Don't touch me," I shrieked, surging to my feet. I didn't want comfort. I didn't deserve it.

"Myra—" he started again.

"No!" I screamed as I turned on my heels and ran, leaving Cole kneeling in the sand alone.

I ran as I had never run before, like a hunted beast. I wanted to escape not just my team, but to get as far away from this tragedy as I could. It was impossible that I would ever be able to leave it behind because I kept reliving it in my head over and over.

I ran north, away from everything I had ever known. After a night of sitting on the cold sand, the sun gave me power, and my legs pumped faster and harder as I picked up speed. It had been a long time since I sprinted all out.

The best thing was that as long as I kept running, I wouldn't have to face anything. I committed every fiber of my being to escaping from what lay behind me.

I couldn't go back to The Clan now. I was stained. Dirty. Broken.

CHAPTER 29
REFLECTION

I don't know how long I continued running. I purposefully kept my mind from thinking about anything besides putting one foot in front of the other. My breath came in great gasps through lungs that felt tight and constricted. Sweat began to trickle down my back, but, strenuous as running was, stopping would have been much worse.

At one point, I felt my stomach heave, and I dropped to my knees to retch in the sand. Being sick left my insides feeling fluttery, but I was up and running again before my brain could register that my legs had ceased moving.

In the end, I only stopped because the beach was cut in half by a wide river. I was knee-deep in water before I finally halted.

Looking down, I saw my face reflected on the surface. Instantly, I recoiled and leapt backward. Somehow, I ended up sitting on the sand a few feet from the water's edge.

Once I was no longer moving, I could feel how tired I was. Not just my legs but my entire body ached. I took a few deep breaths, trying to gather my composure and decide what I was going to do.

Now it was a new face that I saw before my waking eyes: my own. I was a killer, a murderer. Instead of growing calmer, all the feelings I had tried to run from welled up inside me, and I began to cry.

Cry might be putting it lightly. Even weep is too gentle a word for the convulsions that went through my body. Hysterical sobbing is pretty near the mark. I rocked back and forth, letting more tears fall from my eyes than I had cried in my entire life.

It seemed to me that I wept for twice as long as I had run. Before I was ready to be done, I saw a figure approaching in the distance. Part of me hoped it was Cole, but beyond that, I didn't care. Even if it was a member of an opposing team coming to finish me off, I wouldn't have been particularly disappointed.

I did try to stem the flow of tears, more out of habit than because I cared what anyone thought at that moment.

Once my vision wasn't quite as blurry, I was able to tell that the figure was wearing black. It was Astra, of course, the last person I wanted to see.

I turned my eyes from her and stared out at the ocean.

"Nice," Astra said once she'd reached me. She walked past where I was sitting and knelt briefly to scoop up a handful of water, which she brought to her lips.

"It's fresh," she reported.

I ignored her.

She plopped down on the sand next to me, dropping her backpack and mine on the ground. Her hood was pulled up over her hair even though it was growing to be a warm day.

"The others are going to catch up shortly," Astra informed me.

I was still silent. I half wished I had tried to climb the cliffs. Even if I hadn't succeeded in escaping to the seclusion of the forest, falling to my death could not have been as painful as this conversation was going to be.

"We should get out of the sun," Astra announced, nodding toward where a tiny shadow, cast by the overhanging cliff, provided shelter from the brilliant light of the sun.

She rose and lowered a hand to help me up. I looked at it for a moment and then turned my eyes back to the ocean.

"What do you want, Astra?" I finally asked when she didn't retract the hand.

"You talked some sense into me once after a hard time in my life; I figured I'd return the favor."

The day she was referring to seemed so long ago that I had almost forgotten about it.

"Come on," she said. This time she didn't give me the chance to take her hand. Instead, she grabbed my arm and hauled me to my feet.

It was all I could do not to fall over, but she managed to guide me to the shade, where she shed her cloak before sitting down. Once seated, she handed me my knife, which, thankfully, had been cleaned. Otherwise, the sight of it might have made me sick all over again.

As it was, I barely managed to take it from her and drop it in the sand beside me.

We both sat silently for a long time.

"It's hard," Astra said, finally breaking the deafening silence. "It's hard to—to take a life." She wasn't watching me, but she was moving her fingers aimlessly through the loose sand.

"What do you know about it?" I snapped, glaring at her, the tears almost dry on my cheeks. I figured she was about to give me some lecture on 'life and death'.

What I didn't expect was the little half laugh, half sob that came from her. She had been looking down, but at that moment, she looked up. Her green eyes were rimmed with red.

"Didn't you notice?" she asked softly. "I killed two of them."

My mouth fell open.

"How?" I gasped. Suddenly, I remembered something else. "You—you got shot—"

"No, I didn't." Astra looked confused.

"But—you fell," I recalled. "I heard an arrow release, and then you went down."

"It was my arrow," Astra told me. "I was keeping an eye on the big guy with the bow, and almost didn't notice in time."

"The boy, the one with the knife, he was going to throw it at Cole," I recalled.

"Yeah. I shot him. I didn't even think about it. I just did it; right in the chest." She paused and closed her eyes, face creased with anguish.

"Then why did you fall?" I asked.

Her face smoothed, and she opened her eyes again.

"It was instinct. I knew the guy from Treescape was keeping me in his sights, same as I was with him. As soon as I released my first arrow, I figured he'd shoot me, so I dropped to load another."

"He almost shot me instead," I said accusingly.

"Sorry," Astra shrugged. "He had worked out where I was, so I needed to move. I hoped it would take him a little longer to find the rest of you."

I nodded in understanding.

"I shot him too," she added.

We were silent for a moment.

"Are you going to say that it isn't our fault?" I asked.

Astra shook her head. "It might be true, but I wasn't going to say that. It was a bad situation all around, but they wanted a fight."

"What makes you say that? They didn't attack when we first met," I pointed out.

"We had all the advantages then," Astra reminded me. "Last night, they thought we were on equal footing." Her voice dropped to just above a whisper. "If I hadn't shot first, our positions could easily have been reversed."

Astra looked past me, out to the ocean. The wind picked up a little; it blew her reddish hair out of her face, and I could see tears forming in her eyes. She closed them and shook her head gently.

"At least, that's what I keep telling myself." Her voice broke as she spoke, and I knew she was as torn up inside as I was. She seemed to be handling it considerably better. I mean, sure, she was here now, but that was only to find me.

It was worse for me, though. I had actually been close to my victim, not across the beach, picking them off one by one.

"How is Joss? And everyone else?" I asked, suddenly remembering that I hadn't gotten a full update.

Astra shrugged. "He's probably got a cracked rib and a nice bruise on his head. Rollan hurt his leg a little, but he can still walk, and you ran off without telling Kisa you were injured." Astra gestured to my arm.

I looked down and, for the first time, saw the gash above my elbow. Almost my entire arm was coated in dried blood. How had I not noticed?

Because all you can see is her face, I remembered.

"It's nothing," I told Astra.

She nodded without looking convinced.

"Why didn't Cole come to find me?" I wondered, trying to change the subject.

Astra raised an eyebrow. "He thought you didn't want to talk to him."

"So, he sent you?"

"I sent myself. Cole is a great person, but he doesn't understand how you think."

"And you do?"

"To a certain extent, yes. Plus, I understand what you're feeling."

"You don't understand," I told her, finally letting the words flow. "You killed them from across the beach, on purpose. I—I didn't mean to kill her. I turned around and—and I thought she'd block me. I really did. I didn't want to hurt her. I didn't want to hurt anyone, but—but I—"

My voice faltered, and I started crying again, but that didn't stop the flood of words. "I cut her throat. I cut her throat and watched her die. She was so scared. It could have been me, and I would have been scared too. It must be the worst thing in the world to die here, so far away from—from—" I couldn't get the last word out. It was a word I had avoided saying for so long.

"Home," Astra finished for me. She was crying now too, and, somehow, I knew she was crying for me, for my pain. My sobs weren't loud, but they shook my body. In contrast, Astra wasn't sobbing; she simply let the tears run down her face unchecked.

We sat there for a while longer, both of us staring out at the water. Finally, I stopped crying.

"It wasn't like that," Astra murmured softly.

"What?" I was barely able to hear her words.

"I shot the first one, and he died. But when I shot the second one, I only hit him in the thigh." Astra looked at me, her green eyes burning with agony. "I thought maybe he'd surrender, maybe he'd give up. I ran forward and wrestled his bow from his hand. I didn't expect him to attack me when he had an arrow buried six inches in his body, but he did. Almost killed me too.

"We ended up on the ground, struggling with each other. He should have won, but as he was trying to choke the life out of me, my hand fell on one of his arrows, which had fallen from his quiver.

"I shoved it into his eye." I looked at Astra in shock. "He screamed, and there was a lot of blood. Then he went limp, so I guess I beat him in the end."

"I'm sorry," I said, regretting my earlier words. "I didn't know."

Astra shrugged. "I'd do it all again, to protect my team," she vowed. "I just hope I don't have to."

Finally, I understood why she hadn't killed Todd. For the first time, I was glad that she spared his life. I wished like crazy I could have done the same for the black-haired girl.

"We should have moved on yesterday instead of staying by the water," I sighed. "Cole was right, and we didn't listen to him."

"It wouldn't have mattered," Astra replied. "We were bound to end up fighting them at some point."

"But if they'd stopped for the night behind us at the water, we could have outdistanced them," I insisted.

"For a time," Astra agreed. "Until Kisa dropped from exhaustion or someone twisted an ankle. Then they would have caught us and attacked."

"Maybe not," I argued. "What makes you so sure they wanted a fight?"

In answer, Astra gestured to the far side of the stream, which cut us off from the rest of the beach. I strained to see what she was pointing at. Among the rocks, I noticed a couple of objects that didn't fit with the landscape.

"They made it this far last night," Astra explained as I realized that what I was seeing were the backpacks from the other team. "They had fresh water, far more than we did. The only reason for them to double back was to attack us."

A little bit of the weight resting on my chest was lifted.

Why? I asked myself. *They weren't trying to get our water or supplies, even. They clearly were able to survive on their own, so why did they attack us?*

The other part of my brain provided the answer. *They didn't want us to beat them.*

I was competitive, very competitive, but was I *that* competitive? Would I choose to kill someone rather than have to live with them defeating me? I didn't think so; although, my actions of the night before stood in evidence against me.

"The rest of the team should be along soon," Astra told me. "They're having to move slowly because of Joss and Rollan. That was the other reason Cole stayed behind: he's stronger, and it's easier for him to help the others along."

I nodded, feeling guilty that I wasn't there to share the burden. We were a team; I shouldn't have run away. I just hadn't wanted to face them. I still didn't want to face them, but I couldn't run anymore.

I wondered what kind of reception I would get. They knew now that I had killed someone. Would it change how they thought of me? How Cole thought of me?

"It's going to be all right," Astra promised as if reading my mind. "You're their friend."

"I guess," I mumbled, noticing that she said 'their friend' instead of 'our friend'. We were getting along better lately, but that was how our relationship seemed to be. We'd be fine one minute, and then something would happen, and we'd end up arguing for hours. If we did win the trials, we were going to be in for some long council sessions.

I needed to get my emotions together and act normal, like Astra. Then the rest of my team probably wouldn't think any more of the subject.

I would, of course. It seemed to me that I would be haunted by the face of the dead girl forever.

However, there could be no more outbursts like the one that preceded my flight. I would have to bury the feelings of guilt and dread, just as I had buried my emotions of sadness and loneliness after losing my father. Only this would have to be far deeper. Every once in a while, I allowed the memories of my father to rise to the surface, just to make sure I would never forget him. It wouldn't be the same in this case. I didn't want to remember anything about the previous night.

How deep was my soul? How far down could I push the recollection of what I had done? *As far as you need to in order to survive*, a voice whispered in my head. *You're a survivor; you'll make it through this. It doesn't matter what you have to do; you can and will endure.*

CHAPTER 30
RECOVERY

It didn't take too much longer for the rest of the team to arrive. I must not have run nearly as far as I'd thought.

The sun wasn't even close to its high point when they came into view. Seeing them, I felt panic rising in my chest and almost started crying again. I took several deep breaths, bracing myself for our reunion. I wiped the fresh tears from my face and tried to achieve a completely emotionless state. At least that would be better than sobbing like a three-year-old.

As the group got closer, I could see that Cole had one of Rollan's arms pulled over his shoulders, and he was helping the younger boy limp along. I also noted that Todd was assisting Joss in the same way. If the night before had all been just a bad dream, I would have laughed at what a battered and bruised bunch they were.

I hadn't noticed earlier, but Cole had a busted lip and a shallow scratch on his face. I glanced at Astra to make sure she wasn't injured as well. The only thing I saw were faint bruises beginning to appear on her arms and around her neck.

Kisa was the first to spot us. She pointed and called something to the others before taking off at a run toward the spot where Astra and I sat. To my utter astonishment, she flung her arms around my neck as soon as she reached us.

"Oh, Myra! I was so worried about you!" she exclaimed.

Warmth spread through me at her affectionate greeting. Obviously, Kisa was willing to overlook my actions.

"Last night was terrible, but you shouldn't have run off. It could have been dangerous," Kisa went on, still not letting go of my neck.

"Better check her injury," Astra advised before Kisa strangled me completely.

"Her injury?" Kisa asked, pulling back. She gasped when she saw my blood-smeared arm.

"I don't think it's as bad as it looks," I told her.

"Let's get it cleaned up," Kisa suggested, gently taking my other hand and leading me to the little river running across the sand.

We went downstream a bit, and I knelt in the shallows, letting the cool water engulf the lower half of my body. Using my left hand, I began rubbing away the blood. Kisa had dropped her pack by the cliff when she hugged me, but she had a few purple pieces of cloth in her hand. It made me flinch to think of another dead girl who would never wear those clothes again.

Once my arm was mostly clean, I offered it to Kisa. She didn't have any herbs left, since nothing of the sort grew on the sandy shores, so all she could do was clean the nasty gash a bit more and wrap it up.

"You did the right thing," Kisa whispered to me, making sure the others, who were just reaching Astra, couldn't hear. "I'm glad you killed that evil girl and saved us all."

I blinked. Why would she say such a thing? That wasn't how it had happened. If anything, Astra was the one who saved us by taking out the two biggest threats. Someone, probably Cole, must have told it to Kisa differently for my sake.

I glanced at Cole and saw that he was making his way toward us. Slowly, I waded through the shallows to reach him. I couldn't help but wince at our last interaction.

Things were so easy with Kisa. Whatever they told her made me out to be a hero, not a murderer. Cole knew better. He had probably seen the entire incident. He could lie to the others, but we both knew the truth.

"Hey," he said, coming to a halt. Droplets of water fell from my saturated, maroon clothes as I stepped out of the river to join him on the bank.

Kisa nodded to Cole and then headed back to the others, leaving us alone. I longed to follow her, to put off facing Cole. There was going to be nothing more painful than looking into his eyes and seeing his disgust for me and what I had become.

"You lied to her," I murmured, not meeting his gaze.

Cole hesitated before responding. "Not me; Astra. Besides, if you hadn't kil— hadn't done what you did, the fighting wouldn't have stopped, and someone else might have gotten hurt."

I nodded, surprised that Astra had lied to everyone and given me so much credit.

Cole was lying too. He was trying to make me feel better. I'd always known he was a kind person, but I wasn't as naïve as Kisa. I would never forgive myself, even if Cole somehow could.

"She was beaten, Cole," I whispered, trying to make him understand. "I didn't have to—I didn't mean to—"

"I know," Cole said gently. Slowly, he reached out and took me in his arms. This time, I didn't pull away from him. When Kisa had hugged me, it felt good and sincere. Cole's embrace felt awkward. I think he expected me to cry or something, but I had already shed all the tears I had.

When he released me, I still couldn't look him in the eyes. I knew now that I was the evil in the world.

The Clan taught that evil was something that only existed in the Broken. It was a lie. There was evil in me, or I would never have killed that girl. There was evil in us all.

The other team hadn't needed our water or our fire or our food. They attacked us for no reason.

On the flip side, if we really wanted to circumvent a fight, we could have. Not once they were upon us by night, but before that. We could have stopped and let them stay ahead of us, or even gone back to The Land of the Clan instead of pressing on. Each of us knew what the consequences would be, and we accepted them.

Deep down, I knew someone was going to get hurt, but I wasn't able to take my eyes off the prize. Now three people were dead, and two more might not survive the night.

"Are you okay?" Cole asked as I stood unmoving, lost in remorse. It was still a stupid question, but I checked my reaction.

I had buried my feelings.

Now I could lie to him and make it sound like the truth.

"I will be." My voice was as cold as ice.

He smiled then, not a happy smile, but a sad one. Maybe he understood me better than Astra thought.

Wordlessly, he turned and rejoined the others. I followed a moment later, my face dead of life and my emotions securely under control.

Numb. Numb was the best way to describe how I felt that day.

It would have been better if we could have kept moving, gotten back to our routine, and continued the journey. Then, I might have been able to pretend nothing had happened.

However, with both Joss and Rollan injured, we wouldn't have made it very far, and there was an abundance of water where we were.

We only had a few scraps of turtle meat left, which were soon gone. Todd showed Astra and Kisa how to cook some of the seaweed left by the high tide.

I watched but didn't join in. All afternoon, I remained crouched in the shadows close to the cliff. I couldn't remember afterward if the day was hot or cold. I didn't feel anything except the air that periodically filled my lungs and the regular beating of my heart.

I wished they would stop. I didn't want to breathe; I didn't want to live.

Cole gathered a huge pile of wood while the others cooked the seaweed. Kisa offered me some, but I couldn't imagine eating anything. Rollan and Joss slept most of the day, and no one woke them up to try the seaweed.

"We should get the packs from across the stream," Cole said. It was the first time anyone had broken the silence in almost an hour.

"Will they have supplies and food in them?" Todd asked eagerly.

"Probably," Cole answered. "But I wouldn't feel right using them. We could take them back down the beach and leave them for the other—"

"Wait, why?" Todd interrupted.

"They aren't ours," Kisa pointed out.

"So, their owners are mostly dead and—" Todd broke off suddenly as Cole drew a sharp breath and glanced at me. I didn't react; my face remained frozen.

"It just doesn't feel right," Cole began again. "The—the others might come looking for the stuff. They'll need it to get back home."

A little later, Cole and Astra waded across the stream and gathered up the packs. They carried them back the way we had come until they were almost out of sight. Night had fallen by the time they returned and joined the rest of us, already sitting around the fire.

Todd shook his head. "I'm so confused. What is going on? Are these 'others' your friends or enemies? What did you mean when you said 'home'? Where are we going?"

There was a moment of silence. Cole and Astra exchanged a glance.

"Remember how you have to get someone's teeth?" Astra began.

"You mean pass the rite of manhood?" Todd asked, almost as if she was insulting him. "There are many ways to pass the rite; it doesn't have to be getting someone's teeth, you can—"

"Yes, that," Astra interrupted. "The Clan has something much the same. Every fifty years, teams are sent out to complete a task. Whoever does it first and comes back with at least three members will lead The Clan for the next fifty years."

"What's the task?" Todd wondered.

"We don't know exactly," Cole admitted.

Todd shook his head in disbelief.

"So, you're just wandering around without any direction?"

"No," Astra told him. "We were given instructions on how to find a special mountain."

"And what's going to happen when you get there?" Todd asked, turning to Astra.

"We don't know," Cole repeated.

"But—" Todd started.

Astra held up her hand. "Show him the scroll," she directed Cole.

He hesitated and glanced at me as if expecting an objection. I didn't meet his gaze. I was watching the fire consume the wood, much as I had spent the afternoon watching the sea.

Fire and water. Complete opposites, yet so alike. Both had immense power and force. But put them together, and they canceled each other out.

"Here," Cole removed the scroll from his bag. It was tattered and smudged but still mostly legible. He spread the paper on the sand, careful to keep it well away from the sparks that occasionally leapt from the flames.

Cole smoothed the scroll, trying to get it to lay flat, but the parchment had been wound for too long. Astra moved to help him hold it down.

Todd studied it for a moment and then looked away.

"You see," Cole began. "Every team was given an identical copy. We've found the ocean; next is the mountain."

"I can't read." Todd spoke so softly I hardly heard his words.

"Really?" Kisa asked in surprise.

Todd shook his head.

"At all?" Cole asked.

"I can write my name," Todd said. "But nothing more than that. Letters are a waste of time unless you're a priest."

"What's a 'priest'?" Joss asked. He was finally awake. Rollan was stirring beside him.

"Someone who devotes their life to the worship of one particular god," Todd answered.

"Oh," Joss said. "So, how do they do that?"

"They organize gifts for the god and maintain the god's temple," Todd answered.

"I've never heard of a 'temple'," Kisa piped up. "Is it part of the gods' powers?"

I heard the words the others were speaking, but most of their meaning eluded me. Everything in my mind was fuzzy and unfocused, which was fine.

"A temple is a building designed for a god," Todd told her.

"How so?" Joss asked.

"Each of our gods has a large, beautiful temple. We go to the temples of the gods our house follows to offer sacrifices and pray. Those—" before he could finish, Todd was interrupted.

"What do you mean by sacrifices?" Rollan asked. He had finally woken up enough to jump into the conversation.

"To sacrifice means to give something up for another," I quoted. Everyone turned to look at me like I had just materialized out of thin air. I realized it was my first time to speak in half a day. My voice sounded dry and scratchy, even to me. I didn't really mean to answer, but it was a habit.

For a moment, I was back in school. "Myra, what does sacrifice mean?" a teacher would ask. I always knew the answers. I always got the questions right.

"Yes," Todd continued after a moment, still watching me warily. "Usually, we sacrifice an animal."

"How?" Kisa asked.

"By killing it and using the blood to cover the altar of the god, then the body is burned," Todd told her.

There was complete silence for a moment.

"That sounds pretty wasteful," Astra observed.

"It brings a good harvest, protection, and health," Todd replied. "The gods grant their favor to whoever brings the richest and finest sacrifices."

"You make it sound so real," Rollan snickered.

"It's not funny," Kisa protested. "They kill all those poor animals for no reason. I mean, I understand that we have to eat, but killing them just to burn the bodies seems pointless."

"But there is a reason," Rollan declared between giggles. "The invisible guys must be satisfied." As he finished speaking, Rollan dissolved into laughter.

Kisa gave him a sharp nudge.

"You're being rude," Joss told him with a meaningful look.

Rollan sighed, and his laughter subsided.

"You won't think it's funny when a god smites you," Todd warned. This almost made Rollan go off again, but Kisa gave him a fierce look—well, as fierce a look as Kisa could muster.

After reflecting for a moment, I remembered Todd occasionally dropping part of his meal into the fire. I hadn't thought anything of it at the time, but now I wondered if he was doing it because of the traditions of his people.

"There was once a foolish man who mocked the gods," Todd began. "He was born to The House of the Warrior. When he was little, he played along, pretending to believe everything his parents did, but the whole time, he doubted in his heart.

"After he passed the rite of manhood and became an adult, he no longer had to pretend. His father was greatly grieved by his son's lack of faith. He prayed to the gods that they might smite his unbelieving offspring. The gods listened and answered his prayer.

"The fool tripped into the fire a short time later, burning out his eyes. Then, since he couldn't see anymore, he walked straight into the back end of a horse. The animal kicked him and broke his leg.

"No one would help such a fool, and he was left to crawl around in the dirt, trying to find scraps of food to eat and puddles of water to drink.

"He spent a month like that before he finally died, all alone, in great shame."

"That's awful! Why didn't someone fix his leg and give him food?" Kisa asked reproachfully.

"Because he rejected the gods, and no one wanted to risk being punished themselves for helping him," Todd answered.

"That still doesn't seem right," Kisa protested.

"That's because you're a nice person," Rollan told her. "When the gods smite me, I'm counting on you to be the one to take care of me. Not that I have anything to worry about."

"Leave Todd alone," Cole intervened, rolling up the scroll. "We have our beliefs, and he has his."

"Actually," Todd said, "what are your beliefs? If you don't believe in the gods, what do you believe in?"

There was a long moment of silence.

"Ourselves," Astra answered blackly. "We believe that we are a perfect society; the only kind of society that can last."

Now it was Todd's turn to be confused.

"That's weird," he said.

"Not at all," Kisa replied. "We don't run around wasting resources. We have a perfectly managed system. No one is ever hungry or left in pain."

"She sounded like she was from The Paramount there for a second," Rollan whispered loudly to Joss. Both boys laughed.

"How does that work?" Todd asked.

"Everyone pitches in and does their fair share," Joss told him.

"What happens if you don't?" Todd wondered.

"You have to," Kisa insisted with wide eyes. "If you don't do what you're supposed to, you'll get a mark!"

"And a 'mark' is…?" Todd turned to Astra and Cole since Kisa wasn't explaining herself very well.

"A mark is a figurative thing," Cole clarified. "Once you reach three, you are forced to leave The Clan."

"So, then you do leave people alone and without food," Todd pointed out. "It's exactly the same thing we do."

I could see Kisa flush a bright red. "But once they've become Broken, they can't stay with us," she almost shouted.

"Calm down, Kisa," Joss said, patting her arm. "There's nothing to get upset about."

Shamefaced, Kisa ducked her head.

"Sorry, Todd," she apologized. "I see your point. But the man in your story was right about there not being any gods. It was just an accident that blinded him, and the rest followed as a result. We only make people leave when they have done something wrong. The Broken are evil; we can't have them around."

I laughed then—a dark, humorless laugh simply for the irony of it all. It startled everyone. They looked at me like I was going crazy. I raised my eyes from the fire and really looked at them for the first time in hours.

"There's one sitting right next to you," I told Kisa. She opened her mouth, but couldn't say anything. My eyes traveled the circle, examining each of their shocked faces in turn.

"Who do you think Todd's people are?" I asked.

My gaze fell lastly on Astra. Her green eyes met mine and held them. She remembered. All the others wanted to forget and let it slip out of their minds, but she never had.

"But Todd's not evil," Kisa said in a small voice.

Astra spoke then. I knew what she would say before her lips even started moving. It was the same truth that I had spent all day mulling over and trying to come to grips with.

"We're all evil."

CHAPTER 31
THE THREE-DAY LORD

We took the next day off to rest. I tossed and turned, never seeming to be able to find a comfortable position. When I finally drifted off, it couldn't have been for more than an hour or two, and I didn't feel any better when Rollan shook me awake.

My head was in a fog cloud, like the ones that sometimes rolled off the lake in Riverside. They rarely made it as far as The Paramount, but every once in a while, I'd go out the door in the morning and find myself wrapped in a misty cloak. I enjoyed those days. Often, I used the mist to sneak up on Rasby so I could scare her.

I hoped she was doing all right back in The Paramount. The more I saw of this world, the happier I was that she had remained there instead of coming out here with us. When I got back, there were a lot of things I needed to say to her, starting with 'I'm sorry'.

As night fell, we departed. I began feeling hungry for the first time in days and even tried the seaweed, but it was as vile as Todd described. No one seemed to care for it, but boys really will eat almost anything.

Joss and Rollan were walking out in front, hoping to find another turtle or something similar. Meat would have been good, but what I was missing most were fruits and vegetables. Sadly, there weren't likely to be any of those as long as we were on the beach.

The sky was filled with thick clouds that night, so the moon provided very little light. Several times, I felt the sudden cold of a wave washing over my feet. I didn't bother wearing my boots anymore, which made walking easier.

Earlier that evening, just as the sun was setting and we were preparing to head out, I'd found a long crack in the leather of

290

my left boot. I decided then that I would go barefoot as long as we were on the sand.

It was harder to keep up a good pace with nothing in our stomachs. We took numerous breaks. No one had much energy, hungry and injured as we were.

Both Rollan and Joss were recovering quickly. The wound on my arm was mostly closed and didn't bother me in the least. The bruise on my leg was turning an ever-darker shade of purple. My knee-length shorts concealed it for the most part.

I hadn't even mentioned it to Kisa. I didn't want anyone to worry about me more than they already were. Cole hadn't spoken two words to me since the battle. Aside from Kisa treating my arm a couple of times a day, the others left me alone as well. They were so careful in what they said, too, like I might break and do something stupid. I knew myself better. Soon, I would have my feelings completely under control. This tragedy would always be a part of me, but I would not let it destroy me.

When night became morning, we didn't bother pushing on any farther. Instead, we took shelter close to the cliff. The others tried to make a meal of the seaweed, but I immediately lay down and went off to sleep.

The next night was much the same, only with even less light. I was hungry enough to eat a few bits of seaweed myself. It left me thirsty, but I didn't dare drink more than a mouthful from my canteen without knowing how much longer we would have to go before finding water again.

Sometime in the early morning hours, we heard a cry of joy from up ahead.

"A turtle!" Rollan yelled.

There was some splashing as the rest of us hurried to catch up. Joss and Rollan got there first and pulled the creature away from the water's edge.
It was larger than the last one and probably weighed at least sixty pounds.

Finding driftwood in the dark to build a fire was hard, but we managed. I was too hungry to care if anyone saw the light cast by the flames in the blackness of the night.

We began devouring the meat before the first round was completely cooked. It was disturbing to see everyone's gaunt faces, lit only by firelight, with blood dripping down their lips and staining their fingers. We were all becoming feral, nearly as wild as the animals we hunted.

"Tell us another story," Rollan suggested to Todd as we placed more meat close to the fire to cook.

"A happy one this time," Kisa pleaded.

Todd sighed. "I hate happy stories," he complained.

"You'd prefer everyone end up dead and miserable?" Astra asked wryly.

"Well, when you put it like that, no. But when everything works out smoothly in the end, it doesn't seem right," Todd replied.

"Can you try for one that doesn't end horribly?" Cole asked.

"I guess," Todd conceded. "I'll tell you the story of the lord who was lord for only three days. It's a mysterious story that happened nearly three hundred years ago and is recorded in the history of our people."

"Perfect!" Kisa clapped her hands together in excitement.

Todd thought for a moment before beginning. When he was telling stories, he always used a different voice than when he was simply speaking. He still maintained his strange accent, but his words grew richer, deeper, and more mysterious.

"The People of the Brimming Lake are divided into two factions," he started explaining in his regular voice. "The river, which flows from The Brimming Lake to the sea, acts as the boundary, and there are only a handful of bridges. People rarely cross over, since most business can be done on one's own side of the city.

"If you stand on the shore of The Brimming Lake and look down toward the ocean, the followers of the king dwell on the right side of the river and those foolish enough to worship the usurper, the warrior, are on the left side of the river.

"Many times throughout history, The House of the King and The House of the Warrior have clashed. There have also been times of peace between the two. In order to preserve that peace as much as possible, one man is chosen to be ruler over both houses. Whenever he dies, each house holds a tournament, and all those who have completed the rite of manhood—except the priests— have the right to compete to become the champion of their house.

"Once the champions of both houses are chosen, they are pitted against each other in a fight to the death. The winner becomes The Lord of the Brimming Lake and rules over both houses for the remainder of his life."

Todd seemed to have just been giving us a general overview of his people's customs, not actually telling a story, because he suddenly switched to his other voice.

"The story of the three-day lord begins on the day that Lord Husamtaskin died. There was a period of mourning, which lasted three days. He was much beloved by his own house, The House of the Warrior, and was not thought of unpleasantly by The House of the King. He had won the tournament when he was a middle-aged man and was never eager for war. He reigned twenty-one years with only a handful of minor skirmishes between the houses.

"After the three days of mourning were finished, the tournaments began. According to tradition, each house has four days to hold their tournament and select a champion.

"The champion from The House of the Warrior was the old ruler's nephew, Tohopkeion. He was a large man in his early thirties with powerful muscles and a permanent frown etched into his face. He had never agreed with his uncle's peaceful views and was eager to assert the warrior as the rightful leader of the gods.

"When The House of the King learned that Tohopkeion was to be the opposing champion, they despaired, for the winner of their tournament was a young, golden-haired man. No one was quite sure how he managed to defeat opponents so much stronger and older than himself in the tournament.

"His name was simply Matthan. He was the youngest of seven boys. Each of the others had been named for one of the gods. When he was born, his father doubted that his youngest son would ever compare with his larger, stronger brothers, so he gave him a simple name and never thought twice about him.

"Matthan had become a man only two moons before the start of the tournament. Instead of slaying someone to pass the rite of manhood, as most do, he returned with a vast number of gold nuggets. Anyone who finds such treasure is recognized as having been favored by the gods and having completed the rite.

"At sunrise, Tohopkeion and Matthan met in battle. Tohopkeion fought with a massive broadsword, so heavy many believed that he was the only man who could wield it. Matthan chose only a simple, long-shafted spear.

"The battle took place in front of the palace, the only building that spans the river between the two houses. It has a large, open expanse in the front, which is built right over the top of the river. On the left side is the temple of the warrior, and on the right is the temple of the king.

"As soon as the first rays of the sun came up over the sea, Tohopkeion charged Matthan. The younger man was nearly overcome in the first rush, but Matthan was very agile and managed to escape the brutal assault. The two dueled until the sun was high in the sky.

"Tohopkeion did most of the attacking and was exhausted from wielding his massive blade. Matthan, who wasn't even twenty yet, spent the morning dodging and parrying with his spear. He was still fresh and could have continued for many more hours. Tohopkeion realized that his strength was failing, so he made one last, great charge. It was a clumsy action, and lithe Matthan easily blocked the thrust before making one of his own. He stabbed his spear right through Tohopkeion's sword hand. The great man dropped his blade and fell to the ground before Matthan.

"The crowd was shocked, for they had been certain who the victor would be. Once they recovered from their surprise, those from The House of the Warrior called for Tohopkeion to rise and fight on. Those of The House of the King called for Matthan to finish off his opponent.

"Instead of striking a killing blow to Tohopkeion, Matthan surprised everyone by stepping forward and kicking the large sword into the river on the open side of the courtyard. It disappeared beneath the current and was never seen again.

"'Hear me!' Matthan called. 'Three moons ago, while I was completing the rite of manhood, I had a vision of a god.

"'He told me that without mercy, our people would cease to exist. He said that our war-like nature would lead us to doom on faraway shores, where death would come upon us without warning. There, we will be dragged down by our own hatred unless we learn another way to live.'

"At first, the crowd was silent. Such words had never been heard in front of the palace before.

"'Finish him!' Matthan's father bellowed at his son.

"'No,' Matthan said, throwing his spear away. 'I have won the day. I am the new Lord of the Brimming Lake. Things are going to be different now, and I will not slay my enemy. I have heard directly from a god, and I will act upon what has been told to me.'

"The head priests of both houses are the ones responsible for overseeing the duel, and, after hearing Matthan's words, the head priest of The House of the King stepped forward. He was an old man. His hair was white, and he was considered to be the wisest of all the priests among both houses.

"'Who has told you such things?' the old man asked. 'It is against the gods' natures to be merciful to one they consider an enemy.'

"Matthan dipped his head in respect to the priest. 'I admit I was unsure myself, but I saw a vision of us all united for war. We set sail in many boats, ready to conquer a new land. However, every vessel sank before reaching the shores, and nearly all those inside perished. I am convinced that this will be our future if we do not change our path.

"'You have asked me the name of the god who sent me the vision. I believe it was the ninth god, the unknown god.'

"When he said these words, the crowd burst into confusion. No one ever spoke of the ninth god. Some did not even believe he existed.

"Matthan suddenly pointed straight toward the palace. The people there parted like water to reveal the small shrine of the unknown god. A true temple had never been built for him, only a small structure to keep the rain off the few items that were placed there. The largest item was a box made of unknown material, about this size." Todd held his hands about two feet apart.

"It is black with golden markings and sits on an altar in the very back of the shrine. Over the years, many people have tried to open the box, but all have failed.

"'On the day that box is opened,' Matthan declared, 'our future shall be decreed. For life and peace or the darkness of death.'

"His words again caused a stir among those gathered. It was a long time before the head priest could make himself heard over the clamor.

"'Calmly please,' he said in a soothing voice, 'we must inquire of the gods whether this is truly a message from the heavens.'

"The people quieted at his words.

"'But who is our lord?' someone called.

"The priest was silent for a moment. 'At this time, we have no reason not to name Matthan Lord of the Brimming Lake.' There was scattered cheering at his words, but most people, even those from The House of the King, seemed uncertain.

"'But Tohopkeion still lives!' a man from The House of the Warrior called. 'If Matthan is too weak to slay his opponent, then Tohopkeion can still challenge for lordship.' Everyone's eyes turned toward the large man who had been defeated.

"'I will not challenge. Not for today, at least,' Tohopkeion responded, his wounded hand clutched to his chest.

"So, Matthan was made Lord of the Brimming Lake. The iron scepter of the lords was placed in his hand, and the silver crown of eleven points was set on his head.

"The crown was a special relic of the lords. Most lords simply handed it down from one to the next. However, when a lord died who was considered especially monumental, another point was added to the crown.

"Matthan brought his parents and older brothers to live with him in the palace. His first declaration was to abolish violence between the two houses. The twenty-one years preceding his reign had been mostly peaceful, but since the old lord's death, tensions were stirring.

"The night following the crowning of the new lord, several young men from The House of the Warrior attacked a group of men from The House of the King on their way home from a dinner gathering.

"There would have been almost immediate retaliation had Matthan not learned of the attack very quickly. He dispatched the palace guards to quell the outbreak.

"In the morning, he addressed his new subjects from the steps of the palace. He rebuked them for the attack and tried to help them see the future.

"'My brothers,' he cried so all could hear, 'there has been peace among us for over twenty years. Do we truly want to shatter it now? This is our chance to grow beyond what we have always been. If we can band together, we will be far stronger. Together, we could expand throughout the whole earth in peace, instead of squabbling over this small piece of ground. Together we can—'

"It was then that his speech was interrupted by the appearance of a tall, hooded figure shrouded in a black cloak. There was a simple but unfamiliar red design stitched into the dark fabric. On his shoulder was perched a black crow. As the crowd parted before him, the bird let out three high-pitched calls. The figure stopped only when he was directly in front of the young lord, beside the shrine of the unknown god. Then he raised his hand and pointed a gloved finger at Matthan.

"'The path you are trying to follow is closed,' the black figure said in a deep voice. 'It will lead to your death and the death of all who follow in your footsteps.'

"Before the palace guards could react or anything could be said, a great mist rose from the ground and surrounded the tall man. He was hidden from view in less than a minute. When the mist cleared, the man and bird had vanished without a trace.

"There was panic among the people, and Matthan did not finish his speech. The palace was searched, as well as the entire land, but no clue could be found as to where the man came from or where he had gone.

"In the morning, on his third day of lordship, Matthan rose early and watched the sunrise. Before breakfasting, he went to the shrine of the unknown god. Someone saw him kneeling there in prayer, but no one in The Land of the Brimming Lake ever saw him again."

CHAPTER 32
LOST

"So where did he go?" Kisa demanded.

"No one knows," Todd replied in a mysterious voice. "He just vanished, like the man in black on the day before. No trace of him was ever found. He was the last lord to wear the eleven-pointed crown because it disappeared along with him.

"Most preferred to forget that the incident ever happened. Tohopkeion was named Lord of the Brimming Lake three days later, and his reign was one of the darkest The People of the Brimming Lake had ever known. All the peace that Matthan talked about was washed away in the blood that was spilled over the next forty years."

Todd stopped talking.

"That can't be the end of the story!" Cole cried. "Who was the man in black? What really happened to Matthan?"

Todd shook his head. "The common theory is that the figure was a ghost or an evil spirit or possibly even one of the gods in disguise. They were displeased with Matthan for trying to lead the people away from them, so they smote him into oblivion."

Everyone was staring at Todd in disbelief.

"I told you it was a mystery. What were you expecting?" Todd protested. He was almost laughing at everyone's expressions.

"I have a question," Astra said. Todd glanced in her direction. "What was in the box?"

"The box?" Rollan asked.

"The one in the shrine," Astra clarified.

"It's never been opened," Todd told her. "It sits in the same place to this day. No one dares try to open it anymore or even go near that place. It's considered bad luck after what happened to Matthan."

"So, this story is true?" Kisa wondered.

"Yes," Todd answered. "I told you, it happened about three hundred years ago. Since then, no lord has ever spoken of peace.

"Throughout the centuries, there have been many reports of people seeing the hooded figure in black marked with the red symbol. Most are just kids messing around, but every once in a while, someone well-respected claims to have seen him."

"That's so creepy," Kisa shuddered.

Todd grinned. "Well, some people are afraid of him, but not me. I'm a loyal member of The House of the King, so there's no reason a spirit or a god should bother me. The rest of you, on the other hand…"

His voice was grim, but I could tell by the mischievous light in his eyes that he was joking. Astra smiled and gave his good shoulder a gentle shove.

"Don't frighten the children," she laughed.

"I'm not a child," Rollan protested.

"And I'm not afraid," Kisa added, stifling a yawn.

There was still at least an hour before dawn, but everyone was worn out and stuffed with turtle meat.

"I'll watch first," Astra offered.

Even though I couldn't remember the last time I'd slept for more than a couple of hours, I doubted I'd be able to sleep at all. I was wrong. The moment I closed my eyes, I was wrapped in utter senselessness.

Kisa woke me for my watch in the late afternoon. I felt better—much better. Somehow, after sleeping so soundly, the events of the past few days felt far away, like the memories of my bygone childhood.

I moved out of the shadow of the cliffs and sat in the sun for a while, enjoying the heat on my skin. Out of the corner of my eye, I saw Cole rise and begin packing his bag.

In the warm afternoon air, I felt we could have talked more freely. However, much as I hoped he would, he didn't come to join me. After another twenty minutes, I gave up and returned to the shade. The water was running low again, and I didn't want to dehydrate.

The days ran together after that. We would always set out as soon as it started getting dark. The nights crept by slowly. Our only indication of the passing time was the moon. It changed from a half to a crescent, then vanished altogether before beginning to wax once more.

One morning, as twilight came creeping across the sky, I glanced toward the cliffs on our left—or at least, where they had been the night before. Once all the stars disappeared, there was finally enough light to see that the cliffs were gone. They had been replaced by a long expanse of sand and then a tree line about a hundred yards away.

I stopped dead in my tracks and stared.

"What's wrong?" Cole asked.

I shook my head. "This isn't right," I realized. "Did we miss it?"

"Miss what?" Joss wondered.

"The mountain," I told them.

"We couldn't have," Astra insisted. "There haven't been any mountains since the two we passed through to get here, and neither of them had any spires."

"But we've been traveling at night," I pointed out.

"The scroll said a mountain," Astra replied. "There's no way we could have missed it. We don't travel that far in one night."

"What if this mountain wasn't as big?" I panicked.

"If they had meant hill, they would have put hill," Astra sighed in exasperation.

Ignoring her, I turned to Cole.

"We have to go back," I told him. "Look ahead. There are no more cliffs; the land is flat. We must have missed it."

"I—I don't think so," Cole said.

"We must have!" I insisted, practically stomping my foot in frustration. Taking a deep breath, I tried to gather my thoughts. The sun was rising, and everyone was tired. "Let's talk about it while we rest," I suggested, desperate to keep us from going one more inch in the wrong direction.

"Good idea," Astra agreed, even though everyone knew I wasn't talking to her.

After five minutes, we made it to the cover of the trees. It was strange to leave the waves behind. Everything seemed so quiet without the sound of them lapping on the sand.

Kisa and Rollan settled down to sleep immediately, while the rest of us stood in a loose circle. I shot Todd a 'get lost' look, but he didn't seem to notice.

"While it is possible that we've passed the mountain, I don't think it's very probable," Cole said, starting the conversation.

"It's entirely possible and probable," I cut in. "We've been walking in the dark."

"Myra," Cole said, not quite meeting my gaze. He hadn't looked me in the eyes since the battle. "All the other directions have been very obvious; I don't see how we could miss something as large as a mountain, even in the dark." His condescending words sounded like they were directed at a small child.

"Something obvious in the daylight could be completely hidden at night," I couldn't help pointing out.

"Yes, but most nights we've had the moon and some visibility," Joss recalled. "I honestly think we would have seen a mountain."

"There's no way to know that for sure," I snapped, hot and angry. Did everyone always have to be against me?

"If we go back," Astra started slowly. "There is a good possibility we will run into other teams."

There was no need to say more. Cole was already shaking his head. Astra knew exactly the right thing to say to strengthen her position.

"Then I don't see any option except to move forward," Cole announced. He turned to me again, still not really looking at me. "Myra?"

Now what was I supposed to say? That I didn't care if there was another fight? Or if one of us died? Or if I killed someone else?

"Whatever," I muttered and turned away from them. I stalked off into the trees before settling down on a little patch of grass. I was sick of sand and sick of this entire thing.

Didn't they realize that we would have to go back at some point? We were likely to run into many more teams on our way back to The Land of Clan than we had met coming. Was I the only one who ever thought ahead?

No one woke me for a watch that day. Astra took the last shift, and I was awake before I heard her calling my name. It was almost dark, and the others were already assembled.

Cole was addressing them as I drew near.

"The plan is to continue north. Astra and I discussed it, and we still think it's best to keep traveling by night.

"I know it's harder to see, but we should all pay a lot more attention to our surroundings. If you even think you see anything that looks like a mountain, don't be afraid to speak up."

Everyone nodded.

"Okay, let's head out," Cole directed.

I walked past him stiffly. "Thanks for making me part of that discussion," I muttered over my shoulder.

He hurried to catch up with me.

"You disappeared," Cole protested defensively. "Astra thought we should give you some space."

"Because she's the one who knows me so well," I snapped.

Cole lengthened his stride and stepped in front of me, blocking my path completely. He turned around, so we were facing each other.

The rest of the team started clustering around us, uncertain of why we had stopped.

"Keep going," Cole told them. "We'll catch up."

Astra lingered for a moment.

"Are you sure?" she asked Cole. I narrowed my eyes. What did she expect me to do? Murder him too?

Cole nodded at her, and she walked after the others, looking back over her shoulder with a concerned expression as she vanished into the darkening twilight.

"What do you want from me, Myra?" Cole asked.

I met his blue gaze, feeling relieved that he was finally looking at me.

"I thought you wanted me to be a good leader. Well, I'm trying. And I'm sorry we disagree about our course of action, but it was bound to happen at some point. I tried to hear what everyone—"

"Stop, Cole. Just stop," I interrupted him. I could feel tears coming. I didn't know why, but as long as he was carrying on with his prepared speech, I was in danger of breaking down, and I didn't want him to see that. Whatever had been between us once, it felt like it was slipping away.

He did stop. He stopped and rested his gaze on me pityingly.

"I know things have been—rough for you the last couple of days. It hurts me to see you in so much pain, but I was trying to give you time, just like Astra said."

I stiffened. What did *she* know about our relationship?

"Was that the wrong thing to do?" he wondered.

"I don't know," I sighed.

"You said you'd be okay. Astra told me the same thing. She suggested we be patient." Cole didn't seem to understand that what he was doing was the opposite of helping.

"I want things to be the way they were," I blurted out. "Before any of this." Cole nodded as I continued. "Before the trials, before we were on a team, before we met Astra."

I hadn't meant to say that last part aloud. When Cole heard her name, he froze.

"What does Astra have to do with it?" he asked.

"She's always coming between us," I muttered, desperately hoping he would understand.

"No, she's not," Cole protested. "Astra is my second team leader. It's natural that I should turn to her when—"

"You'd rather have her by your side than me, wouldn't you?" I challenged him. "Tell me truthfully, if you had to choose between the two of us, who would you pick to be on this team?"

Cole was shaking his head. "I can't choose between my teammates," he insisted. "You're like my family!"

"So, you can't choose between me—who you've known your whole life—and some girl who just randomly got thrown in with us?" I hissed.

"Why can't I be friends with both of you?" he wondered.

Friends. I felt my heart grow heavy as soon as the word left his lips. Without responding, I stepped around Cole and started trailing after the others.

"Myra, please," he cried from behind me. "I'm friends with you both, but I don't feel the same way about Astra as I do about you."

I turned on him.

"How do you feel about me then?" I demanded.

He seemed taken aback by my directness.

"I—I—" he stammered. "I'm so confused right now. But I told you once that I didn't know what I'd do without you, and that's the truest thing I've ever said. I want you by my side. I need you."

There was a moment of silence, and then he rushed on. "It's good that we disagree. All it means is that we're seeing the situation from different perspectives. That's how I know things aren't slipping through the cracks."

Always the peacemaker.

I sighed.

"Are we okay?" Cole asked.

"Yeah," I lied.

Clearly, he didn't understand why we ever hadn't been. It seemed cruel to confuse him further by saying there was still a problem. Especially since I was starting to think that the problem was named Astra.

"Okay, great." Cole smiled, but even in the near dark, I could tell that it wasn't his real smile. He did offer me his hand as we ran to catch up with the others.

Astra was hanging back behind the rest of the team. She turned when she heard our approach. I noticed that the first thing she observed was our linked hands. It was the best moment of the entire night.

The second best moment occurred about three hours later, when we found a small spring running into the ocean. I had been thirsty for days, carefully preserving what I had left in my canteen. It was amazing to be able to gulp down as much fresh water as I wanted.

We couldn't stay long, of course. However, I felt refreshed, both from the water and from venting to Cole, even though we hadn't really gotten anywhere. There was a distance between us now, and I couldn't explain why. Nor could I see a path back to the place we had once been.

I was losing him, and it was killing me.

CHAPTER 33
VISITORS

I wasn't sure how much the others heeded Cole's words about being observant, but I made it my personal responsibility to keep watch for anything that might pass as a mountain. I still feared that we had missed it in the dark or that we would if we continued traveling by night. The thought of walking across burning sand all day with the glare of the sun beating off every surface was enough to make me hold my tongue.

When dawn broke, we made for the forest once more. Instead of going straight to sleep, we searched the trees to see if there was anything to eat. The meat-only diet we were on was exhausting. After a few minutes, Cole called out for us to come and see something. It was an apple tree. I had never been happier to see a piece of fruit in all my life.

Joss climbed the tree and started dropping apples down to the rest of us. Rollan went up too. He made it to the top, breaking several of the smaller branches on his way.

"Look," Todd said, pointing to another tree beside the first. It was a second apple tree. Without warning, Rollan gave a wild cry and threw himself from one tree to the other.

"Rollan! Be careful!" Kisa shrieked, and then she glanced at Joss, who appeared to be positioning himself to follow. "Joss, don't!" she called.

"I can make it," he said.

"Please don't!" Kisa begged. "You'll fall and get hurt!"

Almost before she had finished, Todd called, "Give it a try; you can do it!"

"Yeah, come on, Joss!" Rollan echoed Todd's words.

Astra laughed and shook her head.

"Boys will be boys," she muttered, taking a bite out of an apple.

"What about your cracked rib?" Kisa reminded him. "Your arms aren't as long as Rollan's. You'll hurt yourself!"

With a great heave, Joss leapt from the tree. I half expected him to end up on his face in the dirt, but he managed to get hold of the second tree and hang on. From the ground, we applauded his efforts.

"See? I made it," he crowed triumphantly to Kisa.

After picking all the apples we could carry, we headed back toward the beach. Once we made camp, Kisa unwrapped Todd's arm. It had been in the makeshift sling since we reached the beach.

"How is it?" Astra inquired, coming to stand behind Todd and looking over his shoulder.

"It hasn't healed completely quite yet, but I don't think there will be any problems," Kisa told them. "You should be able to start using it again. Only for gentle things, though; no heavy lifting."

Todd smiled. "Great! Although, I'm starting to get used to doing everything one-handed." He winked at her.

I just shook my head and lay back among the roots of a tree. We were right on the edge of the woods, which enabled us to keep an eye on the beach.

Rollan woke me around sun high.

"Todd is next up for watch duty," he announced, stifling a yawn.

I nodded and rose. It wasn't as warm that afternoon as it had been the past few days. Was fall beginning already? I tried to count how many days we had been traveling, but there was no way to remember.

That bothered me more than it should have. I was from The Paramount; we always knew the exact number of everything. However, I had let the days slip by unheeded. I dreaded making the return journey in the cold, as summer turned to autumn and autumn to winter. It would be much harder to survive once the snows fell.

I turned my eyes toward the beach. The ocean waves were sparkling in the sunlight, but there was something else glittering just above the waterline. I took a few steps forward, shading my eyes against the glare.

It wasn't until I crossed half the distance to the water that I realized what the object glistening on the sand was. A fish, a huge fish!

It was still alive and flopping around. I ran forward and seized the creature to keep it from wriggling its way back into the water. I ended the fish's life with my knife. Using all my strength, I was able to lift the creature by the tail, my arms fully extended. It wasn't all that heavy, but I refused to let the slimy body touch me.

Quickly, I brought the fish back to our camp.

I had my own piece of flint, but Rollan was the one who held onto the broken arrowhead. I considered trying to find it in his backpack, but decided it would be too hard now that the pack was stuffed to the brim with apples.

Instead, I used my knife against the flint to create a spark. There was a bountiful supply of dry bark for kindling and plenty of branches for fuel, so I didn't have to waste much time gathering a woodpile. I butchered the fish as best I could since it was too large to cook whole.

Either the smell or the sound of sizzling flesh woke Cole. I saw him rub his eyes and sit up.

"Where did that come from?" he gasped, walking over to stand next to me.

"I found it," I told him. "It was washed up on shore."

"Nice," Cole commented, adding a few pieces of wood to the fire. "We got apples and a fish all in one day. What luck."

I glanced at him sharply. "You don't actually believe all that stuff about luck and the gods' favor, do you?" I asked.

Cole laughed softly. "Not really. Todd said it was just an expression."

"Expression or not, I don't like some of the things Todd tells us," I confided to Cole.

"He does have a wild imagination," Cole agreed. "I find it interesting."

"Does that look done to you?" I asked, pointing to some of the fish that was cooking on a rock close to the fire. I was ready to change the subject.

Cole poked the meat and even broke off a small piece to sample.

"A little longer, I think," he told me.

"Cole," I began. I couldn't meet his eyes. "I'm sorry about some of the things I said last night."

"Yeah, me too," Cole replied. I was sure he meant what he said, even though it sounded more like an automatic response to me. He had never liked conflict. He'd probably tell half a dozen lies to keep from fighting again. I let it drop; there was nothing more to discuss.

"Do you want to get some more rest?" I asked. "It's my turn to watch, and I've got this under control."

Cole looked at me with unhappy eyes, as though he sensed that I was pushing him away. Not that he was wrong. At that moment, it was easier to be alone than try to deal with our tangled emotions.

"Okay," he agreed.

Only as he walked away did I realize how much I secretly wanted him to stay. We had been best friends once, and almost more than friends. Where had all those feelings gone? Had I buried them along with everything else?

I always tried so hard to forget the painful moments of my past, but I never meant to forget how much I cared for Cole. People came and went in my life all the time; few ever left any real impression: my father, Golla, Rasby. Those all ended badly, so why would I have expected my friendship with Cole to be any different?

If you're smart, you'll stop longing for the past and bury this relationship with all the others, a voice whispered. *That way, it won't hurt you anymore.*

No! I thought desperately. *I don't want that!*

The noise of snapping branches pulled me back to the present. Everyone was still asleep, but I could hear at least two people walking toward us through the trees.

"Cole, Astra!" I called softly, moving to shake Joss, who was closest to me. Astra was awake the moment I said her name.

I pointed to the woods where the noise was coming from, and she nodded, fitting an arrow to her bow.

"What—" Joss started to say when he awoke, groggy and disoriented. I clapped my hand over his mouth and shook my head.

Cole and Todd were both up and appeared ready for anything. Rollan was clambering to his feet as well. Kisa had a terrified look on her face as she huddled close to Rollan and Joss. We grouped together, weapons raised.

The girl who stepped into view a moment later couldn't have been more surprised. She froze, her brown eyes growing huge with alarm. A boy emerged behind her. Without noticing that she'd stopped, he bumped into her, and she stumbled forward a couple of steps before regaining her balance. Slowly, she raised her hands in surrender. The boy drew his dagger, but his eyes were wide with terror. He knew he didn't have any hope of winning.

Astra was the first to move; she lowered her bow.

"Halin," she gasped. The girl turned to see who it was that had spoken her name.

"Astra," she breathed in relief, lowering her hands. "I'm so glad to see you."

It was only then that I noticed the girl's weather-stained clothing had once been gray. The boy's clothes were a faded light green.

Astra stepped forward, not uncautiously, and took the girl's hand in greeting. Halin was smaller than Astra but strongly built. She was severely underweight, as if she hadn't eaten for numerous days. I wondered if we all looked that emaciated.

The girl's brown hair was a mess. It was curly and fell a little past her shoulders. There were leaves and twigs tangled in every inch of it, as if she had given up on keeping it clean. She was maybe a year younger than I was.

311

"Is it safe?" the boy in green asked Halin. He was slender and only a little taller than Joss, even though he was probably about the same age as Cole.

"Yes," Halin replied. "Astra is a friend."

The boy lowered his knife and then came forward to meet Astra.

"I'm Tusion of The Golden Fields," he introduced himself.

"I'm from The Golden Fields too," Kisa announced, stepping out from behind the rest of us to inspect the newcomers.

Halin's forehead furrowed.

"How many of you are there?" she asked.

I could see her counting us in her head and finding one too many. There was no way to hide Todd now.

"This is Todd of The Making," Astra said smoothly, pointing to him. "The rest of his team died in a rock slide at the cliffs." Astra gestured back the way we had come. "He escaped with only a broken arm, but he couldn't make it back on his own, so we let him come with us."

"I see," Tusion murmured.

Halin was looking past us with hungry eyes at where the fish was cooking by the fire.

"Would you like to eat with us?" Cole offered.

Halin moved to step forward, but Tusion put a hand on her shoulder. "I don't think so, we should probably—" he started.

"It's okay," Halin assured him. "I told you, Astra is a friend."

She stepped forward with Astra, and the two walked to the fire.

"Myra found the fish this morning," Cole told everyone, although he directed the comment at Halin and Tusion. I could see he was trying to hide the fact that everyone else had been asleep less than ten minutes ago.

"And there are lots of apples," Kisa said, holding one out to Tusion. I wondered if she'd seen him before. She couldn't have known him well, or she would have greeted him like Astra greeted Halin.

With all nine of us around the fire, it felt crowded and hot. The newcomers didn't seem to mind, and both began eating with gusto.

"How did you get fire?" Tusion asked.

I hesitated. It was bad enough that they had seen Todd; now we were going to give away all our other secrets too. Before I could stop him, Joss held up a flint and tossed it to Tusion.

"You just rub it against your knife's edge to make sparks."

"Really?" Tusion exclaimed in disbelief. "We might have stood a better chance if we had been able to build fires. Where did this come from?" He was examining the stone in his hand.

"From a river," Joss told him. "We have lots; you can keep that one."

"Thank you very much." He glanced up, and his eyes went straight to Todd.

I held my breath, hoping neither of them had spent much time in The Making.

"You can come back with us," Tusion offered, looking at Todd. "We might be able to make it now."

"You're heading back?" Cole asked.

Halin nodded. She had been too busy stuffing food into her mouth to say much since we sat down. As soon as she finished the mouthful she was working on, she spoke up. "We've had the worst time of it. We got attacked by another team only a few days in and lost two of our team members, including our leader."

Both she and Tusion looked at the ground.

"I couldn't believe they attacked us," Tusion added. "I mean, we're all part of The Clan. Even if this is the trials, it's still a horrible thing to do."

There was a long moment of silence.

"What about the rest of your team?" Astra wondered.

"We had a little boy, Risto of Riverside. He got a fever and never recovered," Halin reported in a sad voice.

"I knew him," Joss recalled softly. "Well, mostly his big brother, but he always liked to tag along. I'm so sorry to hear that he died." Joss looked stunned by the news.

"We kept going, but the day before yesterday, our new leader was trying to catch some fish in the ocean and stepped on something sharp and nasty," Tusion continued the story. "The wound wasn't that bad at all, but he died anyway."

"A venomous sea urchin," Todd muttered softly.

"What?" Tusion asked, giving Todd a strange look.

The tempo of my heart picked up. If they learned the truth, what would we do? Would I be willing to kill members of The Clan to protect a Broken?

CHAPTER 34
SECRETS

"He said that we'll have to pay more attention," Astra cut in smoothly.

Halin nodded somberly.

"I wish we had." She glanced at Tusion. "We should probably get going while there's still daylight. Thank you so much for the food."

"There are apple trees that way." Kisa pointed into the woods. "You should gather some up before you go."

"Thanks, we will." Tusion flashed her a smile.

Halin's attention turned back to Todd.

"Do you want to come home with us?"

Todd shook his head.

"My arm hurts a lot," he told her. "Kisa knows about herbs and stuff. I'd rather stay with her, so she can make sure it heals right."

Todd was almost as smooth as Astra.

"You didn't say it was hurting you," Kisa exclaimed, making me wince.

"I didn't want you to worry," Todd told her. "I'll explain later."

Kisa nodded vigorously.

"We'll leave you then," Tusion announced, rising to his feet.

They started to go, but Astra reached out for Halin's hand again. This time, she embraced the smaller girl.

"Be safe," I heard her whisper. In a louder voice, she said, "I'll see you back at The North Wind."

The other girl smiled and nodded.

"Will do," she replied, following the boy through the undergrowth toward where we had found the apple trees.

"I'm so glad we were able to help them," Kisa sighed blissfully.

"Me too," Cole agreed. "This is how it should be."

Despite Cole's remark, everyone breathed easier once they were gone. I started packing up what was left of the fish. We still had some turtle meat and lots of apples, so the food was sufficient for the time being, but I still wasn't sure it was wise to share it with others.

"Well, that answers that question," Astra announced.

"What question?" Cole wondered.

"We clearly have not passed the mountain yet," Astra replied.

"How do you know that?" Rollan asked.

Astra nodded toward where the two contenders had disappeared.

"They were ahead of us this whole time and traveling during the day. If there was a mountain, they would have seen it."

"Oh," Kisa gasped. "That makes sense."

She was right, of course. Why hadn't I thought of that?

We left Todd on guard duty and settled down to get some more rest before evening. I half expected that Todd would slip away now that his arm was better, but he was still there in the evening.

When I opened my eyes, the sun was minutes from setting. I didn't feel like eating anything. Sleeping on a stomach full of fish and apples had not been a good move. Joss, Kisa, Rollan, and Todd went back to the fruit trees one more time and returned with their bags and arms full. We wedged as many apples as possible into the packs. Mine felt like I added fifty pounds to it.

I saw Kisa staggering under the weight of her own pack until Rollan took half the apples from her and stuffed them into his already overloaded bag. He squeezed some into his pockets as well, but they were still left with a few extras. I sighed and took one from him to eat as we walked. All too soon the packs would begin growing light again.

I thought about the meeting with Halin. Her gray clothing was faded almost to white. Astra's clothes were tattered on the edges, but they still maintained their dark coloring.

"Astra," I began, my mouth half full.

"Yes?" Astra answered, turning back to me.

I swallowed before continuing.

"Why do you and a few of the others at The North Wind wear black?"

Astra sighed.

"I suppose there's no reason not to tell you. But it might take a while to explain, so I suggest we get moving."

Everyone started forward, but we remained grouped tightly. No one wanted to miss what Astra was going to say. I knew several of the others were just as curious as I was about why Astra didn't wear the traditional gray color of her village.

"The Clan is not always as it appears," Astra started, not addressing only me, but the entire team. "Some of you have probably noticed certain things that are 'just not talked about'. There's also the fact that some questions go unanswered. Well, the truth is, The Clan has many, many secrets, known only to a few."

"Like you?" Cole wondered.

"Yes," Astra replied softly.

There was a long pause.

"But why?" Joss asked.

"I'm not sure myself. If I needed to take a guess, I would say that it's to maintain order and control," Astra told him.

"So, the secrets are a good thing," Kisa piped up.

"I wouldn't say that exactly." I could tell how careful Astra was with the words she chose to use.

"Why do *you* get to know all the secrets?" Rollan muttered, almost grudgingly.

"Well, I guess you could say I kind of figured them out," Astra admitted. "I witnessed a few things and started asking questions. When I wasn't satisfied with the generic answers, the

Keepers of The North Wind took me into their confidence. Mostly, it was because my mother was one of them, and everyone had such high hopes that I would be just like her."

"What is a 'Keeper'?" I demanded.

"It's just what it sounds like," Astra explained. "Someone who keeps The Clan's secrets."

"So, you're one of these Keepers?" Cole inquired.

Astra nodded. "Yes. They decided that it would be easier to tell me the truth than to let me cause trouble trying to find the answers on my own. However, there were consequences.

"There is always a price for knowledge. I wasn't allowed to tell anyone what I knew. They also said that, since I was a Keeper of The North Wind, I was never allowed to request a transfer and I would have to stay at The North Wind forever."

That would be a hard price to pay; condemned to remain forever in the isolated north. I couldn't imagine a worse fate, but it probably didn't bother Astra in the least. She actually liked it there.

"So, everyone who wears black is a Keeper?" I asked, a bit confused about how her being a Keeper related to my question.

"Sort of," Astra replied. "The Making, The Quarry, The Golden Fields, and the rest, each has a handful of Keepers. We only know secrets about our own villages."

"This is unbelievable!" Cole sounded outraged. "And the council is okay with this?"

There was an awkward pause.

"The Clan Leaders are the only ones who are aware that this is going on. The council has no Keepers on it."

"How do you know?" I asked. "That could be another secret."

"Possibly," Astra conceded. "But I don't see what purpose that would serve. We have a system that allows us to identify ourselves to each other."

"What is it?" Joss asked.

"Our clothing," Astra replied. "Each village has a color, but certain people wear shades far darker than the others.

"Cole and Myra," Astra addressed us, "I'm sure you've both seen that your parents' clothes are a very dark shade of red."

Both of us were silent for a moment.

"You're right," Cole gasped.

I didn't respond. I had noticed my fair share of strange occurrences. Unlike Astra, I had been raised well enough not to ask. Yet, she was the one they rewarded and took into their confidence.

"There's a woman at The Golden Fields who always wears really dark green clothes. Is she a Keeper?" Kisa asked.

"Probably," Astra asserted. "Keepers are everywhere. We don't normally have much to do with those from other villages, but if you see one of them doing something, you don't interfere or ask questions. You look the other way.

"Most of the villages only have a few. The Barracks is the only place where there are more than twenty."

Rollan cleared his throat. "Why do Keepers exist?"

"I've already told you; they exist to keep the secrets of The Clan," Astra replied.

"Yes," Rollan said impatiently, "but what kind of secrets are there that the rest of The Clan can't know about?"

"She isn't going to tell you," Cole spoke up. "She's not allowed."

"There are no rules here," Astra mused.

"But still," Cole pressed on as if he were afraid to learn the truth. "You probably shouldn't tell us. The other Keepers who have been in the trials didn't, or I'm sure everyone would know about their existence by now."

It took Astra a moment to answer him.

"I'm the only Keeper who's ever been in the trials," Astra finally admitted. "The Keepers watch the youth of their village much as the council watches the potentials. When they find someone that they think is right for the job, they wait until they're an adult, and then approach them."

"Is that why Litis didn't want you to be a potential?" I asked, referencing the woman from The North Wind who had demanded the council make Astra exempt from both the preparations and the trials.

Astra almost laughed. "No, Litis isn't a Keeper, just very opinionated.

"Actually, Core, Myna, and the other Clan Leaders were furious when they found out I had been made a Keeper at such a young age. You see, the Keepers do track the number of years between the trials, even though the council are supposed to be the only ones who know. However, when I was young, I had a bad habit of telling people I was a few years older than I really was so I could skip school more often. I knew it was wrong, but I always hated school and wanted to be in the stables instead.

"It was several years later that I became a Keeper, and they didn't ask me my age or check the birth records. They just assumed I was going to miss the trials because they imagined me a few years older than I was. I'm sure they wouldn't have told me anything if they'd realized the truth. But they didn't see any harm in bringing me into the group a little early, not knowing that I would become a contender."

Are there any rules they actually followed at The North Wind? I thought reproachfully.

"So, what kind of secrets do you know?" Joss asked wonderingly.

Disgusted as I was, I had to admit I was curious now too.

"Well, I've already told you I'm allowed to go into The Valley of the North Wind," Astra began. "But I don't just go there to train horses. That's also where the forge is."

"What's a forge?" Kisa asked.

"It's a place where metal is made and shaped," Astra told her.

"They make metal?" Kisa gasped.

"Where did you think it came from?" Astra wanted to know.

"Don't they dig it out of the ground at The Quarry?" Rollan wondered.

320

"No," Astra told him. "They can get the elements for metal from the ground, but they have to process it in a very specific way. That is done at a hidden location in The Valley of the North Wind. They used large rocks to hide the passage when the trials started.

"Normally, one or two horses need to be taken there every couple of days to be shod. That's the main duty of The Keepers of The North Wind."

"But why couldn't they build the forge in The Land of the Clan?" Joss asked. "I mean, I always assumed they did something like that to make fishhooks. I just thought they did it at The Making instead of in the valley. It's all the same to me, so why all the secrecy?"

"I think—and this is just what I have gleaned from being nosy—it's to keep ordinary people from learning how to make weapons," Astra reported.

Her words were met with silence. The community Astra was describing didn't sound a thing like The Clan I knew.

"What other secrets are there?" Cole wondered.

Astra considered for a moment before answering.

"Myra and Cole, you already know this, but there are guards at the exit to The Valley of the North Wind at all times."

"Why?" Kisa asked.

"To keep people out," Astra informed her.

"You mean, people like Todd?" Rollan wondered.

"Yes. As well as people who have been exiled."

"Well, that makes sense," Kisa responded. "We don't want bad people coming back to The Clan."

Astra hesitated and then added, "They aren't all bad people. Sometimes people are exiled for things that are not against the rules."

"Like what?" I inquired.

"Innovation," Astra told me. "They call it a form of wastefulness."

"What do you mean?" Cole wondered.

"There was a man who was trying to create a new irrigation system for The Golden Fields," Astra began. "It would have saved everyone a lot of time and effort. He didn't hide what he was doing because he didn't think it was wrong. Even still, when the Keepers found out, he was exiled immediately. They told the others in the village that he requested a transfer to be closer to his brother, but the man didn't have a brother."

"That's terrible!" Kisa cried. "Why didn't they just give him a mark?"

"Because he didn't break a law, so there was no justification. No one at The North Wind, not even the other Keepers, knew what was really going on, but I have a knack for finding things out," Astra explained. "Most of them turn a blind eye to everything that isn't their business, but I can't. I want to know the truth, even if others don't."

"How do you know he wasn't actually doing something wrong?" I couldn't help but ask.

Even though it was pitch black, I could feel Astra's burning gaze on me.

"Because they kept him overnight in The North Wind before exiling him. I walked past the place where he was being held and heard yelling, so I stopped to listen. The man was trying to explain himself and was begging to be taken before the council so they could hear him out.

"A Keeper from The Barracks, they're always the ones who handle the exiling, explained the fake reason he was being exiled twice, but the man kept arguing. So, finally, the Keeper told him the truth just to shut him up: that he was deemed a bad influence for the community and couldn't be allowed to remain. Thankfully, I was able to escape unnoticed."

"What's going to happen now that you've told us?" Rollan asked nervously.

"Nothing," Astra replied with humor in her voice. "We're going to win the trials, so you would have found this all out anyway when we got back."

CHAPTER 35
ENDLESS SANDS

After Astra's revelation, we walked along in near silence for the rest of the night. I had a lot to think over.

A year ago, I wouldn't have believed anything Astra said. But in the past eight months, I was starting to see that there was more going on within The Clan than was visible on the surface. Once I had been completely assured of the perfection of my people, but not anymore.

The rest of that night and the following day I was preoccupied, trying to figure out if I even knew what I really believed and why I believed it.

I finally convinced myself that Astra was exaggerating a bit. The average person didn't need to know everything about how The Clan worked. The average person didn't care, and it would not benefit them to be privy to such knowledge. Surely that was why some things were kept secret.

The days became a blur as we continued walking along the beach by night and sleeping in the woods by day. The thing that stood out most in my memory was the warmth of the sand when we set out in the evenings and how quickly it grew cool in the night air. The weather was much colder, and the days weren't as hot.

It troubled me to imagine what would happen if the winter caught us before we even reached the mountain indicated in the scroll. I kept this concern to myself. The others still seemed to be enjoying the journey for the most part. I, on the other hand, was ready to reach the end of our quest.

The thought of coming back all this way was exhausting. I was also haunted by the fear that we might not be the first ones to arrive at the mountain, and our entire endeavor would be for nothing. I couldn't imagine anything worse than making this arduous journey only to fail because we had arrived too late.

As we trekked along, I was torn between trying to push my team for speed and keeping quiet. I didn't want to stir up anxiety, but there was a burning desire in my heart that drove me to walk faster and awaken everyone earlier.

Each time we took a break to rest or made camp before the sun rose, I nearly screamed. The tension just would not go away. I couldn't force it down, and I couldn't bury it.

"Why did the gods come to earth?" Joss asked out of the blue one evening.

We had begun walking earlier than usual, and there was still an hour of daylight left.

"You said they lived in a perfect place, watching the earth from above. Why did they leave it?"

"Because the humans turned away from them," Todd replied.

"But why?" Joss asked. "Why did that matter?"

Todd chewed his lip for a moment. "I guess it was because they were angry and felt that they had a right to be worshiped."

"Oh," Joss responded. His brow furrowed as if he were giving this a lot of thought.

"There's more to it than that," Todd went on. "From above, the gods had blessed mankind. Over the millennia, they watched as humans spread across the world, waged wars, and founded kingdoms. All the while, humankind grew prouder and more arrogant, as if everything they accomplished was done by their hands alone.

"Eventually, they built a city far greater than any that had ever stood before. It was a monument to their pride. Inside, they stored all their knowledge and wealth. Those who dwelt there believed themselves to be wiser than the gods. They thought they knew the answers to all the mysteries of the world.

"That is what angered the gods so much. No mortal, no matter how wise, can ever come close to equaling one of the gods.

The gods saw that mankind had rejected them and left the heavens in fury.

"They smote the great city and tore it to the ground with their bare hands. They then began hunting those who escaped."

"And that's when your people turned the king and the warrior against each other, right?" Kisa piped up.

Todd shook his head.

"Not yet. You see, Peter, whose sons founded The House of the King and The House of the Warrior, had never turned from worshiping the gods. Even after the destruction of the great city, he still prayed to them.

"Instead of fleeing and trying to save himself, Peter waited for the gods to find him. He was an old man and knew he had no hope of surviving against their will.

"Arsh, the king of the gods, came upon Peter as he was kneeling in prayer. When Peter finished, he stood up and saw the king. Instantly, he prostrated himself and beseeched the god to show mercy. Arsh was greatly moved by Peter's pleas and by the fact that, for many years, he had remained faithful to the gods despite the scoffing of others.

"Heeding Peter's prayers, the king decided to gather humanity back together and grant them a second chance. He called the other gods to quench their anger and aid him. This was in the time before the gods' feud had begun, so they all worked together to create a paradise.

"Dezi began by carving out a piece of earth in the shape of a teardrop. Sur brought a mighty river to flow around the land, causing it to be fertile. Zeruiah erected great mountainous walls for protection. Jiya grew a vast garden full of plants to be eaten. Tohopke called for the tamest of the animals to come and serve mankind. Husam supplied tools so that the humans could make dwellings. Todkala gave the gift of language to all who entered so that they would have a common tongue. Finally, Arsh blessed the people with fire.

"Arsh swore, along with the other gods, that, though they might bring destruction to the rest of the world, that place they would never raze. It was decreed that the haven would exist outside the gods' control so long as humanity dwelt there. It was called Edden, The Untouchable Land.

"At first, all was well, and the gods were worshiped once more. Peter governed the people with great wisdom for two and a half years. Unfortunately, after his death, there was one living in Edden who fell prey to the first and greatest of human sins, jealousy. That person, the corrupted one, saw the praise and reverence given to the gods and scorned it. The second chance and all that had been granted by the gods was not enough to satisfy the corrupted one.

"This person influenced the weak-willed who followed as sheep do. The practice of worshiping the gods was abolished, and the corrupted one took control of The Untouchable Land. The two sons of Peter and those who followed them, my ancestors, were still loyal to the gods and would not yield. But there were far too few of them to fight for Edden. They were exiled, driven away from the only haven left on earth.

"At this new betrayal, the anger of Arsh burned against mankind. He began to believe that all humans were faithless and deserving of death. Since he was unable to reach those in Edden, he took his fury out on the exiles, marking them one by one for torture and death.

"He caused the sun to burn brighter than ever before. The heat seared the flesh from men's bones and scorched the earth. It was a miserable time for humanity, trapped between sun and stone, as they tried desperately to escape the wrath of the gods.

"They only survived by leaving the surface of the earth and hiding themselves beneath the ground. It was then that Peter's sons turned the gods against each other so that they might forget the wrongs that humanity had committed. Their plan worked, but it was too late; the world was uninhabitable.

"It was several generations before mankind could leave their hiding place and begin to live beneath the sun again. While the king and the warrior battled each other, the earth recovered, and my people settled on the banks of The Brimming Lake.

326

"In the years that passed, the anger of Arsh cooled. He relented and now blesses his earthly followers once more," Todd concluded.

"Why didn't the gods go back to the sky afterward?" Joss wanted to know once Todd finished the account.

"They couldn't," Todd explained. "They are now trapped here until the end of time."

"You mean, forever?" Kisa wondered. "Is there no way for them to get back?"

"There is," Todd told her. "But in order to open a pathway to the heavens, a god must die. Yet another reason the king and warrior wish to slay each other."

"That's really sad," Kisa cried. "I wish they could go back to the sky and all be friends again!"

"Calm down, Kisa," Rollan said. "They aren't real people; it's just a story. Right, Joss?"

"I don't know," Joss replied absently. He appeared lost in thought.

When we set out the following night, it was harder for me to leave the shade of the trees. I wanted to be off the beach and away from the endless noise of the waves. I longed for the refreshing forest dew, which never settled on the sands. In the woods, there were trees and birds and the occasional deer, but the beach was not a place of life; we could go days without seeing any plants or animals.

Then there was the sand. I hated sand. Walking on it was hard enough, but it also got everywhere. In the mornings, when we would stop to sleep, I would find it in my hair and under my fingernails. My skin, which initially had been rubbed raw by constant friction, was now growing thick and calloused, especially on my feet, since I no longer wore my shoes.

The small streams that we occasionally found weren't large enough for us to wash in, and when I tried to bathe in the sea, it always left me feeling even dirtier. I forced myself to comb through my hair at least once a day with my fingers before tying it back in a ponytail. I didn't want it to get tangled or matted. Astra let her own hair hang free, but she must have been doing the same since it didn't end up full of leaves and brush like her friend Halin's had. I also observed Astra helping to untangle Kisa's hair from time to time.

One morning, just after we had made camp, Cole came over to me.

"Myra, will you use your knife to cut my hair? It's gotten so long it's driving me crazy." As he spoke, he unsuccessfully tried to blow several strands of it out of his eyes.

It was impossible not to laugh at his antics.

"Of course," I agreed. "Sit down."

In my head, it was a simple thing to get his hair back to its normal length. In actuality, it wasn't. Several of the others grouped around to watch. I cut the hair in the front first so that he could see better, and then attempted to make it even all the way around.

Although I had tried to lock up my feelings for Cole, I wasn't completely successful. Never before had I been given an excuse to run my hands through his black hair, and, now that I had the opportunity, I was enjoying the sensation.

"Take off a bit more on the left," Joss suggested, pointing to that side of Cole's head.

"Too much," Kisa giggled a moment later.

I sighed in exasperation.

"If anyone else wants to volunteer to give this a try…" I held out my knife without really planning on surrendering it to anyone.

"Nope," Astra laughed. "It's much more fun watching you."

In the end, I managed to get it almost even. Cole's hair was shorter than I intended, but at least it would grow back.

"I appreciate it," Cole told me as he stood up, touching his head to feel what his hair now looked like. I was relieved to have finished with a somewhat-decent product when Joss plopped down in the spot where Cole had been.

"My turn," he called. I rolled my eyes; his hair hardly reached his forehead. "Just get rid of as much as you can without cutting my head off, please," Joss instructed.

"Are you sure?" Cole asked. "Your hair doesn't look too bad."

"He's always liked it short," Rollan informed us.

It was easier to just shave off as much as possible instead of trying to make everything even. I only nicked Joss once, and he didn't even bleed.

"Awesome! Thank you," he said when I was done.

I turned to Rollan,

"You next?" I asked.

"I'm good for now," Rollan replied. His hair had been the longest to begin with; now it almost reached his shoulders. Unlike Cole, he didn't struggle to keep it out of his eyes. It naturally parted in the front and fell down the sides of his round face.

I glanced at Todd, wondering if he would trust me with a knife anywhere close to his body, but his hair didn't seem to be much longer than when he attacked us. It reached to his eyes, just as it had then, but no further. He didn't ask, and I didn't offer.

I half expected Rollan to change his mind and have me give him at least a little trim, but he didn't.

The following day was cloudy. Rain started to fall in the late afternoon and increased every hour. I didn't get much sleep after that. Finally, I gave up and started packing my bag. It was hard to tell when the night began because the sky grew darker all day. The apples and fish were long gone, but there was meat from a turtle we had found a few nights earlier.

The others also woke up when the rain turned into a deluge.

"We should stay away from the sea," Todd warned. "Storms like this can make the tide come much higher than it normally does."

"Why?" Rollan asked.

"Because of the wind," Todd answered. "It stirs up the waves."

Rollan nodded.

"Everyone, be careful of the water and stay together," Cole called. "It'll be easy to get separated."

As I followed him out of the trees onto the sand, I knew his words were quite true. I could hardly see anything through the rain. It ended up being one of the worst nights we'd spent on the beach. Every step was a battle against the wind and the water. The sand was saturated and clung to our feet and legs, weighing us down.

I struggled to see, trying to make sure everyone was still together. Every so often, Cole would call out his name, and we would call our own names back to make sure no one was missing.

It wasn't until after midnight that I realized with a jolt that we could be walking right past the mountain and completely miss it in the darkness and the storm. I bit my tongue, not wanting to start *that* argument again. I would have to hope that Astra and everyone else was right about the mountain being huge.

The night finally came to an end, but the storm was far from over. We didn't bother making camp. We took to the trees and tried unsuccessfully to sleep.

It was miserable walking all night in the storm, and even worse trying to sleep on the cold, wet ground, knowing that everything we had with us was as soaked as we were.

I offered to take the first watch. I wanted to be as tired as possible before trying to sleep. If I managed to nod off once, I could guarantee it wouldn't happen twice. The rain didn't abate for the first few hours of my watch. It seemed to be letting up a little by the time my shift was over.

Exhausted as I was, it still took me forever to fall asleep. It wasn't raining when I woke up close to sunset—not that you could see the sun, but the sky was a slightly lighter shade of gray in the west.

It remained hazy all night. We were still dripping, and the air was chilly. At one point, we stopped to get out our long cloaks and jackets. They were soaked, of course, and the sensation of dragging the wet fabric over my skin was exceedingly unpleasant, but it did provide some insulation against the wind that cut across the ocean.

Thankfully, the next day was warmer, but not as much as I would have liked. When we stopped in the morning, we laid our extra clothes on the sand in the hopes that they would dry. However, the watery sunlight wasn't strong enough to dry them completely, and we were forced to wear them damp. What made it even worse was that they were also covered in sand.

I was really ready to be off the beach.

By the end of the night, the clothes I was wearing were mostly dry, but not the ones in my bag. At least the sun rose bright and strong, promising that by evening, everything would be dry soon.

Ever since the nights had turned colder, Todd had taken to wearing some of the extra shirts that once belonged to Toruc. It was weird seeing him in clothing from The Clan after he'd run around half naked for so long. I supposed even a Broken felt the elements sometimes. Toruc had been broader than Todd, so the shirts didn't fit quite right. If the owner of the clothing hadn't lived and died in such a terrible way, I would have almost laughed at how Todd appeared in the oversized garb. I supposed one day he might grow into them.

The most disheartening thing about the beach was that every evening when we got up, we would look ahead and see nothing except more sand. The same was true every morning before we stopped to rest. The coast seemed to go on forever and ever without end, just as Todd had once told us. But surely we had to get somewhere if we kept going on like this. How big was the world? How far could one walk in the same direction without reaching the edge? What if there was no edge and we just kept on walking forever?

CHAPTER 36
DISTANCE

Over the next three days, I noticed the horizon finally begin to change. The sand became coarser and rockier—not nearly as comfortable to walk on. The land grew hilly, with fewer trees to provide shelter when we slept.

As morning was approaching on the fourth day, I got a sudden whiff of an unusual and unpleasant odor.

"What is that?" I wondered, sniffing the air.

"What is what?" Cole asked.

"That smell," I replied, getting another, stronger blast of the horrible stench.

"I can smell it," Joss piped up beside me.

"Me too," Astra announced. "I think it's coming from in front of us."

"Should we stop?" Kisa asked fretfully.

It was almost pitch black. The dawn was starting to lighten the horizon in the east, but it would be dark for at least another half hour.

"I guess we'd better," Cole muttered. "I don't want to walk into trouble without some warning."

"Great. Wake me when it's light," Rollan said, flopping down on the sand.

"Good idea," Joss agreed, joining his cousin on the ground.

The rest of us sat and waited for the sun to rise. Todd was dozing in an upright position. Every once in a while, I sensed him jerk slightly to keep from falling over. Kisa went to sleep too, her head resting on Astra's leg.

As the light in the east continued to grow, I stared ahead, trying to figure out where the smell was coming from. About fifty yards down the beach, I could see a blurry shape, but I couldn't quite make it out in the half light. All I could tell was that it was huge and darkly colored.

"You do see that, right?" I asked Cole, who was next to me.

He squinted at where my finger was pointing.

"Yes. Is it a rock?" he wondered aloud.

Finally, there was enough light to see, but I still couldn't comprehend what was on the sand in front of us. It did look like a huge rock, but it was such an odd shape. It wasn't black like I had thought, but gray, and, along the bottom, it was far paler, almost white.

"Is that a mountain?" Kisa wondered sleepily.

I saw that Astra had risen, waking the younger girl. Cole shook the two boys on the ground.

"What is it, Todd?" Astra asked, as the two of them set off toward the gray mass.

"A monster out of the depths," Todd whispered. "It's a bad sign."

"Why?" I wondered, catching up with them.

"If there's something strong enough to kill a sea monster that big, imagine what it could do to you and me," he replied.

Once I was within twenty yards of the gray mass, I was certain that it was the thing producing the terrible odor.

"How did it get here?" Kisa asked, staying well back from the smelly object.

"It's a big fish!" I exclaimed aloud. I had caught sight of what I was sure was a tail, although the tail was larger than I was.

"I've never seen anything like this," Joss murmured in wonder as he drew near the creature.

"Something this size couldn't fit in the lake," Rollan commented.

"And if it did, I would never swim there again," Kisa added.

"I wonder what kind of creature it is," Astra mused to herself.

"It's called a whale," Todd told her.

"You've seen one before?" She turned to look at him.

He shook his head.

"No, but we have stories about these creatures. When Tohopke drops his line into the deepest part of the ocean, this is what he catches. That's why it's a bad sign to see one. It means that the wild one may be close by."

"We're not in one of your stories," Rollan scoffed. "The gods aren't real."

Todd glanced around with a worried expression and hastily changed the subject.

"There are also stories about creatures such as these swallowing humans whole if they go too far out to sea."

Kisa shuddered.

"How do you know they don't get chewed up?" Cole asked.

"Because sometimes they get spat back up—alive." Todd's voice was full of mystery, just like when he told us the story of the lord who had vanished all those years ago.

I laughed.

"Good one," I told him.

"I'm serious," Todd insisted.

"Sure," I murmured sarcastically. "If you say so."

"I don't suppose we can eat this?" Cole wondered, tentatively poking the flesh of the whale.

Why did boys have to touch everything all the time? Even when—no, especially when it was something disgusting and smelly?

"Looks like the birds are." Joss nodded to several white and gray birds perched on top of the enormous animal. Examining them more closely, I could see that they were tearing away chunks of gray flesh with their sharp beaks.

"I'm pretty sure I'd rather die than eat something that smells this bad," I announced.

"I have to agree with Myra," Astra said. "It's been out in the sun a bit too long."

"I wonder if it washed up during that storm a while back," Joss mused.

334

"Seems possible," Cole agreed.

I glanced at the tree line. It was about seventy feet from where we stood, but I didn't want to try to sleep with the stink of a rotting creature in my nose. "Let's move off a little farther," I suggested.

"Excellent idea," Todd responded almost before I finished speaking. The boy was already backing away from the creature. He glanced around several times as if worried a foe might appear at any moment.

"It looks like birds aren't the only things that have been feeding on this carcass," Astra observed. She was kneeling down in the sand. I joined her and saw animal prints that resembled the padded foot of a dog but were much bigger.

"Looks like a mountain lion or something," Todd told her, noticing the markings for the first time as well.

"What's a mountain lion?" Kisa asked.

"A big cat," Todd replied grimly.

"I like cats!" Kisa exclaimed, clapping her hands. "We have them in The Golden Fields. They hunt the mice and squirrels that try to eat our plants."

"Mountain lions hunt larger prey than mice and squirrels," Todd told her.

"Like what?" Kisa wanted to know.

"Like little girls," Todd replied, completely serious.

Kisa's eyes grew wide, and she looked like she wasn't sure if Todd was teasing her or not.

"Probably better to keep moving," Cole decided before Kisa could think of a reply.

We walked on for another hour. The shore was unusually stony and rough. I was glad we weren't trying to cross it in the dark. There were several jagged rocks rising straight out of the ground, which would have been painful to trip over.

"Our nighttime journeying might be at an end," Astra observed.

"You could be right," Cole agreed. "It's not going to be much fun trying to feel our way forward with all these rocks. Hopefully, it'll smooth out a little farther on."

It didn't, and after another half hour, we made camp. There were only a handful of trees to provide shade. It was a far cry from the forest we had camped in the day before, but we made do.

The minute I woke up in the evening, I could feel the damp in the air.

"Going to rain again tonight," I muttered.

Astra nodded, agreeing with my assessment.

We traveled for only an hour before the rain came. It wasn't a downpour this time but a steady drizzle, which kept up for most of the night. It made the rocky ground slippery. I stubbed my toes more times than I could count.

In the early morning hours, there was a sharp cry from Kisa. Everyone froze.

"Kisa," Cole called, "are you okay?"

"Yes," the girl answered in a shaky voice, like she might start crying. "I tripped over a rock."

I heard footsteps in her general direction.

"Don't move, Kisa," Joss told her. "Tell me where it hurts."

I couldn't make out Kisa's reply, but she whimpered something to him.

"She's bleeding," Joss informed the rest of us.

"Better stop until morning then," Cole announced. "Like Astra said, we'll have to start traveling during the day again."

"Do you think you can make it to the trees?" Rollan asked Kisa, joining Joss by her side.

"Probably," Kisa answered. "I don't think it's very bad."

"I'll carry you," Joss offered.

Rollan snorted.

"You're hardly larger than she is. If anything, I'll be the one doing the carrying."

I couldn't make out Joss's muttered reply.

We headed away from the water and toward the woods.

"Try not to run into any trees," Astra advised. "One injury is enough."

The drizzle didn't let up, and the ground was full of rocks, so the night was far from comfortable. I took the last watch—not that there was anything to see. I tried to listen for approaching footsteps, but I couldn't imagine anyone would have been stupid enough to travel here by night.

Except you, a voice reminded me.

Shut up! I growled at it.

I had enough troubles to worry about without that stupid voice pointing out everything I had done wrong on this trip.

I was so sick of walking all the time. I was exhausted, both physically and mentally. My entire body ached from the harshness of the journey. Even still, after everything that had happened, I wasn't sure I was ready to go back to The Clan.

The more time I spent thinking about the situation, the more I was sure that Astra was right. There were many things that we weren't being told. The answers weren't in The Land of the Clan; they were at the end of our journey, and I was determined to find them.

I had been zoning out for some time before I realized that the sun was rising. I glanced up and saw that there was something more than sand on the horizon.

There was a mountain.

"Look!" I cried as I pointed, not caring who I roused in my excitement.

I sprang to my feet, stiffness and misery forgotten, and sprinted out of the trees to get a clearer look.

Hopefully, it was *the* mountain.

We were too far away to see if it had the designated spires, but just the fact that it was there gave me hope that our destination was near.

Cole was the first to reach my side.

"Is that it?" he asked breathlessly.

"I think so," I told him. Then added to myself, "It has to be."

The others joined us a moment later. Kisa cried out in joy and clapped her hands. Her injury from the previous night was little more than a split toenail, and she completely forgot it in her delight. The boys gave whoops of excitement. Cole was grinning from ear to ear. Astra smiled too, but her expression was far away, as if she wasn't quite certain what she was feeling.

"Let's go," Cole called. No one had unpacked the night before in the dark, so we shouldered our bags and set off, munching on some turtle meat along the way.

The ground was much easier to traverse in the daylight. The farther we went, the more rocks we found, and we were basically climbing a pile of boulders.

Even though the mountain had seemed to spring up overnight, it didn't get any closer after another four hours of walking.

"Why is this taking so long?" Kisa complained, echoing my thoughts.

"Because it's really far away," Astra told her. "It's just so big that it looks like it's close by."

"Oh," Kisa muttered, clearly not having expected an answer.

After two more hours passed, I was able to make out something rising from the top of the distant mountain. The spires, I hoped.

"Turtle!" Rollan called. He and Joss raced forward after the animal. It was already at the waterline, but Joss followed the turtle into the waves. If Rollan hadn't been there to grab the back of his shirt, the creature might have gotten away.

Even though it was early in the afternoon, we stopped so we could cook the meat. While the boys built a fire, I investigated the surrounding woods.

Mostly, I was looking for water since our supply was desperately low. I didn't find anything noteworthy and headed back empty-handed.

The turtle meat took a couple of hours to cook. I wanted to put a few more miles behind us before nightfall, but the younger half of the team—namely Kisa—was too exhausted.

As the sun set, I insisted that we extinguish the fire. With the mountain in sight, there was a good chance we weren't as alone as we felt.

I couldn't sleep, and, even though I wasn't supposed to take the first watch, I sent Rollan to get some rest and stayed up until well after midnight. Only then did I feel exhausted enough to lay down myself.

I woke at dawn, full of anticipation. We might be able to reach the mountain, and, if we were the first to do so, we would win the trials. The hours flew by, but our destination was still far in the distance when we made camp for the night.

There was only a trickle of water left in the canteens.

"Should we spend some time tomorrow looking for water?" Astra asked.

"No," I said, shaking my head. "We need to get to the mountain. I bet we'll find water there."

"I'd rather not try to climb that thing with an empty canteen," Astra replied. "Cole, what do you think?"

I expected that Cole would agree with Astra, and we would spend the next day searching for water instead of continuing toward the mountain.

"I think Myra's right. There must be water at the mountain." I was shocked to hear Cole backing me for a change.

"Very well," Astra assented with a gentle smile.

I ground my teeth together, wishing she would argue with him. But *perfect* Astra would never do such a thing.

By morning, the last of our water was gone. The only thing that kept panic at bay was the intense desire to reach the mountain. Around midday, I was desperately thirsty but determined to go on because I could now clearly see the spires rising from the snow-capped peak in front of us.

"We should take to the forest," Astra suggested to Cole and me. "The beach looks like it ends in a cliff down there, but the forest seems to slope up to the base of the mountain more gradually."

"Agreed," Cole said. "We need to end up on the west side anyway."

It felt strange but pleasant to be walking in the woods again after such a long time on the sands. Without the constant noise from the wind and waves, the quiet was unnerving. It was almost as though we were starting our journey over instead of nearing the end of it.

The mountain was tall enough that we didn't have a problem staying on track. It loomed ahead of us, hidden by none but the tallest trees.

Night was rapidly approaching when I heard the flow of water ahead. It wasn't the sound of waves, which we had left behind long ago, but the gurgle of a little stream or brook.

"Listen," I cried. "I hear water!"

That got everyone very excited. We surged forward.

"Over here!" Cole called from my left. We joined him and found a pool fed by a small brook.

"Finally," Joss exclaimed, dropping his pack and plunging straight in. Rollan and Kisa followed him into the water, effectively filling the small space.

"Guess I'll drink from the brook," I decided aloud. A moment later, I was laughing as Rollan and Kisa teamed up to try and pull Todd into the water with them. He teetered on the edge of the bank for a moment before losing his balance and falling in headfirst.

Astra was shaking with mirth as she joined me at the brook to fill the empty canteens.

We all ended up in the little pond before the end of the night. I felt so clean after getting out and lying in the grass. Even though my clothes were soaked and the night was chilly, it was worth it to remove all the dirt and grit of the beach.

I slept peacefully under the shadow of the great mountain. I had finally gotten used to sleeping during the night again. Also, for the first time in a long time, I knew exactly what the future would hold.

CHAPTER 37
THE UPWARD PATH

Around noon on the following day, we reached the base of the mountain. The sheer rock walls rose almost straight up. They were a dark gray color covered by bright patches of green moss.

"Isn't there supposed to be writing?" Joss asked, inspecting the stones close at hand.

"I don't think we're in the right place," Cole replied. "It's hard to tell with the sun directly above us, but I'm pretty sure we're still a little too far south."

We began circling the mountain. I kept a close eye on the rocks to my right, making sure we didn't miss anything. That was why I tripped over Kisa when she suddenly darted in front of me, away from the mountain's towering walls.

"Oh!" I exclaimed as I stumbled and tried to regain my balance.

"I'm sorry. Are you all right?" I asked Kisa, who had ended up on the ground.

"It's okay," Kisa replied, dusting herself off. "Look!"

She was pointing into the forest on our left. I saw a peach tree, a blueberry bush, and, to my surprise, there was also a watermelon vine sprawling across the ground beside a patch of strawberries. The closer I got, the more I saw. There was food everywhere!

Instantly, we were among the plants, eating and gathering all at once. Aside from the seaweed, there had been no food on the shoreline except meat. I reached for a peach and sank my teeth into its soft skin. The flavor was amazingly sweet as the juices flowed over my tongue and down my throat. I closed my eyes, chewing slowly so I could savor every bite. Once I'd finished and tossed the pit away, I reached for another.

After eating my second peach, I moved on to the strawberry patch. Astra was already there, helping herself, but there was plenty to go around. No one felt the need to restrain themselves. There was enough food here that we would never be able to eat it all.

A short time later, we were all sitting together under a large oak tree. The roots formed natural seats. Everyone was stuffed. Kisa lay flat on her back, her small stomach poking up comically under her shirt. Joss was still munching on part of a watermelon he had broken open on a rock. I was so full, I felt like I could burst, but I wouldn't have cared if I had; it felt so good.

"I guess we'll spend the night here," Cole decided. "I'm sure we'll have a better chance of finding the writing in the morning."

Even I was too content to grumble about how slow our progress had been the past couple of days.

"It's like it was planted," I heard Astra murmur to herself a short time later.

"What are you going on about?" I asked her.

She glanced at me.

"The fruit trees. It's like someone put them here."

I rolled my eyes.

"No one's been here for fifty years," I reminded her.

"I know that," she retorted. "But we haven't seen this many varieties of fruit growing together anywhere else. Maybe someone put the plants here a long time ago, and their seeds continued to grow."

"Okay," I agreed to appease her. I didn't want to talk about gardening right then.

I didn't realize I had dropped off to sleep until I was awakened by the sound of someone throwing up. Opening my eyes, I glanced around. It was dark, but it didn't feel too late. A fire burned in front of the oak tree where I was sleeping.

Cole was standing beside a hunched-over Rollan, who was retching on the opposite side of the clearing. The rest of my teammates were clustered around me, all of them wrapped in sleep.

I stood and approached Cole and Rollan.

"What's wrong?" I asked softly.

"I think I ate too much," Rollan admitted, straightening and wiping his mouth.

"Do you feel better now?" Cole wondered.

Rollan nodded.

"Yeah, my stomach's not as upset anymore."

"Good. Get some rest," Cole directed him.

Rollan went back to the others and settled down.

"You feeling all right?" Cole asked me.

"Yeah. You?" I replied.

Cole nodded.

"My stomach was upset for a bit, but not anymore. I guess we all went a little crazy."

"It's been a long time since we've seen so much food," I pointed out.

Cole added another log to the fire. I sat down on a rock and put my hands out over the flames. Everything was so serene. I felt peaceful for the first time in—well, practically forever. I looked up at the stars. They had been visible every night on the beach, but, somehow, they were more beautiful here, where only a handful twinkled through the treetops.

Cole sat on the end of a log beside my rock.

"What are you so happy about?" he asked.

Until he mentioned it, I hadn't realized I was smiling. Slowly, I lowered my eyes from the stars to his face.

"I'm not sure," I whispered. "I just am."

"I know what you mean," Cole agreed. "We're so close. Tomorrow's the day. I'm sure of it."

"I've thought the same thing the past couple of nights, ever since the mountain became visible in the distance," I replied. "It could be tomorrow; it could be the day after. It doesn't really matter."

Cole's expression turned quizzical.

"That doesn't sound very much like you. Are you sure you're feeling all right?" he teased.

I smiled again. It was as if the trials had been stripped away for a moment, and we were just Cole and Myra, not the first and third leaders of a team from The Clan.

Everything had suddenly become so simple. It wouldn't last. Once the sun was up and we were on the move again, this moment would be lost forever. However, it gave me hope for the future. If we could be ourselves together now, then why not after we returned to The Clan?

"Just think," Cole said. "We've come so far. Not many teams have ever reached this place, I bet."

"Yes," I agreed. "I imagine only a handful make it every cycle."

"And maybe only one," Cole continued. "It's strange that the last people to be here could have been our parents."

It was weird when he said it like that.

"Maybe Myna," I conceded. "But I doubt my father's team ever made it this far."

Cole nodded.

"My mother wasn't old enough to be a contender. She's never left The Land of the Clan."

"That's probably for the best," I told him.

"Yeah," he agreed. "I certainly can't see her surviving in the wilderness or sleeping on the ground."

I laughed at the image of Cole's mother living like we had for the past—who knew how many days it had been.

"I can't really see your father doing it either," I pointed out.

Cole chuckled.

"He's tougher than he looks."

"He raised three boys, so I guess he is," I joked.

Cole shook his head.

"Nope, it was my sister who put gray hair on his head." We were both giggling.

"Shhh!" I whispered. "We'll wake the others."

Cole calmed down quickly.

"There's something about this place. It's like we belong here. Generation upon generation of our people have followed the same clues to this very spot. Now we are a part of that history."

I nodded and gave him a cheeky smile.

"Soon we'll be telling that history."

"Nice," he said. "I'll probably leave that bit of the business to you lot."

"Why?" I wondered.

He winked at me.

"Because if I try to tell it, I'll have you on one side saying it went one way and Astra on the other telling me the exact opposite."

I laughed again. Normally, I'm sure I would have been insulted, but the image he conjured up in my head was too good not to enjoy.

"The biggest problem is that somehow I'm sure you'll both be right." I could barely breathe I was laughing so hard at his words. It was a struggle to do so quietly, but I managed not to wake anyone.

When I could talk again, I said, "Maybe we'll leave the tellings to Joss, Kisa, and Rollan. I bet they'd do a wonderful job."

"Sounds good. Then what are the three of us going to do?" Cole asked.

"All the work," I told him. "Can you see Joss and Rollan sitting through council meetings?"

"Not really." Cole shook his head. "I will say that I'm not going to spend nearly so much time in council as our parents do. I mean, how can it take them so many hours to discuss simple issues?"

"You should know the answer to that," I told Cole seriously, trying not to crack a smile until I finished my next sentence. "You've heard Astra and me argue. We can go at it all day, every day."

"True," Cole replied, grinning.

"And you thought we were alike," I said, giving him a gentle nudge.

"You are alike; you just don't agree on anything."

I sighed.

"I suppose we don't." I thought for a minute. "Cole, do you know anything about my father's death?"

"What?" Cole gave me a shocked look.

"You were older than I was when he died," I rushed on. "Do you remember him at all? Or do your parents talk about him ever?"

"I'm sorry, Myra," Cole said. "I do remember him a little, but I probably wouldn't recognize him if I saw him again. He was just another adult to me."

"I understand," I replied. I wasn't really expecting him to remember anything. It was just that with all the talk about parents, the image I had seen in my mind of my father the night before the trials started had come drifting back to me.

"I only heard my father mention him once," Cole continued. I turned intently to Cole, ready for him to go on. "He said it was a shame Rilk, your father, had died so young and that your mother was alone again."

I gave Cole a questioning look.

"Again? Was there someone before my father?"

"I don't know," Cole answered apologetically. "I never thought about it much."

"Do you know how my father died?" I asked him.

Cole puckered his forehead, then shook his head.

"I actually can't recall," he admitted. "I'm sure I knew at one time or another."

"Probably not," I responded. "I never did, and I only found out right before we left. He killed himself."

Cole stared at me in disbelief. I wasn't sure why I was telling him these things. Maybe it was because I had wanted to confide in someone for so long, or because it just felt like the right time to let Cole through my walls.

"I'm so sorry, Myra," he whispered.

I didn't answer him. I couldn't say 'it's okay', because it wasn't. To my relief, Cole didn't ask me why my father committed

347

suicide. I had a hard enough time understanding what Myna had told me the night I finally asked her about him.

All I knew was that he found out something that upset him greatly, and he killed himself soon after. Those scattered details were not something I would ever be able to explain to Cole.

Suddenly, I saw movement on the far side of the clearing out of the corner of my eye. I rose and drew my knife in one swift motion. Cole took his cue from me and was on his feet in an instant, sword at the ready.

Something glided silently through the shadows, and then Astra stepped into the firelight.

Cole let out a sigh of relief and dropped his sword, sinking back into a sitting position. I lowered my knife as well but remained in my fighting stance. I glanced to the right and counted the sleeping figures under the oak tree. How had I not noticed one missing earlier?

"What are you doing?" I snapped. "Trying to scare us to death?"

"I couldn't sleep," Astra replied, joining us by the fire as I resumed my place next to Cole.

"So, you thought you'd go tramping around alone in the woods instead?" I asked.

In the back of my head, I wondered if she had been spying on us and how much of the conversation about my father she could have overheard. Those things were meant for Cole's ears alone. There was no way I would have said any of it if I knew someone else might have been listening.

"I was scouting ahead," Astra told us. She produced a peach from one of her pockets and took a bite out of it. Even from across the fire, I could smell the sweet scent of the fruit.

After she finished the peach and tossed the pit away, she turned her gaze on us. Her eyes were glowing eerily in the firelight.

"Don't you want to know what I found?" she asked.

I was prepared to say 'no', but Cole spoke up first.

"What did you find?" he demanded breathlessly.

Astra smiled, and I knew she was eager to tell us.

"I found the writing on the mountainside."

"What did it say?" Cole asked eagerly.

Astra waved her hand in dismissal.

"I figured it would be best to wait for everyone before reading it," she told him. "Plus, it's all overgrown, and I would've had to make a fire to see it in the dark."

"Wonderful," I muttered sarcastically. "We're so surprised, because writing on the stone is just what the scroll said we would find."

"I know," Astra agreed, sounding very pleased with herself. "But I found something else too."

Cole and I held our breath as we waited for Astra to continue.

"What was it?" I couldn't help asking.

"There's a door."

CHAPTER 38
PUZZLE

Sleep was nearly impossible after Astra's revelation. Even though I told myself to relax over and over again, I couldn't stop wondering what was behind the door. Despite my excitement, I must have nodded off for a couple of hours, because when I opened my eyes next, it was starting to grow light.

Todd was on watch.

"Why didn't you wake everyone?" I asked, springing to my feet.

"It's still early," he protested as I began rousing the others.

I was ready to leave immediately for the place where Astra had found the door, but Cole advised everyone to fill their packs with fruit first. My bag was soon stuffed with peaches and apples, but the others took forever. I waited on pins and needles as Rollan attempted to shove an entire watermelon into his backpack.

Finally, everyone was ready, and Astra took the lead. At first, we just continued following the curve of the mountain around to the west. Before long, Astra guided us into the woods.

"There's a pile of rocks cutting us off in that direction," she reported. "I don't much fancy climbing it, even in the daylight."

She led us through the trees to a place where the ground began to slope up. It quickly became steep and would have been all but impossible to climb if not for the thin pine trees that grew on the mountainside. Holding onto these, we managed to scramble up the rise.

"How did you find this place in the dark?" Kisa asked.

Astra gave her a knowing smile.

"I've always been good at finding things," she replied.

Once we reached the top of the slope, we stood on a broad ledge. Fifty yards farther on, I saw the mouth of a passage in front of us.

An almost perfect rectangle had been cut right out of the mountain. It was eight feet deep, a little more than eight feet high, and at least thirty feet long, before coming to a dead end.

To our left, there was no wall, just open air and a dizzying drop, letting light into the strange space. The right wall was covered in moss, but I could make out letters between the patches. At the very back, I saw the door Astra had spoken of. Ignoring the writing, I walked up to it and reached out, laying my palm flat on its surface.

I pulled my hand back in surprise.

"It's metal," I announced.

The others crowded around.

"I've never seen metal like that before," Cole commented.

"Me neither," Joss agreed.

Most of our metal objects were small, like fishhooks and horseshoes. I had no idea how a piece this large and seamless was crafted, but it spoke of unnatural things. Things better left unknown.

No, I thought, *I must know.*

Cole tried pushing on the door, but it didn't budge. Rollan and Joss jumped in to help him, but it did no good.

"I think we'd better read what's written here first," I said. "That's what our instructions tell us to do."

"Indeed," Astra agreed, beginning to tear chunks of moss from the wall. I reached out to confirm that the wall at least was made of stone. It was.

With the seven of us working at it, we quickly revealed all of the writing. It was written in the high language. Most of the words formed a series of instructions similar to those on the scroll, but there were nine other words spread out along the wall, each about a yard above the ground. They were the names of the villages of The Clan. Under the names were small circles. I leaned down to examine one, noting that it was actually a circular hole in the wall plugged with a colored rock. Checking the others, I realized that the color of the rock corresponded to the color of the village written above it.

"What does it say?" Todd asked.

The words above the names of the villages spanned much of the wall. Cole stepped back to read them.

"It says, 'Welcome. You have reached the end of the trials.'" As Cole spoke, he translated the high language into the common tongue for Todd's sake.

"'If you solve the riddle and the door opens, the truth will be given to you, and you will be prepared to lead The Clan.

"'The scroll contains the key. You will not be able to enter unless you have at least five team members remaining.

"'Members from more than one team may not enter together.

"'Only enter if there are at least two hours of daylight left.

"'If you are not the first team to arrive, do not leave until at least an entire day has passed. If, even then, the door still won't open, you are too late, and an earlier team has succeeded in passing the final test. Return the way you came.

"'If you make it through the door, take enough wood and kindling with you to build a fire. There will be further instructions inside; follow their words.

"'We are The Clan. We were created to be order when all else was chaos. We have lived in peace as our fathers have taught us. We show justice to all without hesitation. We will continue as we have been: the only perfect society.'"

Cole trailed off into silence.

"At least we know we're the first ones here," I said.

"How?" Rollan asked.

"Because the moss over the words has been growing for the past fifty years," I told him.

"Good point," Rollan replied.

"How do we open it?" Joss wondered.

"I bet it has something to do with these," I announced, pointing to the little circles under the writing. I reached forward and touched the one under the name "Riverside". To my surprise, it moved.

I pulled my hand back instantly. Astra was beside me a second later. She touched the round circle lightly, but nothing happened. Then she pushed a little harder, and the middle of the circle moved in. It stopped after having gone back about an inch.

"What do you think?" she asked me.

I felt flustered. "I don't know. I've never seen anything like this before."

"Neither have I," Astra admitted, removing her finger. The circle slowly came back out to where it had been.

"See if the other ones move," Astra said to Rollan and Joss, who were standing by the name that read "The Making".

It moved in and stopped at about the same place ours had.

"What are they for?" Astra pondered aloud to herself.

I moved back over to the door and examined it, looking for another of the circles or some explanation. I didn't find anything useful. Astra followed me.

The others backed away. Clearly, they had no ideas and were giving us space to work. Kisa was on the ground, hugging her knees and watching. Cole seemed to be re-reading the script in his head. The other three were milling about uncertainly.

I turned back to them.

"Joss, Rollan, Todd," I called. "Why don't you go and gather wood as the instructions say?"

"Sure thing," Rollan agreed.

"Be careful," Cole instructed them. "Another team might show up at any moment."

The truth of his words set my heart racing.

We needed to hurry.

Astra was slowly walking down the length of the wall, reading aloud.

"'The Quarry'. 'The Making'. 'Treescape'. 'The Golden Fields'. 'The Paramount'. 'Riverside'. 'The Barracks'. 'The Farm'. 'The North Wind'." Astra came to a stop at the other end of the wall.

"It's all the villages, but what do they have to do with opening the door?" Cole asked.

"I'm not sure," Astra responded. "It's like we should know this, but—I'm just not sure."

We didn't speak for the next half hour. Instead, we stared at the wall. Eventually, I joined Kisa, sitting on the ground. An hour before noon, I ate a peach, still trying to figure out what it all meant. I had no idea what the circles were for, but there had to be a reason all the villages were written on the wall.

The boys made several trips back with armloads of wood.

"Any progress?" Joss asked the first time he returned.

"Do you see an open door?" I snapped.

They didn't ask any more questions after that.

Once they finished their third trip, Cole said, "That's probably enough wood. Stay here and see if you can think of something we've missed."

Noon passed, and we still sat there just staring at the wall.

"Can you read it to me once more?" Todd asked in the early afternoon. Rollan and Kisa were asleep, Joss was fidgeting, and Astra was gazing off into space. Cole and I had been staring at the wall, unmoving, for hours.

"Sure," Cole agreed, and he read it again.

"Maybe you should look at your scroll?" Todd suggested. "What makes it 'the key'?"

"I'm not sure, but it couldn't hurt to take a look," Cole replied. The parchment hadn't fared well in the past couple of storms. It was all but illegible. The border of colors was smudged all over the words in some places.

The border of colors—

"I've got it!" I yelled, springing to my feet.

"What?" Cole asked as I snatched the parchment from his hands. "What's the answer?"

I pointed to the nine names.

"These are the nine villages of The Clan," I began.

"We know that already," Astra replied curtly, coming to stand next to Cole. "What about them?"

Ignoring her, I continued, "They aren't in order."

"How do you mean?" Cole asked.

"Think about it," I told them. "'Treescape', 'The Golden Fields', 'The Paramount'. Why are they listed in such a confusing order?"

"I'm not sure what you're getting at," Joss said.

"Rollan." I whirled to face him. He had just woken up and didn't have a clue what was going on. "Turn around," I ordered. With a shrug, he did so. "Now, name the nine villages of The Clan."

"Umm…" Rollan began. "Treescape, The North Wind, The Making, The Barracks, The Golden Fields, Riverside, The Farm, The Quarry, and The Paramount."

"Exactly," I told him before addressing the others. "You see, he named them in order." I made a circular motion with my hand to encompass eight of the villages, and then a quick dot in the middle for The Paramount.

"You've still lost me." Cole shook his head.

"I don't get it either," Joss added.

Astra bit her lip for a moment.

"I think I know what you're saying," she said. "The villages need to be in the right order. But what order?"

I held up the scroll in answer.

"This one."

"It's a circular pattern; there's no beginning. How do we know where to start?" she wondered.

I smiled at her. "The Paramount first, of course."

"Okay, let's try it," she agreed.

The two of us approached the wall. I went to the circle under "The Paramount" and pressed it in all the way before releasing it.

"The Making next," I said, looking at the colored pattern on the scroll. Astra pressed that one, and then I pressed the one for The Barracks, followed by The Golden Fields, Riverside, The Farm, The Quarry, Treescape, and finally, The North Wind.

"Why are we always last?" I heard Astra mumble as she pushed the gray circle of rock.

She released it, and I sprinted to the door. It still wouldn't budge.

I heard several of my on-looking teammates give long sighs.

"It should have worked," I said in disbelief. "I don't understand…" I trailed off in defeat.

I had been sure I was right. It was the only answer that made sense. I slumped to the ground, still clutching the scroll.

Astra walked over to me.

"It was a good idea," she said. "I bet we do have to push the circles in a certain order. We just need to find out what it is."

She offered me a hand and pulled me from the ground. We tried every combination with The Paramount as the first circle. Astra even made us do it backward, but nothing worked.

"And we're back to square one," I growled, throwing the parchment down in disgust.

"I think we're on the right track," Cole commented. "We'll figure it out soon."

It was already late afternoon. We were pretty high up, and I didn't relish the thought of sleeping so close to the ledge.

In my head, I read the words once more, slowing down when I reached the part about the scroll being 'the key'.

"'You will not be able to enter unless you have at least five team members remaining,'" I said under my breath.

Then I stopped.

"*Will not be able to*," I repeated.

Astra was trying to press the buttons again in a new order.

"I wish they hadn't put them so far apart," she grumbled.

Yes, why had they spread them out so much?

You will not be able to enter unless you have at least five team members remaining, I said again to myself.

"Why doesn't it say 'you *shouldn't* enter unless you have at least five team members remaining'?" I asked.

"I'm not sure," Cole responded after considering for a moment.

Understanding dawned on me in an instant.

"It's because we have to open the door together," I realized aloud.

"What do you mean?" Todd asked.

Instead of answering, I motioned for the others to join me.

"Kisa, Rollan, come here," I directed. "Joss, stand down there, please." I pointed to the end farthest away from the door.

"What are you thinking?" Astra wanted to know.

"I think we need to hold the stones in," I told her. "A winning team must have at least three members. They didn't want just one or two people to be able to enter alone, so they made it impossible to open the door without at least five team members."

Astra was nodding.

"Brilliant," she observed, taking a place by the wall, in line with the others.

"Okay," I announced, scooping up the scroll and stepping back to view the entire wall. "The Paramount first. Hold the stone in. Next, The Making. Don't let go of those circles."

With my five teammates stretched out in a line along the wall, we pressed and held each stone in order, starting with The Paramount and ending with The North Wind.

For a moment, nothing happened, and then there was a deep rumble and a grinding sound. The door suddenly jerked open about a foot. I leapt forward and seized it to keep it from closing, but my actions were unnecessary.

The members of my team released the circles and came over to see what was inside the doorway, which opened into the mountain itself.

CHAPTER 39
THE HALL OF MEMORIES

I was the first one to step inside. The air was surprisingly chilly, and I gave a little shudder. A single passage opened to the left. It was hard to tell after being outside in the sun, but I was almost certain there was a dim glow coming down it.

As promised, more instructions were written on the wall straight ahead. I examined the words with Cole and Astra flanking me. The writing was in the common language this time.

Astra was the one to read it aloud. "'Bring all you have inside with you, along with enough wood to build a fire. Close the door so that it cannot be opened again. Continue forward.'"

We stepped back outside to retrieve our packs. Even though I was inside the mountain for a few moments, it already seemed too bright outside.

Along with my backpack, I also grabbed a large bundle of wood. The others did the same.

Quietly, I turned to Cole and whispered, "I'm not sure it's right for him to come inside." I nodded at Todd as we stepped through the door for the second time.

"I don't think it matters," Cole replied. "The text only said that members from different teams couldn't enter together."

I sighed, figuring that it would be pointless to argue.

Once everyone crossed the threshold, Cole and Rollan pulled the large, metal door shut. As the last sliver of light vanished, we heard a sharp click. Joss gave the door an experimental pull, but it didn't even budge.

"Are we trapped?" Kisa asked in the almost pitch dark. Her voice was worried but not as fearful as it once would have been.

"There's light ahead," Rollan assured her. "That means another way out."

Since there was only one way to go, we set off without any conversation. The stone hallway was about ten feet tall and close to the same in width. It was also a lot longer than it appeared. The floor sloped up, but it was so smooth we had no trouble navigating it, even with limited visibility.

Finally, we reached the end of the passage, mostly guided by touch. There was a one hundred and eighty degree turn on our right, leading into another passage that was identical to the first, except that the upward slope was slightly greater. Four more times we came to turns leading to additional passages. The light increased slightly with each of these, as did the angle of the upward slope. Eventually, it became so steep that I was gasping for breath. The backs of my legs burned. The stress of the climb was making me sweat even though it was chilly inside the mountain.

"Should we take a break?" Cole asked.

He was probably thinking of Kisa, but I just wanted to reach the top.

"No," I replied. "We've got to get to the top before sunset."

Cole nodded, and we continued. After two more hallways, we emerged into a large room. It was rectangular in shape and had a second doorway at the far end. The space was filled with strange objects, the like of which I had never seen before.

I slowly approached the nearest one. It was a piece of paper, but there was a case of something hard and clear around it that looked like ice. I reached out to touch it, and, while the surface was cool, it was not cold enough to be frozen.

The paper itself had words written on it in the strangest, most perfect handwriting I'd ever seen. I read the words aloud.

"'The first skirmish has ended between—'" I broke off, not knowing some of the words on the page. "Something and something. 'It appears to have been a loss all around. Both sides took heavy damage, and neither has gained the upper hand.

"'The' —something— 'are going to have another non-aggression talk in three days. The eyes of the world turn toward them in the hopes that a treaty can be signed to ensure peace. If no solution is reached, we will have to brace ourselves as two of the world's greatest superpowers clash.

"'Already, the other' —something— 'are taking sides and making allies. This truly is a frightening time to be alive.'"

That was all that was written in the perfect script on the paper.

"What do you think it means?" Cole asked.

I shrugged.

"It's not written to us like the other instructions have been."

"It must be very old," Astra commented. "If it's been here through all the trials, I'm surprised the parchment hasn't rotted away."

Joss and Rollan were looking at a second piece of paper.

"What does this one say?" Todd wondered. He was leaning over Joss's shoulder, squinting at the writing.

"'Millions dead after—'" Joss broke off and shook his head. "Something, something— 'struck targets in the heartland of—' something. 'These attacks line up with the threats that were made last year during the—' something 'summit. No one believed that the' —something— 'line would be crossed, but now that it has, can we expect to see more? How far is the' —something— 'willing to go to defend its borders? Is this going to be man's last war?'" Joss stopped.

"There's a drawing too," Todd observed.

"What?" I asked, uncertain of what he meant. I walked over to see. Above the writing, there was a large, colorful image of a human being covered in injuries. I recoiled at the grotesque sight.

"What are we looking at?" I gasped.

"I think it's a painting of some kind," Todd informed us. "But I've never seen one as good as this before."

"A painting?" Cole and Joss asked together.

"You know, when someone makes a drawing that looks like something else," Todd explained.

We all stared at him with blank expressions.

"Like this," he said, breaking off part of a stick from those he carried.

He placed the bundle on the ground and crouched beside it. Then he started rubbing one end of his stick on the floor like he was writing. Some of the wood rubbed off, leaving a faint mark across the stone. A moment later, the markings looked something like a cat.

"That's called doodling, and it's against the rules," I told him. "It wastes time and resources."

"Really?" Todd gasped in surprise. "You guys have no art?"

"Of course we do," Cole replied. "We know lots of arts. Like how to fight, make clothes, fish, grow food—"

"But no one creates images or pictures?" Todd asked, interrupting him.

We all shook our heads.

"Wasteful," I reminded him.

Todd sighed. "Well, that's what you're looking at now. It's a 'doodle' that someone made."

"Is it real?" Kisa asked.

Todd shrugged. "I don't know. It goes with the story. So, if the story is real, then it probably happened too."

"That poor man," Kisa exclaimed, looking closely at the image again. "Do you think he died?"

"This has been here for hundreds of years," Astra pointed out. "So, he's probably dead by now, yes."

"That's not what I meant," Kisa sighed softly.

We moved on to the next item, but we couldn't even get close to it. Instead of just the object itself being encased by the clear, hard substance, there was literally a transparent box around a small platform on the floor. Inside was the strangest pair of shoes I had ever seen, along with a hollow half sphere of a muted gray color.

"I think it's a helmet," Cole guessed. "They don't wear them much, but they have some at The Barracks. I saw them there once with Jase."

"How did they get it so smooth?" Rollan asked. "It's as round as an eggshell."

It was curious. The helmet—if that's what it was—had a perfectly domed top. Cole shrugged. The only other item in the clear box was a folded set of clothing, which was many different shades of green arranged in a strange, mottled pattern. The material didn't look like anything The Clan made.

We moved on to a second clear box. Inside was a single, rectangular piece of fabric. It had white and red stripes and a blue patch with white objects on it.

"What does it mean?" Todd asked.

"I don't know," Astra said, shaking her head.

"Look at this!" Joss called us over to another of the boxes. Inside were a lot of small, foreign objects. They were mostly oval-shaped, but some had pointed ends. They all appeared to be made of metal.

There was a paper close to the square box.

"'Another attack occurred today,'" Cole read. "'It took place at 4 a.m. on the last and largest' —something— 'city. It has been completely leveled. All hope for peace seems gone. Will the' —something— 'rally and retaliate? That is what will be decided today in the' —something— 'meeting.

"'How much longer the world can go on tearing itself apart is anyone's guess. Soon the' —something— 'fallout will be bad enough to make the entire' —something— 'uninhabitable. No reports yet on the body count of the most recent attack. Thousands of people are still missing. Seven hundred and eighty-three thousand confirmed dead. However, we are still within the first twenty-four hours, and more reports are coming in every minute.'"

"So many people dead," Kisa gasped. "It's terrible."

The number was mind boggling to me. I hadn't known that many people had ever lived.

Suddenly, this all sounded very familiar.

"Is this—the history of our people?" I asked. "Are these writings from when the darkness attacked our ancestors?"

No one answered as we moved to the next case, which held a collection of long, black objects.

"How did it all get here?" Astra wondered.

I turned to read another paper. This one was written in a different hand than the others. It wasn't perfect like they were. Instead, it appeared to be more like my own handwriting.

"'The world is destroyed,'" I began, "'and still, the war wages on. Hasn't anyone stopped long enough to consider that what we were fighting over is already lost? There is no point now, except to see which side can annihilate the other first. After one is dead, the other will quickly follow them to the grave.

"'There is no food, no water; the very air is poison. Our' — something— 'weapons have doomed everything they were meant to protect, and for what? Because one' —something— 'had more than the other? Because one people needed to be proven right? Because one man signed the' —something— 'to declare that all others were our enemies?

"'Is this how it was meant to be? All is lost. We cannot survive. We cannot go on. This is the end.'"

The words were eerie and chilling. They didn't sound very much like the account we were taught, where a great darkness attempted to wipe out all our people.

The writer's despair and hopelessness were almost tangible to me. I stood for a moment trying to figure out what it all meant. There must be some reason we were supposed to come here and see this.

The last of the items was simply a collection of what Todd called "drawings". They depicted many things I didn't understand. One seemed to be a triangular object in the sky, like a bird. Another was of a hillside. In the distance, there was a strange, smoky cloud rising from the ground into the sky. Several of the other images were of people wearing the articles of clothing we had seen in the earlier case. Each also held one of the long, black objects.

Kisa looked away from a few that showed people—mostly children—injured or starving.

"I don't want to see this," the little girl cried, covering her eyes.

Cole put a hand on her shoulder.

"I'm sorry, Kisa," he said softly. "I know it's hard, but I think we're supposed to look at them. We need to understand the past if we are going to guide the future."

It was only then that the thought struck me; we had won!

A feeling of excitement swept through me, but I suppressed it. This was clearly not the right time for an elated outburst. Even so, I couldn't help but press forward into the next room. We had seen everything in the first, and I was curious about what else we were going to find.

The second room was much stranger than the one before it. Everything was carved right out of stone.

There were no papers or objects to be seen. However, just as when we first entered the mountain, there was writing on the wall ahead of us and a sloping ramp to the left leading up three feet to a higher floor.

Set in the wall to the right was a door similar to the one through which we had entered the mountain. It was closed, and there didn't appear to be any visible way to open it.

Cole read aloud what was written on the wall.

"'Build a fire in the hearth. Turn the arm until it stops. Observe what you have come to see.'"

"Seems straightforward," Astra commented.

"Everything else has been so far," Cole agreed.

We gathered up the wood, which had been left in the previous room during our exploration, and ascended the short ramp leading to the second level.

The first thing I noticed was that there was a hallway opening ten yards in front of us. This appeared to be the only source of light in the entire place.

To the left was a smooth wall. It was stark white and didn't look at all like the rest of the room's walls. I approached it to see if there were more instructions, but nothing was inscribed on the flawless surface.

Directly across from the white wall was a tunnel-like staircase, which appeared to twist sharply to the right a few steps inside.

Suddenly, there was a squeal from Kisa. I glanced around but didn't see her.

"You've got to come here!" Joss called. His voice was coming from the hall where the light entered the room. "I've never seen anything so amazing!"

I rushed toward him, arriving at the end of the hall just behind Cole. Astra and Todd followed us.

Joss, Kisa, and Rollan were standing inside the doorway of a third room. When I saw what they were looking at, my heart stopped. Their feet were inches from a sheer drop, at least a hundred times farther down than the ledge where we had jumped into the water back in The Land of the Clan. Even the cliffs of The Valley of the North Wind didn't compare.

We must have come right through the mountain and were now looking out the opposite side. I hadn't realized we'd climbed so far into the sky.

There was more of the clear, hard stuff making up an entire wall from the floor to the ceiling.

Hundreds of feet below, there was some sort of enormous ring encompassing a large portion of the ground. On the outside of the ring, a forest of lush green spread out in all directions, but within, everything was grayish brown, and nothing grew.

"Let's get on with what we have to do," Cole suggested after a few minutes. "We need to find the hearth and then turn the arm."

Everyone returned to the second room. It seemed dim and gloomy after the bright light of the sun.

There was no obvious hearth that we could see, and the only place left for us to look was up the staircase. It was narrow, and the tight stone walls made visibility very limited.

I hadn't noticed at first, but as Cole headed for the stairs, I saw yet another door in the wall by the base.

Before Cole even made it up five steps, he called, "I've found the hearth; bring me some wood."

I dropped my backpack on the floor and grabbed a bundle of kindling. Springing up a few steps, I handed it to Cole, eager to see what he had found.

The stairs wrapped around in a half spiral before coming to a dead end. At the top was a small closet-sized area with a fireplace and a long chimney. Gazing into the hearth, I saw a small, round opening in the back.

Just to the right of the fireplace was a tiny space, about four feet deep. In the back corner, a piece of metal stuck out of the left-hand wall. It resembled the cranks we used to draw water from our wells.

"Is this 'the arm'?" I wondered aloud, walking into the small passage and putting my hand on the metal shaft. It was ice cold.

Rollan came up the stairs with more wood and used his flint to start a fire.

I ran my hand over the arm. The surface was smooth and far too perfect. All of this was. It came from a different time, a time long past—a dark and terrible time.

"Okay," Cole called to me several minutes later. "The fire's lit. Go ahead and turn the arm."

I did as he said.

At first, I couldn't rotate the shaft in either direction. Only after I put all my weight into moving it did the arm finally start to turn. It was slow going at the beginning, but then something seemed to come loose, and I was able to move it more easily. After about a minute, the arm creaked to a halt, and I let it go.

At first, nothing happened, then I heard Kisa give a cry of shock. Someone else—I was pretty sure it was Joss—gasped in surprise. The three of us on the stairs hurried down to join the others in the main room.

There, floating just in front of the smooth wall, was a woman dressed in white.

CHAPTER 40
TRUTH

For a few moments, all we could do was stare at her.

"Hello," Cole said at last, approaching the woman. He stopped when he got close, squinted, and then reached his hand out to touch her shoulder. Just before his fingers brushed her arm, part of the woman disappeared from the wall; a piece that exactly resembled an outstretched arm. What was even stranger was that part of the woman appeared to be on Cole's hand. He withdrew it instantly and backed away.

"What is this?" Astra whispered.

"It must be a god," Todd cried, face draining of color. He dropped to his knees and bowed his head.

"Is it another picture?" Kisa asked.

Then the woman moved and looked straight at us. I froze in surprise.

"Hello," she said. Her voice sounded like it was coming from behind us instead of in front of us.

The woman was beautiful, with dark hair, almost black in color, lightly tanned skin, and large, brown eyes. Her hair was brushed back, and it fell behind her shoulders. The clothing she wore seemed to be a long robe; I had never seen anything so white except the freshly fallen snow.

"Do not be alarmed," the woman continued. "What you are seeing now is called a 'projection'. Many years ago, I created this recording for future generations to watch. It is an act of science, and there is no trickery involved. A thin, papery element called 'film' is run through a machine, and when light hits it properly, it creates what you are now witnessing. In this way, you are able to see my image even though I no longer walk the earth.

"My name is Jessica. I am the head scientist on The Clan project."

My heart skipped a beat when she said her name. *Jessica? Could it be* the *Jessica?* I wondered.

"If you are here," Jessica went on, "then you have reached the end of the trials. In order to succeed, there is one more thing you must do to prove yourselves worthy to be leaders of The Clan.

"I am sure you are curious about your final task, but I will come back to that in a moment. First, I want you to understand what is going on in my time.

"This mountain is my laboratory, the place in which my research took place. When my work was concluded, I sealed the lower levels, removed my equipment, and replaced it with what you see now, a few remnants of the past.

"The room you entered through to my right is called 'The Hall of Memories'. The items and records carefully preserved in it probably mean very little to you. But they mean something great to us, your ancestors. What you have seen in that room is the story of our downfall."

Some of the words I was hearing didn't make sense to me, but Jessica continued speaking, so I didn't have time to ponder their meanings.

"To my left is another room, which looks down on the ruins of Axella. I do not know how much of it remains in your time. Some of the buildings may still be standing, or the entire thing may have crumbled to ash and dust.

"In my time, it was the greatest of all cities, an eighth wonder of the world, designed for knowledge, peace, and acceptance. It was the only city ever built which belonged to no country, nor kingdom, nor person. All people from all countries were welcome there. It was the pinnacle of everything humankind had achieved."

Jessica's voice held a proud note as she spoke of Axella, but now her face twisted in sorrow. The next words out of her mouth were barely more than a whisper.

"It did not last long. The fighting started, and then the war began. Less than five years after its completion, Axella was almost completely obliterated.

"And not just Axella, cities all over the earth suffered the same fate. You cannot comprehend the way in which we made our war. Hundreds of thousands of lives could be ended with the push of a button. More people died every day than you will meet in your entire life.

"We used weapons that should never have been created. They poisoned the earth, leaving the ground black. Nothing would grow from it. The sky turned gray and filled with toxic fumes. Death spread among plants, animals, and humans alike. The earth may someday recover from the poison, but it will take centuries."

For a moment, Jessica looked away from us. She slowly shook her head, and I could hear the regret in her words.

"We had found cures to almost every disease. World hunger was demolished decades ago. Our lives were easy. Everyone had everything they needed. We should have been content.

"But in the end, it did not matter, because we could not fix ourselves.

"The human race is broken. We always want more. More possessions, more power, more praise. That is why we are doomed as a species. I have dedicated my life to a single purpose: ensuring the survival of the human race. It has not been easy, for I seem to be working against human nature itself.

"My team, which consisted of my father, Peter, and two of our associates, Roy and Lewis, formed a plan. Our original purpose was to find a way to undo the poison, called radiation, which has destroyed so much of the world.

"Most considered this an impossible task, but it was also believed to be the last chance for humanity, so we were given almost limitless resources. Despite the odds, we succeeded in finding a way to remove and shield areas from radiation.

"We could have saved much of what remained of the earth, but we chose not to."

There was a long moment of silence, and a sense of dread began to creep over me.

"You see, if we were able to reverse the damage that had been caused, the world might have been saved, but for how long? It is inevitable that humans will destroy themselves unless the means are taken from them.

"My team and I decided that humanity's best chance was to wipe the slate clean and start over. We told no one what we found. Instead, we built a land where a remnant of humanity could live.

"We poured the last of the world's resources into building an Eden, The Land of the Clan. A true, last hope for humanity, because it was the only place untouched by the radiation. A mighty river was designed to protect it from large predators, and great mountains were built to break the northern storms before they could ravage the land.

"It took us eleven years to complete, and we almost ran out of time. The war was still raging, although, there was little enough left to fight over.

"We were meticulous when determining which of the survivors were allowed to enter The Land of the Clan with us. The selection process was done very carefully. No one who was weak or flawed was chosen, only the strong and perfect. The rest were left to die in the destruction they had wrought for themselves.

"All those chosen for The Clan underwent a gene mutation to their body's immune system. Roy created this process, and it will be passed on genetically to future generations. The mutation was necessary since medicine has been reduced to the most basic level, and we can't risk the entire population dying off from an epidemic. This boost to the immune system allows the drinking of unpurified water, helps fight off infections, and generally increases each individual's constitution.

"Unfortunately, this causes as many problems as it solves. If no one ever gets sick, and if most injuries heal quickly, then there is a significant concern with overpopulation. To that end, we have altered the females so they will cycle only once a year. This trait will also be passed on genetically and should help to keep the birthrate down.

"Due to these mutations, we have experienced some side effects, including the absence of facial hair for men. As well as a lack of body hair in all subjects. There have also been abnormalities in the blood, making bleeding stop more quickly but allowing poison to be twice as effective.

"Even with all of this, we still fully expected the birthrate to be far too high for the small amount of land chosen to support the community. The others have no solution; they never want to face the hard choices. That is why my father and I have created the trials.

"Every fifty years, a select number of youths will leave The Land of the Clan. A great many will not return. There will be heartache at their loss, but they shall be remembered as having died valiantly in service to The Clan. And so they did, for it is by their deaths that others might live. Since they will not yet have begun to work, their absence will be a relief to The Clan, not a loss. They will have no children, no mate, no one that will miss them for more than a year or two.

"If you are here watching this, I can imagine you are shocked to learn the truth behind the trials in which you have participated. The reason I have left you such a detailed account of our actions is because I want you to understand why they are necessary.

"I have lived my entire life in fear. The fear that I may die at any moment, caught in a bomb drop. The fear that when I go to sleep I will be murdered before I wake up. If some must die for the rest to be able to lay their heads down in peace at night, then so be it. That is the price that will be paid.

"There is much more I would like to tell you, but your time is short. My father and I will be making another recording for you soon with the rest of the information you will need to know.

"In The Land of the Clan, there is a room, similar to this one, in which we will place the second recording. When you return, the current Clan Leaders will show it to you.

"Trust them. They will want to help you, for they have stood where you are standing and have felt what you are feeling. The room is hidden and only accessible by a key."

Jessica held up a small, metal object. It looked vaguely familiar.

"That was in my room." I didn't mean to speak aloud, but I accidentally had. Astra glanced in my direction, but no one else seemed to notice.

"When you leave this mountain, you will immediately find a river. It is the same one that flows around your land. All you must do is follow this river, and it will lead you home.

"When you return to The Land of the Clan, tell the current Clan Leaders 'the price has been paid', and then they will know you have completed the trials and are worthy of leading The Clan.

"One last thing. There is a final test you must perform before you return home.

"Look behind you." Jessica paused for a moment, and we all turned back.

The door beside the staircase was now open. I'd been too distracted listening to all that Jessica was saying to notice, even though it was hardly three yards from where I was standing.

"That door leads to death," Jessica went on. "The same kind of death that was inflicted on the people of the earth all those years ago: the poison called radiation.

"You must make a sacrifice in order to understand why everything I have worked for is so important. This is the same sacrifice my team and I, myself, have made in order to start the human race over. This experience will also serve to bind you together as a team.

"Each team has been designed to include one person who most likely cannot live with what they have heard today. Someone who has no attachments to family and nothing at all waiting for them in The Land of the Clan. That person is the intended sacrifice."

I tried not to look at Astra, but it was obvious who Jessica was speaking of.

"This person will be highly ranked on your team and will feel the need to protect the others, even at the cost of his or her own life. If that person has died on the way here, then another must take their place.

"Do not wait too long to make your choice; the poison is coming through the open door right now. The longer you are exposed to it, the weaker you will grow.

"The chosen one must pass through the door and find the metal arm within. Once it has been turned, the door will shut, and the person inside will die almost immediately. The rest of the team will be shielded and, in the morning, set free.

"If no consensus can be reached, and no one passes through the door, you will all be dead in twelve hours from the poison. The entire system will reset for immediate use, and the next team to find this place will have the same option.

"Once someone has completed the task, the system will reset for forty-nine years, until the next trials are again at hand.

"I am so very sorry, but now is the time to make your choice of who will die. It is the first choice you will make together as Clan Leaders."

CHAPTER 41
LEGACY

The woman vanished from the wall, leaving no trace that she had ever existed. For three seconds, there was absolute stillness and silence in the room.

Then Astra took a step toward the door.

She was close to it and would have reached it in a moment if Cole hadn't jumped in front of her yelling. "No! No! No! We're going to talk about this," he insisted, shaking his head violently.

Astra gave him a gentle smile.

"There's nothing to talk about," she said. "I'm the one. This is my role."

The rest of the team huddled around the pair in a loose circle. Their eyes showed the shock of what they had just heard. Not one of them spoke; they just observed the horrible scene playing out before them.

I was a few steps from Cole and had a clear line of sight into the room. It was really more of a giant cavern than a room. The door was about fifteen feet up the wall. The floor below seemed to be moving slightly.

It has to be water, I thought, *so you don't kill yourself when you jump down.*

And to make it impossible to escape, the darker side of my mind whispered.

There was only a low level of light illuminating the cavern, but I could see a platform just above the water's surface about fifty yards away. That was where I imagined the arm would be since there was absolutely nothing else to be seen through the doorway.

The room had a strange, red glow. I couldn't tell if it came from the water or the roof, but it was a disturbing sight, especially after what we had just heard.

374

Cole was still shaking his head violently, and he started insisting that there had to be another way.

I didn't bother to listen.

I knew how this was going to end.

Cole would try everything he could to convince Astra not to go through the door. We'd have to climb back down all those ramps to make sure that the front door was really sealed. We would spend hours trying to open it, but to no avail.

In the end, Astra would win; she would persuade him, and he would let her go. She would jump into the water below, swim to the platform, and close the door, saving us all at the cost of her life.

We would leave after that and return to The Clan. We would be made Clan Leaders, and I would have everything I had ever wanted. Cole and I would become life mates. We would have a beautiful son, with Cole's dark hair and my gray eyes. We would name him Covil after his father.

Then we would have a daughter, and for some reason, she wouldn't have my gray eyes or Cole's blue ones, but bright, green eyes. Instead of naming her Myla or Myka or something after me, we would name her Astra, and there would be only the six of us who would know why.

The six of us?

I glanced around; the argument was still going on.

No winning team had ever returned with all six members. Now it was obvious why. I looked at Todd, and something dawned on me. We still could. We could be the first team to ever return without having lost anyone. That was the answer to this riddle, the way to cheat the test.

Unbidden, a laugh rose to my lips. The others turned to look at me, even Astra and Cole.

It was all so ironic. This was the truth? This was what I had been so desperate to know all these years? That we were evil but needed to pretend that it wasn't so? That we weren't sent here to earn honor or glory, but to die out of sight and out of mind?

One day, as Clan Leaders, we would have to send hundreds of children to their deaths so that others might live.

What kind of society was that?

We were frozen in time. Unable to move forward or backward. The Clan would be stuck there, in that same pattern, forever. We were stagnant and lost and broken.

Astra saw that my gaze was resting on Todd. Instantly, she leapt away from Cole to put herself between him and the rest of us. Behind her, Todd's dark eyes grew huge, as if he had just figured out what was going on.

"No," Astra growled, looking not at me alone, but at everyone, as if any one of us might pounce.

I turned away. It was just a passing thought. I never planned to act on it.

Astra was the chosen one; it was true. She would never be able to accept life in The Clan after what she had seen and heard here today.

But maybe that was what The Clan needed.

Cole was blocking the entrance to the cavern. I took a slow step forward, and then another until I was directly in front of him. He gave me a wary look, unsure of my intentions. I slowly raised my hands to his face, brought it down close to mine, and then pressed my lips against his.

It was the only thing I could think of, and, I won't lie, it was something I had always wanted to do. The kiss was as amazing as I imagined it would be, so sweet it almost made me waver in my resolve.

The moment seemed to last forever and not nearly long enough. I pulled back. He was completely stunned; everyone was. I was already without my pack, but I pulled my knife from my hip and let it fall to the ground.

Astra realized what I was going to do and tried to jump forward to stop me, but she was too far from the doorway and couldn't reach me in time.

I jumped without the hesitation I had struggled with on the clifftop the first time. There, the fall was full of exhilaration and excitement. I felt none of that now. I felt nothing until my head vanished beneath the surface.

The water was icy cold. I wondered if it had ever seen the light of day. I glanced back up at the doorway I had just jumped through. My greatest fear was that someone would follow me down, but no one did. It seemed that Cole recovered himself in time to stop Astra, or maybe the other way around. Regardless, they were all there in the doorway. I think they were calling to me, but I blocked them out of my mind.

Ridiculous as it sounds, as I swam toward the platform in the center of the cavern, I thought of Todd's gods: the king and his lost friend, the warrior, and the rest. I had lived for them. Not in the way Todd did with sacrifices and worship, but in a far truer way.

My entire life, I had been ruled by anger, jealousy, conceit, sorrow, hatred, and all the other things they stood for.

Astra was right, there must be more to this world than what we could see. Something greater. Maybe the last god, the unknown god, stood for something good. Something like kindness or hope or love. If I had lived for the other gods, then couldn't I die for the unknown one?

Looking back on my life, if I could have changed one thing, I would have changed everything: the way I treated Rasby, my relationship with my mother, all my mean thoughts, and my cruel behavior. I had hurt so many people. Astra and I could have been sisters, and I made her my enemy. My future, all of my hopes and dreams, were given to her now.

I reached the platform and pulled myself out of the water. It was made of metal, and my feet crunched softly on a layer of dirt or ash. My breaths made clouds in front of me a moment before I walked through them. In the eerie, red light, it seemed as though the sun had just set and the horizon was still tinted pink from her departure.

I reached the arm and tried to turn it. The metal was stuck just like the last one, but I gave a great heave and pulled with all my strength. It began to move. I turned it until it wouldn't turn anymore.

I looked back toward the doorway. I couldn't see it from where I was; a large chunk of rock was hanging down from the ceiling, blocking my view. The red light seemed to be coming from it, pulsating brighter then softer.

Quickly, I moved to the end of the platform just as the door began to shut. They were all standing there, and I saw them again for just an instant—safe and sound.

Pain filled my body suddenly, causing me to lose my balance and topple into the underground lake. The cold water numbed the pain. My head felt light and fuzzy, almost warm. It was like being wrapped in a giant blanket.

I closed my eyes, and the water was calling me home.

I have given all I have to give, and this—is my legacy.

THE GODS

HOUSE OF THE KING

ARSH – The king – He that is the crown upon the head

Arsh was the ruler of the gods until his best friend, Husam, betrayed him and tried to usurp his throne.

JIYA – The fair one – She that is the heart in the chest

Jiya is the most beautiful creature in the entire world. She is the first wife of Arsh.

SUR – The hater – She that is the dagger in the soul

Sur is the younger sister of Tohopke. She was in love with Dezi once, but, after being forced to become Arsh's second wife, she erased all emotion from her heart save hatred.

TODKALA – The trickster – He that is the fox creeping through the night

Todkala is the younger brother of Arsh. He prefers manipulations and deception to direct confrontation.

HOUSE OF THE WARRIOR

HUSAM – The warrior – He that is the edge on the sword
Husam and Arsh were once good friends, but Husam grew jealous and tried to steal Arsh's throne.

DEZI – The weeper – He that is the sorrow in the tears
Dezi was in love with Sur. After she was forced to wed Arsh, his sorrow overtook him and he now mourns day and night, preferring his dreams to the waking world.

TOHOPKE – The wild one – He that is the beast in the forest
Tohopke cared very little about the conflict between Arsh and Husam until Todkala tricked him into giving his sister, Sur, to Arsh in marriage. Now he longs for revenge against Todkala.

ZERUIAH – The torturer – She that is the pain in the wound
Zeruiah is the wife of Tohopke. She is cruel and has a special disdain for Jiya.

OTHER
THE UNKNOWN GOD
The unknown god is the ninth god. He did not descend to earth with the others. Very little is known about him. He has no temple, only a small shrine. Inside is a black box, engraved with golden writing.

ABOUT THE AUTHOR

Photo by Brian Prewitt and Prewitt Studios

Danielle N. McDonough spent her childhood exploring the world through books. These stories, paired with her imagination, took her on hundreds of adventures to different times and places. Her favorites were about heroes, dragons, mysteries, and magic.

As a young adult, Danielle continued in her love of art and fantasy. She graduated from Full Sail University with a degree in film. After spending several years working on television and movie sets, she decided to step away from the film industry and pursue her passion for storytelling by writing her debut novel, *The Preparations*.

It was in Colorado, on a mission trip with her church, that Danielle had a dream about one of the members of The Clan. This dream was the inspiration behind *The Legacy* series. It took her four years to finish writing the series, but the journey was the greatest adventure she's ever been on, and she welcomes you to share it with her.

WWW.THELEGACYBOOKSERIES.COM